THE KILLER
FLIES
OF LUXOR

ALSO BY AGUSTIN BLAZQUEZ

Cubriendo y Descubriendo/Covering and Discovering
(with Carlos Wotzkow)

The Agustin Blazquez Art Gallery may be found online at:

https://abartgallery.com

PRAISE FOR AGUSTIN BLAZQUEZ

I had the privilege to come to know Agustin Blazquez during the Elian Gonzalez saga, over 20 years ago, on which he made several documentaries.

A first impression of him, while visiting him at his Maryland home, was an 8 mm short film which he had done almost by himself. It was full of allure, rich though delicate, and as a filmmaker myself, I was impressed by his prowess. Still, it was but a little sample of his multifaceted talents and abilities that I came to know during our 22 and some years of friendship.

He painted and, in fact, had done quite a collection of Egypt inspired art, with which he attained a certain success. He was his own cinematographer, having shot all his films, mostly documentaries. He created his music out of thin air, with the most disparaged objects and sound effects.

He wrote, mainly about political issues, always in the forefront of activism against the left and in defense of the real Cuba, the one he grew up in and was forced to leave at an early age. He was an interior designer, a remodeling Architect, a furniture restorer (sometimes inventing out of discards!) an actor, a fashion designer.

His presence was odd, often dressed kind of campy (he used to say that he bought his clothes at Goodwill), while always conveying a very serious demeanor. At first glance, no one would dare to make a humorous comment about some serious subject at hand. Except him, unexpectedly blowing the dull atmosphere with some hilarious comment, born out of his delirious fantasy.

And he had a delirious fantasy! It was a ride to see him taking off from a known situation and climb the ladder of the absurd. Take as an example the story "Cinnamon Skin" in this book, or his character The Painted Woman, from the chapter of the same name.

Still, he never stopped passionately fighting against the forces of evil that took away his country, which was his childhood, and which he noticed were sneaking into his adoptive country as well.

He was exquisite and vernacular, trivial and grave, realistic and fantastic, absurd and very down to earth. And he was a magnificent friend.

I would invite the readers of this book to sit down and dabble in his stories, imagining him cracking up in his Chayanne bandeau with a ponytail!

—VIVIAN GUDE, Filmmaker and Journalist

We will never know if it was a Pharaoh's curse or the simple fact of being born in Cuba (which is a curse in itself) that prompted my dear friend to write this book. What is certain is that one feels the great urgency in the life and art of Agustín in a time without clear generational boundaries and in the stories he tells us. The subtext is another exile-only book that humorously recounts the feelings of a chaotic and often lonely existence. Few could describe such a suffocating plot with such intimate prose or feel those burns in the soul that guide our dreams along uncertain paths.

The reader will find in these pages a unique and humorous way of seeing the political and social turmoil mixed with the daily uncertainty, hourly fears, minutely doubts and anxieties of this wonderful artist and writer. Agustin, one could say, was a pioneer victim of the Cancel Culture since he was born. The artistic beauty of the ruins of his beloved Egypt are described here as masterly as the ruin of his entire homeland. His pain for the destruction and death in both cultures is excruciating, as are the hopes, joys and sorrows of his imprisoned soul in exile.

This is not a book of short stories, but a timeless essay of a Cuban nightmare. Those who lived 40 years ago, and those who will live 40 years after reading this book will feel the same fear, the same fanaticism, nostalgia, sorrows or joys of the artist in a landscape lost in oblivion, or in streets that have already changed their names. It's not in Luxor or in La Habana (as it's spelled in Spanish) that PAIN (with capitalized letters), reaches its climax. It is in the heart of this artist where everything has arrived to an end, knowing that as he types the last words of this book, he leaves the reader with the terrible news that all will disappear, or that we will never be able to visualize those wonderful sites again.

—CARLOS WOTZKOW
Co-author of *Cuba: Cubriendo y Descubriendo*

The great French painter George Braque famously said that "Art is a wound turned into light." Agustin Blazquez's *The Killer Flies of Luxor*, a fictionalized memoir about an artist's confrontation with his exile from Cuba and subsequent escape into a dream-world of art and movies, is a testament to the power of Braque's insight.

—SCOTT DOUGLAS GERBER,
Author of *The Art of the Law: A Novel*

Over the years, Agustin had told me bits and pieces of what life was like in Cuba before and after the Castro revolution, but when reading the chapters "Escape" and "The Flight of the Rooster", I felt like I was in the driver's seat. It was quite a ride! All the anguish, fear, desperation, loss, determination, and relentless struggle really hit home.

—STUART GOODMAN

Thrilling!

—DODI MOSSAFER, Saatchi Artist

SARA MONTIEL AND AGUSTIN BLAZQUEZ IN NYC, 1975

THE KILLER FLIES OF LUXOR

Partial Autobiography
Travel Chronicles
Dreams
Fantasies

AGUSTIN BLAZQUEZ

Penny-a-Page Press
Clearwater, FL

PENNY-A-PAGE PRESS
CLEARWATER, FL
HTTPS://PENNYAPAGEPRESS.BLOGSPOT.COM

ISBN: 978-1-7331178-5-2 (HARDCOVER)
      978-1-7331178-6-9 (PAPERBACK)
      978-1-7331178-7-6 (EBOOK)

To **SARA MONTIEL**, the only star
that shines in the sky of my fancy,

To my mother and father

To Tiri

To Terry

To Jason

To Kelly

To Maecy

To Ladee

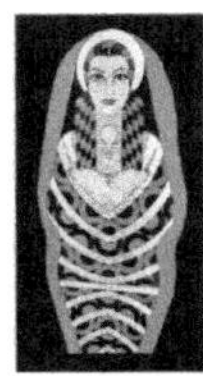

TABLE OF CONTENTS

FOREWORD BY LAURENCE JARVIK

The author of this book, Agustin Blazquez, passed away October 27th, 2022 in Bethesda, Maryland at age 78, from a stroke.

He was my dear friend of thirty years, and also my artistic collaborator as producer-director of *The Trump Effect: Deprogramming the American Mind* (2017). I first met him at a hearing in the 1990s where we both testified to Congress about serious problems at PBS and the Corporation for Public Broadcasting. His testimony struck me as both honest and courageous, paying no heed to any careerist considerations.

In addition, with his ponytail, beard, and wearing a colorful outfit, there was no way that anyone could see him as anything but a blacklisted artist. Years later, I attempted unsuccessfully to help get his *Covering Cuba 7: Che: The Other Side of an Icon* aired on PBS. Even though Agustin had met Che personally in Cuba, and even though PBS had broadcast numerous pro-Che Guevara programs, and even though at the time the Corporation for Public Broadcasting was headed by a supposedly anti-communist Republican, and staffed by purportedly anti-communist filmmakers Michael Pack and John Prizer, they would not help get his film critical of Che Guevara on-air.

It reinforced everything Agustin had told me about the degree of protection that Cuban communism enjoyed even from so-called conservative media. But this did not stop Agustin, because he was unstoppable. I watched in awe as Agustin made movie after movie, building testimony for future generations about the horrors of communism, at first released on DVD, later on YouTube. He was thinking of the future, not the present.

So I was delighted when he and his co-producer, James W. Sutton, decided to make *The Trump Effect* after the 2016 election, in order to explain the significance of the election of Donald Trump as the 45th President of the United States. Not surprisingly, PBS didn't show the film, nor did any film festival. The only review it received was published in *Frontpage Magazine*, for which we were very grateful.

But none of this fazed Agustin in the least. Like Bach writing music for the Glory of God, or Solzhenitsyn keeping careful notes in the Gulag, he made his movies for Posterity, not for the moment.

Agustin Blazquez was a Renaissance Man—actor, painter, sculptor, graphic artist, portrait photographer, author, essayist, novelist, and a truly independent filmmaker whose oeuvre included music videos, documentaries, and art movies—and he left a legacy of personal integrity and courage in every medium in which he worked.

Born to Elisenda Martin and Francisco Blazquez in Cardenas, Cuba on April 17th, 1944, he grew up in the small towns of Coliseo and Limonar. Even in childhood, he said he knew that he was an artist:

"From a very early age I was drawing and painting everywhere, including on the walls. I developed the sense of a strong force pulling me to a life devoted to art…While I was studying in high school, I discovered that the style of my early childhood drawings bore a remarkable resemblance to the ancient Egyptian murals that appeared in my ancient history textbook. I took this as a sign of a mystic affinity between my inspirations and those of the ancient Egyptians…During the early 1960s I also painted abstract compositions and around 1963

I returned to my first love-Egyptian art-and completed a second collection of Egyptian paintings."

In addition to his art, Blazquez pursued a singing and acting career, graduating from the Municipal Academy of Dramatic Arts of Havana in 1962. He began his acting career before graduation, appearing in Cuban theatre, radio and television. While studying at the academy, he and a fellow alumnus purchased a Keystone 16mm camera and made two short films, shot in sequence because of lack of access to editing equipment. They were only able to view the films once, and unable to otherwise screen or distribute them.

He auditioned for the Instituto Cuban de Arte y Industry Cinematographic (ICAIC), the official government film studio, in 1962. In 1963, he was cast in *En Dias Como Estos* (1964) , directed by Jorge Fraga, as the supervisor of a group of volunteer teachers in the Sierra Maestra Mountains named "Responsible." He also played a bartender in *Cronica Cubana* (1963) and a bit part in *Preludio 11* (1963).

As he testifies in this novel, Blazquez had to hide his discomfort from pro-revolutionary relatives (some very active in the Communist Party):

"I was put under contract with a theatrical group the government created to present plays in the countryside around La Habana. It was of course in a legitimate revolutionary company that I was sure my little cousin would have approved and even been PROUD of me. What he didn't know was that at that time I detested THE REVOLUTION more than ever because I had more information and first-hand experience with the actual 'REVOLUTIONARY JUSTICE.' But I didn't see my little cousin during that period. He was busy involved in defending the indefensible. Even my mother was afraid of him and asked me not to talk to him anymore!"

Finally, after many twists of fate, Blazquez escaped Cuba on July 18th 1965, leaving his beginning acting career and two reels of film hostage to an unknown fate. He subsequently lived in Montreal, Paris and Madrid, prior to arriving in the United States in 1967.

In Montreal he worked as a busboy, in Paris cleaning floors, in Madrid as a dress designer, in addition to acting.

In Spain, he acted for Television Espanola (TVE) from 1966 to 1967 in numerous dramatic, musical and comedy productions. In the USA, Blazquez appeared on *America's Most Wanted* (1989) as a drug dealer, and in voice-overs as King Juan Carlos of Spain and Barcelona guitarist Jordi Pujol in Maryland Public Television's (MPT) *The Immigrants.*

He also narrated the Cuban Spanish version of *Welcome to the USA: A Guidebook for Refugees,* produced for the US State Department.

Meanwhile he continued to work as an artist, initially exploring "Op-Art" in Paris and Madrid, exhibiting there for the first time as a professional. He arrived in America in 1967 and had his first gallery show in 1968, shifting to Egyptian themes in the 1970s:

"In 1974, after a hiatus of 11 years, I resumed painting in the Egyptian style and in 1976 my one-man-show 'Egyptian Sculptured Paintings' opened in Washington, D.C. I received an official invitation from the Egyptian Embassy to visit Egypt as a guest of the Ministry of Higher Education in March of 1978. After my return from Egypt other one-man and group shows followed in subsequent years."

One of his films was shown at the US State Department, and reviewed in *State Magazine* by John Bentel under the title "An Egyptian Montage," as follows:

The concert series offers a diverse selection of talent to Department employees. One of the more intriguing examples of this occurred on Sep-

tember 18 in the East Auditorium when filmmaker Agustin Blazquez debuted "Memories of Egypt," a chronicle of the artist's odyssey from childhood to the present.

Mr. Blazquez was born and raised in Cuba and at an early age showed a gift for drawing and painting. As a child, he had recurring dreams influenced by Egyptian images, something he claims he had not yet seen. In high school, the artist said, he became aware of the remarkable resemblance between the Egyptian murals in his textbook and his own childhood drawings. Blazquez left Cuba in 1965, feeling his freedom imperiled by the oppressiveness of the Castro regime.

In 1974 the vivid dreams returned and became his art form: his murals evolved into three-dimensional shapes in the form of Egyptian mummies. In 1978 the government of Egypt invited him to be their guest for a month and interest in his artwork later resulted in over 80 private and group showings. His collection since 1967 totals 504 pieces.

"Memories of Egypt" is a montage of Blazquez' artistic evolution. He has an uncanny eye for the balance between imagery and music, and the special effects were captivating. The sounds of harp and piano seemed to simulate the images shown on the screen. I left longing to see more of this artist's work.

The Egyptian tour was so remarkable that Blazquez began this auto-biographical novel afterwards, inspired by his trip. It remained unpublished for over forty years.

He was revising the manuscript for publication at the time of his death.

PREFACE

Since everything Agustin did was without boundaries, he sometimes needed a collaborator to provide a bit of a stepping-stone to his next ability in order to complete whatever it was, as he completed everything he started. His expression of appreciation for my part was profound, but the enrichment that I received was also without boundaries.

Many, if not most, of Agustin's talents had a visual foundation or component, including this book, which, as he says in his Introduction, he drew with words.

I was always curious to try to understand why he said what he said and did what he did, this book reveals more than he would reveal of himself in life, here just lightly cloaked in, as he wrote on the title page: Partial Autobiography, Travel Chronicles, Dreams, Fantasies.

James W. Sutton
Silver Spring, Maryland
December 9, 2022

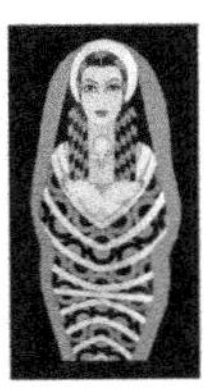

INTRODUCTION

Why have I written this book?

Well, I guess for the same reasons a painter paints, a sculptor sculpts, a singer sings, etc. I just felt the need to do so, as has always happened in the past when I wanted to say or to express something. Of course, I have expressed myself more often with the brush on canvas, that's why I became a professional painter. But this time, what I wanted to say couldn't be done with the paint of a brush but with ink on paper. As a creator I always felt free—thus my broad background—this need made me sit and draw my stories with words to convey my feelings, emotions and experiences, creating with them the imaginary colors of my life in your mind.

It took over a year to put everything together in writing. But it came out easily, as if it was being drawn by something governing my mind and my hand. Chapter by chapter, in order, kept coming to the paper. All coordinated in a way that nothing was there for free, everything had a purpose and a reason to be there. Even though the chapters are not in chronological order—except the ones concerning my official trip to Egypt—the information you will receive in one of them, will be of relevance for the next. Going back and forth into my past, dreams and fantasies, will explain and offer you a clear picture of why I am the way I am.

Apparently, I wanted to express certain things for a long time, since two of the chapters, "Escape" and "The Flight of the Rooster," were originally written in Paris in 1965—the same year I left my country and while memories were very clear in my mind. However, when I wrote them for this book, I discovered what I had not forgotten and more detailed, traumatic memories came back. But this isn't a total autobiography. I only went back to certain episodes of my life, the ones that were my building blocks and ones that had left scars, contributing to form my character, personality and goals.

I do not intend for this book to be a literary masterpiece. English obviously is not my language, even though I have lived in America longer than in my native country where Spanish is the main language. Sometimes I am actually able to make myself understood, somehow, by people close to me, while new acquaintances look disconcerted at what I try to say… And my American friends have barely understood what I have said for over 50 years! I am very lonely and discouraged. The way I have written this book is the way I think in English, which is not the same as real Americans do. But, I hope you can understand me! When you read it, have in mind that it is a Cuban telling the story although not quite *I Love Lucy's* Ricky Ricardo. And most important: this is a book with an accent.

I must point out that in this book I have made no attempt to describe the extraordinary beauty and grandeur of the Egyptian antiquities. I was so lucky to visit Egypt thanks to the generosity of the Egyptian Embassy in Washington, D.C., the Egyptian Government, the Ministry of Higher Education, the Cairo Museum and its Director and all the officials that made possible this extraordinary three-week tour of most of the antiquities throughout Egypt.

If something has saved me from the cruelties of living in our increasingly troubled world and its political nightmares, it's my sense of humor. And that's what I want to share with you, not just my unknown life and odd experiences. Many do not know that I exist. My own private sense of humor saved me in order to live. It's always there, moving around inside my mind, in my dreams and fantasies. Now, I am using my humor in this book as I used it in my 1980's painting series."Fifteen Pharaonic Fantasies." I hope it will amuse you so you can laugh with me in this surreal world. Your amusement and entertainment will be my delight! But don't forget about "the accent" and keep your tongue in your cheek!

Yours,

Agustin
August 9, 2022

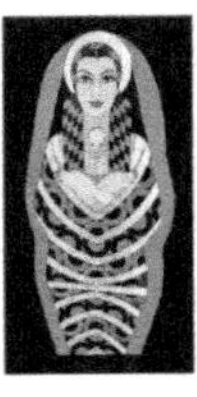

CHAPTER 1

THE ARRIVAL

When I stepped out of the door of the plane, there was a crowd waiting for me at the bottom of the stairs. They seem to be dignitaries, reporters and photographers. And there were TV cameras. I heard a band playing the familiar *The Star-Spangled Banner*. Tears came to my eyes under the binding midday Cairo sun. In the distance, I could see a lot of people in the distance on the upper balcony of the terminal waving and carrying signs with my photograph and what appeared to be my name and welcome signs. After the American anthem they played the Egyptian one. It was grand and unexpected. I marveled to see all these smiling welcoming faces concentrated on me. It was so much more than the rejections I received in American art circles. Down at the end of the stairs was a red carpet, a warm and friendly offering for my feet. After the Egyptian anthem was over, I went down to the tarmac where I was greeted by what appeared to be the Chief of Protocol who introduced me to the dignitaries. Soft warm Egyptian hands and ear to ear smiles. What a pleasure and joy to feel myself wanted for a change. After meeting the dignitaries, I turned around facing the crowds on the upper balcony of the terminal and lifted my right arm in salute to them. The response was like a roar in a sports stadium repeating my name. I was ushered by the Chief of Protocol to the waiting black Cadillac limousine. I followed him walking in the middle of photographer's flashes and TV cameras asking all kinds of questions. I was overwhelmed and couldn't say much but kept smiling and waving. Thinking of my fellow office workers, my supervisor and manager back in America I thought, "If they could see me now . . ."

Inside the limo I sat comfortably while the door was closed promptly and immediately the regal barge was smoothly sailing. We left the airport grounds and went fast throughout a wide street toward Cairo. There were people on both sides of the street throwing lotus flowers in our path. There were even welcoming billboards with my face and pictures of my Egyptian paintings.

We are passing by Heliopolis and the Chief of Protocol, sitting on my right, was explaining. "Oh," I replied while noticing the famous fig tree passing by where the Virgin Mary stayed with baby Jesus and Joseph. But a dog was peeing on it. Surely it was a Jewish dog, I thought. However, he looks like the god of the dead, Anubis . . . Well, our world is not perfect.

The sky was a bright and vibrant blue, not a single cloud. I had never seen one like it! The Chief interrupted my contemplation saying, "We are heading now toward Giza. You will be staying at The Mena House, just across the road from the great pyramid of Giza." What a detail, I thought. I was trembling with emotion. I could hardly wait. The Egyptians are really going all the way to make me feel at home, while some had said that in a prior life I lived in Ancient Egypt, which I didn't quite believe. But, let's see if this trip will unleash memories. . .

I could see in the distance the pyramids approaching and I felt a chill throughout my body. "You know," the Chief said, "actually the pyramid that looks smaller from our angle of view is in fact the great pyramid of Cheops." I stayed in awe and complete silence for the rest of this trip to heaven while looking with my eyes wide open as that real wonder of the world came closer to me. Its enormous size and grandeur is unbelievable.

I could not believe I was really there! It was like those dreams I have been having for quite a number of years–for as long as I can remember. Tears came to my eyes again. The Chief interrupted the solemnity of my state and looking very serious at my complete silence. We were there. Cheops was there and became the building down the block. The limo reduced speed and did a right turn into the entrance driveway of The Mena House. I was still silent when the chauffeur opened my door and I went out to the reality of the entrance staircase of the luxurious hotel. The Chief escorted me through the doors and under the magnificent golden ornate ceiling of the lobby. I signed the register at Reception and was ushered to my room past beautifully carved double doors. God have mercy, I thought, it's a suite! I wasn't expecting this. It was luxuriously furnished with reproductions of ancient Egyptian furniture and objects. "Everywhere the glint of gold," as the man who discovered Tutankhamen's tomb in the Valley of The Kings in 1922, Howard Carter, said when he peeked through a small hole on the stone wall at the interior of the treasure room of King Tut's tomb. But in the 20th century I had the benefit of a free 360-degree open view of the suite interior with electric lights. The Chief guided me to the next room, the bedroom, crowned by a splendorous canopy bed in the shape of an ancient Egyptian barge. It was the divine barge indeed; Cecil B. DeMille eat your heart out came to my mind thinking about the iconic Hollywood Golden Era epic films.

Next was a bathroom with a golden sunken tub! To finalize the grand tour, the Chief, ceremoniously, took me to carved double doors with Egyptian god motifs at the right of the bed and voila, a balcony facing The Great Pyramid (!!!). "We hope this room will be of your satisfaction," the Chief said. What could I say? I didn't have words to express my real feelings. And he added, "In four hours I will come to take you for a camel caravan tour to see the sunset at the pyramids."

Smiling as a child, I managed to reply, "I'll be ready." He turned away and left with the bellboys.

I was alone in this 1000 Arabian Nights' set. I was so excited that I did not know what to do next, so I stayed on the balcony relaxing and enjoying the incredible view for I don't know how long.

Later I walked into the room and began removing all the clothes I wore since I left the U.S., leaving them scattered all over the room until I was nude. I got a luscious tangerine from the fruit basket on the middle table of the sitting room. I walked slowly, jumped on the barge and the deliciously beige satin, I set the tangerine on the night table and concentrated on looking at the pyramid through the open balcony doors. I felt like a pharaoh and decided to rest for a while and later take a bath to get ready for the next Egyptian treat.

About two and a half hours later, I woke up looking at the summit of the Great Pyramid. I got up and carefully sneaked out onto the balcony, I was nude and didn't want to be seen since I was an official government guest. After the stasis of the view, I ran to the bathroom to fill the tub with warm water. I got in and felt so relaxed… It was my first contact with the Nile waters.

After a soothing bath, I decided that for the caravan tour I should wear the typical Egyptian garment. I unpacked the sand-color linen *gallabeah* with its matching Arab pants my mother made for me. Then I must wear a turban as the Bedouins wore in Cairo. What the heck. I always liked to go all the way on my first dates. And I dressed up for a glorious evening ahead.

Just four hours to the minute, The Chief was knocking at the door. He looked pleasantly surprised and smiled at me. He was also wearing a *gallabeah*! We walked out of the hotel through an inside garden with elaborate iron gates to the outside. There was a group of Bedouins dressed the same as I was outside with their troop of camels. Two of them helped me to get on the kneeling camel. It felt very unusual to be on such a tall, strangely built and ugly animal. I had ridden horses in the past, but they were beautiful. It doesn't feel very comfortable or safe being on a camel. But do as the Romans do. After all, the Bedouins and The Chief were on their camels, and we began to move toward the pyramids just across the highway but actually much farther than they looked. The Chief stayed on my right explaining the sites we passed. I felt a nice breeze and the sun was getting low and the sky was filling with a glorious array of colors. I was not asking any questions, just enjoying the unusual exotic view. I was immensely enjoying the breathtaking surroundings. The mystifying Sphinx in the distance on the right and on the left the majestic Cheops, Chephren and Mycerinus pyramids waiting for our feast at sunset. The temperature was getting cooler and more breezy as the sun was rapidly declining to the horizon. Each minute, each second, the beautiful coloration of the sky was getting more and more sensuous. My linen clothes were waving with the breeze. The back and forth of the camel movement–yes, those movements–there is something very suggestive from them. And the enormous structures reaching the heaven. And those camel movements . . . The breeze increasing… Oh no, I'm having an erection. I hope The Chief won't notice it. Those damn camel movements! This is embarrassing. It seems we are not far from the base of Cheops pyramid and it is getting dark pretty fast. I glance at the sky and its a phantasmagorical dark purple. God those movements… I can't get my mind distracted on other subjects so the damn erection will go away. The Chief looked at me and smiled. The breeze was becoming a strong wind. Why does The Chief keep smiling at me? I felt some particles of dust getting in my eyes and suddenly sand was everywhere and the wind was whistling. The Chief got closer to me and almost screaming over the howl of the wind said, "We are having an unannounced light sand dust. Let us get close and try to reach the opposite side at the center of the pyramid to seek shelter until the wind subsides." The other Bedouins tried to form a tight circle and advance to the other side of the pyramid.

My clothes were battling against the wind. My turban flew away. My hair into my eyes. The visibility was very bad. The Bedouin guiding us was fighting with the force of the wind and the stubbornness of the camel, trying to pull him to the other side of the pyramid for shelter. I couldn't see the other Bedouins of our caravan. Suddenly my camel was producing unusual sounds and became restless. The Chief jumped down from his camel to help the Bedouin control my camel. But with a fast stroke, my camel moved his neck to the left and ran away. It was so windy and surrounded by sand that I was blinded. The only thing I was able to do was to keep myself on the camel. I heard what appeared to be the voice of The Chief in the distance. He was screaming something to me, but I didn't know what.

Apparently, the turbulent sounds of the wind was too much and my camel was galloping away, out of control. But somehow in the middle of that unusual situation that I never had before I kept my cool and was not afraid. I knew that the pyramids were just across the street from my hotel and there were buildings and villas around the area. I felt the spirit of adventure. I felt really free and wild in the middle of this unusual situation. My only worry was staying on the camel. He will stop eventually. He will get tired, of course. It was a shame that I could not see much. I would love to be able to see. Suddenly, something hit my head! Oooooh, I lost balance and I'm falling. I fell to the ground. I probably passed out.

When I eventually opened my eyes very slowly. I still couldn't see much because of the sand and the burning I was feeling. I opened and closed my eyes to get tears and finally I was able to open them. God, is it completely dark. Where am I? In the distance I kind of see what appeared to be some light of candles or kerosene lamps. I gathered I was in the desert because I felt the sand under me and on my fingers. I was lying on the ground facing up and I turned my head to the other side. Just a few feet away from me was The Chief. I felt so relieved! He was standing with the full moon behind him, observing me in silence, lying on the sand. "Can you help me get up?" I asked. "My back is in pain and I cannot get up." He didn't answer. He didn't move. He was standing there and he smiled like he did before. It was an unusual smile. There was something sinister in it. In my state I was beginning to feel apprehensive and noticed a cool sweat in the palms of my hands. I felt helpless lying on the sand.

I tried to reason and said, "Chief, I am a guest of your government, help me please."

Then, between his feet appeared a cobra as represented in Ancient Egyptian art. Oh no I am terrified of snakes, I thought to myself, but I couldn't hold my feelings and panicked and screamed at him, "Help me please, help me!" But he had the same sinister smile on his face. I began shaking all over and losing control because of my helpless physical state. Making an extraordinary effort and overcoming the excruciating pain, I was trying to crawl out of my nightmare situation, faster and faster… But I can't…. I can't move faster… And I could see more damn cobras moving around me. They are creeping on their noxious slimy bodies and looking at me with their jaws wide open, showing their mortal fangs. I have to get the hell out of here! I don't know how but I have to… Getting strength from I don't know where and overcoming my back pain, I miraculously managed finally to get up and start running. I was running incredibly fast. Suddenly my feet felt like lead. I was trying to continue going fast but it was impossible. I was slowing down and they are going to get me. I turned my head and The Chief was running behind me. The cobras are moving fast and getting closer and closer. I can see the silhouette of the Sphinx in the distance and I wanted to get there. Somehow I was sure she will save me. But my feet didn't respond. Against my will I am slowing down as in slow motion. I look back again and see that the Bedouins were also running behind along with the cobras on both sides with their clothes in pieces, destroyed by the sand storm. I saw a tent not far. I can see lights inside and hear music…. I changed direction and ran there almost without breath. Come on legs, go faster! I am almost reaching the tent and the music is louder. I am almost there. My back hurt badly. Come on… I'm almost there… Closer… Closer. . .Without air in my lungs I entered the tent collapsing on the carpet. I was saved, I thought and closed my eyes.

When I slowly opened my eyes I saw what appeared to be a mummified cow in the middle of the floor. Also, there were musicians, dressed as in ancient Egypt and belly dancers almost nude. I asked for help. Abruptly, in the festive tent, the music and dance stopped. It was an eerie silence and everybody was looking in my direction. Then, one of the dancing women came close to me. She was offering something to drink in a black container and in surprisingly perfect English said, "This is the blood of Mother Hathor." And she pointed to the dead cow. And I replied, "Do you happen to have a Root Beer?" She seems to be without words and looking at me very seriously she said, "No, you have to drink her blood!" "Ugh… it's revolting," I exclaimed and vehemently screamed, ``Get me out of here! I made a wrong turn and landed here! But I want to go to the Sphinx…" They all started laughing and running in circles around me. The women were making noises with their voices that reminded me of American Indians. Some of them began tearing apart what was left of my clothes until I was completely naked in front of the laughing crowd. I wanted to get out and run but my feet were glued to the carpet. Then they began to dance around me chanting something that even though it was not in any language known to me, I was able to understand clearly their monotonous repetitions as "You died here and you came back to die here again." Realizing what was going to take place I began screaming, "Oh no, no, no , no! Help! Help! Help! Oooooooh…!"

Opening my eyes, I saw the ceiling. I looked around. I was full of perspiration. I was glad to be saved… In my own bed, in my home, in the good old United States of America.

"Oh say, can you see, by the dawn's early light…"

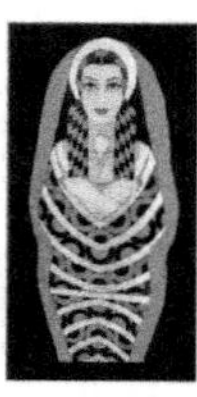

CHAPTER 2

CRY OF THE WITCH

I was really excited about the first gallery exhibition of my Egyptian paintings.

I first did ancient Egyptian-style art when I was little in the country of my birth. I did more in the early 1960's. In April of 1974, I developed the form of a three dimensional canvas in the shape of the lid of the sarcophagus after trials and errors. I very much enjoyed this form and the creativity that resulted from it. I felt like I now had something worthy of being exhibited in a gallery. Previously I exhibited in a private residence for two princesses and two commercial galleries in Spain in 1966 and 67. But I was mainly doing Op-Art at that time. That change of style happened when I lived in Paris in 1965. Then in the U.S. I had shows in 1969 and in 1970, exhibiting my Colorist Geometric collection.

In May of 1975, I started looking for a place to exhibit my new Egyptian collection inspired by sarcophagus lids. It wasn't until July, 1976 that I finally got a gallery. It was not easy but I got a "recommendation" as usually happens in this subjective art field that is based on "who you know." It isn't very often solely for the merit of your work but instead on your political leanings, a big surprise for me. I am not very lucky in general, but this time I was introduced by a wealthy and prominent art collector to the Dean of the art school of a reputable and well known museum. He saw my work and found it unusual and merited an exhibit. He said, "However, this museum will not exhibit your work because you are not an American artist." But I had been an American citizen since 1974 and America was, then and now, my only country. I didn't understand this objection but I didn't want to say anything to antagonize, it was not the proper time for that. Nevertheless, he advised me to go to a few art galleries. He said, "You should mention that I have sent you." So that was a very good recommendation!

That very same day I went to all the places he suggested with no luck whatsoever. They were all booked or not interested in touching the subject of my art. I found that in Jewish owned galleries there was some animosity against Egyptian art even though my work and subject matter was not political at all. At the end of a very long day, there was only one gallery left. It was supposed to be at a very good location but I couldn't find it. I kept walking back and forth on the same block where the gallery was supposed to be, but it was not to be found. I went to stores in the block asking for the gallery. It was as if I was speaking in Chinese. No one knew anything about this now mysterious gallery. When I was getting ready to abandon my search for that forgotten place, I decided to inquire in a liquor store I previously discarded from my quest. As the late actor *Jim Nabors* would say in the 1960s TV show *The Andy Griffith Show* as his character *Gomer Pyle, "Surprise, Surprise, Surprise!"* In the liquor store they knew all about the gallery! Bingo! The entrance was just beside the liquor store, so, when I was back on the sidewalk I was able to decipher on a very dirty bronze wall plaque with the name of the gallery I was looking for. What was the point of having a bronze plaque so dirty that it was unreadable? Well, that's not my business, so I entered and the gallery was upstairs. The fact that it didn't have a window facing that lively street disappointed me a bit… Anyway, I will try, what do I have to lose? The staircase wasn't that clean either, but that's all right. I was coming up with excuses in my mind. After climbing the first flight of stairs, I came out to a bigger, charming, oval staircase open in the center and with an old translucent dirty skylight on the top. I liked the architectural design. So, I continued climbing to the fourth floor where I saw a door to the right bearing the same name of the gallery the Dean gave me. I went in, entering into a medium sized room, with white walls and track lights. Some prints here and there were scattered on the floor and leaning against the walls. There was a tacky sofa with a horrid coffee table with a clear glass top resting on a real, stuffed crocodile. I hate reptiles. I am terrified by them—something I was glad to leave behind on the "tropical island paradise" of my birth. Along with lizards, iguanas, tarantulas, mosquitoes, scorpions, flying roaches and all the fauna of big, disgusting, large, epic, insects that ruined my otherwise idyllic childhood!—I swallowed my pride and tried to console myself: Oh well, that must be a sign of good luck this encounter with the Egyptian god Sobek himself, mummified, holding for eternity the glass top of the coffee table. Could this be the place this god is reserving for me?

Getting me out of my occult Egyptian thoughts, two middle-aged ladies approached me. One of them with dark hair. The other, tall, attractive, with abundant natural gray hair. I identified myself and stated "Who" had sent me there. Both appeared very interested and flattered that such a person had referred me there. The tall gray hair said she was the director and the other her assistant. I gave my portfolio to the director and she seemed to be favorably impressed and excited at what she was seeing. Then she called her assistant over to see it. She also seemed to be impressed as I kept explaining my work and my ideas about an exhibit and when it should be held. Actually what I was dreaming of was to have my exhibit at the same time as the National Gallery of Art in Washington, D.C. was to have the exhibit of The Treasures of King Tutankhamen. It was coming up soon—the timing was perfect. Perhaps, judging by the way the gallery looked to me, they were probably not usually booked too much time in advance. They may be desperately looking for anybody. I may have seemed to them as sent by divine providence in the form of the Dean of a museum. They appeared sincerely impressed (thanks to the Dean) and they loved the idea of exhibiting at the same time as the National Gallery of Art. We were already in early July and the National Gallery exhibit was to be in November. My collection was completed and ready. We had three months to do all the promotion, etc. It seemed like I was right, that they didn't have anybody booked for that month. I came as a blessing with a perfect, if unusual show at the perfect time.

I left the gallery very happy. I wanted to run and laugh. I was feeling so excited, like Gene Kelly "Singing in the Rain." I hadn't felt like that in a very long time. Everything had been so difficult in the past year looking for a place to exhibit and now, in a few minutes, my luck had changed because of the magic of the recommendation of the Dean. The art world would be nothing without recommendations or connections with other people with a name and power. Sad but true. The artists are at the mercy of this reality and in many cases difficult to overcome. This is not that I had made it, this is only a chance to exhibit in a professional gallery on a good street in Washington, D.C. on top of a liquor store and I don't drink! Could this be my big chance? The opportunity I had been waiting for? Could I be just dreaming again those vivid dreams that I have been having all my life? No no! I am quite awake this time. It is true. It's not a dream or one of my fantasies. I became worried that for some reason I would lose the chance. If I have this show, it's going to be my first big show in the United States. My prior shows in America have been in institutions, and clubs. When I arrived home I told my roommate how important this exhibit was for me and asked him, "Please, stop me from doing anything that could jeopardize the realization of this exhibit."

A few days later I received, as promised, a letter from the director of the gallery agreeing to show my "Egyptian Sculptured Paintings"—which is the technical name I created to classify them–"sculptured" because they are three dimensional. But, people called them "mummies" for short and I eventually called them "mummies" too. I promptly answered the agreement and what I'll do to set up-and promotion of the exhibit. At the end of July, I received a letter from the gallery agreeing to my proposals and stating the gallery conditions. Also agreeing to have a meeting at the gallery on August 2nd to discuss the brochure for the exhibit.

I took Jaums to this meeting, because I wanted to be one hundred percent sure of understanding everything. We met in the gallery room with the uninspiring tacky sofa and the mummified crocodile coffee table. She was charming, nice and polite. I agreed to provide the design for the brochure, which I'd mail to her in plenty of time before the opening. Then she asked me, "Could a friend of mine, who is a curator of a Washington museum, go to your studio to see your "mummies?" "Of course", I said, liking the idea very much.

A few days later, I mailed her my designs for the brochure. After a week or so, her curator friend called me to set an appointment to view my work.

The curator came as agreed. He, too, seemed nice and polite. However, he liked some of my early Egyptian flat paintings best. He was very impressed by them. And said, "As a matter of fact, I like them very much and they will look beautiful in the show." Since he was a curator, I much appreciated that he liked my early work. I'll include them in the plans for the exhibit, although there were not so many at that time since I had grown to prefer my friendly "mummies." Other people who shared my excitement with them like, at-the-time, leading well-known Interior Designer, the late Anthony Child, who came to my home to see my "mummies" by recommendation of the owner of the well-known Pyramid Gallery, in Washington, D.C.

Back to Mr. Curator who asked, "Has she seen photographs of this kind of work?" He asked. "No, I showed her only the photos of my 'mummies.' They are the most representative of my current work. There are many pieces of Tutankhamen and with the upcoming exhibit at The National Gallery of Art of Tutankhamen, they would be more attention getting for the gallery." He asked, "Do you have more flat paintings?" "Yes, I do" I replied, "But not enough for a solo show but enough to fill in. Come with me and I'll show you the rest." So I did. They were hanging in many places in my home. I said before he left, "I can make a few more before the exhibit."

A few days later the owner of the gallery called me asking if she could come to my studio to see my work in person. That was fine with me.

On the agreed-to evening, after opening the door of the foyer, there she was, tall and attractive, but in a mood I hadn't seen before. She arrived with the same curator friend. She looked frantic and panicky. The first thing she said before entering was, "Where are the paintings?!" What was she expecting? I had the paintings hung all over my home. Some were in the foyer right in front of her nose! Okay, my "mummies" are paintings too, just a different shape, the iconic shape of a sarcophagus lid. And, I was not the stereotypical artist depicted in films wearing dirty clothes, greasy and unkempt hair living in a dump with paint drops all over the floor and the paintings thrown around helter-skelter. I have never been able to create with a mess around me. I always managed to live in a restful, balanced and beautiful environment, otherwise I am not inspired to create anything. So, I replied to the out of control gray hair lady. "I have my paintings displayed in various rooms of my home, some are just here in the foyer, you can see I have four "mummies" here. Can you come in please?" When she came in I found myself beginning to point at the walls at all of the Egyptian paintings I planned to show that I had shown the curator on his previous visit. Then she repeated,

"Where are the paintings?!" I replied to the gray hair lady on the verge of a nervous breakdown, "You'll be seeing more of them." The gray hair lady replied, losing her "composure." "I came to see paintings, paintings!" "Oh I see," I said, "Do you mean the regular flat paintings?" Realizing that's only what she wanted to see—even if the exhibit will be titled and promoted as *Egyptian Sculptured Paintings* alluding to the three dimensional "mummies." Without saying a word, she made assenting movements with her head of gray hair. "Well, I have them all over my home mixed with my 'mummies.' You see, they are not concentrated in one place. I'll show you everything so you will see them," I explained and proceeded to the living room. When we entered this room, it was like a shock to her. Apparently she was not expecting that I would live in an environment like this. She glanced at the four corners of the room fast and with an expression of disapproval and disgust reflected on her face. I guessed she thought I was an starving artist; just a little Latino found on a banana leaf basket floating in a piranha infested creek, rescued by Juan Valdes, the coffee picker; living in a dump with "carved" plastic Mediterranean motifs on crushed velvet furniture sealed in clear plastic slipcovers; a pair of tin enameled peacocks and photos of dead relatives on the falling apart wooden walls... No it wasn't like that. I wondered what the curator told her about my home... Obviously, she had no clue. I didn't have a clear glass coffee table held by a mummified crocodile or tacky sofas, heaven forbid! Who knows what it was in her tiny head of gray hair. All of the sudden she became frightened of my "mummies" and didn't want to see them at all. She walked fast through the living room. I followed her to the next room, the library. There I had three flat paintings on the walls that she appeared to be anxious to see. I pointed at the paintings and she looked very fast. Then, at that very moment, in front of my incredulous eyes, a transformation, and unreal metamorphosis took place like a film special effect: she became a full-fledged WITCH in front of my eyes and demanded, "I want to see more flat paintings!" There will be three more to come in the gallery hall. We left the library immediately and rushed through the dining room in a frenzy toward the gallery hall where, along with the smaller "mummies" I had three more of the flat paintings she was so vehemently demanding to see. She became so terrorized of the three infant "mummies" there that she refused even to see the flat paintings! At that moment I became frightened by the WITCH that was in my home. And she walked very fast like escaping the gallery hall of horrors. Next was my studio which had a twelve flat paintings depicting an Egyptian theory of Immanuel Velikovsky making a parallel between the story of the Pharaoh Akhenaten through Tutankhamen, with the Greek Tragedy of *Oedipus Rex,* as well as other flat paintings inside two of the closets. I remembered that in the previous visit of the curator, he particularly liked the two, big flat paintings I had on a back wall which he called "very handsome." She glanced at these two paintings and nervously looked at the curator for approval. He made a positive gesture with his face after which she seemed reassured enough to like them. Apparently that insecure "director of an art gallery" needed somebody to fill in for her lack of backbone. She cannot decide for herself! I was getting a little bit upset about her attitude and behavior and I noticed that Jaums was making a gesture behind her back to communicate to me his displeasure with her frantic conduct. I decided to show her the other paintings in the master bedroom which she hardly glanced at demanding to see more flat paintings. Well, I didn't have any other alternative than somehow take that WITCH to my studio again! Running and as fast as I could I opened both closets to show her the rest of the flat paintings. She glanced at them fast and, exasperated, demanded to see more. "That's all I have," I replied.

Frantically she asked me, "Can you make more for the show?!" The date for my exhibit was getting close and I had a full time job at an office and cannot ask for vacation. So I said, "I think I could do two or three small flat paintings, no more." And we walked back to the living room and I made them sit down. I still have a few things to talk about the show. I had cheese and bought wine to offer them. However they didn't want to eat or drink anything, except water for the curator only.

Then she categorically stated, "I received your design for the brochure but I didn't like it. It was too busy."

Nothing from my production was good enough for her now. Her displeasure with everything was total. But I decided to bite my tongue and not say anything to disturb the rage of the gray haired WITCH. This exhibit was too important for me. If I lose this chance, I would not be able to exhibit during the Tutankhamen exhibit in any other gallery. So I kept my cool even if in reality what I wanted was to commit a *WITCH-icide* on the spot. There would be no blood since she didn't have any. If she doesn't want to have my exhibit at all, she should be the one to tell me, after all it was her gallery and she has the *WITCH-right* and we didn't have a written contract. If she was experiencing so much disgust with my work, myself and my environment, she should say that herself. I should not have to pull it out. I wondered what Mr. Curator had told her about my "mummies" that made her change so completely after she had seen all the photographs of them and the with the recommendation of the Dean of a prestigious art school and museum? Who knows.

I proceeded to ask the WITCH about the promotion she was planning for my exhibit. She replied, "The usual, Galleries magazine and the galleries section of the local publications." I said, "Since my work is so unusual, I had in mind something more than that. I had found recently that I am the only artist doing this specific type of three dimensional work inspired by the Egyptian sarcophagus lids. If that's all you are planning to do, I would like to ask your permission to make a press release on my own to send to The Egyptian Cultural Department of the Embassy in Washington, D.C., and publications specializing in this kind of ancient art in America, provided that you review it ahead of time before I send them. I want to work with you." She seemed a bit scandalized at my proposal and pointed at me in a not very polite way to say the least, "I don't want my gallery to become a carnival!" And she got up indicating she wanted to leave followed by the curator, so the WITCH went. I guessed on her flying broom into the dark night. Fortunately, as fast as she came, she went. When I closed the door the smell of sulfur was left on the air. Jaums, an American-born with cold Anglo-Saxon blood in his veins said, "I was ready to kill her! I was very glad she left because I was getting red hot." In my case, my Latin blood was fuming in all directions getting ready to explode like a 50 megaton atomic bomb to incinerate that WITCH on that tranquil spot in the Washington, D.C. suburbs known as Silver Spring, Maryland.

To hell with HER! I decided to write the press release without HER consent. Of course it was sedate and informative, not designed in any way to create a "carnival." That was never my intention. I sent it to the WITCH's assistant since thankfully, SHE was out of town. HER assistant thought that was all right and with the best interests of the gallery. So I released it on my own at the end of October.

The date of the opening was getting close. FORTUNATELY the WITCH was very busy all the time or out of town but I needed to set the date and time to take all the pieces for the exhibit to the gallery. There was a lot of press coverage, excitement and ballyhoo about the exhibit of Tutankhamen at the National Gallery as I predicted. Inspired by mine, the WITCH gallery assistant also decided to write a press release from the gallery to send to local news media. She did a good job and the WITCH approved its release six days before my opening.

Set-up day arrived and I was there, sharp-on-time for the delivery and setting up of the exhibit. Jaums came to help me. The station wagon was packed to the brim and the paintings were carried up the staircase to the fourth floor gallery. Fortunately for "Peace on Earth" the WITCH was not there. The morning was ticking away and SHE still hadn't arrived. I usually know how to hang art, including an entire exhibit. I have been doing it since the early sixties and especially my new unusual art. I had also been a professional display artist. But waiting for HER to "materialize," I decided, with the consent of HER assistant, to at least distribute the pieces resting on the walls of the gallery to see how the show would be looking, but not actually hanging anything, awaiting HER approval. The time continued ticking with no flying WITCH landing. The assistant was getting nervous. She liked very much the way I distributed my pieces in the two rooms. She gave me some suggestions for minor changes which I did. The exhibit certainly would look great! But I couldn't hang without the WITCH being there. Jaums and I sat in the small office, under the tacky fluorescent tube waiting.

After another hour or so passed, the assistant told me, "You know, I have no idea where she is. Why don't you start hanging the exhibit to see if she arrives? I mean, what you did looks very good. You have done a good job. I am sure she will like it." It sounded like a good idea. It was getting late and I didn't want to spend the night at the gallery, so I began to hang my pieces. After a few hours and just when I was finishing to hang the last piece, the frantic WITCH landed, walking-very-fast-just-glancing-at-the-art as SHE had done in HER most memorable visit to my home and spat out: "This cannot be! Everything is horrible! You have to change all your pieces!" I saw despair reflected on her assistant's face. I got upset and told HER, "You had agreed to be here early this morning with me to supervise the hanging. And, ahead of time, I showed you a floor plan of what I was planning to do and you said that it looked alright to you." SHE coldly said, "I could not be here this morning." Without any excuses. Her assistant looked at me highly apologetic while the sulfur-distilled WITCH added, "There are too many 'mummies!' It's too… too busy."

So, I turned my back and went to the next room to cool down

because I was getting ready to jump over that despicable WITCH and set HER on FIRE. However, on my way to the gallery that morning, I made an agreement with myself that if something went wrong with HER, I should avoid confrontation by all means possible. And I found Jaums in that room cooling down too! I asked him to go out and ask HER what changes SHE wanted to make. Jaums went and asked for the specific changes. SHE walked with him back and forth with HER through the main room gallery and SHE could not come up with any suggestions. SHE wanted change but SHE could not come up with any! I went out of my forced cooling down seclusion and followed them to the entrance staircase. Then, I asked HER, "Do you like the selection of pieces here?" SHE thought for a short while and said, "It's all right, but I would like one of the big flat paintings to be placed in the main gallery room." I replied, "I arranged the paintings historically. Here at the entrance I placed the Egyptian Trinity of Osiris, Isis and Horus in the form of three 'mummies' and two paintings. These are the basic three characters of Egyptian mythology." I explained. "The main room," I continued explaining, "is dedicated to my versions of the Tutankhamen collection. Historically, your change would break the idea of the beginning of the Egyptian mythology that prevailed for many centuries before Dynasty XVIII which is the period of Tutankhamen's life and death. That will not add anything to the main room exhibit." SHE thought for a moment and said, "I like the way the entrance looks." And walked again to the main room. I TOOK A DEEP BREATH OF RELIEF!

Then SHE added, "I want to eliminate some of the Tutankhamen mummies." I clarified, "Remember that they are the highlight of this exhibit. Remember that the Tutankhamen exhibit at the National Gallery will be very popular now. These pieces will attract attention to your gallery." HER reply was, "They have to go! Too many 'mummies.' Too busy," SHE insisted while looking around completely scandalized and terrorized at the sight. Then, abruptly, SHE ran to the phone for HELP, apparently to call 911! But no, SHE was calling her "fixer," the curator to come to help! So we had to wait again, this time for him to decide on changes. During this waiting period SHE apparently went to the downstairs liquor store to get some courage . . .. That's why SHE was well-known at that place! HER assistant came to Jaums and me and very apologetic said "She is an extremely moody person. She is really very difficult to work with." I replied, "I am PAINFULLY aware" and smiled.

The sulfuric WITCH came back holding her drink and a second one for her curator savior. After an excruciatingly long wait the curator arrived and the WITCH automatically gave him his drink. SHE immediately told him loud enough for me to hear clearly, "I do not like this hanging at all!" while they walked through the gallery. "Changes have to be made!," SHE dramatically said. He was displaying agreement but wasn't saying anything. Then SHE suddenly flew to the tiny office indicating with an obvious gesture that SHE was leaving him "in charge." And he walked to me. "Well," I said to him, "I have been asking what SHE wanted to change in this room and SHE seems unsure." After a short pause the curator said, "She wants to eliminate the 'mummies' and hang flat paintings. "But there are not enough flat paintings to fill the exhibit, even with the extra ones I have done" I said. "Then, let's remove some 'mummies,'" he said. "All right. Which ones?" I asked.

Then he walked around and I followed him. He proceeded to eliminate the three most important "mummies" of the Tutankhamen collection and in its place he hung a flat painting that completely destroyed the balanced composition of that entire wall. The one flat painting was quite obviously too small for the space and the history that had inspired me would be violated. Then, he separated a Tutankhamen triptych of 'mummies.' But this change, after it was done, I liked and I told him so. He walked to the other room and after carefully examining everything, he left it the way I had done it. I thought, "He likes it! He likes it!" But then he walked to the small office where I had hung some of the flat paintings and he changed them around, making the room look pretty bad. To make things worse, he demanded that I remove spotlights that I supplied for that room the WITCH approved. That room's only light was an anti-art fluorescent tube which changed the colors of my paintings, making them appear faded. And he said, "No gallery will do that." To avoid confrontation, I took the ladder and took down the spotlights. Actually, what "No gallery will do" is display paintings under fluorescent tubes.

Well, at least I should consider myself lucky because he didn't make me remove my other spotlights in the other gallery room where the only source of lighting was another single fluorescent tube office fixture! I realized that "the curator" didn't have much aesthetic or art gallery sense. Besides, he was already sounding a little drunk. By the time the WITCH was inspecting the two rooms with an evil victorious smile on HER dried, old, *none-kissable*, thin lips, Jaums and I got our things together and as fast as we could get the hell out of that toxic place, alas, leaving my "mummies" to fend for themselves. "She will cry someday . . ." I thought.

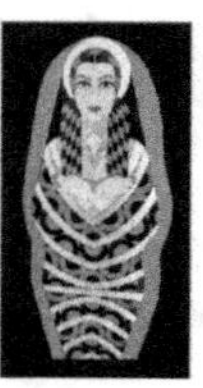

CHAPTER 3

THE EGYPTIANS ARE COMING!

Since the gallery was on the top floor and difficult to spot from the street, I thought of making two advertising banners to hang from the two dormer windows of the gallery facing the avenue. On them just the name of the gallery, name of the exhibit, my name, and the floor it was located. After all, the National Gallery had two banners announcing their exhibit. My banners were to be simple, in black and white and the WITCH approved the idea. So, I worked hard for two weeks —I never had done this before— to have them ready before the official opening. For the same reasons I also made a simple black and white medium-sized poster, so people walking on the sidewalk could easily find the "forbidden" staircase to the elusive gallery. The poster had the title of the exhibit *EGYPTIAN SCULPTURED PAINTINGS* with a simplified silhouette of a "mummy" and my name. For it, I got a plain, metallic gold easel from none other than *Saks Fifth Avenue*, where I worked in 1969 and it was complete with a built-in-light (since the entrance was dark). Well, the WITCH hated the poster. SHE said, "It's too busy." SHE also hated the easel and prohibited its use. However, SHE said that the poster could be placed on the glass entrance door of the building, fastened with *Scotch Tape* to the glass… Very tacky, but APPROVED.

The evening of the opening, I arrived half an hour ahead of time. The banners were still hanging from the fourth floor dormer windows of the gallery. The poster was still up. I was very much relieved. I was afraid that the WITCH might have changed her mind in one of her recurrent, "professional" mood swings and removed everything.

I got upstairs to the gallery and I found her assistant very busy getting ready for the opening. She was very nice as usual. I always had a good rapport with her. She went out of her way to balance and make up for the vicious WITCH. There was a young guy who was working part time to set the table with wine, cheese and peanuts. I was very nervous and went in to stay in the main room, I didn't want to face the tacky fluorescent lights at the entrance reception office raping the color of my paintings. Fortunately the WITCH was not there yet. I was wishing deep in my heart that HER broom's transmission fell apart that evening so SHE could not show up. I was looking forward to a nice and relaxing evening.

So, at 6 o'clock, the people started arriving. For being my first exhibit since 1970, there were a lot of people. The reactions to my work were of awe and surprise. They haven't seen a commercial exhibit quite like that. The words that I kept overhearing throughout the evening were, "magnificent," "marvelous," "incredible." All were very favorable. I was very pleased to hear all these comments since I became worried because of the attitude of the WITCH against my "mummies" which eventually created feelings of insecurity on my side. But the reactions were positive, restoring my confidence in my work. Among the people who came was a talented artist that I respected a lot. We worked together in the first job I had in Washington, D.C. at a shop building and painting props for the windows of a big department store downtown. I hadn't seen him since 1967! And there he was. He saw the announcement of my exhibit and came to see my work. He was very impressed at what I had produced.

My only disappointment was that no one from the Cultural Department of the Egyptian Embassy came. I had invited them and asked the assistant if they had called back, but no call. The only real Egyptian there was Ramses, the husband of a fellow worker from the office where I was working. He was the first Egyptian I met in America. He was very excited about seeing my work for the first time. He shook my hand and his had a different feeling, it was strong and at the same time it was warm and soft as a velvet cushion. I have never noticed that feeling before or since. He talked to me about his own art and he was amazed at my work and said that he had "never seen anything like it." I appreciated his reaction. But the other Egyptians never showed up that night. I was sad because it was a tribute to their ancient art, inspired by them and for them. I felt abandoned by the people who had inspired me since my childhood, because my affinity to this kind of art was manifested in the early days of my imagination. Later in the evening, disturbing the reigning peace in the gallery and while people were still there, I heard a whistling sound followed by a strong stench of sulfur and voila, the WITCH, riding HER old broom made HER uncalled-for entrance through one of the dormer windows of the gallery. SHE was wearing black of course. Oh well… We ignored each other. Fortunately the curator didn't come, hanging from the broom. I was very glad, I didn't want to see him again and probably that feeling was mutual. I am very understanding.

Oh no… The WITCH is coming in my direction! Politely, SHE introduced me to a couple that wanted me to explain my work. So I did while I was noticing that the WITCH was looking surprised about the amount of people in the gallery and the favorable reaction to my "mummies." Apparently they were not "scared" at the sight of them as she suddenly had become. Also there was the co-owner of a well-known commercial art gallery who was there complementing the exhibit! At the end of allocated time for the opening night, I went home satisfied with the reactions of the public to my new collection of Egyptian Sculptured Paintings (ESP).

The next day I had tickets to see at the National Gallery of Art for the exhibit *Treasures of King Tutankhamen*. I decided to risk my life on the way and stop by at the WITCH's gallery to check if there were any sales. I was surprised that the WITCH was there! But apparently SHE was in a different mood toward me—perhaps the favorable reaction of the night before or who knows. SHE even complimented my Canadian Nutria coat! I certainly was speechless! SHE was obviously happy to tell me that there were no sales or any other news. So I left, I didn't want to stay there long in case of a sudden mood change.

As the days passed, the WITCH decided to remove the banners from the dormer windows. SHE called me to go to the gallery and take them down. Her excuse was, "No commercial galleries in town have display banners." SHE also made me to remove one of the "mummies" from the show, alleging, "One of my partners did not like that "mummy because it's casting a shadow on the translucent glass door that is very eerie." I dutifully carried out all of HER requests in order not to antagonize.

One day her assistant called me to tell me that a local television station contacted the gallery to do a report about my exhibit, but the WITCH was not interested. The days were passing and no one was coming to see my exhibit, no sales or inquiries. I was very discouraged. I had the idea to have a special reception for the Egyptian Embassy before the closing of the exhibit. I called the assistant and talked to her. She liked the idea but she had to consult with the WITCH. SHE was as usual "out of town." Finally she was able to get in touch with HER. Apparently SHE was in a good mood and accepted the idea. So the reception was scheduled for the evening before the exhibit closed.

I was very concerned that evening, because that afternoon I had called the Egyptian Embassy to confirm if they were coming. After a long time on the phone being transferred from one department to another, I could not get any assurance whatsoever. So I was very apprehensive.

In the early evening when I arrived at the gallery, my poster was not taped to the street door, so I rushed upstairs, got the poster and went down and fastened to the glass street door. I wanted to make sure that if the Egyptians showed up they would find the entrance of the elusive gallery. I rushed upstairs again. The assistant and the other part-time guy were getting things ready and she told me that the WITCH would not be able to attend the reception. I could not contain myself and like an involuntary scream from the depths of my soul exclaimed in relief, "Gooood!" At least that eliminated the tension I was feeling when the WITCH was buzzing around me on her broom.

As a miracle from all the Egyptian Gods, at 6 o'clock, the Egyptians arrived! All at the same time! They all were amazed at what they were seeing! They looked very happy and proud. It was like a discovery for them. Most expressed their feelings that it was a shame that they found the exhibit just the last night and could do little now to promote it. But it was an impossible situation since I had already agreed to the mandate that I take down the exhibit the next morning. A last minute change of plans with the WITCH was something out of the question. I was sure SHE wanted me and my "mummies" out of there in a hurry since my exhibit did not sell anything. I think if SHE had allowed the TV reporting and other opportunities to properly promote the exhibit, the story would have been different. It was HER fault for not handling my exhibit properly due to HER stupid fear of my friendly "mummies". Even removing banners and poster I provided at no charge! From that busy avenue far below, people cannot imagine that upstairs there was a gallery having a second exhibit of historic Egyptian art, this one accessible with no long lines and free of charge. People in 1976 were excited and curious about ancient Egyptian art. And the only place in town to buy <u>an original piece</u> was this gallery. In my opinion how stupid SHE was, what an opportunity SHE lost; what an unique exhibit SHE mismanaged!

Back to the last evening at the gallery, I recalled the most exciting thing. A group of Egyptian diplomats were talking in a corner of the main exhibit room and suddenly they all turned to me to join them. They told me that they did not know of anybody in or out of Egypt that was doing original sarcophagus lids like mine. They expressed how excited and amazed they were and knowing that I had done all of it without having been in Egypt. So "they were thinking of extending an official invitation to visit their country as a guest of their government." They said it will take about a year to put together "but it will come. We all going to sign the petition to our government." I was speechless! I was not expecting anything like that. It was beyond my wildest dreams. Now I understand how Cinderella felt when the shoe fit and the Prince selected her! From then on I was on cloud 9!

Dr. Mafouz, one of the Cultural Counselors from the Embassy, who was very nice and charming, gave me a kiss on my forehead before leaving and she said, "You should go to Egypt. . ." `` Then, unexpectedly, the WITCH arrived flying on her broom to destroy that sweet moment looking despotically at everybody, obviously displeased at the sight of "my" Egyptians.

Fortunately as fast as SHE landed SHE took off leaving her sulfur in the air and giving the order to turn the gallery lights off. The assistant had to do it, forcing the rest of the Egyptian diplomats to leave in the near darkness with only the light of the tacky fluorescent tube at the entrance. The WITCH spoiled that evening but not my future. Some time later SHE had to close HER gallery business. And in 1978, I went to Egypt as an official guest of the Egyptian Government.

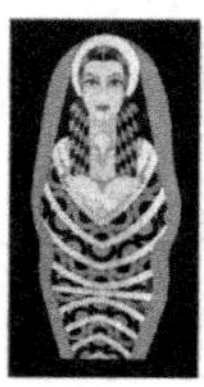

CHAPTER 4

IN THE PYRAMID

I was climbing the huge limestone blocks up the side of the pyramid. A few feet ahead was my self-appointed guide, a dark skinned Bedouin, equipped with his turban, traditional long shirt, *gallabiyah*, and his will to make a few bucks (Egyptian Pounds). We were careful so no one could notice us from below. After all, it was against Egyptian law what we were planning to do. Fortunately it was getting dark. The sun was almost reaching the horizon. The temperature was getting cool, perfect for my plan.

We should be the last ones entering the pyramid before the guards close the iron gates. It was really exciting but somehow I was apprehensive at what we will be encountering… I could get in trouble with the law but my curiosity was insatiable and I was there. How many would have this opportunity? I had to take the risk. We are already reaching the level where the entrance gate was. We are hiding behind a boulder, in silence, without moving a single muscle in our bodies, extremely quiet so the guards fairly close by will not notice our presence. The Bedouin is smiling, I am not and am in a solemn silence…

The last group of tourists is coming out of the narrow entrance tunnel. There are many old foreign ladies and gentlemen coming out in a group. By their comments they sound like Germans. The guards are trying to help them on the way down steps ahead to descend from the level of the entrance. The steps are very steep. By helping these elderly tourists, the guards are abandoning their post at the entrance and the gates are still open. So that's our chance to get in. My guide signals to me. We walk fast, and reach the entrance and rush through the low, narrow corridor. It's very dark inside despite the light bulbs here and there hanging by their wires. The atmosphere has completely changed from what it was outside. The air was heavier and full of dust particles. We rush to the end of a low corridor until we find the second iron gate. At that point my "loyal guide" told me that he will not go any further. The rest will be on my own. Then he gives me the backpack with the provisions for the evening and indicates that the Great Hall to the King's Chamber was ahead and he ran. So, his plan all along was to get out before the guards closed both gates for the night. I turn and I see him running and vaporizing into the dust hanging in the air.

Resigned to my fate, I walk ahead to the Great Hall. It's very tall and inclined toward the entrance of the King's Chamber. It was dark at the top because of the very high, narrow ceiling but at my level the chain of single light bulbs more or less allows me to see the hall ahead in the dusty air. I begin trembling with emotion in my solitude. But I had to continue climbing ahead on the crackling wooden steps—who knows when they were installed, for the convenience of tourists. All of a sudden my climb is interrupted. I hear footsteps approaching from behind. I freeze in place, my excited heartbeat in my ears and, now, in the distance the sound of keys. The footsteps are getting closer, wait . . . they have stopped . . . again the rattling sounds of keys. So the guard has come back to lock the second gate. This is it. My fate is sealed. I thought they would lock only the entrance gate, allowing air to come in. I wondered, why both? His footsteps are fading away in the dark… I am in silence not moving a single muscle except the uncontrollable trembling of my diaphragm and legs. The silence is an eerie and profound silence, fear racing from my head down to my feet. Suddenly the sound of a metallic lever… Oh, it's the electricity. And all of the lights are suddenly off. God, the darkness is as profound as the silence. Am I still standing on solid ground or am I suspended in space? There is no point of reference. I waited a few minutes in silence for the sound of the main entrance gates closing for the night. My flashlight permits me to continue my slow climb and my fear is gone. I am enjoying the eerie experience now that I am…alone. I point the flashlight and its beam of light up, but the beam doesn't reach the narrow ceiling of the Great Hall, but I know it's there. So I continue my climb toward the top. The sounds of my steps on the crackling wood are now very loud, echoing . . . echoing . . . echoing in the long and tall hall. Am I sending a coded message to the Egyptian Underworld warning them that I'm on my way? Why in the HELL am I thinking of spooky things?! I am shaking again. A chilly breeze now against my face, I aim the flashlight up—maybe I am reaching the end of the climb and the entrance of the King's chamber. It's a very low entrance, so I need to be prepared. This chamber has two very long inclined shafts on two opposite walls that go to the outside of the pyramid in the directions of two stars. Air will be entering from them and that's the breeze I am feeling. So I crawl through and finally enter that iconic room with the back sarcophagus at the center of the black wall to my right. It was very dark, the blackness fading my flashlight but I can manage! I am excited and relieved to reach my goal. I can see the empty sarcophagus and look inside and around the King's Chamber. Then I went to one of the shafts to breathe some cool, fresh air of the desert. Suddenly I am hearing a chanting sound and am frozen on the spot. "This, I cannot explain," rambles through my head. But it seems somehow familiar, an Islamic chant. But now it's gone. "That's good," if I was in my previous country and in the city of Perico, I'd be running the HELL OUT OF HERE! For this night, though, there is no way out.

Maybe somebody else has my same idea and stayed behind… Could it be my imagination? But there is no one else in this chamber. Waiting a few minutes . . . or was it an eternity . . . No more chanting. I direct my flashlight toward the low entrance of the King's Chamber at the end of the Great Hall and the chanting starts again … And again I freeze! After a minute or so and making an effort to get my voice back, I almost whisper–expecting no reply–"Anybody… there…?" "Answer me please, but you don't really have to…" I just hear the echo of my silly questions. And now the eerie silence again. I am really afraid like never before with a long night with nothing much I do until morning. Perhaps it's some sort of initiation for my violation of today's laws and probably yesteryear's as well. Trying some logic to try to restore my courage. Perhaps that was a recording that they play over and over to discourage intruders. I certainly was one. However, I remember the story of Napoleon Bonaparte staying one evening in the King's Chamber and having a horrible experience. For me this is turning out to be pretty horrible, too. I turned my flashlight toward the area of the empty sarcophagus, but now I didn't need the flashlight. The black stones seem to emanate a white, subdued light that allows me to see inside the whole chamber! I remember that on my first visit to the King's Chamber some days ago I saw two single fluorescent light fixtures dimly illuminating the room. But now the fixtures were not there! And that light couldn't travel that far from the two shafts. The chamber looks bigger than ever now and the triangular ceiling even higher than before. I simply couldn't explain what's going on. So I make the decision to walk to the sarcophagus, after all, that was the experiment I intended to conduct that night, sleep inside of it alone.

The walk to the sarcophagus is longer. Time and distance are stretching. I keep hearing the echoes of my steps on the dusty black floor that seem to be an exotic music. Now the sarcophagus looks longer than before! I'm just in front of it. There I am! I look inside and can't see the bottom, it looks like a deep well … Recovering from the shock, I am seeing my face reflected in what appeared to be water. That was not there before a few days ago! Who put that mirror there? But the water has begun to move, clearly reflecting my face. I turn my flashlight off and place it on the floor beside my backpack and decide to get inside after all. I wonder what will happen to me inside. How do I come out from this unknown experience? Anything could happen. It could turn out to be an ugly sight that I may not be able to handle…

But so far I have been braver than I thought I would be. But before climbing in I decide to walk around the sarcophagus to see if there is a way to escape in case of emergency. I walk behind between the back black wall parallel to the sarcophagus and around. It seems to me that in the worst case I could make my exit from the left side crack in the top of the lid. I can reach with my arm and prop myself up and jump out of it. So, I finally decide to jump in and "Que sera sera, whatever will be, will be…" I take a deep breath, fill myself with courage and jump! I land on a warm wave of a thick ocean and take another deep breath and go through the deep waters and emerge in another side where I can see the stars around me and the blue planet earth below.

What a sight! The sarcophagus and its constraints are non-existing now. I am floating in space like in a mummy position with my arms crossed over my chest. So far not a bad experience at all. I wonder what scared the hell out of Napoleon Bonaparte?! In spite of the unexpected and unimagined pleasant experience I wonder if I can get out of this inexplicable situation. Who will believe me? Perhaps it's best to be silent in order not to be ridiculed, like Napoleon, who never explained in detail what happened to him in the King's Chamber in 1798… And thinking about my return to my reality I find myself standing alone, silent, outside the sarcophagus in the middle of the familiar King's Chamber with the walls emanating light. The moment of truth had arrived and I decide to walk back to the sarcophagus and see whatever was necessary for me to see in order to complete this weird experience. I take another deep breath, just like when I was going to get immersed in water and approach the lid. Finally at the edge and trembling all over, I look… Oh! No no no no! I CANNOT BELIEVE IT!

Dolores..!!! Dolores Del Rio..!!!

Then, she slowly opens her eyes, smiling and very matter of fact, she says "How do you think I keep myself so young..?"

Damn. I woke up late this morning and now I have to rush to work.

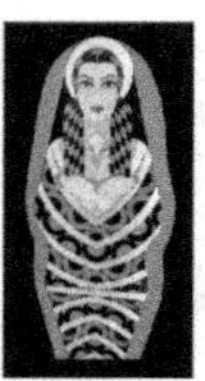

CHAPTER 5

UNDER THE INFLUENCE OF PROFESSOR LLOVERA AND THE VIRGIN

I am a dreamer. I have been a dreamer in the past. I am a dreamer in the present and apparently I'll be one in the future. This has its advantages and disadvantages. The advantages: I always think they will come true, therefore I am an optimist. The disadvantages: My mind wanders very often and makes me waste my precious time in this world. We all are here for a limited amount of years so time becomes even more and more important to me, because it will allow me to complete the tasks I need to complete in this life. Time is always running short when I am doing what I love the most: creating something with my hands.

Years later, after I grew up and was living in another country I wanted to be content with the regular office job I got since life would be simpler for me, but even there I got pulled into my dreams, inspired by them and created art. So I was distracted!

Since my childhood I have been having very vivid dreams and always in "Technicolor" with many details and characters with makeup by William Tuttle and hair by Sidney Guillaroff. And the sets are spectacular! The best of Cecil B. DeMille's visionary versions of ancient Egypt! But in the country town where I used to exist I didn't have any idea that they were Egyptian (I was a kid!), but I was attracted to them. The overall view of my dreams' scenery appears to be seen by the eye of the movie camera of my mind. Later on when I left my country and was living in Paris, I met the Oscar winning cinematographer, Nestor Almendros, who was living at the same address where I was living. At that time he was working with famous "new wave" French directors in Paris like Jean Luc Godard, Francois Truffaut, Claude Chabrol who were influenced by "Cinema Verite" where the camera was mainly hand-held, which is supposed to give a more in the moment experience, which in prior years I had grown to detest immensely because of the resulting wobbling image. So I used to tease Nestor about it until one day he listened to me and placed the camera on a tripod again! Based on my early dreams I always view life as through the eye of a camera on a tripod, a dolly or a crane, not floating around aimlessly.

Coming back to my childhood dreams again, even fully awake, as a new being in this world, I had a problem that I could not sleep normally. That drove my poor mother crazy, making her spend countless nights on a rocking chair holding me in her arms trying to get me to go to sleep. I learned to speak early and unfortunately very clearly, specifically because the son of the doctor next door gave himself the "duty" to teach me all of the most indecent, BAD words in the Spanish language and I repeated them without warning with my full clear voice in public! I became a certified "bad boy" that was dreaded in my town. My mother didn't know what to do and most of the time the front door was locked from the inside so I could not go out. It got so bad that a lady gave my mother the "final solution" so I would stop once and for all repeating that filthy vocabulary. Her wise advice was, "every time he repeats any of those words, rub this red hot pepper on his lips. My poor desperate mother did it and that was the end of my embarrassing foul mouth period. So I was again presentable in civilized society. But I never forgot those words.

Later I developed another bad behavior once I was allowed to play on the fairly large front porch of our colonial house. I stood at the open gate of the porch which reached the sidewalk. Every girl or lady who passed by I dutifully lifted her skirt exposing their undergarments. Ladies stopped passing by our porch preferring to walk in the middle of the street. But one day a black lady, perhaps from out of town, came to see our doctor-neighbor and I proceeded with my stunt, exposing this new victim to the healthy country air. Well, she stopped, fixed her skirt, approached me and slapped my face with all of her strength. I fell to the ground crying. My mother came out. The lady explained and my mother who THANKED HER FOR WHAT SHE DID! Again I was locked in my house. And my well deserved solitary confinement began again.

Then my father gave me a rabbit that was kept inside the house for company. I loved him and he came when I called him. He was very sweet and relaxing. But I begin to draw on the walls what I was seeing in my vivid dreams. And later on I ate plaster from the walls. Then I acquired a predilection for new processed food so that I didn't need to work so hard with my fingernails on the walls. Then it was the easily found rabbit "do do." Imagine if my mother discovered what I was doing! Yes, I was doing it secretly. I guessed that it was a "no no."

It was around that time that kindergarten age hit me and I had to be allowed out to go to the public kindergarten on the main street of the country town. My mother dressed me in my some sort of "sailor suit" with short pants and a little cap with the insignia of a popular baseball team which was the scorpion! Maybe a subliminal message my poor mother missed.

My father's youngest brother, who was a photographer, came to document the "memorable" procession party from my home to the kindergarten class on the other side of the railroad tracks. I was kind of proudly exhibited through town for the first time after my forced seclusions in a home reformatory. I still have at least two photos of that day and they reveal my enormous disgust of going to the hell hole that I imagined kindergarten to be with screaming and jumping children that I haven't been exposed to during my years of confinement. The photo tells everything about my violent state of mind that day. To make the story short, fortunately my kindergarten exposure lasted only one day. When my parents came to pick me up, the teacher said that I had caused so much havoc, hit so many children and even broke her piano (!). Very apologetically she said "So the best is for him not to come back any more." I was glad I was liberated from that place where for sure I didn't belong. Imagine ME in kindergarten!

Fortunately, my refuge during those times, after I graduated from eating and drawing on the walls, was to draw on wrapping paper that my father brought from the grocery store much to the relief of my poor mother. I spent countless hours out of trouble concentrating on my drawings. Peace and tranquility finally reigned in my household. I still had the rabbit but stopped getting nourishment from him, just his sweet love.

Later I was enrolled in a private school a block from my house. But my behavior had changed. I stopped being a menace to society. My first teacher and owner of the school was a black lady who was the daughter of a veteran of the last War of Independence of 1895 in Cuba. Her looks reminded me of the Hollywood film actress, Joan Crawford. She looked, dressed and conducted herself like her. I'll never forget her flaming red lips and her 1940s up-dos. She was always very dignified, nice and respectful of all the children, all of the races and all of the colors. I remained in her school until the third grade. I don't recall what I learned there, but I didn't cause any further trouble. In the bottom of my heart, though, I didn't like the obligation of going to school. Daydreaming saved me from being there at all. Memorizing the lessons allowed me to recite them in class. That was the only way. Fortunately, I had a very good memory.

Since the solitude of my early years I always knew what I wanted to be in life: an artist. The word "artist" has a broad meaning in Spanish and to me, at least in my small country town it meant to be an actor or a "movie star," a singer, a dancer, a painter or even a circus performer. I was particularly fascinated by the trapeze artists and practiced their peculiar wrist movements in the mirror. In my dreams I could see myself as any kind of artist. Of course, a movie star was also my favorite because I could live all of my fantasies being just that. Dreaming, I grew up apart from reality. It was a fanciful childhood in a normal home environment, with two loving parents, but creating my own games and my own rules. No wonder no other child in the neighborhood wanted to play with me. So I withdrew more and more to a point that I did not know how to relate to other people. Instead, I related to the animals.

At about 7, we moved to a bigger country town not far from the first. The new colonial home was in the shape of a "U." Therefore it had a fairly big central patio of dirt to play and have animals. First, we got a couple of rabbits and fairly soon they became 47! With my creativity and inclination for carpentry, I built a big, multi floor wood cubicle housing condominium—maybe the first in Cuba! It had open doors and windows with ramps to get to and from each floor. The rabbits understood all the mechanics of it, loved it and they were living happily ever after. The rabbits were very docile, knew me and played with me. But a sudden epidemic killed them all. It was very sad for me.

Then, unexpectedly and without a formal invitation, the notice was given to the white doves around the area that good and safe real estate was available in the neighborhood. So a massive move took place to the coveted rabbit condominium. They were docile and I could play with them, but sometimes they were nasty to each other and I didn't like that.

Then my father got me my first dog. His name was Terry—in Cuba dogs were given American names! Terry instantly became the light of my life. For the first time, somebody besides my mother and father and some far away relatives that didn't have to live with me, I had unconditional love–Terry loved me with all his heart and we were inseparable. He loved to play with me and sleep by my side. One of the saddest moments of my life was when I had to leave Cuba and I had to say goodbye to him. There is nothing like the companionship, sweetness, love, loyalty and humanity of a dog. He will always live inside me.

Things grew very fast in Cuba. I planted in the central patio mango, avocado and papaya trees. I was able to eat from them after about five years. We had three harvests a year. What we ate was mainly produced in Cuba. There was one cow per inhabitant so milk and milk products were abundant. All of the records were in the United Nations archives before 1959, if they have not mysteriously disappeared.

I began to add painting to my drawing on paper and cardboard using anything that could produce a color. I used earth for brown plus fruits, toothpaste, Merthiolate, Iodine, topical tonsil tincture, blue laundry whitener, regular enamel house paint, bubble gum for texture and of course some other unmentionables. Mainly those early "masterpieces…" were abstracts, complete with odor. I called this early experimental stage my "Icky Period."

Not knowing what to do with my aromatic abstracts, one day my mother took a bunch of them, not knowing what they were made of and mailed them to a well known national TV painter. His name was Professor Llovera. He appeared on a well known early Sunday evening TV show circus for children called "The Circus with Valencia." Professor Llovera gave mini lessons for children to show how to draw and paint using the color pencils Mirado and Prismacolor. They were the main sponsors of his show. If my paintings were shown on the air, Professor Llovera would send me a jumbo box of Mirado and Prismacolor pencils. Perhaps that's was my mother's hope for me to quit using my experimental coloring techniques and adopt the established proven odorless ones, and keep the tropical flies away.

A few weeks later my mother received a letter from Professor Llovera! He was returning my abstract collection which stank even more after a few days inside the sealed envelope along with Professor Llovera's long and very nice letter. He complimented my unusual work and said "true artists are born with the gift" and that apparently I was one of them. He advised my mother not to send me to any art school because the teachers would tend to "influence and guide, thus limiting me. He said that I should be given "total freedom of creation." So that was it. And I was never to receive any instruction on how to paint so I developed my own style and techniques. After that my mother bought me a set of "Temperas" and paint brushes to keep me busy and keep the flies away.

But what my mother really wanted for me was a career as a doctor, dentist or a lawyer, just like all good Jewish mothers—Cuban mothers are the same! But as I went through my primary education my only good grades were always on "Drawing." I barely passed the rest. I was physically there but my mind was always elsewhere in the universe. So I was sent to La Progresiva, an American Presbyterian Boarding School founded by religious educators in the 1920s in the city where I was born–as was most of my family. My mother's family had many connections with that school. My mother's uncle was the concierge and one of his sons was the owner of the "Commercial Department" that sold all the supplies and textbooks for the school.

La Progresiva was about an hour drive from the town where I was living in my own world. That was a long distance at the time. I had to live away from my security blanket. That was the first time I had to separate from my parents, my environment, my dear animals, especially my dog Terry. It was not easy for me. I'm sure not for my parents either– especially my mother. Even though it was a great and beautiful school with young teenagers from all over the island. When my parents left me there I sat and cried. I didn't know what to do or where to go. It was like I was left stranded in outer space surrounded by aliens. The only consolation was that if my behavior was excellent, I would be allowed to go home every other weekend. With that incentive I became a saint. I barely talked or socialized with anybody, Anything to stay out of trouble and GO HOME!

The weekends at home went too fast. The bus would pick me up to take me back to school at 6 pm. Damn, it was the time for *I Love Lucy!* I loved that show and still do. My sweet dog Terry knew the routine and always came and ran behind the bus until it left town.

At school I had to share a room in the dorm with two other teenagers. I had never seen so many students together before. It was a big school, for boys and girls. The dorms were separated by about two blocks. We were together in the classrooms and in the morning gathering in the great room where a religious session was conducted before class. The only thing I liked were the anthems which I learned very fast but sang very quietly so no one would hear me. I was petrified to call attention to myself. I was very timid then. Teenagers at boarding school can be very cruel with the new students, and I was one of them. When I was admitted they totally shaved my head even in front of my mother. No one escaped that! Also, at night they used to throw the newcomers into the cold swimming pool—I hated cold water and never cared about swimming! So I sneaked out from the dining room after dinner and disappeared under my bed until the disgusting rite ended! I really hated those stupid, cruel and uncalled for punishments against people or innocent animals. So I stayed hidden as much as possible.

It was during those invisible days that I fell deeply in love with my Spanish Grammar teacher. She was like an exquisite porcelain doll and I only had eyes for her. To hell with the complicated Spanish grammar which I never understood anyway. My eyes are just fixed on her during class. When the class was over and she left I felt sad and desolate. After the first semester I realized that it was an impossible love. Probably she didn't know that I existed since I was so quiet in class and never raised my hand to ask any question because I was an introvert. In reality I was very unlucky with girls after spending most of my childhood with animals who certainly were easier than girls. I could handle a rat better than a girl! I remember my first love was "Candy" when I was about 6. She had been in an automobile accident and had a little bandage on the upper part of her left arm. She became a famous celebrity and much admired in the small country town. Candy was about my age and looked to me like the Mexican actress Isabela Corona who I had seen in a few films. Actually now when I think about her, she was pretty homely. But she was very much in demand by the children's costume dances. At one of them that I was forced to attend, my parents arranged for me to dance with her against my will. However, I fell crazy in love. But since she was a famous celebrity, she couldn't care less about me and I suffered my first love rejection. So, I sought refuge with my loving animals who were nicer to me than girls. Years later when I was in 4th grade in another very good school in the town, I felt miserably in love with another girl. Her name was Juana Rosa. But this one was very pretty, a real beauty queen with exotic eyes and an air of superiority. In that school we were separated in two rooms, one for girls and another for boys. But sometimes somebody from the other group could visit to ask questions. Every time that Juana Rosa visited I became flushing red and my heartbeat reached the far side of the moon. Apparently she noticed me but she ignored me. After a long time of suffering for her, one day I decided to take matters in my own hands. When the classes were over I decided to follow her to her home keeping a safe distance of course in order not to call her attention. Apparently she noticed that I was following and didn't like it at all. After she entered her home she told her mother who immediately came out and gave me a huge scandal and neighbors came out due to the commotion. I was embarrassed and completely crushed by this incident. And I never looked at her again! And I went back to the safety of my home and the unconditional love of my animals. My "Don Juan" career was over before it began. Years later I saw Juana Rosa at a neighbors' house and she put on a lot of weight and didn't look like before. I couldn't help but feel extremely glad that she became a FATSO and hardly fit in the rocking chair! I pretended that I didn't notice her obvious pretty full presence. That was my revenge for what she did to me.

It was during the first year of high school at La Progresiva that I studied Ancient History. There was a chapter about the Ancient Egyptian civilization and I was surprised that the photos of the art I was seeing in the book were so close to what I had been drawing since I was a child! The Egyptian murals and freezes were surprisingly similar to what I drew on the walls of the house before I ate them. I was never aware of any of this before. How can it be possible? Well, living in a small country town apparently no one knew to make an assessment of my art or established their resemblance to Egyptian art. Once I began high school I hadn't been drawing or painting anything. I was not inspired by the new environment I was in. I was too busy trying to pass undiscovered and trying to memorize my new assignments.

Then something terrible started happening to me! My memory was failing! I couldn't memorize my lessons no matter how much I tried. I told my mother and she took me to a doctor who prescribed medication for it. But it didn't help. And studying became a nightmare. My grades went down even lower and with a private tutor I finally narrowly passed the test for the second year. After that my mother took me out—THANK GOD!!!– of the boarding school and we moved to La Habana–that's the correct name in Spanish. There we were provisionally living with her parents, sister and brothers until we found a house. Meanwhile she enrolled me in a private school so I could continue the second year of high school. I loved living with my grandparents and uncles. It was big with a lot of relatives around. I liked that! The school bus would take me to and from the new school. It was located in a very plush residential and commercial area of La Habana, just about half a block from the biggest and tallest condominium building in the world constructed of reinforced concrete against hurricanes. The basement of that building was housing the new, biggest TV studios in America. This building was some blocks away from the very important and powerful CMQ commercial radio and TV studios in Cuba built in the late 1940s. By 1958 we already had a total of seven commercial channels and one with all programming in color. There were also many theaters and 100 movie houses in La Habana and one of them had CINERAMA. So all of this was very exciting and like a dream come true for me.

At lunch time I used to walk from the new school to the CMQ studios to see the popular TV stars of the late fifties. Even the son of a TV and theater star went to my school! But I never dared talk to him, I was too shy and they were untouchables, like deities to me.

La Habana was a beautiful, clean and exciting city, full of life and plenty of places to explore and enjoy. All the people that I had admired through the radio and TV were there in the flesh. There were a lot of tall buildings and big, luxurious, well kept hotels, night clubs, cabarets and casinos—where minors were not allowed so I never saw anyone inside except when they were arriving or leaving. Men and women very elegantly dressed in tuxedos and long evening gowns. You can come and go and enter wherever you please, except for the casinos. The musical extravaganza shows were like in Las Vegas today. I felt very free in that wonderful city.

Many movie theaters were spectacular as from the "Gilded Era." One in particular called my attention because of a peculiar unsuspected feature that amazed me the first time I went. In the intermission, during the previews, I heard an unusual sound coming from above. I looked up and discovered that the unusual sound was the huge roof opening to the night sky. So I was watching a film under the stars! The walls inside looked like a big Spanish Square!

During my early days in that wonderful city, one of my younger uncles took me to see a very popular film from Spain that was number one in Spain and all the Americas, breaking all of the box office records everywhere. The title was *El Ultimo Cuple*. He told me that in a close up in a pivotal scene the star of the movie looked like the Virgin Mary, because of her perfect, classic beauty. The star was none other than Sarita Montiel who I had seen as the star in many Mexican musical films of the Golden Era of that industry in Mexico while in my country town. So I certainly knew who she was when I went to the movies every night to see the double feature for 5 cents before we got the 21 inch TV set. I had seen most of her Mexican films, but not her last two made in Hollywood. *Veracruz* and *Serenade*. I thought that she was from Mexico but in fact was born in La Mancha, Spain. While I was watching this musical hit I realized that my uncle Ofrey was right on target and she was the image of The Virgin Mary. From that moment on I fell in love with her until "death do us part" and beyond. She became "The Virgin", the one and only! I saw *El Ultimo Cuple* more than 15 times! Despite my bad memory, I was even able to memorize her lines!!!

Her film was so successful that she became the most important and famous Spanish speaking female movie star in the world and the absolute ideal of beauty and everybody's sweetheart. Then in 1958, she got a 10 day contract to appear on TV in Cuba nightly and do two shows a day in the over 6,000 seat Blanquita Theater, one of the biggest theaters in the world at that time. Of course I went to see her at the TV studio and saw one of her theater shows, singing and sharing her personality. The lines were for miles. But I saw her finally in person! She was real, in the flesh, making miracles on the stage, returning sight to the blind, hearing to the deaf, healing the terminally ill and making quadriplegics stand straight on their feet and returning dexterity so they can play their castanets on their final road to rehabilitation. Well, okay, but she certainly was a miracle.

I tried to get close to her in the theater, to get her blessing, but it was impossible. Too many screaming women, men and teenagers in my way rioting around her. Those 10 days were glorious and unforgettable for me and many other adolescents. And just like magic, she vanished, leaving behind my broken heart and many others that had to be content with seeing her blinding light in dark movie houses. I decided that in order to get close to her, I must become an actor…

Despite the idyllic life I and so many others in Cuba were having, one morning everything changed for me and everybody else. The "Revolution" came and took all of the power from the Republic of Cuba. With the change of government there was a lot of confusion and happiness in the beginning–hope for a brilliant future ahead. No one imagined in their wildest dreams what was included with this change. We thought a new era of freedom and prosperity was at hand for the already advanced and prosperous country. But this "Revolution," like the "French Revolution," started executing all people who opposed what they wanted to do or were part of the previous government. They even publicly broadcast the executions on TV to terrorize the population. First they said that they were all collaborators with the previous government of Batista, but afterward there was a full war against the people in general and, in particular, anybody who criticized the Revolution.

You could not say anything that could be interpreted as an attack on the newly implanted system. This "Fundamental Transformation" canceled the Cuban Constitution of 1940–one of the most socially advanced in the Americas. People accused in fake revolutionary trials were sent to jail or executed.

During those horrible times I was young, but old enough for it to have a serious impact on me. What was happening around me reminded of the films that I had seen about the Holocaust. Education was radically changed to political brainwashing and Marxist indoctrination. The "Revolution" began expropriating all private schools of all denominations that existed in Cuba to impose the new political curriculum. Teachers and professors were fired and substituted with new Marxist indoctrinated ones. Everything became "political." Many parents were desperate to avoid the indoctrination in schools so sent their unaccompanied children to relatives, foster parents and Catholic orphanages in the United States. By way of one clandestine operation, 14,048 unaccompanied children were able to reach the United States between 1960 and 1962. It was the biggest exodus of children in the Western Hemisphere. It's known as Operation Peter Pan. Two of my cousins were saved by this exodus.

All the big media networks in Cuba were confiscated from their private owners and converted into propaganda and indoctrination outlets. There was no escape from the constant bombardment of Marxist political junk. Despite my young age, I knew through my mother that her father and uncle were "communists," but I did not know what that meant—no background whatsoever. My mother's father died in 1959, shortly after the "Revolution" took over and he had been "gaga" about Castro and his road to Communism. That year we still had the house and the grocery store in the small town. My mother's family moved to La Habana and she wanted to be near them—it was a very close and loving family. So in 1958 my mother and I were living at my grandmother's home in La Habana and I was in my second year of high school there in a private school. But in 1959, she wanted to move there for good. So my father found a job and we finally moved there. I loved the idea, I loved that city and everything it had to offer. But after the "Revolution" was in total charge of everything, it was not the same as freedom began to disappear from the panorama.

When classes began in La Habana, I went back to a new private school and my tutors, but I was very much distracted by what was happening around me. Suddenly, the school, owned by a black couple, was expropriated by the "Revolution." I heard that the professors who owned the school had to leave for exile in Miami. I was sorry about that because they were very nice people who founded the school many years earlier and loved the school very much. So to continue high school, I had to enroll in a public school many blocks away and use public transportation back and forth. The public transport was excellent in La Habana and very economical with reliable GM and Leyland British buses but that changed with the new government bureaucracy whose goals did not include efficiency. All the political agitation everywhere and intrusions in daily life was very distracting so my bad grades in the new high school meant I had to repeat the 2nd year. I hated school and now to repeat a year was very discouraging for me!

This new public school that I am forced to endure now due to the "Revolution" is further away from my exciting show business area where the other private school had been. I loved that area very much, even though with the "Revolution" things are not the same any longer. Well, I could walk there after classes but it was many blocks away. The day I went to fill out the entrance application for the school, by accident I met a guy who told me that he was an actor! This was very important, I had never met one before. He became my instant idol! My eyes were wide open and my ears tuned to listen to his story about how he was discovered and his other show business anecdotes. Then he revealed that some blocks away on the same wide street there was The Municipal Academy of Dramatic Arts, and, I decided that one day after class, I should venture to the Academy to find out what I could do to enroll. I didn't say anything to my mother and father so they wouldn't discourage me.

The public high school, I soon found out, was a chaotic place. Most of the students were not interested in the curriculum, neither was I, but I was trying hard not to have to repeat anything again. The problem was that there was constant political agitation coming from the "Student's Association" controlled by the "Revolution's" political commissars. There were constant political rallies during classes that you were forced to attend or you'd be accused of being "counter revolutionary." That would be THE KISS OF DEATH! You would be expelled from the school and become a non-person. The fanatic members of that association were nothing more than gangsters without scruples. This group also kept an eye on the political behavior of the professors. If one was suspected or accused of not sympathizing, their classes would be sabotaged and a meeting organized in the main square of the school to demand the immediate resignation of the professor. I remember Dr. Llelensky, the math teacher. She was excellent, even though I never understood math, but that was my deficiency. She was an exile from communist Hungary and she and her family experienced the reality of Communism in her own country and was able to realize that Cuba was going in that lethal direction. One day she explained it to her class. (I didn't believe her at that moment in time, I later realized that she was right on target). Well, another day the Association got news of what she said in class about her Hungarian experience that her family was killed by the communists and they entered the class to call her a liar and everybody had to laugh at her. That was her last day. She was expelled that same afternoon as a "counter revolutionary." Later on I found that she was able to leave Cuba for exile. I hope that wherever she is, she is living in a free society where individual freedoms are respected. As Dr. Llelensky, one by one the good professors were disappearing from that hell hole called a High School Institute. But this was not the exception but the general rule as this "Revolution" was to extend its tentacles all over that now lost Republic. It was getting increasingly difficult to stay at school and even to study while all aspects of life were being politicized all around you every single day.

During breaks I would look from my upper floor window to watch my actor former-idol in the courtyard surrounded by many girls in an activity not forbidden yet, chanting revolutionary tunes praising the revolting "Revolution" that was strangling the population of Cuba. Very sad sight to witness. One day in the Spanish grammar class which I detested, we had a new teacher. She had horrible acne which she unsuccessfully covered with tons of bright pink makeup and rouge. Also, thanks to the "Revolution," hair dyes for women became scarce—typical in communist countries—and very difficult to locate anywhere in La Habana, especially with the bad public transportation now. So the problem was that the latest shade of hair dye she was able to find gave her short hair a color which I would have to describe as "parrot green." Poor woman! So the students began to call her "Chlorophyll."

One day Chlorophyll made me get up from my invisible anonymous presence in that dreaded class to read to the class a well known piece of poetry about the defeat of the troops of Montezuma at the hands of Spanish conquistador Hernan Cortez. I wanted to kill her, kill Chlorophyll first and myself afterward—some sort of reverse Romeo and Juliet—I was trying to pass the class unnoticed! I do not like to be in the spotlight! Or the center of attention of anything. Leave me alone! I was really shy. But, I didn't have any other alternative than to manage to walk to the front of the class with my shaking legs and read the damn poetry. Trying to get that situation over as fast as I could, I read the best I could … I cannot remember how I did it but I finally finished with it! To my surprise the entire class gave me a standing ovation even the damn gangsters from the "Student Association." Maybe they won't expel me now . . ..And, I kind of liked it. From then on they called me "the dramaturg." That shows how well educated they were thanks to their "Revolution." Actually that alias was not applicable to me, but it was the only word that those gangsters were able to find in their limited jargon.

Perhaps I should thank Chlorophyll, because shortly thereafter, during afternoon break, I sneaked out of that crooked school and with new courage I walked to the Municipal Academy of Dramatic Art of La Habana. Well, it was close by, but I was still afraid to walk on their sidewalk, so I crossed the street just in case. From that vantage point and with something jumping up and down in my stomach, I looked at what to me looked like a two story classic temple for deities and I wandered around that temple of hope to see it from different angles. Afterwards I would often make that sacred pilgrimage after class and stay in front of that temple and dream of belonging inside–to become an actor and follow The Virgin… Then I found in the newspaper that new classes will start soon at the Academy in a few months. But, even though the Academy was closed now I began going every afternoon after class, in a kind of religious pilgrimage.

Finally the day came when the Academy of Dramatic Arts' doors reopened and I could enter the temple! Since I got up that morning I was trembling inside. But first I needed to get through another day at the highschool of hell. After a very long day of waiting, finally the time came to abandon that tense environment and escape to the relative freedom of walking on a sidewalk of La Habana, although it meant facing the reality of those difficult times. I was wearing my best clothes and shoes bought before "The Revolution," because each day there was less to buy in the stores. When I finally got to the temple I was so nervous that I began to shake all over. That morning I stood in front of my bathroom mirror and rehearsed my gestures, expressions and tones of my voice. I hope that I can deliver! But my main apprehension was that I didn't have the slightest idea what I would be finding there. I had never been where Dramatic Arts were taught. Would they laugh at me? I had heard stories of corruption in show business… Would it be a place of corruption? The whole idea was frightening to me. I was worried I would be disappointed. That place was sacred to me and in the deepest of my heart I wanted for it to continue being that way. My walk that pivotal afternoon seemed much longer than usual, it was like time was stretching slowly. I wanted to walk faster, but like in a dream, I couldn't. My hands were ice cold on that hot September afternoon. And then I realized that I was finally there! Right in front of the temple. This time on the same sidewalk for the first time. In front of the elegant black iron fence around the temple. My legs were shaking but they somehow moved back and forth until I was at the beautiful wooden door. I could see what seemed to be a marble staircase to heaven. I didn't know if I would be able to make it. I was ready to turn and run away, but then, I thought of The Virgin and that if I want to go to her, I would have to conquer the mysterious staircase ahead. I stayed in silence for a few seconds and took a deep breath and all of a sudden, a force dragged me quickly up the staircase. In a matter of seconds I reached the first floor, excited and out of breath, but actually there!

It was a small, white reception room with a desk and two benches, one on the left where the stairs ended and the other in front, making a square angle with the other, only separated by a door leading to a big terrace facing the wide street. Beside the front bench, a desk. There was a tiny old lady with reddish hair in a 1940s up-do sitting behind the desk. She smiled at me and looked friendly. She said "My name is Adelaida." I forgot what I had fully rehearsed that morning and, not in a very articulate manner, I mumbled to her what I was doing there. She smiled and gave me an application to fill out and a pen. I managed to sit at the bench without falling and began to fill in the information. Fortunately I was 15 years old because if I was younger, they would not have accepted me, according to the application. I also had to provide two 8X10 headshots. That would not be a problem, my photographer uncle can have them ready in no time at all. I worked on the application slowly. After I had suffered so much to get in I was not going to leave that soon!

Apparently a rehearsal was finishing because a French door opened and a group of very happy looking young people came out. They were young guys and girls older than me looking very wholesome and well put together. For a moment I envied them because they had something I didn't. They looked secure. They look fearless, not like me, hiding most of my life. I wanted to be like them! Some of them went to the open terrace to talk and others sat on the benches near me. Some left, not without kissing each other and Adelaida. Some went through an open door beside the classroom leading to a big room with a lot of mirrors, lights and counters. It was a make-up room! The first one I had ever seen. Others pulled out what looked like their scripts and began reading, making gestures and expressions with their faces as if they were on stage. Everything looked so normal and relaxing. It was the opposite of the tension and self-censoring in my high school for fear of saying anything that could be deemed critical of the "Revolution." It was politics all day long and pretending that you love and support that intrusive, oppressive new political regime imposed on us. It was asphyxiating. At least in this Academy of Dramatic Arts the students are free and able to openly express themselves without fear of reprisals or being expelled. This was what freedom was all about. I cannot wait to pass the entrance test! I hope they will admit me to this heavenly place. I felt sorry when I finished with the application and returned it to Adelaida, I didn't have an excuse to remain sitting there any longer. So I decided to take extra time and extend my stay. I was too timid and didn't know how to start a conversation with those lucky superior beings.

Suddenly the classroom door opened and an impeccably dressed lady in full makeup came out. After the shock, I recognized her immediately. It was Eva Vasquez, the theater and radio actress married to the popular radio and TV actor Carlos Badias!!! She came out and asked a question of Adelaida who replied back completely naturally… as if Eva Vasquez was a normal human being… I would have died on the spot if she looked at me and asked me anything. Imagine meeting an in-the-flesh actress in real life! And that's what the Academy will introduce me to! At that time she was doing a popular play titled "La Señorita" (The Miss). Already the Academy, that sacred temple, had made possible my first contact with a well-known actress! That was very promising indeed. Today Eva and tomorrow The Virgin, I thought. Miss Vasquez quickly disappeared like a vision from heaven behind the double French doors.

Shaking, I returned the application to Adelaida and she gave me what appeared to be a printed monologue. She said that I had to memorize it for the admission test that would be in two weeks. Well, what am I going to do here now…? What would be my justification for staying here any longer? So, I had to leave. My legs started moving me toward the staircase, but I had the idea to walk out to that ample terrace facing the wide street. I had seen that empty terrace so many times before from the other side of the street. But now those superior beings from the academy were there talking and laughing. I stayed alone with my eyes lost in the distant sky, in silence, completely unnoticed, as the sunset began. The sun was getting lower and strong blues, reds, oranges and golds were capriciously forming, making this experience even more significant for me, still concerned to be unnoticed by the others since I would not know what to say about my previous life. I am not at their level and I was afraid to be uncovered. Such fears are difficult to recover from. I didn't want to disappoint them. Perhaps they will be my new friends… Then in silence I left unnoticed and crossed the street and stayed there until it was dark.

As the days passed by I became concerned about my memory and inability to properly memorize a script, so I spent countless hours reading and re-reading the monologue Adelaida gave me, trying to figure out the best way to deliver it. I had never acted before, except silently in front of a mirror when I was playing as a child in the country town. Now I didn't have the benefit of a mirror to tell me how I was aesthetically doing. I keep forgetting the lines and going blank from time to time. I was terrified to fail because perhaps this would be the opportunity to come out of my shell and become like those lucky beings I saw at the Academy. Those two weeks were excruciating. I didn't tell anybody that I had gone to the Academy of Dramatic Arts and I applied for acceptance with the opportunity for a scholarship. Not even my mother and father knew, only my best, loving and loyal friend Terry knew, and he didn't bark about it. Dogs have a sixth sense so he knew it was best for my future development and success to keep my secret. He kissed me and gave me my nice hugs. I was counting the hours to go back to the temple.

The day finally arrived. I have been sick to my stomach since I woke up snd after an excruciating day, I found myself at the Academy, seated again on the same bench but with other youngsters waiting to pass the admission test. To say that I was nervous was the understatement of the twentieth century. There were a lot of fears I would have to conquer. This will be the first time that I will be intending to act in front of people. The previous time in Chlorophyll's Spanish Grammar class was completely accidental and without any preparation, so my nerves didn't have time to begin their insidiously bad influence. But this time was a MEMORIZED text and that was my weak side. The classroom door opened and a young girl probably my same age came out wearing a huge skirt with thousands of noisy crinoline petticoats ready to parachute from an airplane and looking very happy with an ear to ear smile. She left the French doors wide open and for the first time I was able to see the classroom. It looked like a long theater with an aisle in the middle and the stage in the front. Then I saw an overweight gentleman walking down the aisle toward the main door, carrying a sheet of paper in his hands. I felt something unpleasant inside my stomach. When at the door, he looked at everybody waiting, smiled and proceeded to read a name. Oh no my god! It was my name. My heart literally jumped in my chest. My heart began beating very fast. My blood rushed to my head and I could hardly hear. I felt that I was glued to the bench but I managed to get up and move my shaking legs into a kind of unnatural walk. Somehow it worked because I cleared the door frame entering the classroom and moved through the aisle toward the front and the stage, the altar on which I will offer myself in voluntary sacrifice to The Virgin. I turned around facing the audience I saw on the left, seated behind a small table, none other than Miss Eva Vasquez again! Beside her were a gentleman that I didn't recognize and then an empty chair for the other gentlemen who followed me to the stage. Miss Eva Vasquez asked for my name!!! Actually she talked to me!!! Now she knows that I exist! The other gentleman sitting beside Miss Vasquez asked me to go to the stage. There were three steps to climb and I prayed to The Virgin that I could make it without falling over, because my legs were out of control shaking. And She listened and helped me to save my pride and get safely onto the stage. I was on stage for the first time in my life and facing an audience of seasoned professional theatrical deities. My first impression was to feel the heat of the lights on my already overheated face. The lights were really hot! After a silence, during which I noticed that the gentleman who called me was the Theater Director, Modesto Centeno and the director of the Academy. Miss Eva Vasquez asked me to begin the monologue. It was then that I lost track or notion of time and I have no memory of what happened. Suddenly, I woke up and it was all over! I thanked The Virgin for this miracle and felt great relief. I looked at the three members of the jury and they looked very pleased and were smiling at me kindly, even Eva Vasquez! I was SO GLAD IT WAS OVER! I didn't say anything about this potential new and life-changing chapter of my life to my parents or any member of my family, only Terry, of course. He always understands me.

A month later I received a telegram saying that I had been accepted by the Academy and that I should go to pay the small tuition. I thanked The Virgin again and thought that this new and improved chapter of my life will begin. Actually this was the first time in my life that I passed a test without the help of private tutors. Maybe this is what I should do in life… And do it for Her. I had tried other things with little or no success. This may be my real break, and a break it was.

When I went to pay my tuition, Modesto Centeno, the director of the Academy, was talking to Adelaida at the reception upstairs. As soon as I arrived, he recognized me and invited me to go to the classroom with him. There was Miss Eva Vasquez again! She also recognized me and, smiling, walked over to me to congratulate me for my test and welcomed me to the Academy. Can you imagine, Miss Eva Vasquez, the actress that I had heard in hundreds of radio soap operas and married to the most famous actor in Cuba congratulating me?! I was flabbergasted. Then, Modesto Centeno, told me that the Academy was preparing an event and a play for a show at La Habana Amphitheater and a tour to the interior of the island and that they needed a strong voice like mine to recite some solos for their Greek Chorus that would be directed by well known female theater director Cuqui Ponce de Leon who had her own company.

All of this was an invigorating breeze of fresh air for me in the middle of the toxic Marxist political agitation in the education field that was resulting in the progressive loss of individual freedoms that was permeating all stages of life of the previously free and happy population.

Well, The Virgin really did it all. She was setting the path for me for sure for our future meeting in Spain. I haven't even begun and she opened some doors for me. Finally, I was liked, accepted and welcomed for the first time in my life, thanks to The Virgin.

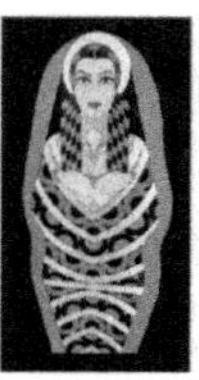

CHAPTER 6

THE CASE OF THE MISSING MUMMY

The next morning after the Egyptian Embassy reception, I picked up all my works from the WITCH'S gallery. I was very glad to end that disgusting experience. I had already made plans to take one piece to a commercial gallery in the Watergate building. It wasn't exactly what I wanted because that gallery was mostly selling prints and frames and they didn't have solo or group shows, but at least it was in a shopping center with a lot of affluent people traffic and just across the street from the Kennedy Center. So I took my favorite piece from my Tutankhamun collection which I hung myself on a prominent column facing the busy arcade. I had very good relations with this gallery owner since she was a normal human being not the typical neurotic gallery owner that artists suffer with. I was very glad. After my experience with the WITCH I needed a good rest and the Betty Ford Center had not been founded yet. Time passed and she had gotten a lot of very good comments about my work but no purchase. So, I need to get more exposure for my unusual work. I had faith in my work and I enjoyed the time consuming and complicated construction of them. I used the carpentry abilities developed in my childhood, but what I enjoyed the most were the stretching of the fabric over the structure and the application of the coats to harden the structure and the application of the colors. They became my children and friends. I never got tired of them and I let them evolve with all kinds of different shapes and techniques.

The Treasures of Tutankhamun's success at the National Gallery was still going strong and the excitement about this ancient Egyptian Art was very much thought about. Original work like mine couldn't be bought anywhere in the world, but I needed to find an art gallery that shared the values that my work represented for me. So I began looking for a gallery again. In my search, one day I went to the Latin American Museum to see its director. Surprisingly, I found an acquaintance from two years earlier. He had been the M.C. of a show that I participated in as an actor. He was Cuban and was working in that museum, but he said that as a Cuban I couldn't exhibit in this museum either. I was surprised by this discriminating statement because there were already works by Cuban artists in that museum. But, no, no, no, I could not exhibit there! Another strangely closed door. He did give me the name and address of another commercial gallery in Georgetown, an affluent area of Washington, D.C. I left and went there right away.

I found the gallery on a street corner but it was closed, odd since it was in the middle of the afternoon. I looked inside through the gallery street window and it looked nice. It had been snowing the last few days, and I found,in the snow in front of the main entrance, a bunch of pennies, which I took as "pennies from heaven" and as an omen for good luck and good things to come. I left and kept calling the gallery until I got hold of its director who had a Spanish name. But according to him, he came to America when he was eight years old and he only knew a few words in Spanish. We arranged an appointment and met at the gallery a few days later.

I took some of my Egyptian inspired work to our first meeting as he requested. He became extremely excited when he saw them. He kept saying, "magnificent, magnificent!!!" I took Jaums to help me transport my work in and out of the gallery office.

Then, after getting out a bottle of sherry wine from his desk drawer he asked us, "Do you want something to drink?"

We declined since neither of us drink alcohol. "Not even a little bit…?" He asked.

"No thank you. We just don't drink, but thank you anyway," I added while he poured sherry into his glass.

After drinking the wine he said, "I want to show your paintings in my gallery."

"That's very nice," I said, very surprised.

"Yes, they are magnificent pieces. It will be an extraordinary show," he added while drinking more sherry.

"What dates do you have available?" I inquired.

He filled his wine glass again and said, "Right now."

"Do you mean, right now?" I surprisingly questioned him.

"Yes, right now. Could you go back to your studio and get them all here today?" He said very matter of fact while sipping more of his wine. I was finding this all very strange but didn't want to lose an opportunity. But I did not like the idea of doing an exhibit in a rush. So, I asked him for a future date instead.

"What about February 14?" He proposed while pouring more sherry.

It was January 29. I was thinking that it was still too soon and I let him know my feelings about it. "Two weeks are enough," he said, "that will be plenty of time to arrange everything including the invitations," he insisted, talking around his wine glass.

I didn't want it to be difficult. After all, I needed another exhibit. So I finally agreed to open on that date.

Then, while sipping more wine he began taking about a "gentleman's agreement" which he explained consisted of: Since he will provide for the exhibiting of my paintings from now on, his gallery will be my sole representative and that I couldn't exhibit in any other gallery and that I couldn't sell my paintings on my own, and if I do, I will have to pay his gallery a 40% commission.

But, "I already have contacts I have made on my own with other people and places. I think that since those have already been arranged, they should be left out of the 'agreement' you are taking about," I told him.

Then he said, "It's not professional to do that, you know."

And I replied, "I had those contacts before this meeting. Your gallery does not have anything to do with them," I explained. "I feel you should respect all my prior contacts before the date I formally agree to show in your gallery."

He said, "OK, I will accept to share some percentage of any sale resulting from your previous contacts."

"I'm sorry, I cannot agree to that either." I said.

"You just have to make up your mind if you want to exhibit in my gallery or not," he said while finishing off another glass of wine.

"I'll have to think about it." I said.

"You have to make up your mind now. I have to know now. I have other engagements, you know." He pressed me while filling his wine glass.

"Well, I cannot give you an immediate reply now. I have to think it over." I replied.

He wasn't very happy about my answer and he gave me until the next day in the afternoon. But he insisted on keeping two of my works in the gallery on consignment and I did sign an agreement to that specific temporary arrangement.

After I left the gallery I was worried. There was something odd about that man, plus his drinking I did not like at all. He was too pushy. Probably I was to him what six months ago I was to the despicable WITCH: the artist of the desperados. And in my little experience with these commercial art galleries, I had never heard about these "gentlemen's agreements" in the air. These types of vague things were not for me. I always like to have everything clear and in writing. Maybe that's the way some galleries operate and I wanted to find out. I decided to call some people and research and ask for advice before making up my mind. First I called my acquaintance at the Latin American Museum—who sent me to that gallery in the first place. I told him what happened at the meeting. He was funny about the gallery owner whom he called, "that old lizard," which actually was a very accurate description of him. However, he advised me that under no circumstance should I accept his verbal agreement, because that would tie me forever with his gallery. Then I called a friend of mine who was the co-owner of a reputable commercial gallery, and without mentioning the name of the gallery or owner I asked for his opinion. He told me pretty much the same thing. But he also explained that sometimes galleries have formal contracts with some artists to represent them for a period of months to a few years. But he pointed out that "always" with a written agreement needs the provision that can be voided if one of the parties desires to do so. He emphasized that I should not accept such a verbal agreement and he was very specific when he said, "everything must be in writing." I called a well known newspaper art critic and his opinion was the same.

I called the gallery the next day in the afternoon as agreed. I was completely sincere and open about my worries about his "gentleman's agreement" and my worries and the result of my three source survey. He was kind of apprehensive and his only concern was if I mentioned the name of the gallery which I didn't to two of them but the person who referred me in the first place knew, but it was between us only. "Did you mention it to anybody else?" He inquired again and I assured him that I did not. He calmed down and became nice and persuasive about what he had told me the previous day.

"You know," he said, "You didn't understand me very well when I said that the gallery would be your sole representative in the Washington, D.C. area only," he carefully stated–that was not what he said last night! Also he said now, "You will be free to conclude your previous engagements and to follow through with your previous contacts too, without my gallery as intermediary, and of course, with no compromise about any commission."

"That sounds fair to me," I said. And he added, "You also will be free to exhibit in any museum in this area," he added. And in the event of a sale, my gallery will share the commission."

Since per this phone conversation the basic points of the agreement were clarified. I told him, "Under these reasonable conditions, I will accept to exhibit in your gallery if you agree to sign a letter of agreement based on this conversation."

"OK, but you write the letter and bring it to me. If everything there is of our mutual agreement, I'll sign it," he said and we finished our phone conversation. After I hung up, I was kind of confused and I asked myself if I had misunderstood him the day before. I told Jaums about my doubts. Jaums replied that I did not misunderstand anything and in fact he was changing his "gentlemen's agreement" now in order to have my exhibit. Apparently he really wanted my work in his gallery.

About an hour later he called me back. He was very nice and began telling me how "talented, great, extraordinary and marvelous" I was. How "magnificent" were my paintings, etc. As his conversation went on, I realized that he was drinking. His voice was sounding different and he began having difficulty speaking and making no sense. He began calling me "Joselito" and "Antonio." After a while he became nasty and he was shouting at me that I was being very greedy and only concerned with money "like a Jew," and he went on and on… He kept me on the phone for an hour and forty minutes. I felt sorry for him because he seemed to be a lonely old man. But finally I have to convince him to end the call.

OK, now I have to get ready for my next show. Since I finished at the WITCH gallery the last December, I had not had much time to produce more new pieces, so I would have to show more or less the same works. I needed to rush if I wanted to produce new pieces. I decided that I should at least try to do a small piece to put on a pedestal in the gallery window that faces the street. a piece that would be different from the rest, free-standing with faces on three sides. It was going to be a representation of the birth of King Tutankhamun. It became a one of a kind piece, 36" tall, free-standing sculpture with three sides, each with a face. In the gallery window two sides could be seen from the sidewalk and face on the back only from inside the gallery. The birth of the pharaoh was portrayed by the sun disk from where the pharaoh was symbolically born. One face was looking east and the other west. The face of the pharaoh was born from a lotus flower. I was able to finish it in time and it was very striking, especially when it was perfectly framed in the center of the gallery window. The title was *Tan-Kha-Ten* and its code number in the bottom of it was #109, it's finishing date, "2-9-77" and my signature "Blazquez" and "©" symbol as appeared in all my pieces for future identification.

On February 5, I delivered all the paintings to the gallery for the show, except *Tan-Kha-Ten* which was not quite ready yet. The gallery owner approved and signed the agreement letter. I hung the show with a few suggestions from the owner. It looked very good and I was extremely pleased, so was the owner of the gallery.

On February 12 I delivered *Tan-Kha-Ten* to the gallery and placed it on the pedestal facing the street window. It looked magnificent. It just belonged here. The owner was very excited about the extra piece. That day I noticed a few changes from my original display a week ago, but I didn't have any objection. Since this exhibit room was bigger than the WITCH gallery and didn't have a single office fluorescent light, everything looked more artistic and dignified. Actually the exhibit looked impeccable.

The opening on February 14 was very well attended. The visitors were fascinated with the Egyptian Sculptured Paintings and the display. Some Egyptians from the Embassy came Dr. Ezeldin Ali Mostafa of the Cultural and Educational Bureau came with his wife. They were charming people and loved the exhibit. Also an assistant of a Congressman attended and some friends. After the reception was over and the guests left, the owner was very excited and asked Jaums and me to stay. We went to his office in the back and immediately he got the sherry bottle from the drawer and began to drink glass after glass. He got drunk and we left as soon as possible.

Two days later, the owner called me very excited asking me to come right away with the station wagon to the gallery because a lady had come to see my exhibit and was very interested in buying more than one piece. She wanted to take a few of them to her home to see which one looks the best. I drove to the gallery that afternoon and with Jaums' help I put a few pieces in the station wagon. I found out that the lady lived in a Georgetown mansion not far from the gallery, so we arrived very soon. I had seen that house many times before. It was big but not particularly impressive and in my humble opinion it needed some outside work. The lady was the wife of Mr. Gordon Gray who was a politician with high official government positions during the administrations of Presidents Harry Truman and Dwight Eisenhower from 1945 until 1961. During the drive to her mansion the owner of the gallery told me, "You know, she is a very wealthy lady. I have known her for quite some time and she loves ancient Egyptian art. She has a few residences in different places, but she wanted one of your pieces for her main mansion in Georgetown."

Before we entered the home he looked very apprehensive and seemed to want to say something to me, but he didn't know how to say it. After some hesitation he finally said, "You know, I don't think you should enter Mrs. Gray's house." "Why not?" I inquired. "You know," he carefully said. "Artists, sometimes, say things they shouldn't." I was very understanding and smiled at what he was trying to say and replied, "Don't worry about it. In Spain I met two princesses and other very high class people and I know how to conduct myself. I'll do whatever you consider necessary. The most important thing is to sell." After what I said he was more relaxed and decided that I should go inside Mrs. Gray's home to help him hold the three pieces in place for her to make her final choice. We walked to the main door and rang the bell. A while later, a black maid opened the door and let us in the foyer. The maid went to let the lady of the house know that we were here. She promptly came down the staircase very matter of fact still buttoning her house dress. I acknowledged her presence but kept my mouth shut as the owner of the gallery requested. I guess he never believed me when I told him that I had met princesses in my European past.

We followed her through a few beautifully decorated rooms to the dining room. Indeed it was a great house inside. I tried the pieces in various places. The gallery owner was nervous, anxious and a bit pushy. Mrs. Gray was very logical and reasonable. In my mind I was agreeing with her decisions. After some tries she made her selection of one of them for her dining room. She gave me a hammer and a hook and I hung it in a wall niche in that room. She looked very happy and excited and she thanked me for coming and helping her. Afterward we left with a check for over a thousand dollars to the gallery. He told me that it was an honor that a lady like her would buy one of my pieces. He was very excited about the sale and after we got back to his gallery. He was still too excited and asked Jaums and me to stay in the gallery with him for a while. We stayed and we sat in his back office. He brought out a bottle of orange juice and offered us a drink, which we accepted. Then he got a bottle of vodka and mixed it with the orange juice and immediately started drinking. He wanted to talk more about Mrs. Gray and her wealth and he was getting a little drunk and he told me, "You know, *Hor*"–my piece inspired by the Egyptian God Horus–"speaks to me at night… He made me do certain things . . .."

"What?" I asked him incredulously about his statement.

"Yes, he does. He talks to me at night. I light the incense stick and I sit in front of him in the gallery and he talks to me. He tells me things and makes me do things…" I certainly didn't want to ask him what sort of things *Hor* made him do.

This must be some of his drunken talk I thought and apparently he noticed the skepticism reflected on my face, because he looked very upset at me. Then he got up from the chair behind his desk and said, "Oh…you'll see… I'll show you!" Then he walked to the patio. Jaums and I looked at each other. He came back bringing a painting and said, "You see, *Hor* made me do it!" The medium size painting from the distance looked like a Jackson Pollock. And as he was getting closer to me the painting looked like the amalgamation of drops of color paints of an unbalanced, abstract composition. But when he got closer, it actually was a collage of broken pieces of cardboard in a Pollock-style imitation print pasted on top of another painting that I had seen previously lying down in his office. Apparently he combined all of them together into a crazy composition. That was weird, especially when he was claiming that my piece about Horus was talking to him and made him do it. And he kept repeating, "*Hor* made me do it. *Hor* made me do it." This was very strange..

According to the ancient Egyptian legend, "Horus," a falcon god, was the son of the god Osiris and the goddess Isis. Osiris was murdered by his brother Seth, and his body was chopped in many pieces by Seth, his wife Isis and his son Horus decided to put all the pieces together again and to restore life to Osiris. I have no idea if the alcoholic owner of the gallery knew about this ancient myth… Could he be telling the truth? Could it be possible that My version of *Hor* was giving him instructions to carry out the process to bring Osiris back to life? All that resulted in a very eerie sensation. Maybe I should have had a swig of the vodka…

As I thought about what the owner of the gallery did by putting together all those fragments of a few paintings to restore a broken painting to life was not far from what Horus did! So this bizarre behavior of the gallery owner was not far away from the reality of this myth. Did he already know about this myth? Or not? It was getting dark outside and the room we were in was painted in a spookie Dracula dark gray. The gallery owner was standing in front of us proudly holding his "masterpiece." At that crucial moment where survival may be at stake and saying anything could make matters worse, with the vodka flowing, we didn't think he'd notice if we left, so Jaums and I looked at each other and without saying anything we decided to get the hell out of there, just in case! Who lets these gallery owners out of the asylum?

Another lady in Georgetown that had seen the exhibit requested to take three pieces to her house to see which ones go better in her environment, so I delivered them. She couldn't make up her mind and requested some photos so she could take it to her other homes. So I returned the paintings to the exhibit. When I got to the gallery I noticed that one smaller piece, *Kah*, hanging on the wall, had a black dot on the label. I asked the owner, "Did you sell this one?" "No, no," he nervously replied, going to the piece and quickly removing the dot as if he was caught by surprise. Then in a flash I remember a telephone call I overheard the last time I was at the gallery. He said in that conversation "Yes, I'll give it to you. Yes, the small one… the $350 one… Yes, I'll give it to you." The $350 that was only 37.25" tall he was referring to was *Kah*, an early piece code #75 which was the third mummy-form piece I produced in the U.S. in 1975. Apparently he had a client that wanted that piece. That day he also begged me to stay longer. I felt sorry because obviously he was a lonely old man and I stayed a while.

I was working at an insurance company office during the day. So at night was the only time I had to paint. I treasured that time very much. I knew that eventually my unusual Egyptian work would set me free and give me the independence that would allow me to create even more work and new collections I had in my mind.

The next evening, while I was painting, the phone rang. It was the owner of the gallery calling me "Joselito" and "Antonio" so I knew he was already drunk, interrupting my work with more drunken nonsense. I kept trying all possible ways to get him off the phone with no success. I am not a nasty person and I couldn't just hang up the phone on that lonely man who perhaps did not have anybody in his life. After almost one hour on the phone, he kept asking me again to give him *Kah* as a gift. This was the one I overheard him on the phone a few days ago talking about to sell for $350. And the one he put the black dot indicating that it has been sold. This caught my attention, but I rejected the whole thing because he was so drunk. I kept telling him "no" that I wasn't going to give him that piece. But he kept insisting, begging and crying for it as a child. At the end he was so drunk that I ended up hanging up. Exhausted, I continued painting.

On the way back from a radio interview about my exhibit, I dropped by the gallery to take photos of the exhibit. I noticed that the piece he asked me to give him the night before was not on the wall. I asked him, "Why did you move that piece?" "Oh, it was too crowded where it was." he replied while walking away toward his office. Well, I was glad, I never liked where he hung *Kah* so I began to take photographs when I saw *Kah* resting on the floor, against the wall in the back room and without its label. When I finished photographing all the pieces of the exhibit, I still had one more frame left before the film was over, so I asked him to pose in front of one of my pieces for me to take his photo. His reaction was like *Count Dracula* when threatened by the rays of the sun. That was very weird!

That night he called me at home with the same story as the night before begging and crying to give him *Kah* as if he didn't remember what I said the evening before. Apparently he doesn't remember anything while drunk. I could not afford these interruptions at night, using up my precious time to paint!

Then night after night these drunk calls and I opted for not answering the phone. So he began to call me at odd hours of the night waking me up. In those calls he didn't want *Kah* any longer but kept talking about strange things and that *Hor* was commanding him to call me. I never took his petitions seriously and unplugged the phone at night. One day in his gallery I mentioned to him his calls and he looked completely ashamed, quickly changing the subject saying, "I never remember what I say on those occasions."

When the time for closing the exhibit was approaching, I called him to arrange a time for me to pick up my work. He said he wanted to extend my exhibit. That was fine with me. I didn't have another engagement. During that extra time another lady who was a friend of Mrs. Gordon Gray saw my work in her home. She lived in another mansion in Georgetown. She called the gallery and asked if I could take one of my works to her home to see how it would look there. The owner of the gallery told me that she was the producer of a daily TV talk show on the local CBS station and that she was "a difficult person" but said that he would take the piece to her house not far from the gallery. So that was fine with me. However, later she decided to invite me to her TV show to interview me about my Egyptian art. I was pleased since it was a very popular show which I used to watch in the morning while I was having my breakfast. The host of the show was Carol Randolph, a very pleasant local TV personality. The producer called me and asked me to take my best pieces and they were going to be shown on a set made for them for the show. So I selected my most attention getting pieces and took them to the TV studio the morning of the show and that's the day I met her in person.

Also on the TV show that morning was J. Carter Brown, the director of the National Gallery of Art which still had *The Treasures of Tutankhamun* exhibit, as well as survivor of a gunshot, the Washington, D.C. politician and future Mayor–rather infamous–Marion Barry.

So I placed my pieces in the specially made set. To my surprise at each side the set-builder put two Greek columns! That anachronistic detail was amusing to me but I didn't say anything about it. The producer came to take me to the "greenroom." There she introduced me, mentioning my Egyptian work to J. Carter Brown who was a snob and couldn't care less about me or my work. I was used to this treatment from others in art circles in the U.S. Probably he didn't know that during the Tutankhamen exhibit, the director of the Cairo Museum, Ibrahim El Nawawi, met me and gave me a VIP tour of the exhibit in his National Gallery of Art. About two years later, I met El Nawawi at his Cairo Museum office in 1978 as an official guest of the Egyptian Government. So I sat in silence while I waited for my turn to be interviewed. I thought, probably when Carter Brown has to go out for his interview, seeing the set with my works will be unavoidable–it was right beside the interview set. I watched him as he walked out of the "greenroom," and saw that he turned his face the other way as he walked by the set with my art so he didn't have to look at it. What a disgusting man, I thought.

After the show was over I began to take my pieces from the set to put them in the station wagon. The producer approached me and sat on a bench beside me and she said, "You know–pointing at one of my pieces said–I like that piece very much. It'll look terrific in my home… Would you like to sell me that piece?". "Of course," I replied, the owner of the gallery told me that you have a magnificent home." "Thank you, you are very kind," she said. "You know, I'm not a salesman," I said, "and the gallery owner already told me you like that piece very much." I pointed out to her that I had already talked to the owner and I had told him to lower the price as an exception just for you." After a brief silence she said, "I don't like him. He is a horrible man." I was surprised by the statement she made with profound conviction. Apparently she knew something about him. Also I remember that the gallery owner said that he "knew her very well." And she just performed as he predicted! I proceeded to explain to her further, "You see this is a different situation and I cannot sell you one of my pieces. I have an agreement with the gallery and he is the only one who can sell you the piece that you want." Understanding the situation she said anyway, "Can you make an exception?" I told her that I had to respect the agreement, and reminded her that I had already made an exception for her asking him to lower the price. She replied, "I don't want to deal with him. Your pieces are very expensive, do you know that?" "I don't think they are considering what they are and the amount of work required to make them. You are buying a one of a kind original piece of original pharaonic art that does not exist anywhere in the world." I left the TV studio with my piece and I never saw her again until eight months later, November 17 of the same year, 1977, in a different gallery on M Street in Georgetown, the new one that was representing my work and where I was also the curator of all of the exhibits. This occasion was the opening night of the paintings of the wife of the President of PBS who was a very good artist and was very pleased with the way I set up her exhibit. As expected there were a lot of people from the TV fauna who normally attended such gatherings if the artist was connected to them. So there she was! The TV producer dressed in an all long, sequined, light blue gown. However, in one of the six exhibit rooms coincidentally was an exhibit of some of my Egyptian pieces. I could see that she and her companion were attracted to my two rooms. I don't think she saw me because the gallery was packed. She walked to my pieces and I heard her commenting to her not so formally dressed companion, "His paintings are magnificent and I particularly like that one." I was standing just behind her. And at that very instant I noticed that a sequin had fallen from her gown to the floor. I carefully bent down immediately and picked it up and dropped it in my pocket and amused myself thinking that I may use it for a future *voodoo*! She was really cheap when I realized that other people who had bought my work were not wealthy and never discussed the price. Later on that evening she saw me but pretended she didn't. I did the same.

Coming back to March 15, 1977, after the TV show, I returned to the gallery to hang my pieces again. The owner was very happy with my interview performance and kept saying "how good, natural and lucid" I was. I don't think I ever told him of my experiences in show business in my former country and later in Spain and a few acting jobs I had done in the U.S. I told him of the TV producer trying to buy a painting from me at the end of the show as he warned me. "She is a horrible person," he said. Maybe that's why she wanted to have me on the TV show she was producing after all. He said that I did very well and I acted "like a total professional not wanting to sell a piece on your own." He said that he was proud of me and then paused and became enraged screaming, "She is a bastard! Bitch! Damn!"

After this explosion he controlled himself and told me about a man from the Metropolitan Museum in New York who came to see the exhibit a few days earlier and he liked it so much that he asked for permission to photograph all my work. "What did you say?" I asked. "You know," he explained, "I said yes." Then he went back to his hotel for his camera and came back later that day and took pictures of everything." "Did you ask him why he wanted the pictures?" I inquired since I was very curious about the whole thing especially since he didn't tell me until a few days later. "Well," he replied, "He liked them and wanted to have them for himself." He then suddenly remembered and added, "Before he left, he recommended that you should meet with the Chief Curator of the Cairo Museum who is now at the National Gallery taking care of the Tutankhamun exhibit. He also said that he will talk to him about your work. He left the Chief Curator's name and phone number and said that you should mention his name." Then he got up and went back to the back room and brought back one of the opening invitations of my show on which the guy wrote down the information. I immediately called the Cairo Chief Curator, Dr. El Nawawi, whom I met back in November 1976 when he gave me a VIP tour of the Tutankhamun exhibit. And he gave me an appointment for the same day in the afternoon.

So I went to the National Gallery and found, once more, a very sweet and unassuming man, not a snob with a superiority complex like J. Carter Brown. We talked about my possible official invitation to Egypt and he insisted that I should visit him at the Cairo Museum. He said that he will try to visit my new exhibit before he leaves town for Egypt. Unfortunately, an illness struck him and he was at Walter Reed Hospital in Washington, D.C. and couldn't come to this second exhibit of my pieces. But we will meet in Egypt later in 1978.

After March 31, I didn't receive any more drunk phone calls from the gallery owner at night. I was very glad because producing new work was very important to me. I found out later that the miracle was due to divine intervention. He closed the gallery for a few weeks and went out of town. That's why some people had called me saying that they could not see my work! After the middle of April, I finally got in touch with him again. At that time he informed me that he was having a new show opening on April 30. That was fine for me and we talked about the setting of a day for the removal of my exhibit. We agreed on Saturday, April 23. My exhibit had been there a little over two months, so it was time to end it.

But, for the new show opening in May, he asked me if I could come and move my exhibit from the main room to the back room rather than ending my exhibit. I decided to go along with his idea even though the back room was not very big. After I rearranged my pieces in the back room, I helped the owner hang the new exhibit in the main gallery. I went to the opening of the other artist whose work I liked very much and I met her. During the evening, he called me to his office in the back and said, "You know, I like your show better. Tonight after everybody leaves, I want you to help me to switch the shows." Thinking that I didn't hear him well I said, "Can you repeat what you just said?" Very matter of fact he said, "Yes, change the shows. You're in the front again and her in the back." I replied, "I think both shows look fine where they are now."

After a momentary silence he said, "No no, you just don't understand"–with a glint in his tiny eyes–"I want to put your show in the front and the other in the back, it's simple…capisco… comprendo…?" "But what is she going to say? That's not right!" I replied. "Oh, she'll never find out. She is from New York. She will be leaving town tonight after the opening." He answered and I said, "I will not do that. I know what being an artist is and how difficult it is to find a gallery to exhibit. I would not do that to anybody."

"OK, OK," he rapidly said. "I promise I'll get her permission."

Later on that evening he approached me, "I talked to her about it. She said that's OK with her." The way he said it didn't sound very convincing to me. I felt uneasy about the whole thing. I couldn't understand how she had agreed to that and at the same time I felt completely inadequate going to her behind his back to ask her for a verification. I didn't want to cause any trouble or friction between the three of us. Somehow I had to trust the gallery owner. After the reception was over and everybody was gone, I expressed my feelings to him again. He then became irate and screamed at me, "For God sake, do you think I would do that to anybody?!"

I felt sorry for that old and alcoholic, lonely man, who recently I had discovered, didn't even have any place to live but the basement of the gallery and I decided to take his word for it and ended up hanging the artist from New York's work in the back room and mine in the front again. By the time I was finished, he was completely drunk and passed out on his office floor. I went to the basement which was in a chaotic disarray and got a dilapidated old mattress and took to his office and helped him lay there. By the time I was ready to leave he was waking up and was asking me what I was doing. I explained to him what I had done and he asked me to help him to get up so he could see how his gallery looks. I told him that I was planning to take two of my pieces home. He mumbled, "All right." So I took one of my pieces and placed it in the station wagon and came back to the gallery for the second one, but I could not get in since the main door was locked and all the lights were off inside the gallery. I knocked on the door and called him to please open the door to get the other piece. Then I heard a scream from the inside of the gallery, "Get out! You are a thief, you are a thief!" I replied, "No no it's me Agustin… Remember?" I said, trying to make him reason, "I have to get the other piece, remember!" "You are a thief! Get out!" He shouted again.

"To hell with him," I thought and left. What an unpleasant evening…

Early next morning he called me to apologize for the night before. I was getting fed up with him and told him, "Listen, I have been very patient, but I'm getting tired of trying to help you. What you did last night was uncalled for." "What did I do? What did I do? He interrupted. "Oh come on, I said, You know what you did." "No!" he emphatically denied. "I honestly don't know. I can't remember." I told him about the night before and added, "You see, that's not the way of conducting a serious business. I was there last night to help you. If I go to your gallery again, I don't want to see you drunk." Then, he apologized again and promised, "I won't do that again."

I had never dealt with any alcoholic relatives. No one in my family drank alcohol and didn't have any acquaintances who were heavy drinkers, at least to my knowledge. So I didn't know how to deal with it. The owner of the gallery said that he lived in a house nearby, but he was very vague about where. He pointed at the distance, somewhere… But when I went to the basement of the gallery the night before I figured that the basement was his only home. I felt very sorry about him and his lonely life. He said that he had a brother and a sister living in a different city. He called them "horrible" and "greedy." That's why he lived alone.

One evening I had to go to the gallery with Jaums. When we arrived we noticed that he had been drinking, but he wasn't drunk. Then we asked him to go with us to dinner at Martin's Tavern nearby. He accepted the invitation. Before we left he said he had to go to the bathroom to freshen up. As soon as we left the gallery he began walking strangely and by the time we arrived at the tavern he could no longer control his intoxication. We managed to get him into the booth. He became very impertinent clapping his hands demanding services from the waiter. We ordered food and he requested a *Bloody Mary* which I managed to hide from him for a while. He was so drunk that couldn't even eat for himself. So I got the fork and began to feed him. He cooperated without hesitation as if he was used to it. He was demanding more and more tartar sauce from the waiter who finally got upset with him. He wanted to pay for our food but we didn't accept because of the state he was in. We carried him to the station wagon and asked for his home address. He refused to provide it and asked to be taken back to the gallery. We made sure he got in and locked the front door and we left. After that night we realized that the gallery truly was his home and felt even more sorry for him.

On April 21, I had to go to the gallery for business. Everything was in order. I asked him, "Have you received any more inquiries about my pieces?" He replied with a negative gesture. I was surprised and I insisted, "Not even for the one I specially made for the gallery window?" His reply was a fast and nervous, "No, no," and rapidly walking away to his back office. That struck me as strange, since a few days ago he told me he removed the pedestal from that one-of-kind free standing three-dimensional piece to show a client." After finishing business at the gallery, I asked the owner, "Can I start taking some of my pieces today so I can save an extra trip on Saturday?" "Sure it's all right with me," he answered.

So I proceeded to take some of them and put them in the station wagon. At the end I had some space for a smaller piece and I thought of the other 36 inch tall piece, *Kah*, since I didn't want to take the eye-catching free-standing *Tan Kha Ten* from the gallery window. So I ended up taking *Kah*, the third art piece made since arriving in the U.S., done in 1975. That piece is the one he had removed from the exhibit and placed on the floor leaning against the wall in a corner of his back office. This was the piece that he began requesting as a gift in his first drunken night time phone call. He never said anything about that piece when he was sober. So I really wanted to close that chapter. After I took this last piece to the station wagon, I walked back to his office to sign the inventory of the pieces I was taking that day. Okay, one more encounter with him behind me.

When I opened the door of my apartment the phone was already ringing and I ran to it. He was already drunk and crying like a child, "I want *Kah*." I was exhausted, I was already having my annual allergy attack plus a swollen knee. I was not in the most minimal disposition of wasting an hour or more listening to his drunken wails. I told him that I was exhausted and still had to unload my work from the station wagon. His reply was a scream saying, "I want to talk NOW!" "Listen to me," I said, " I just entered my home. I have many things to do. I cannot talk to you now." Then he became completely irrational, screaming and insulting me using all kinds of dirty words and saying that he not only wanted *Kah* back, but also wanted *Hor* too. Then he became even more irrational and hysterical and shouted "You are a fucking liar! A goddamn liar and a cheat!" I hung up and left the phone off of the hook.

When Jaums arrived that afternoon I told him what happened and I said, "I don't want to answer the phone so leave it off the hook. I cannot deal or reason with him when he is so drunk. Later on that evening when we thought it was safe, we hung up the phone. After 10pm the phone rang and Jaums answered. It was him and as drunk as early on. He was demanding from Jaums the same two pieces he was asking early afternoon. "I'm sorry I cannot do that I am not the owner of those pieces, and he shouted, "You are a fucking liar too!" And demanded, "Let me talk to the other fucking son of a bitch!" Naively, Jaums tried to calm him down and kept asking him, "Why do you want those two pieces?" But he didn't answer that question. Jaums hung the phone and left it off the hook for the night and said to me, "Know what I think? I think he wants those two pieces because he has two buyers and he wants to pocket all the money. 'Sticky fingers' you know…"

As a trivia, I would like to add that on November 18, 1977 *Kah* was sold at the next gallery I was associated with, which also was located in the Georgetown area of Washington, D.C.. *Hor* I lent to a very good friend and after he died in 2017, it was returned to me as well as other pieces I lent him for his home along with one of the God Anubis he had purchased.

But the story of this unfortunate second gallery was not over yet. The best and most unpleasant and traumatic experience for me was lurking around the corner…

On the morning of April 22 I called the gallery. When he answered he appeared to be sober, but he had an aggressive attitude. I was extra careful handling him. I mentioned his two phone calls the previous evening, his insults and obscenities and that he shouted at Jaums and me. I told him that we had been extremely considerate and respectful with him and that we adhered to our contract agreement. We helped him in every way we could. That he must know perfectly well that we had not taken advantage of him. "You are a liar!" He shouted interrupting me and continued irrationally, "A god damn liar! A fucking liar! Those two pieces are mine! You know it! You gave them to me!"

"Those pieces are my creation and I am the sole and right owner of them. You never talked to me about them rationally. You had mentioned them only when you were drunk. You told me on multiple occasions not to pay any attention to what you say when you are drunk. But even if you were in your right state of mind, I wouldn't have agreed to give those two pieces to you for the simple reason that my work is very complex and it takes me a long time and a lot of work to produce them. From 1974 to this exhibit in 1977, I was able to produce just 24 pieces. So, I can't afford to give my work away."

"I don't have to ask, they are mine!" screaming and sounding completely deranged on the phone. "You owe them to me!"

"Listen," I said, "I do not owe you anything but your 40% commission for the sales.

"You owe them to me because I had your show here for three months!" He was obviously looking for an excuse to support his claim.

Clarifying his ridiculous claim I said, "I never requested the extension of my exhibit. That was at your convenience and was your decision and you made some extra money in commission during that time."

"I had to cancel other shows in order to have yours," he said.

"That was your choice, besides, you never told me you had other shows. And the other one you had you decided to move to the back room in order to have mine as the main event. Remember it was your idea not mine. I did it reluctantly."

"For God sake, don't be greedy! You had your show for three months!" He shouted.

"I didn't ask you for that," I replied.

"I let you stay for THREE MONTHS!," he screamed.

I said, "If we are going to be technical about it, my show was in your gallery for two months and your gallery was closed for over two weeks during that period of time, as you very well know."

He irrationally screamed, "Three months! Three months! Three months! Those pieces are mine, mine mine! I'll take them to my house in Pennsylvania and you'll never see them again!

Now he is mentioning he owns a house in Pennsylvania! Perhaps it's like "the house down the block" near his gallery that never materialized. I felt sorry for that drunken man. I tried to calm him down to no avail. I neeed to go back to my office to work, so I had to terminate that futile phone call to oblivion by hanging up on him again, escaping to the sanity of my auto insurance office job… I don't know why in the HELL I had the curse of being an artist. Life is so simple and boring for a regular office employee. I may be in need of electroshocks to conform, adapt and to shut up as people do in communist countries!

After I came back home for the evening I left the phone off the hook. I could not tolerate being yelled at by that unbalanced, drunken man. I tried to sleep but I couldn't. Probably he had buyers for these two pieces he so vehemently tried to get from me as gifts so he can keep the extra money for himself. Actually in this equation he was the greedy one. He was being dishonest. Perhaps his mind was already affected by his excess of alcohol.

I was hurt, upset and disappointed by him, his insults and irrational demands. And he never said that he wanted those pieces because he really liked them. Jaums tried to probe his mind the day before by asking him, "Why do you want those pieces?" He was silent and didn't answer that simple question. Actually he became enraged at his question. It seemed to be something cooking underneath that was not smelling good. That night it was a long night. I was quite awake thinking about my relationship with that strange man. Everything was a film that I cannot stop over and over in my mind. I could have privately sold the piece the TV producer wanted and kept the money and her favor, but I didn't because it would have been unethical and disloyal to him. I remember the phone conversation I overheard in his gallery with a person who was trying to buy the piece that later he asked me while drunk to give to him. Another time while I was at the gallery I overheard another similar conversation about another of my pieces and he was promising to sell it to that person. I didn't think much about it, but now both came to my mind that long night and made me suspect even more what he was planning to do behind my back. Probably he also had a buyer for the special free-standing piece that I specially made for the window… I remembered his strange behavior when I asked about why it was removed from its pedestal and placed on the window seat…

I was suspecting that something would happen the next day when I'd be going to the gallery to pick up the rest of the pieces. I remember the first time I went to his gallery and he tried the scheme of the "gentlemen's agreement" that he was trying to force on me that would tie me economically to his gallery forever… And the next day, based on my research, he reversed everything he had said the day before. He was dishonest with me from the beginning. And I felt hurt because in spite of him being a sick and obnoxious alcoholic, I went out of my way to help him. I had not been very lucky with this experience with this second gallery either. This might well be just another bad experience to make me act even more carefully in the future. Being desperate for a gallery can be the kiss of death.

Finally it was dawn… April 23rd, 1977, had arrived. I could not stay in bed any longer and I got up early to get ready to pick up the rest of my pieces from the gallery. That was not such a relaxing event now to return my pieces home. Who knows in what mood he will be or if he will be already drunk or not… Jaums was going to come to help me load my work into the station wagon. I called the gallery before leaving home. The tone of his voice sounded very "dry" to me.

It was 11:25 am when we arrived. We parked in front but across the street. From that point I could easily see the gallery where the free-standing, three-sided piece had been displayed. I noticed right away that it was not there. I thought he may have taken it to the back room, so I didn't say anything to him about it when I entered the gallery. Inside the main gallery room I noticed that the two pieces that he was demanding for him, *Kah* and *Hor* were hanging in the original places in the exhibit. I thought it strange that he walked from the back room to where the empty pedestal was inside the window and was standing just to the right of the pedestal looking through the window at the street outside. I was kind of alarmed about the missing piece for a few seconds, but then I thought that perhaps with the main door of the gallery wide open which was beside the window, he removed that small piece and put it in his office for security. So thinking that it was in a safer place I didn't worry anymore about it. While we began removing the pieces from the gallery walls, he stayed by the window watching us outside, putting the pieces in the station wagon, and when we were inside the gallery he was watching our movements. I thought that was very odd because he had never done that with us in the past. He trusted us. However, he was very silent and reserved this morning and didn't say anything to us. On one of our trips going inside the gallery and with him standing beside the empty pedestal I said to him, "Good morning Mr. Perez." Very hush and dry he replied, "Good morning." Then I proceeded to inform him that I thought I would be able to do it in one trip but I miscalculated and instead I will be doing another trip. He listened in silence and didn't say anything. However, he finally said, twice, that on this first trip I should leave the most expensive pieces in the gallery. I didn't want to upset him and provoke another attack of rage against me so I accepted his request. And we continued walking back and forth placing more pieces in the car with him keeping an eye on what we were doing all the time. Actually, what I was doing was going inside the gallery to pick up the pieces from the wall and take them out to the station wagon on the street where Jaums was helping me to slide each one inside and with fabric to protect them from each other. We had done this routine often in the past. He seemed very nervous and kept walking from his observation post beside the empty pedestal looking at our every move. By this time Jaums was able to move the station wagon from across the street to a new parking space just beside the sidewalk of the gallery. Two ladies across the street were completely intrigued by the unusual movement of what appeared to them as "mummies" being placed inside a red station wagon! After I finished loading, there was a little space where I could place the small piece, *Tan-Kha-Ten,* that had been in the window, so I asked him for it. "It's there on the pedestal," he nervously replied, turning his eyes avoiding mine. "No Mr. Perez it is not there," I replied, completely baffled by his absurd reply. How could he say that when he had been standing by the empty pedestal all morning. How could he overlook that fact? Is he crazy?

"It's there," he repeated, to my astonishment! Then pointing to the empty pedestal just beside him, I said, "Don't you see that it is not there?" He screamed, "It was there when you arrived!"

"Mr. Perez," I said, trying to be conciliatory and lowering the volume of my voice to the minimum, "The piece was not there when I arrived this morning."

Screaming irrationally, "It was there! It was there! You know it was there!"

"It was not," trying to be patient and pointing out to him, "It was the first thing I noticed when I arrived this morning. I thought that you put it in the back room."

In an accusatory tone of voice he shouted, "You took it, you took it! It was there! You took it! You are a thief!" He seemed to be trying to call attention to any passerby.

Trying to make sense of the absurdity of that situation, I said, "Mr. Perez, it was not there when we arrived this morning. I noticed it was not there as did Jaums when we were parking the station wagon on the other side of the street. I thought that you put it in the back room as you had done in the past. The pedestal was empty as well as the window sill. There was nothing there."

His reply was to scream in a theatrical way for anybody to hear, "You are a thief, a liar and a cheat! Oh my god you are a thief! You took it, you took it!

During all this time Jaums and I were trying very hard to control ourselves in the middle of this uncalled for and grotesque situation and make him reason to come back to his senses. He didn't seem drunk, just completely deranged trying to get us to accept a situation that obviously had not taken place. He watched us since we arrived and had observed all of our actions. We never went to the window or the place where the empty pedestal was. He was standing beside the empty pedestal from the time we arrived. We never approached it.

As he continued screaming, accusing and following behind me, I went inside the gallery to the back room to see if I could find the missing piece somewhere there and I didn't see it, so I went to look in his office and it wasn't there either. I checked in the bathroom and nothing. I managed to go to the back patio and down his basement. In it I looked the best I could because it was dark with a single light bulb. The floor was an ocean of tossed newspaper pages almost knee high. Two box springs with broken mattresses amid cardboard boxes, bags and locked trunks in total disarray making it an easy place to hide something. I reached the conclusion that my search of the basement was overwhelmingly futile and went upstairs.

There he was following me screaming like a malevolent beast. His screams were so loud that I noticed that two ladies across the street were watching in disbelief. He kept repeating like a broken record the same accusations behind my back. His voice was getting affected by his louds screams that he was sounding like a pig before being killed. It was a grotesque spectacle that reminded me of the surrealist films of Luis Bruñuel.

Then he pointed with his finger at the open cargo door of the station wagon. Inside he could clearly see all my big pieces and no small ones. I yelled at him, "Can you see that it is not here?! The missing piece is not there and you know it!"

His irrational reply was, "I know it is there! Open the hood!"

Exasperated, I said, "Mr. Perez, under the hood there is only space for the motor!!!"

"Open it you thief!" He screamed hysterically at me.

To prove his stupidity, I opened the hood to show the motor. "You see," I said, "even if I wanted to, I could not hide anything here."

He said, "You are very calm. There is something fishy here…" Trying very hard to control myself again, I took a deep breath and said, "My piece was not in the window when we arrived this morning inside the window. Why don't you admit it? We can call the police and report the robbery…"

He rapidly responded, "There is no robbery"! He shouted, interrupting me, "You took the piece!"

I turned my back to that disgusting irrational being, closed the hood and the cargo door of the wagon, got inside, locked the doors, turned the motor on while he was outside yelling and accusing me like a mad man and I drove a block away from that hell and parked the wagon in front of the home of the only person I barely knew in that neighborhood, who actually was an admirer of my Egyptian work and had come a few times to see my exhibit and brought some friends. Her name was Rachel and she was married to the lawyer James Tracey Welch who by many accounts was the lawyer who made the decision to transfer the famous *Hope Diamond* by First Class U.S. Mail from New York to the Smithsonian Institution in 1958. I didn't know any lawyer at that time so I hoped that she or her husband could direct me to the right one to handle the situation I was in that horrid morning.

Her husband was not at home but Rachel told me that Mr. Perez didn't have the best reputation in the neighborhood and that she had heard many bad stories about him. She proceeded to call her husband and he recommended a lawyer that may help me and may not be that expensive. While I waited for the lawyer, Jaums and I spent part of that morning at the Welches' home. She let me talk with the lawyer on the phone in a private alcove of her lovely upstairs French parlor. This was the initiation of our long friendship with the Welchs, who were very nice people living for many years just a block away from the gallery. It was during that time that the Welches were looking for a place to move after Mr. Welch retired. They were looking in a few places, but after they met me they took that as an indication that their best place to retire was Saint Augustine in Florida, because my name was Agustin and my family came from Spain.

Rachel, who was a civil engineer, decided to design their new home in the style of a typical old Spanish home in the Historic Area of Saint Augustine and she was given permission by the city to build their home on Cordova Street. While their home was under construction they invited Jaums and me to see the progress and she commissioned me to paint two small mural-type paintings on top of two mirrors in the upstairs parlor in her favorite Egyptian period of the pharaoh Akhenaton and Nefertiti. I loved doing those paintings for the Welches. I saw the size of the room, the configuration and I took the measurements where my paintings were going to be inside the mirror frames already in place. I liked the truncated pyramidal ceiling she designed for her parlor.

She didn't know what color she would paint that ceiling, but when

I finished the two pieces and they were installed on top of the mirrors, she decided to paint the ceiling in the sky blue color that I used in my paintings. By that time the house construction was more advanced and I did some work on the back door accessing the central patio and that door was named *Puerta Blazquez*. Jaums did some work on the brick floor of the patio and it was named *Patio Jaums*. Rachel asked me to make signs for both of our contributions and I did and both signs were up.

Unfortunately her husband James Tracey Welch died on April 13,1990 and Rachel S. Welch on December 14, 2000. Some years later I went to Saint Augustine and visited the cemetery where a pyramidal grave already existed and where they are resting nearby.

Knowing the Welches was an enrichment to my life, so perhaps that makes the pain of Mr. Perez worthwhile. But, his pain is yet to be completed…

Back to the gallery mess, I called the lawyer from the Welches' home and he said to park the station wagon in front of the gallery and he will meet us there in one hour. So, Jaums drove the car back to find a parking spot close to the gallery.

I later left the Welches' house and walked to the gallery to face that HORRIBLE experience again. I had never been involved in a situation like this before. As I approached I noticed that Mr. Perez was screaming and gesticulating to Jaums and that he was taking all the pieces out of the station wagon and placed them standing resting against the wagon to convince Mr. Perez that nothing else was hiding inside. But he kept screaming "You are a thief! You took the painting! You are a liar!" So I told Jaums, "Don't waste your time. He is crazy. He doesn't know what he is saying." I helped him to put my pieces inside the car again.

One of the ladies across the street who had been witnessing what was going on and saw the searching of the station wagon and the demands of Mr. Perez, walked toward me and said, "You ought to call a lawyer. That man seems to be completely insane. His demands and his rage and accusations against you both are inexcusable. You both were more than nice and patient with him. Look, I know a lawyer. I think I have his card in my purse, let me see…" She began to search inside her purse. I was very glad that she was there and was trying to help me in the middle of this ordeal. She was like an angel in the middle of the storm. I thanked very much and told her that we were waiting for a lawyer. She finally found the card and gave it to me anyway just in case.

Meantime, Mr Perez, witnessing the lady talking to us from the gallery window, came out full of rage running and screaming like a madman at the two ladies saying, "Get out of here! Keep moving! Keep moving! Get out!" The ladies were outraged by his attitude and one of them replied, "The sidewalks and streets are public places and you don't have any right over them."

Then Mr. Perez went inside the gallery and locked the door. Both ladies gave me their names and business cards. We finished placing the rest of my pieces inside the station wagon again and locked all the doors and sat and waited for the lawyer. I said to Jaums, "If that madman comes out screaming again, ignore him and do not move this car out of here under any circumstance."

Time passed slowly as always happens when you are trying to get through a bad experience. It's like a perverse and diabolic being is rejoicing with every microsecond of your agony.

Later a tall, slender guy I had seen before with Mr. Perez arrived at the gallery and was knocking at the door. Mr. Perez opened and looked at our parked station wagon. He said something to him and pointed to the station wagon. They went in and locked the door again. After a while, another man arrived that I hadn't seen before and the same scene was replayed. I was getting apprehensive. Who knows what that crazy man was concocting now. Some of my paintings were still inside that gallery and I felt completely helpless. The one hour the lawyer told me it will take him to be there was over fifteen minutes ago. I was very concerned about the security of my work still inside. I remembered what he had done in the past with the work of another artist which he tore apart and pasted over another painting saying that my piece *Hor* "made him do it." I was concerned that my creations were still kidnaped inside with that unpredictable weird old alcoholic man. But my lawyer was still not there. If Mr. Perez sees a lawyer he may refrain from doing harm to them.

Then I decided to find a policeman because I thought that if he sees one around he will not do anything drastic. So I got out of the station wagon and went to the main street, Wisconsin Ave. After quite some time I was able to get the attention of a police patrol car, but to my surprise, I had to literally beg him to come to the scene. Apparently the policeman was not interested in getting involved in any other thing but a traffic violation. It was to me another disappointing experience that day… I dragged the policeman in his cruiser to the front of the gallery and told him what had happened that morning there and that I was concerned about my work virtually kidnaped inside and that my concern was that he could damage it as he had done to the work of the other artist. I wanted an official record that they were there undamaged. He was not interested at all in what had happened there that morning or the missing piece. He said it was "my word against the word of Mr. Perez." He didn't care about witnesses. He said, "How can you prove that the art pieces are yours and you are the artist?" They are all signed, dated and had a code number that identified each one, beside I have the inventory of all of them. He said that what I had to show him wasn't valid! But he will go inside the gallery to check the pieces inside the gallery. So he crossed the street, knocked at the door. A different guy that I didn't see before opened the door and let him in. Very soon after that, the policeman came out and told me that there was a lawyer inside the gallery and that it was a civil matter. "Oh gee, thanks a lot,"

I thought, I wondered what he would have done different if a woman was screaming "rape!?" Well, that could be a "civil matter" too…

A dilapidated avocado green *Pontiac* convertible passed by and its driver was signaling to me. It parked across the street and its driver actually looks to me like a cheap version of the TV character *Lieutenant Columbo*. After about over two hours my lawyer finally arrived! He parked his car across the street and he came out walking toward the station wagon. My god, that's my lawyer? Well, at least somebody that I hope will be my savior. I hope. The end of my nightmare is near, I thought. My sense of humor was somehow coming back after a grueling day. I was becoming myself again.

After the formal introductions, he asked me some pertinent questions and I showed him the documentation I brought with me. Then he went with me to the door of the gallery and knocked on the door. Shortly, the same guy who opened the door to the police appeared and identified himself as Mr. Perez's attorney. He certainly looked much better than my Salvation Army shopper. He must have eaten caviar and champagne for lunch while mine only had a 25 cent hamburger at the Little Tavern with a Billy Carter beer. Well, we went in and I saw my work hanging on the wall.

After an excruciating, more than two-hours of negotiation, I felt exhausted and with a terrible headache but somehow protected. I thought my lawyer did the best he could and he witnessed by himself the hysterical and theatrical manners of the ridiculous behavior of Mr. Perez. Even his lawyer at a point of the negotiation realized that fact, telling my lawyer that he was the one with the "honest client."

My lawyer wanted to get all my pieces out of the gallery that same day. But Mr. Perez was opposed to that. He didn't even want to accept my check for the commission I must pay him as a result of a sale and he came up with a demand: a certified bank check if I wanted the rest of my pieces back by the next coming Saturday! So my pieces became his hostages. It was really unbelievable!

He also refused to account for the "mysterious disappearance" of *Tan-Kha-Ten* from the pedestal of the inside gallery window, accusing me again in front of the two lawyers of stealing my own property! This whole situation was ridiculous and apparently there was nothing my lawyer could do in order to change that fact. Then I requested that if my pieces were going to remain there, a detailed inventory of all of them should be filed, because I did not want to come back next Saturday and find anything damaged or missing. The inventory was done, an agreement was typed and that was the end of that horrible and excruciating Saturday afternoon of April 23, 1977.

My lawyer requested that I write down all I remembered about my unfortunate relationship with Mr. Perez. That night I was unable to sleep. I couldn't stop the film inside my mind of the relationship with this troubled man and the horrible experience that he put me through. With this horrible plot running relentlessly in my mind and with no way to stop it I got out of bed and sat in front of my typewriter and wrote down everything that was still fresh in my memory of the turbulent 84 days of personal and business relationships with Mr. Perez.

It was an excruciatingly long week until the next Saturday…

When the day came at last, I went to the gallery with Jaums and his father as a witness of the process to retrieve my pieces once and for all from that gallery at the hands of that "horrible man" as many before me knew him to be and for me to learn the hard way.

When we entered his office, a lady—as, I suppose, his witness—was sitting there, looking very stern, on a chair to the right of his desk. He also was very controlled and unemotional sitting at his desk. But the atmosphere without any doubt was tense since no one knew where and how an explosion may materialize. Everybody seemed forced into being civil and guarded. There was no introduction of the lady or of Jaums' father. It was a chilled and uneasy atmosphere in an irregular situation. Sound and voices were kept to the minimum in both camps.

I extended my hand to him with the signed certified bank check and he carefully inspected the check and gave it to her to look at and she returned the check to him and he placed it in the middle drawer of his desk. There was tension in the air as the closing of the desk drawer seemed to echo thunder in the room.

Jaums, his father and I turned around and proceeded to remove the paintings from the walls and prepared to carry them to the station wagon outside beside the sidewalk of the gallery. We tried to do our work as fast as we could to get the hell out there as soon as possible without damaging any of the pieces. From that god forsaken gallery of horrors we headed to the police station to file a robbery report. This was because Mr. Perez told my lawyer that he was not going to file a report.

I always asked myself, "Why would he accuse me of stealing *Tan-Kha-Ten* when we all knew I didn't steal it? I guess it was the best he could come up with with his foggy mind. I would like to know who the new owner is, not to take it away from him or her. Just knowing its whereabouts–I always like to know where they are. They are my children."

After reporting the theft to the police, I made and distributed a flier with a photo of the missing "mummy" in the window of the gallery in case somebody was to see it in somebody's home and let me know. But no one ever contacted me and much less the police, what do they care?!. I reported the stolen painting to The Art Dealer Association of America and the Stolen Art Foundation. But no news.

According to police the gallery was closed all the time and the police detective in charge of the case wasn't able to contact Mr. Perez. Later he was able to get hold of Mr. Perez, but he refused to talk or cooperate with his investigation. According to the detective's own words, "He threw me out on the street."

Eventually, the detective was able to talk to Mr. Perez and he simply told him that I had the painting. So that was it. He took Mr. Perez's word as the only truth and he closed the case, insinuating to me that in reality I took my own painting. I couldn't understand his logic at all…

During this long ordeal, I found out that what had happened to me was not unique in the art world. It happened to other artists. "Mysteriously disappeared" artworks from exhibits was a fairly common occurrence by dishonest gallery owners that apparently are an abundant species. There was no legal protection for the artists who were left in limbo. The laws protected the art dealers and the galleries. Not even insurance was the answer, because it specifically does not cover "mysterious disappearance." So we are at the mercy of the galleries.

During this period I had problems sleeping. All of the episode became like a film that was playing and playing inside my mind. I had to be treated by a doctor who prescribed Placidyl, which was generally used to treat insomnia. With it I was finally able to sleep. I have always hated being dependent on drugs and getting into a habit for them. So after a few months I stopped taking that medication for good. I hate vices, that's why I never drink coffee or tea, never smoke or drink alcoholic beverages, even though my ancestors in Spain have produced wines since 1785!

I ended up suing Mr. Perez for the "mysteriously disappeared" three-dimensional painting/sculpture. The litigation back and forth took a year. He didn't want to go to court and he finally agreed to pay me back for it. The legal agreement was signed by both parties. He began paying monthly installments, but they were never on the promised schedule. One month his payment did not come at all. I called my lawyer who advised me to wait another month. But then, Mr. Perez vanished. The gallery was permanently closed. The gallery phone was disconnected. He was gone. No one knew where he went, not even the ones who thought of themselves as his friend.

After a while, I had the idea to produce a collection called *Tan-Kha-Ten Where are you?* It was composed of a group of three-dimensional free-standing pieces with three faces, two in the front and one in the back inspired by the "birth of a pharaoh," just as the stolen piece but slightly taller than the original. My plan was to exhibit them with the hope that somebody in town had seen the original piece somewhere. Making this new collection was therapeutic to me. But to this day no one has made the connection with the "missing mummy."

I have never seen that piece again. I know it's somewhere. Somebody out there is enjoying it. I do not want that "mummy" back. I just would like to know where it is, as I know where all my paintings are.

After that incident, every time that I made a new collection, the first one was dedicated to the "missing mummy."

Tan-Kha-Ten, where are you?

CHAPTER 7

THE SECOND COMING

Almost a year after the special closing reception for Egyptian Embassy guests at the WITCH's gallery, I received a phone call from Dr. Ezeldin Ali Mostafa of the Cultural and Educational Bureau of the Egyptian Embassy in Washington, D.C. He was excited and wanted to give me a surprise, he said, "I have received the official invitation from my government. You will be traveling to Egypt as a guest of the Ministry of Higher Education." Well, I was so excited that I could not say much. I was extremely surprised indeed, since I had almost forgotten everything about it. I was flattered and happy. It was like a dream and I refused to wake up… But I was not dreaming this time. I was living the reality. Certainly I was excited and nervous at the same time. So far, this is the most important recognition of my work I had received and from the people who are the authorities in ancient Egyptian art. I could not imagine what it would be like being a foreign government's guest. What an honor! And just for the merit of my unusual work! I felt very lucky and as usual, I couldn't help but fantasize about my future trip… Dr. Mostafa asked me to drop by his office to pick up the official invitation letter and to talk about when I was planning to make the trip.

First, I would have to ask for permission from my supervisor at my office job in order to decide when to go. I found that March was a good month to be in Egypt because of the weather, so I asked for a one month vacation–fortunately I had already accumulated a lot of vacation time. And, it was a slow month at the office and nobody else had requested vacation around that month. So my petition was granted. I would be able to leave for Cairo during the first week of March 1978. I communicated the dates to Dr. Mostafa as he requested. Now he can notify the Ministry of Higher Education for them to make all the arrangements for hotel reservations and travels inside Egypt. He said that as a guest of his government, I would be staying only in first class hotels, like the Hilton or Sheraton in Cairo and other good hotels throughout Egypt. I asked Jaums to go with me as a photographer to document the trip and he liked the ancient Egyptian civilization. Of course, he had to pay his own way, but that was all right with him since this was going to be an unique opportunity.

All of a sudden, I was there in Egypt, the land of my dreams. I could not believe the wonders in front of my eyes. The official guide was taking me everywhere I wanted to see, temples, monuments, tombs in the Valley of the Kings, pyramids… All these fascinating and incredible places flashed across the land, mighty symbols of bygone splendors. However, they all looked to me perfectly preserved, all brand new. That was remarkable! I was not expecting this. The wall murals' colors were as bright as when they were first painted, thousands of years ago. It was a feast of colors. I had seen those colors before! They were the colors of my own paintings! I was wondering how I knew. I saw a huge sarcophagus standing up vertically. The wood was in perfect condition, but to my surprise nothing was painted on it! That was very unusual. It was only a highly polished and smooth wooden surface. It appeared to be stained in a rich walnut color. Actually its finishing reminded me of some German and Chinese radios I had seen in my younger years. The curious detail about this sarcophagus was that the area where the head was supposed to be was of a trapezoidal shape. That made it completely different from most sarcophagi I had seen. And to my amazement, it had a complicated mechanism that opened a sliding window lid so you could see the face of the mummy inside. This highly unusual sarcophagus was located in some sort of museum, on the second floor corridor with open balconies facing a central patio. Actually that museum resembled a Spanish colonial house. I was familiar with this style of house. On the ground floor there was a museum shop which was decorated inside like a Middle Age castle. And on the counters there were many reproductions of the unusual sarcophagi I had seen upstairs. Even though they were small, they had the same complicated mechanism that opened the sliding window. I took one of them in my hands, I operated a tiny lever, instead of seeing the face of the tiny mummy inside, only a skull came into view. The whole thing transported me to the annual Mexican festivities of the Day of the Dead. I decided to buy a bunch of them to make a version of that oddity when I come back home.

From that museum, my guide took me in a limousine to an airfield. There was a helicopter waiting for me. As soon as I was aboard, it lifted up. Sitting beside me in the small cabin was a tiny old lady. She introduced herself as the museum director. She had a strange sounding name that I was not able to repeat. She had very tiny dark eyes and she didn't talk much, only the necessary, I guessed because of the loud noises of the helicopter. She had long and curly gray hair that appeared to be greasy. Her hands were old, dry and boney. She indicated to me that she was going to be my guide at Queen Hatshepsut's temple. At that time I had no idea where that temple was located but the tiny lady said that it would be a long way out. So, I tried to sit as comfortably as I could in the middle of all the helicopter vibrations. One of the pilots threw a pillow at me which I put between my face and the square window to entertain myself looking at the barren Egyptian landscape below… After a few hours I saw the monumental temple with its ramps in the distance. I was excited. That was an intriguing temple to me since I saw its picture in my first year of high school. I used to think that was King Salomon's temple. I never figured out why I thought that! How could I have known what his temple looked like?!

At last we landed just about 300 feet from the base of one of the first ramps of the temple. The day was very clear and hot. There were some dogs around. They warned me that they were wild and to be careful with them. They had eyes far apart that reminded me of Jackie Kennedy. In general they looked like the god Anubis and they were beautiful. I stretched my hand to one of them and he came, sniffed and didn't do any harm. The site was empty, except for the two pilot crew, the tiny lady, the dogs and me. I would have liked to wander around, but I had to stay with the tiny old lady all the time, otherwise it would be impolite on my part—at least, that was my sense as a government guest. So I followed her and listened to her explanations. Sadly, all of sudden I realized I knew more than she did about that marvelous, haunting place. Every time she pointed to a highlight, her detail was mistaken and I bit my tongue. I suffered in silence, I didn't want to embarrass her. But, for unknown reasons, I knew the place better than I ever thought.

The whole temple looked very familiar. It was as if I had planned and designed it myself in a prior life. It had my style. The columns and the hallways were straight and simple. It was like I had gone there in the past thanks to a time machine. Only one thing was gone: the people that used to be there and the solitude was mystifying.

We walked through in almost religious silence for a long time, until she stopped and turned to me and said, "You know that Queen Hatshepsut is still here…" I didn't doubt that her spiritual presence was there, but I knew her mummy was not. Apparently this tiny old lady was able to read my thoughts, because she emphatically said, "Yes, she is here. Her body's here and she wants to see you. She is listening!" To her very much absolute statement, what could I say? I wanted to be polite to the tiny lady, so I followed her once more and this time to meet the thousand-year-dead Queen. I wondered what would be the reaction of this tiny lady when she fails to show me the real mummified body of the ancient queen. But she was so convinced that she was going to find her, and walked so decisively to the royal encounter that actually she was putting her credibility to task… I kept walking behind her. The inner hallways of the temple were narrow. The farther we walked, the darker it got, but somehow I was able to see the dim surroundings. We made a turn and the hallway seemed to be slightly descending and in the distance I could see a blue-green light that turned out to be the end of the hallway. But to the side there was an entrance to a big chamber which was kind-of glowing from a round light that was resting on a *Djed* Egyptian symbol that with a twenth century mentality looked like an electrical device. But it wasn't the only one, there were many scattered throughout the chamber. The ceiling of this chamber had the most unusual mural I had seen in Egyptian art. It was not the traditional representation of the sky full of stars. This was a realistic and three-dimensional one! I was completely shocked by this find! It appeared to be a representation of the inhabited worlds of the universe. I received the information just by looking at it! How is it possible that such an astonishing wonder had never been reported or written about in any of the books dedicated to the ancient Egyptian civilization?! And this was easily reached without an excavation, just by entering an open hallway! The tiny lady guiding me stopped and turned to me and said, "There is more to come…" Gee, I was already dumbfounded by what I had witnessed and there is more ahead…?! What would it be at the end of this amazing chamber? As we approached I saw a trapezoid shaped door similar to the one I had seen on top of the sarcophagus in the museum earlier. I thought that maybe the idea for that rare sarcophagus came from here! That door rapidly slid down to the floor revealing ahead a long inclined corridor that resembled the great corridor of the Cheops' pyramid. But unlike that one, this one is inclined down. In opposition to Cheops' that was dark, this was irradiating a sudden golden light. I entered following the tiny lady who apparently was very familiar with the surroundings. I noticed that our skin had a golden tanning effect. There were a lot of echoes. The sound of our footsteps began to grow, until resounding forever as our breathing grew into thousands of hurricanes. The corridor led us to an antechamber not very big with an important looking doorway in the center. We stopped in the middle of that room, just where it had, on the floor, a round highly polished surface, that was like a mirror. I looked down and could see ourselves reflected from head to toe. Above our heads, I noticed what appeared to me at that unsettling moment, something resembling a spaceship. I thought it might be painted on the ceiling, so I looked up to admire the mural. But no, there was nothing painted on the ceiling except again billions of shining stars on a velvety black background. The spaceship wasn't painted on the floor either, it was somehow only reflected on the mirror below us. I could not comprehend this optical illusion and the significance in this very strange situation we were in. Then the tiny lady walked away to the center door and I immediately followed her. Just when we were in front of it, it slid open and disappeared to the right! This is the second sliding door of this unexpected adventure. My brain was spinning, wondering how the ancient Egyptians were able to accomplish such sophisticated technology! The tiny lady entered the next chamber and I followed her like an obedient dog. But what else at this juncture can happen inside this labyrinth? In the next room I felt immediately a drop in temperature. It was really cold there. It was almost like being inside a refrigerator. The tiny lady walked toward an elaborate ancient looking Egyptian trunk placed in a wall niche, opened it and brought out two ivory colored fur coats, apparently for us. I helped her and I put mine on and we proceeded through an archway opposite the niche to another corridor. In it I noticed that the floor felt like velvet for a few seconds and immediately we began to float!

Oh… I loved that! I always liked the idea of flying! It was easy. We move forward effortlessly, gliding through the air. I didn't feel cold any longer. Just right. It was pure perfection! We glided through until we reached the end of another long corridor with no door ahead, just an opening in the ceiling. We turned a 90 degree angle up and continued gliding. We encountered the same geography many times. It was a maze! But apparently the tiny lady knew where she was going. I certainly underestimated her. I was immensely enjoying the experience, as we entered another gigantic room, full of towering columns and a highly polished black granite floor, creating the illusion that the columns were even higher. It was amazing! However, what was the object of this experience? It began as a way to somehow get in touch with Queen Hatshepsut but this had become a trip to a fantastic and very sophisticated amusement park in the middle of the Valley of the Kings. So far there is no end in sight and I began to worry…Now we are gliding until finally reaching what looked to me like a huge black granite sarcophagus. Just in front of it we regained our normal vertical position and softly landed on a hard floor. Apparently we were at the location where the tiny lady wanted to take me. This must be the secret resting place of that elusive Queen Hatshepsut, I thought. "Yes," she said, reading my mind.

There were four statues of the jackal god Anubis guarding the sarcophagus. The four of them were in a sitting position. The tiny lady walked to one and said, "Give me your paw." The statue lifted his right arm and immediately the lid of the sarcophagus went up smoothly hovering. I looked inside and I exclaimed, "It's empty inside! I knew it! I knew it! Queen Hatshepsut is not there! She is gone!"

"Wait," the tiny lady said, "Don't jump to conclusions," and she showed me that there were steps inside the open sarcophagus and she climbed in it and took a few steps inside. Then she stopped and turned to me, indicating to follow her. What the heck, I thought, I had gone all this way so why not climb down inside a black granite sarcophagus.

So I went in and to my surprise the sarcophagus lid closed behind our backs. I froze on the spot but the tiny lady said, "Don't be afraid" And I proceeded to follow her once more.

The descending steps went forever. Our fur coats were no longer necessary. We dropped them onto the steps. To my further amazement, when they touched the steps they became living lambs! That was not normal to say the least, I thought. As we kept descending I began to hear what appeared to be tapping sounds in the distance and as we advanced the sounds were getting closer and I could begin to see daylight at the end of the steps. It was blinding in comparison with the previous softer golden light. The rhythmic tapping sound was getting much louder as a sign that we were getting closer to unraveling the mysteries. The daylight was becoming so bright after such a long time under the subdued gold that my eyes were hurting and I had to close them. The taps were there loud and clear. I could hardly see. It was like looking at the sun. I began to realize that despite their speed, the taps were rhythmic, like for the musical number "I got rhythm, I got music…" I could sing it inside my mind! The tiny lady had vanished. I tried to open my eyes again and began to see a silhouette of a dancing woman in the middle of the light of what appeared to be one of the one of the monumental central ramps of the exterior at the entrance of the Queen Hatshepsut temple. Gradually the woman's image was becoming more in focus and I decided to circle around the dancing woman to see what she looked like. After I completed my circle it became evident that she was a consummate professional, dancing like I had seen in films and on Broadway before. She was tapping in a near uncontrollable frenzy, hundreds of taps per minute. What did this have to do with Egypt or Queen Hatshepsut? I questioned myself. More and more I circled around that mysterious dancer completely out of place here, trying to make sense of her presence at that ancient site! She was wearing a bright, light blue and dark blue dancing costume with long, light blue gauze sleeves, jet black hair and carrying a two-shades-of-blue matching top hat. She was tapping her way up the ramp toward a huge pyramid in the background. I still could not see her face very well because of her turbulent hurricane speed. However her back hair stayed strangely stationary and untouched by the speed no matter what she did or where he went. I tried in vain to follow her to get close so I could ask her who she was and what she was doing there and why. Yes, why?

She was moving so fast that it was difficult to follow… I ran in her direction and finally caught up with her. But as I got close, she was spinning so fast that I still could not make anything out of her blurry face. "Hey!" I said, calling her attention. "What do you think you are doing here?! Who are you?!" In an instant she stopped spinning in the spot and kept her balance like a ballet dancer, nailed to the floor. Then, I finally saw her. And, she looked exactly like Ann Miller, the famous tap dancer from the Golden Era of Hollywood! Disbelieving my eyes in front of that anachronistic vision of an ancient Egyptian temple, I asked her, "Aren't you Ann Miller…?" She looked at me very seriously and surprised and said, "I am the one you are looking for."

"I am not looking for Ann Miller," I said, "As a matter of fact, I was not looking for anybody. I was not expecting to see anybody. I knew **she** was not here."

To my surprise she replied, "You are wrong. She is me and I am her. I never left. I have been here many times in the past. I am Queen Hatshepsut. This is my temple."

I said, "I cannot believe you." And just in front of my incredulous eyes she became two persons, one dressed as a queen and one dressed as a pharaoh, making evident the duality of the legendary historical character! In fact she was a queen and a pharaoh!

Indeed she was the one and only legendary queen Hatshepsut! I felt that my whole body was falling into a vacuum and pulled by a powerful magnet.

As a trivia: based on this complex vivid dream I made four paintings. Two *mummies* about the double transfiguration of Hatshepsut, as a queen and as a pharaoh and about Ann Miller, one of them dancing tap on the Queen Hatshepsut temple.

There was hardly a night that I didn't have a dream about Egypt or my future trip as an official government guest. There were so many that I could fill the chapters of many books if I wrote them all down. But that's not practical when you have an office job and paint at night and on weekends. Sometimes I had to rely on memories about the most impactful and traumatic events from dreams that I kept remembering sometimes for days. I wonder if some of them will be premonitions of things to come. In general, I don't sleep well, so I prefer to sleep, rest and not have any dreams. I was counting the days, hours and minutes to be in Egypt. If I lived there before, like some people suggested, would I be able to remember some familiar places? I am skeptical about reincarnation, but many people believe in it. Apparently Ann Miller did since she talked about hers many times in TV interviews.

Finally one day was the day! Jaums' parents took us to Dulles Airport, and we boarded the Pan Am night flight to London as a friend who worked in that airline, Pedro Nuñez, advised me. Under normal conditions, I can not fall asleep on a plane, and now, with the excitement of this trip, much less. So I decided to take a sleeping pill after the plane took off. But it didn't do anything. I was quite awake during the whole flight.

The suitcases were packed way in advance as I didn't want to forget anything. I was carrying clothes and shoes for all possible occasions, even a tuxedo since I was going to be an official government guest and had to be prepared for any eventuality. A lady friend of Jaums who had been in Egypt in 1967, advised us, "Do not drink the water. Do not even brush your teeth with it." She recommended taking a gallon bottle of kelly green mouthwash. Jaums packed it in his suitcase with his clothes. My doctor prescribed muscle relaxing pills for back problems because it happened before on a trip to Europe. Also some sleeping pills to help with the initial jet lag. We certainly were ready!

When the time finally came for My Trip to Egypt, there had to be a change of planes on my way to Cairo. I decided to go through London in order to see my friends there, the internationally known writer Guillermo Cabrera Infante and his wife, model and actress, Miriam Gomez, even though in 1966 while we all lived in Madrid she gave me some pills to stop menstruation! Yes, it was an error. She was very absent minded. I forgave her for that a long time ago but keep reminding her, as a joke. She and her husband had a very good sense of humor. My wait at Heathrow Airport was going to be five hours, so my plan was going to be to call them and go to their home in Kensington. However, what I didn't know was that my next flight to Cairo was overbooked and there was pandemonium to get onto the flight. So Jaums and I had to remain put in the airport for five excruciating hours.

At Heathrow airport I went to the EgyptAir desk to check our suitcases and get our seats reserved. The desks were closed and no one around knew when they were going to be open. Meanwhile, people were arriving and forming some sort of line in front of the ticket window. So I got in the line. Of course there were a lot of Egyptians there all speaking at the same time—I thought only Cubans did that. After a while it became very noisy indeed. I wondered what they were talking about in such a passionate way. After about an hour, an employee from EgyptAir arrived and opened the ticket window. Then was when everybody began to be real loud! Most of them appeared to be demanding something and they began pushing each other in order to get close to the window. After that it was impossible to keep an organized line. After a lot of struggle, finally I was able to reach the window and talk to the airline representative. He said, "Sorry we don't have any reservation for you on this flight." I was speechless. I couldn't believe it! Everything was arranged months ahead of time and now the official was saying that they don't have any reservation for us! It has to be a mistake! What are we going to do here in London now?! Visit the Queen and talk to her about her collection of purses? No! It has to be an error! So I got my official invitation letter, the press release from the Egyptian Embassy in Washington, D.C. that Mr. Hakki, the Minister Counselor for Press Information of the Embassy had written and other pertinent documents about my official invitation and that they were waiting for me at Cairo airport on that specific flight! Sorry, the EgyptAir official said to me again. "Sorry, this flight is already overbooked because another earlier flight was canceled. The next one will be in a few days." No, no, no. This has to be a nightmare that I'm having… Actually, I am sound asleep inside the plane due to the sleeping pill that the doctor prescribed… This is another of my typical realistic nightmares and dreams I had been having for decades! I refused to believe my thoughts and, waking up to the reality, I finally said to the EgyptAir official behind the counter, "Sir…you have to be kidding! You see, I have to be on this specific flight no matter what! I have to be. There is no other choice. The officials are waiting for me in Cairo! You know, you have to put me on this flight!" He didn't reply. He observed a grave looking silence like he was think-ing how to handle my situation… Then he turned around and went to talk to another man in a back office. I stayed in place at the window observing and hearing the conversation in a foreign language trying in vain to decipher their facial expressions, body language and the tone of their voices. To that talking duet, another man and a woman joined, forming an Egyptian quartet. Later they called another employee to join them, forming a small orchestra and all taking at the same time in an Arabian rhapsody titled *Shipping a Sucker to Cairo*. Later on I witnessed this rapid formation of collective meetings on many occasions during my trip. After an abrupt, however grandiose final fanfare, the original same single official came back to the counter window and said, "Sir, it will be OK for you to be on this flight." "Thank you," I said, very much relieved that this nightmare was over. It was like coming back to life again! However, "I just realized that I forgot to tell him about the other party, my photographer, Jaums. He has to go with me on this flight too." A deadly silence was observed this time by the EgyptAir employee on the other side of the counter. Then he went away to the back office and a carbon copy of the prior performance was neatly executed to the very last note. Then he came back to the window and said, "Yes, the other party can go with you on this flight." Well, that was another good news I thought and felt very much relieved. Then the employee said, "But you have to be here in the airport in case of a last minute change. Besides, we don't know the hour of the departure…" "OK," I said, "I want to check our luggage to Cairo and I want to reserve our seats." Then he pointed out, "Sir… There is not such a thing as reserved seats for this flight. It's first come, first served." "OK," I replied, what could I say? I was very glad that at least they were allowed to be on that flight. Would we…? We wouldn't be able to leave the airport, we have to stay there and wouldn't be able to visit our friends in the Kensington area of London. We are stranded in the airport for about five hours or more. So I decided to walk to the gate carrying our heavy suitcases to try to be the first in line to board (our?) EgyptAir flight. But seeing how our fellow travelers were behaving, screaming and pushing each other at the ticket counter, probably an organized line would be an impossibility to keep. Surely most of them would be striving to be the first in line in order to get a seat. Could they have standing room in these unusual overbooking conditions? So, Jaums and I joined the crowd and began to run with our heavy suitcases toward the departure gate. However, our flight was announced at more than one gate! So Jaums sat at one of the gates and I sat in the other… After waiting there a while, I went to the public phones to call our friends Guillermo and Miriam and tried to conduct a conversation on those awful 3-minute European phones. I explained to them what had happened and our inability to leave Heathrow Airport. After a 9-minute frustrating conversation, the communication was cut off for the third time and I decided not to call again and went back to my post at the gate. When I arrived there, I found that most travelers were all concentrated around Jaums' gate. So I decided that they probably knew more than I did and moved to that gate. After a few excruciating hours, an EgyptAir employee came and announced that we were all standing in the wrong gate and he indicated which will be the correct one. Suddenly, pandemonium! People got up and began running with their suitcases like crazy to the new gate and began taking seats in a flurry. When we arrived out of breath at the other gate it was already full. I began to imagine what those people would do when they announced the boarding of our flight! That may become a Word War Three battleground! So our hopes were bleak! Well, we'll sit on the floor and wait… If our destiny is to be on that flight, we would be on it somehow…

Over five long and frustrating hours passed since we had landed at London's airport and we were still waiting and not even knowing the hour of departure of our flight yet. The EgyptAir flight number was no longer visible on the screen monitors. It disappeared about one hour ago. I was worried that our flight was canceled. As far as I know there was somebody from the government waiting for us at Cairo's airport…

About two hours later we noticed on the monitors that our flight was rescheduled! At the appointed time, everybody at the gate started getting up and forming what a very optimistic person would call "a line." Actually it was some sort of a battlefield, where pointed elbows and hand luggages became the preferred weapons of mass destruction. I had never seen anything like it in my life. Apparently, they were used to this kind of thing and they all knew what to do in order to survive the relentless attack of elbows from every direction. So as the famous phrase goes "When in Rome, do as the Romans do," we had to incorporate that indiscriminate form of warfare and went into attack mode by incorporating our heavy artillery, our heavy suitcases! After a few minutes on the battleground I lost sight of Jaums. Somehow we had been pushed apart and I found myself in the middle of the conflict. I finally looked back and saw Jaums waving his arms so I could see him like a person who was drowning in the ocean. I managed to get one of my arms up in the middle of the battle and shouted, "Here! Here!" He saw me and tried to squeeze in my direction. I was letting myself be pushed by the out of control crowd in the direction of the exit door of the gate to the plane. I was moving, yes, but I was not doing anything to move. I was just part of that uncontrollable mass. It was a frightening experience until I was miraculously deposited inside the one of the buses that will take me to the plane. The bus was filled to capacity in a matter of seconds. And I was still holding my suitcase with my two arms! Jaums apparently wasn't on the bus but there were other buses on the tarmac. He may be next because he wasn't that far from me at the gate. After the bus got there and opened the door another wild rush began to get to the plane. But they didn't let people in. First we have to set the suitcase on the tarmac and identify the owner's name before it's put inside the cargo compartment of the plane. At that time the second bus arrived and I saw Jaums with his suitcase. He stood beside me and we identified our suitcases. We had to wait on the tarmac until all the buses arrived and the suitcases were identified and placed inside the plane. But the next battle was to form a line and go inside the plane and grab our unreserved seats–in the directed pandemonium, what were the chances that the number of people on the tarmac would match the number of seats on the plane? The officials tried to convert the undulating crowd into an orderly line. Before entering the plane each passenger had to be individually checked to see if anybody was carrying a firearm. After each person passed, they were allowed to enter the plane. This operation was another pandemonium of people running to make sure they got a seat. Jaums and I ended up completely exhausted after this operation and we collapsed into our seats in disbelief of what we just witnessed and went through. After thirty more minutes of sitting and waiting inside that crowded and hot airplane, we got ready to taxi for departure for the *Land of The Pharaohs* (1955) with Jack Hawkins, Joan Collins and Dewey Martin…

It was late in the afternoon in London, so our flight will be landing late at night in Cairo, four hours behind schedule! I prayed to Osiris, Isis, Horus and, just in case, to Anubis, that the person appointed by the Egyptian government would still be there waiting for us for the grand welcoming reception at the airport for my second coming. The takeoff fortunately was uneventful. By this time I was expecting anything. But, we rapidly gained altitude and London quickly disappeared under the clouds. It was a shame that we were flying at dusk, because I wanted to see the Mediterranean and the African coastline. I have never flown to Africa before. I was excited with the idea of seeing the Sahara from the air–if indeed we were to fly over it. There was not a single brochure onboard with a flight path, as I had seen for my previous flights. So there was not much to do but sit, relax and wait. After some hours, the pilot announced that we were flying over Egypt. The passengers cheered! He said that we will be landing in half an hour. I got a jump in my stomach. I never thought that I would be there! But I also felt very tired of the tension and ordeal that we went through at the London Airport. By now it has been a total of 30 hours since we left the U.S. without sleeping. I tried to look out the window. It was completely dark. I was able to see fires from time to time. They may have been towers of oil wells in the desert. By now the airplane was getting ready to land. I felt the slow descent and from time to time I saw electric lights in the night. We were getting close to Cairo. The "no smoking" and "fasten seat belts" signs were on. We were descending and my ears were popping. I was trying to swallow in order to feel better. The airplane was rattling, jumping and vibrating like crazy, obviously there was some turbulence around. The passengers that were so brave before and were ready to attack and fight against each other at the London airport, now were very still, subdued and muted… The plane seemed like it was going to disintegrate while it descended and descended forever… I could not see any lights indicating that the airport was near. It was total darkness outside. There was a lot of anxiety in the cabin judging by the faces of the passengers… And surprisingly an unexpected touchdown! There was an applause of relief that we were now on the ground of Cairo! I looked at my watch and it was exactly 10:40 pm.

When I went out the door of the plane, it was very dark and I didn't see an official crowd waiting for me down the stairs on the tarmac. I saw the airport terminal in the distance. There were no dignitaries, reporters or photographers, no TV cameras either like in one of my vivid dreams. Then they discharged all of the suitcases and put them on the tarmac. Then another pandemonium of the passengers trying to identify their suitcases in the dim light. This operation was exhausting, but we found ours and held them very tightly. However, I noticed a few people that seemed to be officials standing at the doors of the bus. Could they be my reception committee? But not a single belly dancer dancing the hula-hula… And it seemed that these officials were not waiting for me with a band playing *The Star Spangled Banner* as in my dream… So we passed by them unnoticed and joined the pandemonium to get into the bus to take us to the distant airport terminal. I thought that there would probably be my reception committee. After the bus was filled beyond capacity it left toward the arrival terminal. On the way to the terminal I saw that a lot of people were on the upper balcony of the airport and they were waving. I couldn't see the signs with my name and the word "Welcome." It was a big crowd and were screaming I don't know what— maybe it's my name in their Egyptian language. Yes, they may be the people waiting for my arrival, the dignitaries, reporters, photographers and TV cameras. That was a welcome relief after a complex 30-hour trip! Even though I was exhausted I had to do my best to please them.

The bus got to the arrival terminal and we got out to a huge smiling crowd. It was grand. These must be the crowds waiting for me in my dream. They were screaming something–that must be my name! So, I decided to enter that terminal with Jaums and our heavy suitcases to see if we could see our reception committee. I was saluting the crowd. It was a grand reception! It was marvelous to see all these smiling welcoming faces… But I noticed that they were not concentrating on me. They were concentrating on their relatives coming in the same flight with me! After what we had all been through, they must have been relieved to see them. Signs that I couldn't read were not for me! It was a very noisy and confusing situation. I didn't see any sign with my name! No one was coming toward us! "Welcome to Egypt!" I said to myself.

There were many guards carrying machine guns. Jaums was very apprehensive about it. But I had gotten used to it in communist Cuba. Even their olive green uniforms were very similar to the ones in Cuba after communism was imposed. Actually, it looked to me as if I had gone back to Cuba, mainly because of these guards with their machine guns, not because of the people waiting for their relatives. Many of them were wearing the typical *galabiya* and many variations of headdresses. We decided to join the group that came in the bus with us and began walking slowly in the middle of what appeared to be a line to pass customs. We were almost at the end of the line and outside the terminal. The line was advancing fairly quickly and after a while, we entered the arrival terminal. The room was big but it was already almost full to capacity. Again I let myself go with the crowd, after all, I didn't know where I was going. I continued to scan for a sign with my name and I was getting very worried. If no one was waiting for us, I didn't have the slightest idea where I should go to notify my official host that we were there. I didn't even have the address in Cairo of the Ministry of

Higher Education. Well, after we passed customs we will sit all night in this airport and wait for some official to pick us up, I thought. Our fight arrived so late that whoever was in charge of us left. But how could they do that? They should have waited, after all the delay was not our fault. By this time we got in front of the customs officer and gave our passports and asked him where to exchange our money. He said he could do it there. So we proceeded to exchange… Then, *The Bells of Saint Mary* started ringing! I overheard my name in the crowd! That must be them, the reception committee that finally found me! I turned around looking "across the crowded room" as the song goes. And I overheard my name again closer! Even with the accent, I was sure it was my name. I turned my head in the direction the voice seemed to come and I saw my name written on a piece of cardboard! Jaums and I were elated! I began to wave to the little man with the sign. Well, he wasn't little, but he was all alone, tall and slender. He saw me and rushed toward me in what appeared to be in slow motion… When he arrived he introduced himself and said "Welcome to Egypt!" He asked the customs officer for our passports and told him that we were official government guests and that we didn't have to pass through customs. I was amazed how fast everything became after his statements and he began taking excellent care of us. Our suitcases reappeared out of nowhere, like a miracle, and he said, "Follow me to the car waiting for you."

What a relief! I was very excited! I was also very flattered by the fact that we didn't have to pass through customs. That was very nice. The red carpet had finally arrived! While we were walking through the crowded airport in the direction of the exit, many people around were saying "hello" to our savior. Apparently, he was well-known there. He was explaining to us that the other people could not come to welcome me because of the delayed arrival of our flight. And he added, "But not to worry, they have arranged everything and you will be taken by car to your hotel tonight and your reception will be tomorrow at the Ministry of Higher Education." I was very glad, I needed to hear that. I need to rest tonight after all this ordeal. Then he pointed out, "I will not be able to go with you tonight to your hotel, because I still have to wait for other guests arriving later on. Your official chauffeur has been instructed and he will take care of everything." So, we walked out fast from the terminal to the parking lot where the car was waiting. We got into the lot and followed him… There was the other car and the chauffeur who flashed a friendly smile, shook our hands and introduced himself as "Abulela." Our suitcases were in the trunk and we said "goodbye" to our savior. Abulela left, speeding through dark streets and boulevards toward our hotel. At the speed he was driving we may be having an accident! So Jaums and I adopted the "crash position" just in case.

CHAPTER 8

NEW GARDEN

I was anxious to arrive at the Hilton or the Sheraton to take a shower and go to bed. I was hoping that the ride in Abulela's jumping car would not be very long, at least the Cairo streets were empty. "That is Ramses statue," Abulela's pointing out while passing by the train station. Jaums and I raised our heads from crash-position and peeked out the window at the tall statue, which was swiftly fleeting behind the speeding car. A while Later, he said, "We are passing across Heliopolis." "Oh…" I replied. And he added, "There is the famous fig tree where the Virgin Mary stayed with baby Jesus and Joseph…" I peeked again at the sight, but unlike in my vivid dream, I could barely see it since it was dark and the car was going so fast. The lights outside were not particularly bright. However we had a full moon, the sky was very black and not a single cloud. A while later I was surprised to see a dead horse on the pavement. Then Abulela said, "We are heading for the New Garden Hotel." I thought he was heading to the Hilton or the Sheraton… Well, the New Garden sounded nice, maybe another good hotel, probably associated with an European chain unknown to me. It had a good sounding name, "New Garden." Surely it must be a beautiful new hotel with spectacular hanging gardens, like the legendary ones of ancient Babylon with waterfalls, fountains and ponds with water lilies, like it was portrayed on the ancient Egyptian papyruses… Oh sure, I was so tired that I wanted to get to the New Garden to bathe and go to bed. That was my priority after so many hours of traveling, I thought.

The car made an abrupt sharp turn, sliding Jaums and me to the right. We were now going through narrow, dark streets. It seems that our chauffeur may be taking shortcuts to get to our hotel as quickly as possible. After a short while the car stopped and very proudly, Abulela announced, "Here we are!" He got out in a rush, opened our doors and went to get our suitcases from the trunk. I stepped out of the car, and very much surprised, looked at the dark building in front of my eyes. On its main double-door entrance, it had a tiny sign that said, "New Garden Hotel." I didn't say anything, I just turned to Jaums and I saw my same feelings reflected on his face. I didn't like the looks of that hotel at all. It reminded me of the old, beautiful residential homes built at the end of the nineteenth or beginning of the twentieth century in La Habana that after the 1959 communist revolution were expropriated from their owners and converted into something else that was not being maintained well. Those beautiful homes deteriorate and become dilapidated multi-family dwellings and always look very sad and depressing. That was my first impression of the New Garden Hotel. It was a beautiful home in the past but it was not in the best condition now to be a hotel. I couldn't figure out why its name was New Garden because I didn't see any sign of vegetation. At the entrance was a single low voltage light bulb hanging from a long electric wire.

Abulela, already carrying our suitcases, was walking through the main doors and we followed him in silence. As soon as we went in we were greeted by a strong and disgusting urine stench! I don't think it was human, it must have been from a horse or a camel. So my second impression was worse than my first… In my mind I was trying hard to justify this hotel as an old, quaint, perhaps charming and exotic place that later on we will learn to love and even as the time passes by after we leave Egypt, we will feel nostalgia for the New Garden…

The entrance staircase of white marble was grand in spite of the picturesque stench. Actually it was two flights to reach the reception desk where sat an elderly gentleman. Abulela was in charge of talking to him because he didn't speak English. After they talked for a while in spite of the invigorating stench they seemed upset. And Abulela was screaming at the elderly man. Then, Abulela called down and very politely explained to me the gist of that long loud voice interchange, "He said that he didn't have any reservation for you." I WAS SO GLAD INSIDE!–But I tried not to show my true feelings. This cannot be bad after all. We can go to another hotel, maybe not as "charming" as this one… Then the elderly old man turned to me and, interrupting my hidden deep jubilation, said to me in English, "We can put you in two different rooms. We don't have a vacancy with two beds." That was like a hurricane on my parade! Even Abulela was surprised by the elderly man's contradictory statement–in English!– and he was smiling at me looking very much satisfied. So I thought, well what the heck. I don't want to be difficult. One night is one night. We are very tired after so many hours awake since we left the U.S. We can spend one night here and tomorrow we will find something better. So I replied, "OK it's OK with us we will take the rooms."

We walked toward the elevator which was in the middle of the stairs like in European countries but the elderly man indicated that it was out of order. Who knows how many more things are out of order in this hotel… So we walked to the 3rd floor followed by Abulela helping with our suitcases and another man who apparently was a bellboy without the customary uniform plus another man, which I had no idea why he was following us. On the 3rd floor, we stepped into a big room which looked like an empty dining room, living room or the waiting room of a train station with an old sandblasted Kelvinator refrigerator in the corner. There were several French double doors with translucent glass. I assumed one of them was for Jaums and the other for me. What seemed to be the bellboy opened one of the doors, turned the light and got the two suitcases in. At that point Abulela left and reminded us that tomorrow morning he will pick us up at the doors of the hotel. We entered the room and I was astonished! There were three very narrow, extremely concave beds!!! They have to be kidding! First the elderly man said that they didn't have any room. Second, they only have rooms with a single bed! And now a room with three concave beds! My train of "logical" thoughts was interrupted by the supposed bell boy indicating the sink inside the room and beside the separate private tiny bathroom with a shower and a toilet that was out of order and full to the brim! After seeing that spectacle I made the firm decision to never set foot in that bathroom. Our panorama was bleak!

The pronounced concavity of the beds were concerning to me because of my back problems, also each bed was no more than 24" wide. How am I going to sleep there? But most concerning to me was the third bed. I got bad vibes about it. Could it be for a third person? Everything was possible at the New Garden… Jaums decided to open his suitcase for the first time since we left the U.S. to get his clothes ready for tomorrow's visit to the Ministry of Higher Education. He woke up from his exhaustion to the cruel reality that the recommended one gallon bottle of mouthwash for the brushing of teeth had burst open on the plane and all his clothes were green and smelling like mouthwash! That was terrible in the middle of the trauma of the New Garden hotel. He could not use any of his clothes until he could get to a place where he could at least rinse things out. So he closed his suitcase but decided to take the risk of a shower in that very small bath. To make matters worse, the water coming from the shower was little more than a mist! He came out of the shower very upset, mumbling something about getting a helicopter to Silver Spring, Maryland. I was already trying to get in position to see if I could sleep inside the convexity of that 24" wide valley called a bed. But I could not remove my worries about that empty third bed… I turned off the only small light bulb hanging from the electrical wire from the ceiling to try to see if I could go to sleep.

A short half hour later the door of our room suddenly burst open and a figure of a man entered as if he belonged there. My worries came to fruition! The third inhabitant of the convex third bed came to sleep convexly! I don't know how but jumped out of my cavernous bed and walked to the man who was saying something to me—I guess in an Arab language—and I placed my two hands against his chest and pushed him out of the room like a bulldozer and closed the door in spite of whatever it was he was saying. Immediately I slid a nearby armoire in front of the door-with-no-lock so he would not try to open that door again. So actually I wasn't far from reality about that suspicious third bed! After all that commotion it took me more time to fall asleep mainly out of exhaustion after all our ordeals of that day…

All of a sudden I was awakened by the unusual ringing of an old Egyptian telephone—not quite from the time of the pharaohs, but a was a free-standing original derelict from 1920. I opened my eyes, totally confused about where I was. The voice on the other side sounded upset and said, "I am from the Ministry of Higher Education. Why are you not waiting at the door of the hotel as I requested?!" I just vaguely remembered something about that the night before. "Oh good morning" I replied while still confused and surprised by the tone of his voice. He sounded upset. "Your chauffeur, Abulela, has been waiting for you," he added. "Well," I said, "It's not eight in the morning yet. I think he said he will pick me up at nine…" He replied., "You had an appointment with me at nine. It's after nine now." "How come…?" I said I was extremely confused. "I believe we set the alarm for 8 o'clock. It's not eight yet…" "I believe you got confused, it's after nine, believe me." Jaums, who was awakened by the call, looked at his watch and he realized that he did not set his watch last night from London to Egypt time. So he jumped out of his hut and began dressing in a rush. So I explained to the guy on the phone what had happened and told him we would be down as soon as possible. "Fine," he said, "Your chauffeur will be waiting for you downstairs. So long." And I nervously try to get dressed with the same clothes I had been using since I left the U.S. I felt dirty but there was no time to find clean clothes. Jaums also got dressed with the clothes he had been using since leaving the U.S. We decided to carry both of our suitcases because I was planning to request they get us in a better hotel. I did not want to come back to the New Garden. It's time to say "Goodbye" to that stinky chapter. Many years have passed now and I hope the owner of that hotel got their act together since that building had possibilities of being a really charming place.

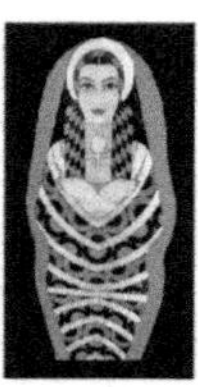

CHAPTER 9

VIVIR DE LOS RECUERDOS
(LIVING ON THE MEMORIES)

It was a new day and, thankfully, we left the New Garden Hotel's adventure behind us, over and done with, except that we were still wearing the same clothes that we had been wearing since departing the U.S. Our government appointed chauffeur, Abulela, was dutifully waiting for us in front of the hotel. He put the suitcases in the trunk and he nicely opened the doors for us. I decided that I would carry my portfolio with the photographs of my Egyptian work for our meeting at the Ministry of Higher Education. As the night before, Abulela drove very fast through the now crowded and twisted streets of Cairo, apparently that's the way to drive there. There are people moving in all directions in every imaginable type of vehicle from gasoline to animal powered. They drive in all directions with little regard to traffic rules. Gas pedal and horn, no brakes. You are on your own and you survive by chance. The pedestrians also move in all directions, also surviving by chance. The buses are filled to capacity and people enter and exit the buses by door and window with the dexterity of the performers of Cirque du Soleil! But, people help each other in that eternal survival of the fittest, arms extending from door and window to give a hand. At the beginning it was shocking to me, but after a while you begin to see the crowd goodness because they are all in the same boat, together. The Egypt I visited in 1978 was under President Anwar Sadat. He had very good relations with the U.S. and the country was under a period of relative peace. There was no aggression against Americans and American tourists on the streets. Actually we felt at ease and safe walking the streets of Cairo. If you were lost and asked for directions, a group formed instantly with many Egyptians clamoring to help by providing directions in all possible directions. After a while I opted not to ask for directions because of the diversities of routes emphasized the complexity of the Cairo streets where many streets had the particular hobby of changing their names at every block.

So while riding in the car under the care of the friendly Abulela, when we saw danger, we learned to quietly "duck and cover" as in the 1950's nuclear age in the U.S. Also to close your eyes when a crash seems imminent. You have to have a good sense of humor like his as he laughed at situations of mortal danger while deftly carrying us to our destiny. During this perilous trip Jaums explained to me the mistake he made the night before when trying to adjust his watch to Cairo time during the excitement of the New Garden Hotel. Yes, it was very diffi-cult after the ordeal of that long exhausting trip. I understood.

At intervals when the car stopped, we lifted our heads and looked out at the surroundings. In reality, Cairo reminded me of La Habana. And that brought back old memories. Actually, the architecture of most of the old buildings of the old section of La Habana was known as La Habana Vieja (Old La Habana). Well, at least the area where we were traveling now. But of course the buildings that were built before the Castro communist revolution of 1959. These buildings in Cairo were apparently built during that early era too, when La Habana was a vital and vibrant cosmopolitan city, full of lively people, open to the world and all kinds of architectural styles and specially with total artistic freedom of creation—without the impositions of a totalitarian government. The most beautiful buildings and homes were built during those early years of the new Republic of Cuba. The only difference I was observing was that there were two ways of dressing in Cairo, one was the typical European style and the traditional Egyptian galabiya. However, in Cuba because of the proximity to the U.S. they dressed more in the American way. In Cairo there were all kinds of animals on the sidewalks and streets. In La Habana only dogs and cats and in the countryside, horses, donkeys, cows, sheep, goats, pigs, chickens and other farm animals. Cairo was much more picturesque than La Habana in relation to their urban animals. It was very entertaining to see the variety of honorable animals in the middle of a cosmopolitan city.

In addition to the human and animal crowd, there were thousands of cars coming and going from all unimaginable directions. Some of them had fancy iron work as some sort of armor in the front and back in case of collision. I noticed that the horn was used in place of the brake. I realized that the horn was as necessary as any other part of the car. No horn? You don't belong on the streets of Cairo. I saw all kinds of carts, cars and trucks being pulled by animals. I saw a '55 Chevy being pulled by a donkey! It all seemed very normal in Cairo. In Cuba I saw old fashioned carriages, *carretas*, only in the countryside to transport cut sugar cane to the mill being pulled by two oxen or the typical landau carriage that were used as a taxi in Cardenas—the city were I was born in Cuba—that was pulled by a single horse. It was very picturesque and charming in that city. There was another city in Cuba, Sagua la Grande, that has the same old fashioned traditional taxi transportation. But in Cairo, anything that goes, goes.

Then we were no longer driving on the wide main streets of downtown Cairo. Abulela has been confidently turning onto narrow streets of what looked like an old section of the city. They appeared to be neighborhood streets. There were children, dogs, cats, goats and chickens playing on the streets and Abulela drove very carefully and at a low speed. In the distance, I spotted a woman standing on a corner. As we approached that corner, that woman looked exactly like the famous and popular, great, Cuban bolero singer Olga Guillot–I couldn't believe it! Traveling all the way to Cairo to find her standing on a corner! To my further amazement, Abulela slowed down the car and stopped just in front of her! She looked at Abulela, smiled and got inside our car and sat beside Abulela! I wondered if the Minister of Higher Education had planned this surprise encounter to make me feel at home. But then Abulela spoke to her in Arabic, and she replied! God… I didn't know that Olga Guillot spoke Arabic! I was really surprised. She was more educated than I thought. As she entered the car a magnificent perfume fragrance wafted through the car. It was delicious! Well that is something that Olga Guillot would do. I was flabbergasted with the unexpected surprise and I was getting ready to sing for her one of her greatest hits of the early fifties *Vivir de los recuerdos*. When she interrupted speaking to me in English without a Cuban accent, "Welcome to Cairo. My name is"–I knew her name!–"Madame Ahlam…"–Oh no, I don't…"I will be your guide today."

I was speechless for a few seconds and when I woke up from the dream state of my misunderstanding, I introduced myself and Jaums. Even all that close she was a perfect clone of Olga Guillot! She even smiled like her! That was uncanny! Then we were immediately moving again as Abulela began driving again. But her delicious fragrance reigned inside the car like magic. Well, I was not totally disappointed that she was not Olga Guillot. I have been used to Egyptian reproductions for quite a long time. My immediate problem was that I could not pronounce her name properly. It would be impolite to call her "Olga" or "Miss Guillot" and also to explain the whole thing. So from then on every time that I would have to talk to her or ask her a question, I had to refer to her as "Madame." And "Madame" she was until the last time

I saw her. She went out of her way to be nice and helpful. Her delicious perfume was a mystic, haunting experience. Something to look forward to after my arrival.

Trivia: I finally met the real Olga Guillot at the Chateau Madrid in NYC. Later I saw her on various occasions during my trips to Miami. She even sent me a Christmas card. She died on July 12, 2010. She was a great singer. I never found out the name of Madame Ahlam's perfume, alas.

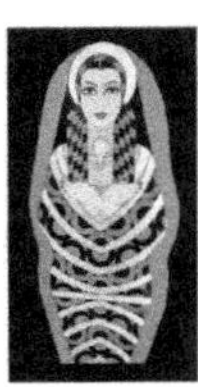

CHAPTER 10

GENTLEMEN, WHAT ARE YOU DOING HERE?

A while later, after we picked up Madame, we arrived in front of a building that looked like a 1950's apartment building, painted in the dark green of more than 20 years ago—Is this green the color of hope?

Madame got out and kindly asked us to follow her. We entered a small lobby furnished by a three legged desk with nothing on it except a thin layer of dust. Sitting behind the desk was a seriously armed official. Madame approached the desk and apparently explained to him the reason for our visit. Then he looked at us and he let us in. We followed her up a few flights of stairs and through narrow hallways. Just like outside, the inside was not in the best condition. Through a narrow door in the middle of the dark hallway we entered a small office with three big desks considering the space in that room. There were no papers or anything else on the desks except the universal layer of dust. The room looked crowded because there were a number of people standing there, maybe having a meeting all talking at the same time just like Cubans. A lady who was a perfect reproduction of the Indian Prime Minister, Indira Gandhi was standing beside her desk with an old 1950s handset and repeating with a French accent, "Allo? Allo?... Allo?..." Then Madame said something in Arabic which apparently was a magic word because suddenly everybody looked at us and left the room. The only ones left were Indira Gandhi who continued repeating "Allo?, Allo?, Allo?..." and what appeared to be the man in charge sitting at his desk.

So, the gentlemen at the desk, with everyone else standing, Madame, Abulela, Jaums and me, smiled and invited us to come and sit on a bench facing his desk. He introduced himself as the Director of the Delegation Department and we shook hands and I introduced myself and Jaums. Madame and Abulela remained standing.

After a brief silence and looking very puzzled at us, the Director said, "Gentlemen, what are you doing here?"

I was paralyzed and surprised by this sudden unexpected question. For a moment I visualized Jaums and me in a jail like in the film *Midnight Express*, 1978 starring Brad Davis...or Lucy in the *Bastille*, Paris, 1956. I looked at Jaums for some kind of moral support. I didn't know what to say to justify our presence in Egypt and he was as perplexed as I was. The image of the guards with big guns we had just seen in the lobby flashed by and I saw us being led into the grand dungeon. No no, this cannot be. I have to get back to … to reality and be logical. How come he is asking me that question? He should know. They invited me and he is in charge. Obviously he had gotten word from the Embassy in Washington—he knew to pick us up at the airport, put us up in a hotel and sent Abuela to bring us here. Well, there must be an error somewhere. All of sudden I knew exactly what to do: show him the photos of my art. Shaking all over I picked up my case, opened it and put the binder on his desk without saying a word. He silently began to pass the pages and called Indira Gandhi who was still repeating "Allo?...Allo?..." Immediately his face adopted a pleasant understanding as to why I was there. Their faces as well as that of Madame were showing surprise and amazement at my work.

He looked at me, smiled and very friendly said, "Oh, I see now. I am sorry for the misunderstanding. You see, what happened was that two days ago we received a cable from the Washington Embassy telling us to pick you up at the airport and take care of you and nothing else… We didn't know why you were coming here… Now after seeing your extraordinary work it's very clear why you are here. So, now, in Cairo, we are in the peak of the tourist season and there is an international fair going on… With that short notice we could not get reservations at a better hotel. All hotels were booked… I am sorry for the hotel."

To this last statement I reacted immediately laughingly saying, "I'm glad you mentioned that… I wanted to tell you but I didn't know how. You know in America maybe we are spoiled but, we are used to a different kind of hotel. A Holiday Inn will be alright for us. The New Garden leaves a lot to be desired."

He laughed and said, "I know but with that short notice we couldn't find any other. I am sorry." I reply, "Maybe today we can try to find something else." And he said, "This afternoon I will go with you to find a better hotel. But now let's get to work with Madame Ahlam to organize the schedule for your visit here. Where would you like to visit in Egypt?" I proceed to enumerate sites that would be interesting to visit throughout Egypt. Then he asked me to make a list and give it to Indira. She was in charge of arranging all my trips to antiquities and appointments with other artists and officials. He introduced me to her but her name was too complicated to remember and pronounce. So I will continue respectfully calling her Indira. She was very nice and helpful and she said she would be able to organize all the trips except to Tel El Amarna, the city founded by pharaoh Akhenaton. She explained that it was in the middle of nowhere and transportation was very difficult to arrange. Well, that was fine with me. It was much more than I expected to accomplish that morning. As a matter of fact, they were very generous with me. Egypt was not a rich country and I felt uneasy that they were spending so much money on me. The director told me that from now on Abulela was my exclusive chauffeur during my time in Cairo. That was nice, I liked him very much in spite of his Cairo way of driving…

While waiting for the afternoon to go with the Director of the department to look for a new hotel, I asked Abulela to take us to the Cairo Museum and visit its Chief Curator, Dr. El Nawawi, as he suggested at the National Gallery of Art in Washington, D.C. in 1976. So we left the office and went down to the street with Madame and Abulela. This time Abulela was given a bigger and better car to drive us. We arrived at the museum fairly soon. Madame went with us, maybe she announced our visit because Dr. El Nawawi was expecting us and was extremely nice and he appointed one of his staff curators to give a VIP tour of the museum, allowing me to photograph anything I wanted except the mummies. The Cairo museum is an experience. At that time, it was old, dark and dusty. I felt very sorry because the extraordinary treasures and in many instances the lights were not working. The natural light through the translucent skylights was tempered by the accumulation of sand and dust on the outside. The Tutankhamun collection was even larger than I thought. I saw pieces I had never seen before. We had to rush because we had to cross the street to the Hilton for a delicious lunch and went back to Dr. Nawawi's office to wait for the Director of the Delegation Department to take us hotel hunting in the afternoon.

Just at two o'clock, he arrived at the Chief Curator's office and we walked out to the waiting car at the entrance of the museum, we entered and left. Our first stop was the Sheraton. Abulela stayed in the car. We went to the reception desk. The Director asked the attendant for a room. Before a determination could be made, others joined in on a long conversation. After a while it had grown to some sort of town meeting. It took quite some time. At the end the Director turned to me and said, "They don't have any room available." From there we went to all possible hotels in Cairo. In all of them the same scene of the town meeting was staged in order to conclude that there was no room for us.

From Cairo we went toward the Giza plateau. The Director said, "We will go to the Mena House." I almost had tears in my eyes thinking about the possibility of staying there, so close to the pyramids. The road was long and straight. I could see in the distance the pyramids getting closer and closer, just as I had seen them in my dream… I was speechless, trembling with emotion thinking that soon I'll be so close to the legendary pyramids and the Sphinx. I was wishing so badly that we could stay there.

I felt the anticipation of the great news that we could stay there. The afternoon sky was a bright turquoise blue and not a single cloud. It was like a dream and I was completely silent inside the car, almost as if in a catatonic state with my eyes fixed in the distant approaching sight of the pyramid complex. After a while I began to see to the right of the road the long silhouette of what appeared to be Mena House Hotel. Then I could see its name. I was trembling all over. Abulela turned to the right at the entrance driveway toward the main entrance of the hotel. The Director broke the silence inside the car and said "I'll go to the reception to see if we can rent a room." And breaking my silence I said, "I'm going to go with you." Jaums wanted to go too. Abulela stopped the car just at the entrance doors. We came out and followed the Director. The interior lobby of this hotel was like an epic Hollywood movie set, "Everywhere the glint of gold" as Howard Carter, the discoverer of Tutankhamun's tomb would have said if he would not have died of Hodgkin's disease in London on March 2, 1939 at 64.

What a beautiful lobby the Mena House has! So we followed the Director to the reception desk and he asked for a room for two persons.

I was praying to Osiris, Isis and Horus for the pleasure of staying here so close to the pyramids. Then more and more people joined in the search for a positive answer. Soon the customary town meeting was in full force. I don't know how long it took for the final conclusion to be reached and announced but… "There is no room available." That was a lethal blow for me that I wanted so badly to stay and sleep so close to the pyramids! I was incredulous and I said to the Director, "Are you sure? I can sit in the lobby to wait for a cancellation." He laughed at my desperate proposition and replied, "They are not expecting any cancellations. They are booked throughout the entire month." That was the perfect place for me to stay, just across the street! So close and so far! Even an official from the government can't get us a room! There is no justice in this world! And for you Osiris, Isis and Horus for ignoring my petition: GO TO HELL!

From the Giza plateau we left like dogs with their tails between their legs. We were completely defeated by the reality of the tourist season and the international convention in Cairo and now the best hotels were booked. Now the unwanted New Garden is on our horizon again with their three concave narrow "beds." And I am condemned to move the heavy chifforobe every night to block the mysterious third guest from entering the room! This was a depressing prospect to say the least! Maybe it was a good thing after all–I consoled myself–since in a previous dream there was a horrible ending. Resigned, we got in the car returning to Cairo while seeing the pyramids and the Mena House rapidly fade away.

Back in Cairo late in the afternoon, the Director said that there was a small hotel we hadn't checked yet, so we went directly there. It was near a busy area of modern Cairo near a very big elevated rotonda built just for people to move around without being killed by the crazy-busy traffic below. The location of this hotel was not far from the Sheraton. But it was located at the mezzanine level of what appeared to be a fairly modern apartment building. Abulela stopped the car just in front of it so we could all go in for the town hall ritual in the lobby. Now, to get to the hotel from the sidewalk we had to escalate a very wide, tall, straight, stairway. Outdoors. An unexpected and unique but somehow somewhat appropriate fixture of this long outdoor staircase was that, inexplicably, on each step, was, a, proudly, resting, toilet. I should have, but I never counted the steps nor the toilets on this thankfully open-air display because I was speechless contemplating this peculiar architectural adornment that I had never seen before, not even in my vivid nightmares. The closest thing I have seen to this repetitive architectural adornment was the famous ancient Egyptian "Road of the Sphinxes" at the entrance of a very old temple. So based on this precedent I named that unexpected architectural entrance, "The Staircase of the Toilets."

With that grandiose entrance waiting for us, we climbed the tall staircase to the lobby of this unusual hotel. I arrived out of breath because of all the steps with no elevators in sight. It had a big reception desk and the Director went promptly there. The employees explained that they were doing renovations in the apartment buildings and the toilets were the old toilets of the apartments. Could this be an omen of the shape of the things to come? So Jaums and I sat patiently in the lobby waiting for the next unknown to happen. Of course the ritualistic town hall meeting took its usual time. The answer this time was positive according to the Director, "But there was one problem. The room will be only for one night" because they are booked from the next day on." We were desperate and we took the room anyway, there was no other alternative in our bleak panorama. We signed the register and the Director went with us to see if the room was satisfactory, which it was and it had a complete and clean private bathroom. Then the Director told me that Madame and Abulela will be coming next morning at 9:15 am to take us to see the Chairman of the State Information Agency and he left. After we made sure our watches were synchronized.

The first thing I did was to take a long hot shower and brush my teeth with water of the almighty Nile…

"What are you doing?!" Jaums said, alarmed. "You are going to get sick to your stomach!" I replied, "I have decided that If I'm going to be here for three weeks, I'd better get used to the water."

"If you get sick," he added, "it's your problem."

"I'm not going to get sick," I explained, "while taking my shower, I figured out that if I get used to the water step by step, I will not get sick. First I start brushing my teeth, later on by using the ice in my drinks and after that I will try drinking juices and last I'll try the water. This is not the first time I brushed my teeth this morning. And so far nothing has happened to me."

"Yet," he interrupted, "you'll see… I will use bottled water."

" If I lived here before," I added, "as some people suggested, the Nile water will not affect me."

Jaums opened his suitcase for the first time to face the horror of his green and mouth wash-scented clothes. He began to distribute them all over the room with the hope that by the next morning the strong smells would dissipate. After he finished, he took his second Cairo shower and we went to have dinner at the Sheraton. And, what did we eat for our first dinner in Cairo? Lasagna! It was delicious. Well, at least for two hungry fishes out of water.

From the Sheraton, we walked back to our hotel with its triumphal Steps of the Toilets for one-night-only. We went to bed at 8:30 pm–the correct time in Cairo. But we needed to rest! It was an early *Hard Day's Night*, 1965 with John, Ringo, Paul and George.

CHAPTER 11

GUESTS WHO ARE COMING TO DINNER

Years later, I went back to Egypt. At that time the reservations were done way ahead of time and I finally stayed at the Mena House! It was as grand as I thought. I would visit the pyramids in the afternoon when there were not many people around. The sun sets were really spectacular. On my first trip in 1978, one night I had collected some small unusual black shiny stones I found by Cheops' pyramid with the help of a flashlight. Upon my return to the U.S. I kept the smallest ones inside a small pyramid pendant talisman that I wore hanging from a chain around my neck.

On one of these afternoon visits while staying at the Mena House, as I wandered near some newly unearthed ruins around the base of the great pyramid, my pyramid talisman fell to the sandy ground. First I thought the chain had broken, but no, the chain was intact and perfectly secure around my neck. Probably the pendant hook broke, I thought. I kneeled on the sandy ground and was able to find my pyramidal talisman and carefully examined it. To my surprise, the talisman was intact too! Then, what happened? I was extremely puzzled...

At that point, I started remembering that some years earlier a lady I knew did a research about my possible reincarnation one evening in her home. I went along with her research, not because I particularly believed in such "occult" things as she did but because she was quite intrigued with the process and it was fun working with her. She found that I lived in two periods of ancient Egypt. The first was during *Queen Hatshepsut's* reign. In this first one I was an artist working on the construction of her temple of *Deir El Bahari*. But I was not Egyptian. I was brought there only to work for her on that project. But I died before I completed my assignment. According to that research, I had an accident involving my knees and couldn't work anymore.

And the second was during the transition from the reigns of Akhenaton to Tutankhamun. I was part of the royal family and closely related to both pharaohs. But I met a violent death at the age of eleven at the hands of general Horembeb because of my religious inclinations for the only god, Aton, and his belief of "Living In Truth."

Coming back in time to Egypt on that afternoon and the spot where my talisman fell on the ground, I wondered if the strange falling of my pyramidal talisman was an omen, or an indication that I should pursue the reincarnation research further with the same lady. I asked in my mind for guidance and help. Then I began feeling some chills throughout my body and I had the feeling, at that point, that my past history was there, buried under the ground. Should I pursue it? Then I felt stronger chills! Well…definitely **NOT!**

But during this visit to Egypt, staying at Giza, living at the Mena House, and having the benefit of a clear day, I began digging the sandy ground with my bare hands, just as an eager dog would do. Digging and digging… It became kind of frantic, digging away as a broad daylight operation I kept finding rare stones and pottery fragments… This ought to be the place! I begin to think about how I would react if in fact I found a sarcophagus and a mummy! Could the mummy be me in a prior life? Then I got more chills. I got scared about these chills, but to my surprise I continued my eager digging… I was going at a fast pace when I noticed some tourists wandering around the area. They were looking at me and I flashed back to reality. I decided to stop for a while and wait until they were gone. I sat on a stone and waited…

At dusk the scene was clear and the temperature was cooler, so I went back to my dig. I couldn't keep track of how long I was digging because I was so concentrated on what I was doing. It was exactly as when I was painting and lost track of time so suddenly it was late into the afternoon and the sand started to feel different—obviously there was something hard under the sand. I got a putty knife I kept in the top pocket of my *Indiana Jones* shirt—I didn't want to take the usual digging utensils in order not to attract much attention from people and tourists walking around. So I was pretending that I was playing in the sand. With the putty knife I discreetly keep moving the sand around the contour of the wooden container I was uncovering to uncover its dimensions. Well, it seems to be that it wasn't too big. I was relieved! After all, I didn't want to unearth a coffin with a mummy. But I kept wondering what was going to be inside this box…? The clue about my previous life? I got more chills after I entertained that thought. Even though I was excited I made the decision to stop again and wait for the sunset when people around will be retiring to their hotels. So I sat patiently at the sight I found.

After dusk and with no one around I went back to unearth what appeared to be a wooden box until the four sides were exposed. I got my tape and measured. It was 10 X 15 inches. I dug down at one of the corners to find its depth. I stuck down the tape to measure the height of what appears to a box and it seems to be about 8 inches deep. So I was excited and my heart was beating fast in anticipation of what my discovery will mean to me and perhaps the archeological world! I began to dig frantically, protected by the darkening sky. The box was getting loose and I saw it was moving around. There was some space to introduce my hands and try to pull the box out from the place it has been resting for who knows how many thousands of years. Finally, I was able to get it out and carefully place it on the ground beside me. It wasn't very heavy. I became very nervous and got my brush and flashlight to clean it and observe its exterior. But it didn't have Egyptian hieroglyphics or other markings. It was a plain dark wooden box and it was sealed. Well, I decided the best thing to do was take the box to my hotel room and try to open it there. So I decided to cover the hole in the ground the best I could.

After I completed filling the hole, I picked up the box and rushed back to the Mena House some distance across the road. I tried to be inconspicuous as I entered the lobby and walked to the elevators. Now, in the safety of my room, I put the box on a desk and looked for anything that I could use to try to open the mysterious box. A while later I realized that there was nothing there that could be used as the tool I needed to put between the box and the top to try to open it. Well, I thought, I'll have to wait until tomorrow to see if I can find a hardware store to get a crowbar…

I took a long bath and called room service for dinner. While I was eating I got the idea of trying to open the box with the different kinds of silverware. But that didn't work. So I went to bed. However, I could not sleep at all because I was very intrigued by the box.

Next morning, very early, I went to look for a hardware store. Finally I found one. I bought the tools I needed and rushed back to my hotel room. Now, with the proper tools, I was able to begin to loosen the metal seal around the top until it was broken and was able to remove the top. A kind of hot air with a very strange pungent scent came out of it. But to my surprise, the only thing there was a very ancient looking piece of paper–not papyrus–written in what appeared to be Arabic and some sort of map that clearly showed the Sphinx. I could not make much of the manuscript, and the map was puzzling. One might have been related to the other. So I decided to take both to an antiquarian in a nearby bazaar.

There I found a little antique shop and its elderly owner who spoke fluent English. I showed him the manuscript and the map but I told him that I had bought them at a Khan El Khalili's bazaar.

He smiled and asked, "Did you pay much?"

"No, not much" I answered, "A pound to a child vendor."

"You paid too much," he said smiling, "probably a fake... What is what you want to know?"

"Well" I replied, "I would like to know what it says..."

"Very well," he said while he pulled a magnifying glass from a drawer and began to carefully examine the manuscript. On a few occasions, he seemed to smile. After a while he put the magnifying glass on the counter and very amused said, "Well...it says that if you follow the path indicated on the map, you will find petroleum... But everybody knows that there is no petroleum in Sahara City... Only sand, sand and tons of worthless sand... You know, it has to be Sahara City because of the Sphinx and the direction of the path to follow. This is a fake. I'm sorry... What can I tell you? That's all it says."

"That's all right," I said. "How much do I owe you?"

"Nothing, nothing at all," he replied and added, "You already paid too much."

I said, "Thank you very much for your time." And I left.

But I was convinced that he was wrong. It was very strange what had happened the day before. It was no reason at all for the talisman to fall in that spot. There was nothing wrong with my chain or the pendant. It was very mysterious what happened. It was an omen that I must pursue to the end.

From Khan El Kalili's bazaar I went directly to the Sphinx, and with the map in my hands, I followed the map printed on the ancient looking map on the paper. I had to walk a great deal until I reached the appointed mark on the map at Sahara City. At that point I found a falling apart villa ... which happened to be for sale! Should I buy it? I asked myself. And I got the strongest chill of them all! Yes, definitely I thought I should…

So, a day later I got hold of the seller and after some negotiations, I purchased the villa! And soon after I hired a drilling company and we began the process of drilling for the precious black gold. Some of the neighbors and other people around the area were laughing at me the whole time. They thought I was out of my mind. They kept telling me and insisting that there was no petroleum. Even the drilling company I hired didn't have faith in me or my project. They kept drilling because I kept paying them. I became the laughingstock of Sahara City. People used to come everyday to watch the drilling operation and to make all kinds of jokes and comments about me… It became a carnival. But I didn't care. I just knew that– it– was there for me to find. The box I found at the Giza Plateau was an unmistakable signal for me to follow to the end. Whatever I find there it was meant for me!

After over a month, it was hit and up it went!!! People didn't laugh at me any longer…

And with the black gold, came the money, a LOT. I was no longer "trying to make it as an artist." I became THE ARTIST. Even my paintings became very expensive!–as if I needed more money… As the saying goes "Money follows money." From one day to the next I became a well-known and famous internationally known artist." One day an elitist and snobbish New York publication was now crazy about my work and offered me a position as an art editor. In the past they looked down on my Egyptian inspired work: "Too decorative." "Look," I replied, graciously declining their offers, "You already had Jackie O. You don't need another millionaire in your staff. Why don't you hire somebody with real talent for a change?"

I had been looked down upon so many times by publications and the art world in the U.S. but I really didn't need them anymore. I can produce any kind of art and I didn't have to care about what those elitists and discrimination circles said. Now with all the money that was coming I have total freedom and I can produce what I really like.

On my first trip to Egypt as a guest of the Egyptian government in 1978, I visited Aswan and I discovered that it was extremely beautiful and peaceful with the most beautiful blue sky that I had seen. And about a year later I decided to buy a magnificent classic villa in Aswan, perched on a hill overlooking the peaceful Nile and Elephantine Island with its spectacular rounded rocks forming soft rapids with the Nile waters. The villa was built in the early 1930s. From it, I could see the Aga Khan wife's residence in the distance and its own mausoleum on the top of the sand-colored hills opposite to Elephantine Island and the old city of Aswan.

The villa was refurbished and redecorated with classic furniture to my taste to the last detail, including a chapel dedicated to Rona Barrett.

At that time I had contact in France with somebody in the film industry because I decided to marry Danielle Darrieux, the French actress, whom I had met back in 1971, at a hot dog stand, when she was playing "Coco" on Broadway. With all the money I have, she married me without hesitation to avoid a nursing home… She was kind of old. Before we married we got two puppies! She badly needed some repair work on her face, neck and other parts of her body. She didn't look any longer like in the 1954 film *Le Rouge et le Noir/ The Red and the Black* with actor Gerald Philipe… So I had her interned in a plastic surgery specializing hospital in Brazil where her accordion style wrinkles were ironed. However her usual sweet smile was not the same anymore and slightly crooked—which was a trait bearing many other contemporary stars, who had chosen that method of artificial rejuvenation. That was the price of youth.

Then her body was shaped up with silicone from the knees up and she gained a figure as curvaceous as Dolly Parton. Unfortunately her boobies didn't heal right because of complications with her scar tissue and honestly they look like two silly cones. But overall, she looked pretty good. It was a shame that she was walking with some difficulties. And to solve that problem, our close friend Marlene Dietrich–who was still around doing her show in Haiti with a protective net over the orchestra pit–recommended a rhinestone walker for Danielle. So I ordered one specially made from the Hollywood Boulevard Veteran Movie Stars Medical Supply Boutique, also with a branch on Rodeo Drive. There I also ordered a Tina Turner wig and a Frederick's of Hollywood hostess gown with the three colors of the French flag. Believe it or not, the repair job that I paid for made Danielle very happy indeed! She really was looking ravishing. In perfect form for the remake of her 1936 film *Mayerling*.

Danielle had the idea to celebrate her comeback to her social life by throwing a big party in the magnificent home in Aswan. But honestly, I am an enemy of parties. The only type of social gatherings I would enjoy was an intimate sitdown dinner of no more than six to eight of a very selected group of people. I consulted my feelings with Danielle and she graciously agreed with my idea. This was going to be the first social gathering dinner since the restoration of our home which was named *Le Plaisir* honoring Danielle's 1952 French film, so I thought we should go all the way for our first social dinner to make it a night that would be forever in our and our guests' memory.

In order to create that special night, my petro-dollars would be the magic wand. To prepare the lavish and exquisitely presented dinner we had in mind, I called Saint Mary's County, Maryland to get my friend, *haute traiteur* Bill Taylor, to ask him to fly to Aswan, first class of course, and all expenses paid. I really trusted him and I wanted a relaxed atmosphere but with elegance and good taste. However, I didn't want professional waiters to serve at the dinner table, I wanted real show business personalities acting as waiters and waitresses. After a lot of phone calls and negotiations with their agents in the U.S, I was able to get my choice of players. I got Charo, Joan Rivers, Pia Zadora, Mia Farrow, Julie Christie, Daniel Craig, Pierce Brosnan, Timothy Dalton, John Travolta and Pee-wee Herman.

I wanted a subdued entertainment during the dinner, so I was able to hire the tiny, little and whimsical twin sisters from the Japanese Godzilla movies singing *There's No Business Like Show Business*. After dinner I wanted to be more lively, so I booked the Trocadero Ballet to dance Martha Graham's last choreography, *Roots Adagio for the Dukes of Hazzard*.

I wanted very much to achieve the perfect chemistry among the people invited. I began making a selective list of possible guests having in mind their backgrounds. I decided to invite them as a couple not necessarily married, convincing them via singing telegrams. And after I received their confirmations I began to arrange their transportation. They would all fly first class to Aswan and then on private helicopters to our heliport at the top of the mountain where our home was located.

Since I was living in Aswan I began to wear the typical turban most locals wore. Since this was a very special ocassion, I decided to contact my previous stylist, Norbert, who lived in Maryland and was a Seventh Day Adventist. I asked him to come to Aswan with all the expenses paid to do my hair as well as Danielle's. He loved the idea. But he explained to me that he was not a man any longer… And he said, I am a woman and my name is Norah! It took me a few seconds to recuperate and then I remembered Joe E. Brown's last line in *Some Like It Hot*. And I replied to Norbert, now Norah, "Nobody's perfect."

Miss Norah Ralston arrived a week later carrying 21 pieces of lavender luggage. Actually she looks great as a woman! She looked like a version of the country singer Dottie West with Mae West mannerisms and the voice of a deep bass like Vera Charles, the friend of Mame Dennis in the Broadway play "Mame." Norah was a lot of fun to be around and Danielle liked her very much. I didn't tell her about her sex change. But she was intrigued about her deep bass voice.

The morning of the dinner party I told her, "Norah, give me a haircut and set my hair in a John Davidson eat-your-heart-out style." She did it and my hair looked very good!

After that, I went to inspect everything in the villa. And everything was in its place as I had planned, especially the impressive dining room with the Bill Taylor touch. The setting of the table was flawless. The fresh bouquets of yellow roses and the twenty-two karat gold rings, goblets of Bohemian crystal on the rectangular glass table top with the eighteen karat goldware and equally gold charger plates and yellow napkins. Everything looked impeccable in the dining room. The guest will be arriving by the typical Egyptian sailboats called *faluccas* with a uniformed Venetian gondolier singing *Santa Lucia* to the pier where two helicopters will transport them to the other side of the Nile where the mountain and our house rest.

At 4:30 sharp, Herve Villechaize, who asked to come in order to meet the Godzilla Japanese tweens, came running announcing, "The helicopter! The helicopter!" Well…

I ran to get Danielle. She automatically sat in her wheelchair looking ravishing with her Tina Turner wig styled by Norah. I wheeled her out to the heliport and she got up and stood by me. From the heliport we could see the majestic Nile below with its serene *felucca* sail boats silently passing by. Danielle, standing by my side, was radiantly smiling. I was very happy, because after all, everything I was doing was for her enjoyment after everything she went through with all her operations in Brazil.

The first couple arriving was Charo with Mr. Daniel Craig while the Mariachi band from Tijuana played *GoldFinger*. And to the surprise of Mr. Craig, Charo began dancing in a conga tempo. Slightly confused by the tempo of the Mexican mariachis. The second helicopter can be seen in the distant clear blue sky and the first took off. I thought to myself–I shouldn't have invited Charo… They approached us and we greeted them.

The next couple to arrive was Miss Pia Zadora and Mr. Pierce Brosnan. Gosh she is very petite–I thought to myself. Since Mr. Brosnan was a former James Bond, the mariachis continued playing Goldfinger. Actually it sounds very strange when that tune is played by a mariachi band. Mr. Brosnan looked quietly amused. As they approached us they were delighted to see Danielle looking so good. She was very pleased with their comments.

The other helicopter was seen in the distance and the landed one had to leave to pick up the next couple. Our staff guided the four celebrities already on the heliport to the interior of the house for drinks and relaxing while the others were arriving. The next helicopter arrived with our third couple, Miss Mia Farrow and Timothy Dalton while the mariachis were playing the same *Goldfinger* tune. I thought–Miss Farrow looks like a street person and her kinky hair looks terrible. I must talk to Norah to see if she can do something with it–she interrupted my line of thought to introduce herself to Danielle and me and she looked even worse up close. Then Mr. Dalton, looking very dashing, was very proper and nice to Danielle telling her how much he admired her in her films. Danielle was very flattered by his nice comments. Staff came to take them inside the house. I suggested to Miss Farrow that if she wanted to take a bath she should just let the staff know. She was speechless…

The previous helicopter was on the way back while the next was getting close to landing. In about 2 minutes it landed with the impeccably dressed Joan Rivers and John Travolta while the mariachi finally changed its tune to Staying Alive. Both Rivers and Travolta were very gracious and excited to see Danielle looking so good. She was flabbergasted. She knew about John Travolta but didn't know about Joan Rivers and she complimented her beautiful gown, Joan replying, "I found it on a camel and I couldn't resist it." Travolta and I laughed at Joan's reply but Danielle, not acquainted with her, didn't understand why we were laughing. But I explained later and she understood Joan's joke.

So they were the last guests of the evening. Danielle sat on her Egyptian wheelchair and we left for the living room of our home to join the previous guests… After about 10 minutes, we heard the helicopter landing. That's strange I thought since we didn't invite anybody else. I overheard the mariachi band trying to play out of tune and out of tempo the *William Tell Overture*. So I excused myself and went outside to the heliport to see what was going on…To my surprise I saw what appeared to me an impossible situation, Gina Lollobrigida and Sofia Loren together at last! But both were full of bruises and lacerations, apparently they had been fighting inside the helicopter because both were wearing their identical metallic gold evening gowns which were all torn apart! I wondered who invited them here?! I have not allowed either of them in our home fearing problems. I signaled the pilot to put them back in the helicopter and take them both to the pier. I just wanted a nice and peaceful evening at home! So I returned to my civilized guests for an evening to remember.

It certainly was an occasion none of our guests will ever forget. Just as Danielle wanted and deserved, "a truly unforgettable evening," as Danielle said afterward. Suddenly her face and figure and the home on the hill in Aswan disappeared like multi-color confetti and I saw darkness with my eyes closed. I slowly opened my eyes and saw the ceiling of my bedroom and the faint sound of a helicopter disappearing in the distance and then, silence…

CHAPTER 12

POLYGAMY AND STUDIO 54

After a much needed good night's rest, we got up around 7:00 AM. We had to go to breakfast early, because we had an appointment that morning with the Chairman of the State Information Agency, Dr. Morsi Saad Eddin, and I wanted to make sure that this time there will not be confusion with the hour. I planned to be ready much ahead to time.

On my way back from the cafeteria, I stopped by the reception desk to find out the check out time, since we were supposed to move out of the "steps of the toilets" hotel today. But to my surprise, the lady attendant said that we could stay one more day! But, only one more day because "Tomorrow we have overbooking." That was very welcome news since we didn't have any place to go! At least we won't have to spend another afternoon driving around Cairo looking for a place to stay. Not today.

However, Jaums couldn't unpack his green stained and mouth-wash-smelling clothes from his suitcase, so he had to wear the exact same clothes he had been wearing since he left Maryland a few days ago. However, since he cannot send anything to the hotel laundry because we are supposed to check out next morning! My clothes didn't fit him!

So he had the idea to empty his suitcase and place his clothes everywhere in the room and leave the window open. At least today the mouthwash smell could be dissipating.

At 9:15 am sharp, Madame and Abulela arrived at the majestic "steps of the toilets" entrance of our hotel. We proudly descended to the street and got in the car inundated by the delicious fragrance of Madam's perfume. That was a relief in opposition to our mouthwash permeating the environment of our room! But Madame seems nervous this morning. Obviously Dr. Morsi, as she kept referring to him, as the Minister of Higher Education in Egypt, was a very important man.

The Ministry was not very far from our hotel and we arrived soon. It was a medium height building, probably built in the late 1950s, not in the best condition but I already noticed that many of the buildings in the old section of Cairo were just like that. Maybe due to previous unrest, wars and expenditures in defense, their general budget has to be deviated to other more vital directions. Their economy did not seem strong enough for those kinds of refinements we took for granted in the U.S. So I felt bad that they were investing so much money on my trip and I really felt that I wasn't worth everything that they were doing.

We were searched by the guards as we entered the building and escorted to a very small elevator perhaps for two persons. Madame, Jaums and I managed to fit inside. The elevator moved up very slowly and hesitating at times, but it managed to get us to the top floor, where Dr, Morsi's office was and we entered the waiting room. To my surprise Jackie O. was sitting there! What a small world I thought… She was all in black of course. But looking at her much more carefully I eventually realized that it was another Egyptian reproduction, just as I thought that Madame was the Cuban singer Olga Guillot!

The waiting room was a big room and its architecture was fairly similar to other rooms I had seen in La Habana in 1959. Certainly there were striking architectural similarities. I was always very interested in architecture, as a matter of fact when I was a child living in a country town and on a trip to La Habana, I went to the main Woolworth's Ten Cent and bought a set of *American Plastic Bricks* that allowed me to construct many types of houses and buildings of my own creation. I spent countless hours playing with it. When I got to the U.S. in 1967, I tried to find those sets again but they were not available any longer. In about the year 2000 I was able to buy many sets on a site that sells older merchandise. I was very happy to have them with me again!

After a while sitting in Dr. Morsi's waiting room, a man came from the swinging doors of his office. Madame nervously smiled and I thought that perhaps it was her first time there. But the man went to Jackie O. and indicated to her that it was her appointment. She got up without looking at anybody and rapidly made her regal entrance in Dr. Morsi's office as if she was a very important personality, leaving the swinging doors swinging after her.

During her time in Dr. Morsi's office, other people went in and out. I guessed that her meeting wasn't as important as Jackie O's. was pretending it to be. Later on, the same man who ushered Jackie O. in, came out and called us for our meeting with the Minister of Higher Education and Madame with her delicious fragrance came with us. Inside it was a big penthouse office with a big window behind Dr. Morsi's big desk and a big terrace to the left. This time the desk had documents, photos and mementos unlike the other desks we had seen. We advanced toward his desk. I noticed a man seated on the first chair on the left and seated on a chair on the right was none other than Jackie O. I thought that now we will find out who that reproduction was.

Our party was in front of his desk and the Minister got up from the central chair and Madame introduced us to Dr. Morsi, who was a distinguished looking, middle aged, very charming and naturally friendly man who made us feel welcome and at home. But he didn't introduce Jackie O. So her mystery continued… However, he introduced the other gentleman sitting there. He was a well known Egyptian artist who also wrote a column in the Egyptian magazine *My Country*. His name was Rushdi Iskandar, artist born in Cairo on April 23rd 1918. He has the same zodiac sign as I have, Aries. I was born on April 17.

As soon as we all sat, Dr. Morsi and Mr. Iskander began looking at my portfolio. They were really fascinated and excited about my work. Dr. Morsi asked me for slides and I gave him a set. Then he told me about his television show and invited me to be his guest to interview me the next Thursday. That was all right with me, as a matter of fact, it was an unexpected honor. Then I told Madame to include the taping of that show on my schedule. After our meeting concluded some photos were taken with Dr. Morsi and the artist Rushdi Iskandar. However, Jackie O. managed to be out of the photos. So her mystery continues…

Later on, Dr. Morsi arranged for a private screening that same morning of a documentary about the ancient past of Egypt. I loved the idea. He said it would be a nice introduction for my trip. We were ushered to the screening room. However, Madame said that she couldn't attend, but she would be back with Abulela to pick us up in one hour. So, she left.

Jaums and I waited in the screening room while they got the film ready. A waiter came to offer coffee, but we declined since Jaums and I do not drink coffee but requested Egyptian Pepsi instead. As we witnessed *Joan Crawford* doing in a retrospective of her films at the American Film Institute, in the early 1970s, we also drank the Pepsi directly from the cans. The Egyptian Pepsi had a more rich flavor than the ones sold in the U.S. In my modest opinion the Egyptian ones were better, at least in 1978, when my trip was taking place.

The screening room only had a few rows of wooden chairs. But they were like the ones in the old movie house in the country town in Cuba where I grew up. I had not seen them since. It was amazing to find them so many thousands of miles away! They brought back memories… After a short time, the lights went off and the documentary began. It dealt with the importance of death for the ancient Egyptians.

It was a very interesting study. It lasted for about 45 minutes, after which we were ushered to Dr. Morsi again. In addition to him, Rushdi Iskandar was still there but Jackie O. disappeared as the vision she was. Rushdi asked us to visit his studio. I said "of course," I will talk to Madame to put that on my schedule. Then, we left and one of Dr. Morsi's secretaries took us to the tiny elevators. Madame and Abulela were waiting for us downstairs with the car.

From the Ministry of Higher Education we dropped Madame at her home and I asked Abulela to take us to the American University, because I wanted to locate John Van Deerlin, an English teacher I had met in one of my exhibitions about a month prior at the Washington World Gallery on M street in Georgetown, Washington, D.C. I had told him about my upcoming trip and he asked me to visit him in Cairo. After we arrived at the university, I began searching for him. But the place seems to be not very well organized as often most of the time happens with the U.S. universities. No one knew him or where his class room was. Jaums and I were in the main building for some time, going here and there and walking up and down. When we were going to give up the search, we accidentally found ourselves in a central patio crowded with students and I saw John in the distance, then we rushed toward him. He was very surprised to see us there as he would have been if he saw a Martian. However, his reaction was quickly understood when he told me that he never received my letter announcing my visit. He explained to us how bad the communication channels are in Egypt, even the phones. Then I understood the delay to receive the cable from the Egyptian Embassy in Washington, D.C. announcing our arrival, even the phone problems Indira Gandhi was having her futile efforts repeating "Allo, Allo, Allo…" to my futile attempts to call John Van Deerlin from the Sheraton the night before… Well, that afternoon I was scheduled to visit the pyramids of Giza and John lived in a villa nearby, so we arranged to meet later that evening on our way back from the pyramids. John has to go back to his class. Abulela will be dropping us at the Sheraton for lunch and he will pick us up at the "Steps of the toilets" hotel at 4:30 pm. So after a relaxing lunch eating American food at the Sheraton, we walked back to our hotel a few blocks away.

After we returned to our room, Jaums found that the smell in his stinky clothes subsided a little and while I was taking my shower he began washing some of his clothes in the sink and hanging them outside from the room's window that had more air circulation. For my first real date with the pyramids, I decided to wear the typical Egyptian galabeah that my mother reproduced for me for this trip. So I unpacked the sand color galabeah. But instead of the matching pants she made for me I wore a pair of blue jeans and knee high boots because of the irregularities in the terrain as Abulela recommended to me, since it can get windy and chilly sometimes at night in that area. Once I was fully dressed, Jaums made fun of my clothes. But I didn't care, I just wanted to wear the same as the Egyptians and I want to be dressed properly for the pyramids. I didn't want to look like a ridiculous American tourist.

At 4:30 pm we ran downstairs and while passing by the reception they gave us notice that we could stay one more day. But after that, "We have overbooking." That was good news!!! We were out of breath as we got into Abulela's car and down we went again on the road to the pyramids of Giza. Madame couldn't come with us on this trip. As government guests, our official hosts gave us a document that we can visit any antiquities and archeological sites as many times as we wish and didn't have to pay any fee or wait in line. That certainly was another great thing for me and saved us time at the sights!

The traffic toward the Giza plateau was heavy and as disorganized as usual with the customary bumper to bumper use of the claxon and the brakes. We were getting used to it by now and didn't *"duck and cover"* any more. We could see the mythical pyramids slowly growing in the distance. They were looking orange because of the sunlight. The road was already looking familiar to me because of our previous trip looking for a room at the *Mena House.* We finally arrived at the pyramids at 5:15 pm, with plenty of time to see the tourist *Sound and Light Show.* The pyramids looked majestic at that time. Then, I asked Abulela, "Can we go inside the pyramid now?" "Well, not now. It's too late. They are getting ready to close at 5:30 pm, perhaps another day. Today we can see the *Sound and Light Show* and walk and look around…" "I'm disappointed, what a shame, I said. Abulela replied, "I can take you to a shop in a bazaar while we wait for the 7:30 show. Lets walk there now, I cannot take my car there."

So we started walking and got to the shop. We entered and immediately our senses got hit by thousands of all kinds of merchandise made specially for tourists. I am a serious and selective buyer, there was nothing there that I would like to buy. Immediately the owner came in our direction dressed in a typical colorful folkloric costume to our group offering Egyptian coffee. We declined. I didn't want to be impolite with this jovial salesman. He kept offering some other trinkets and jewelry which I am not interested in buying and he was trying to offer me at a lower price. I kept trying to leave his store and he was following me around. Finally I managed to escape that unexpected situation but I didn't want to be nasty to him, because that's the way he had to make a living. However, just outside that shop were a Bedouin with two camels ready to receive two American tourists on the ride of their life with the pyramids silently watching! Well, at least I don't have to buy the camel and I had ridden horses before so I tried to happily accept being on top of that poor, homely animal… So the Bedouin helped me to get installed on it and began to pull the innocent animal forward. The most *espeluznante* ride of my life was when I was 15 years old aboard the roller coaster at *Coney Island Park* in La Habana. That experience was my first and last and now in Egypt with the pyramids as my silent witness I was experiencing something similar! I very politely screamed my way through this uncalled-for experience. The nice Bedouin ordered the poor camel to make reverence and I slid down from this unwanted ride. Jaums was subject to the same unwanted experience. After I recuperated from this ride, I very politely explained to Abulela that "we were not crazy American tourists and that we are in Egypt to see and appreciate the ancient art only." He asked me, "Would you like to climb the Great Pyramid to the summit?" I replied, "No, thank you Abulela." We both laughed at the impossibility of his suggestion. He was very apologetic about it. After we recuperated, we relaxed and experienced the *Lights and Sound Show*. I would have enjoyed it better if only they would have shown the lights and music and tune down the over dramatic theatrical narration.

Afterward Abulela came back and said, "Stay here, don't go anywhere, I'm going to find a guide for you. There are tombs around here. I'll be back," and he left.

After a while he came back with the same Bedouin from the camel incident. Previously, because of the situation, I didn't notice what he was wearing. But now I did. It was a sky blue galabeah and matching turban and a navy blue turtleneck sweater. I turned toward Jaums and pointed, "You see, I was not crazy when I decided to wear a turtleneck under my galabeah as recommended by Abulela. It's kind of cool here.

This Bedouin, who was the first one I met in my life, spoke better English than me and appeared to be well educated and said, "I will take care of you from now on. I will show you things that other tourists will never see." Well, that sounds promising to me. So, we followed him around and very soon I found us entering an underground tomb. It was exciting! It was a very small one, lit by a single candle that an attendant was holding in his hand. We almost had to crawl inside. It was very dark and I couldn't see much. The attendant was showing me what appeared to be the side of a stone sarcophagus with a skull and some bone fragments… Well, there was nothing remarkable about it. Not a single painted hieroglyphic, not a hint of a fragment of a mural and no mummy in sight. The only thing was the spooky feeling of being inside a tomb. We crawled out and the Bedouin took us to another tomb. This one was much better and bigger. It had some eroded stone sculptures inside, but no murals, no sarcophagus and no mummy. So we visited a few more. But there was nothing remarkable about them either. That's not what I wanted to see. "My interest was seeing tombs with painted murals like I had seen in books" I told the Bedouin guide and his reply was, "Would you like to climb the Great Pyramid to the summit…?" I kind of smiled at his illegal proposition and replied, "No, I am not interested in that either. I'm not a thrill seeker. I am very serious about examining the ancient Egyptian work in the museums and archeological sites. I had read stories about unusual phenomena at the summit of the Great Pyramid and I'm not ready to test my luck with that enterprise. That's not why I came to Egypt. I am not an average American stereotypical tourist wearing a Hawaiian shirt, Bermuda shorts, dress shoes with knee high socks, a red cap with attached green sunglasses and an 'Instamatic' camera hanging from my neck. No, I am a Cuban American wearing a galabeah who is in Egypt to observe the real archeological findings throughout the country and in museums and so it can be incorporated into my art creations." He replied "I see, I see." "I was planning to do some shopping but at the end of my trip, not now," I added.

So we went to where Abulela parked his car. Jaums and I took our usual place in the back seat. To my surprise the Bedouin sat in the front seat beside Abulela. I didn't know that we were going to give him a ride but it was fine with me after he spent his time with us. The Bedouin was very friendly, pointing out highlights of the road. Then, Abulela took a sudden turn leaving the main road onto a bumpy road leaving the desert area into a fertile valley near the Nile with a lot of vegetation around. Then the car stopped, "Here we are," said Abulela and he and the Bedouin got out of the car and Jaums and I followed them. I could see the roof of what appeared to be a house not very far away. Whatever it was, it's certainly a secluded place. We kept following them until I was able to see the whole thing. It looked like a house with a tall masonry fence and a walkway leading to a door with one step. We all stepped up and very soon we found ourselves in an Egyptian nightclub! I don't drink, I never go to night clubs except in Cuba to see a friend, singer or dancer performing. I asked myself and probably Jaums did too, "What in the hell are we doing in a nightclub?! There were no other people there, no other customers around. Obviously, this is the Egyptian version of *Studio 54*! But *Liza, Misha, Jackie* and *Halston* were nowhere to be seen!! What a shame! The place wasn't even decorated, just a few color spotlights. Only a big room with a bar, an area for dancing and a lot of simple tables and chairs. We sat by a long row of windows. Actually, the view was the only worthwhile feature of the place. It was an endless valley of tall grassy vegetation undulating in the soft late afternoon breeze and in the distance the Giza plateau with their monumental pyramids and the last rays of the sun colorizing the surreal display. I kept silent with my eyes lost absorbed in that enchanting view…

Silence was interrupted by the drinks being served–Jaums and I got Egyptian Pepsi. The Bedouin began talking about the villa he was building near Sahara City for his wives (!). After all he was modest, he had only two. But he was still a young man. He may add more wives and children in his future and enlarge his villa. He explained that one of them was British (!) and she didn't have any children yet. But he had many children with the Egyptian one. He explained to me that the British wife came to Egypt as a tourist a few years ago, met him and immediately fell in love with him. According to him, she asked him to take her as his wife–Queen Victoria must have turned in her grave! He took her, of course, and introduced her to his Egyptian wife and children and they all were very civilized, and slept in the same room. Then he said that she had to go back to England, but she kept writing to him. And every opportunity she had she flew to Egypt to be with him. From England she was contributing to the building of his new villa. Then he proceeded to show me her letter but due to respect to both of them and his family I will not disclose that private communication here.

Well, it was getting late and I told Adulela that we had to go to meet John Van Deerlin and we should take the Bedouin back to his villa. Certainly this lesson on Polygamy in the Egyptian version of *Studio 54* was very enlightening to say the least…

When we were walking out of this "night club," I discreetly approached Abulela and asked him if on our way back to Cairo we he could drop the Bedouin at his villa or a place nearby. Also I wanted to know how much tip I should give him for his time. He replied, "Whatever you want." I responded "I'm not familiar with the money here yet. Can you give me an idea how much would be a fair amount?" And he casually said, "Give him two pounds." "Two pounds?! I said, "That sounds so little. Are you sure it's correct?" "Yes," he replied, "One per each one of you."

"OK," I said, but I got Five pounds instead and turned to the Bedouin, thanked him and gave him the money. He took it without looking at how much it was and put it in his pocket. But out of curiosity a few seconds later he got the money out of the pocket and looked at the bills. I noticed his facial expression of disgust and irritation and he said out loud "THANK YOU!" Well I gave him more than what Abulela, an Egyptian, advised me. So I didn't understand after he dropped us on top of a Camel and later conducted me to a tourist trap shop full of trinkets and took me to see boring and probably fake tombs… I noticed that he almost threw the five pounds on the floor, but decided to keep it after all and put it back in his pocket and turned his back to me and walked away in a different direction. I felt terribly embarrassed. He made me feel bad, then I walked to Abulela and commented, "I think he didn't like the tip." And he replied, "It's all right, two pounds is all right. Don't worry." And I said, "I gave him five pounds instead." Then Abulela's eyes were wide open, surprised at the amount.

However, I couldn't help but feeling sorry for the Bedouin polygamist and his way of life with an active wife in Egypt and spare one in England sending money to enlarge the villa so she can have more space and privacy as a proper British citizen—I hope—with their unusual arrangement. And I decided that if I ever see him again working freelance at the Giza plateau, I would give him another five pounds. As a matter of fact in another trip to that area I saw him again, and I walked very friendly toward him and he looked at me very offended and turned his back to me. I was perplexed and didn't give him anything. I never saw him again.

So Abulela drove us to John Van Deerlin's house in Cairo. Poor Abulela, he worked very hard trying to find his address. Obviously it was not easy to find, We drove around a lot on the complicated Cairo streets until he finally found the elusive villa.

I was glad to be in the house of an American. He explained many things about Egypt and their way of life, which was very helpful to us. However, there was one thing I could not do, and that was the fact that a servant was to be treated as such, if you want for them to respect you—and that included Abulela. That was why John did not invite him to enter his house with Jaums and me and told him to stay outside in the car. I thought I cannot do that, it's against my principles. I treat everybody as equal. For us Abulela was a very important part of the team. Without him we would not be able to visit the sites and take the time to explore without any rush. We like him very much. He was kind and always ready to get us wherever we wanted to go and with advice that was very helpful.

I was not upset at John for his advice, but we were not going to follow that with Abulela or anyone assigned to us by the government.

It was getting late and tomorrow we have an early schedule to follow. Abulela honked the horn of his car. And John said, "Don't worry, let him do it. He has to wait. His job is to wait for you."

"No, no John," I replied, "it's getting too late and tomorrow we will have an early schedule. We'll see you again." And we left.

In the car I apologized to Abulela for staying there so long. He was very surprised and at the same time very pleased about our different attitude. From them on we noticed that he respected us even more and went out of his way to please us. That evening we arrived at the "Steps of the Toilets" at midnight.

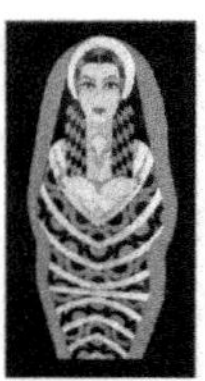

CHAPTER 13

THE PAINTED WOMAN

Next morning, after we came back from breakfast at the Steps of the Toilets' Cafeteria and while passing by the reception lady of the hotel, she called us over. I had the premonition that there was bad news that we could not stay one more day there… Jaums and I were petrified with the prospect of going to look for another hotel in Cairo. However, this morning it was to let us know that we can stay another day! "But tomorrow we have overbooking". Maybe I should write a song….

We went back to our room with all of Jaums's clothes everywhere in the process of drying after he was able to wash them in the bathtub. Yesterday he was able to wear one of his outfits. Today he will wear another one. He smells very fresh. At least it's not *eaux de Listerine*.

At 9:15 am sharp Madame and Abulela will be arriving to take us to the Art Institute to meet the artist Mamdouh Ammar, and later on, the Dean of the Faculty of Fine Arts at Helwan University, Professor Abbas H. Shohdy.

Madame, as usual, was wearing her delicious perfume, inundating the interior of the car with her distinctive fragrance. On our way I could not resist any longer and I took the indiscretion of asking her the name. She smiled and said that it was French—which I already suspected, but poor Madame, she was unable to pronounce it well and I didn't understand a word but I didn't have the heart to possibly embarrass her by asking her to say it again. But probably it was for the best because I don't think she would have been able to repeat it with more clarity. So, nevermind, and I politely smiled at her. It was a shame she appeared to be a very nice and proper lady. My idea was to buy her another bottle and give it to her as a thank you present because at the rate that she was using it, I don't think it was going to last very long, and it really suited her.

Mr. Amar and Professor Shohdy were very nice, receptive and appreciative of my work–I carried my portfolio with photos of my art almost everywhere we went. They insisted that no one in Egypt was doing the kind of three-dimensional paintings that I was doing inspired by the ancient sarcophagus lids. The rejection that I was receiving from the U.S. art critics and academia immediately came to mind. So opposite! These people were the real authorities in this ancient art and they valued my work. In general there was a very good chemistry between us and we talked for a very long time at Prof. Shohdy's office. Hanging on the wall of his office, I noticed the project drawing of an airport that was going to be constructed in the future. Its radar was going to be enclosed inside a sphere, just like at Dulles airport in Northern Virginia. I remembered that I had read that Dulles was having some troubles with the radar enclosure and I conveyed him that information. Then he said they decided to do some research to avoid the same problems as at Dulles. We also talked about the enormous potentials of the tourism industry for Egypt if it's truly developed. More hotels and restaurants were needed and good communications, especially a better phone system. The telephone system in Egypt–I was told–and was installed by the French and had been untouched all these years. I mentioned the superiority of the American phone system. Prof. Shohdy as well as the artist Mr. Ammar was very interested in this subject. The fact that their system was installed by the French explained the very French-sounding ""Allo?…Allo?…" we heard so often.

Before we ended our meeting, Prof. Shohdy invited me for dinner at his Heliopolis flat and Madame made the arrangements.

After leaving his office, Abulela dropped Madame at the Ministry of Higher Education and drove us to the Hilton, just across from the Cairo Museum. At the Hilton, Jaums and I went to their Italian restaurant. To my surprise, it had live entertainment, a young Egyptian man playing the accordion and singing familiar Italian songs while walking between tables. My mind traveled to my childhood and was singing along with him from our table–of course not with my full voice!

It was then when the famous American singer Eydie Gorme made her entrance in the restaurant!!! Well, she has to be Eydie Gorme! She has a lot of show business make up, I mean pounds of it! She looked like she used to look back in the sixties. I was glad she was looking like that again, because the last time I saw her on TV she wasn't looking that good any more, she was made up by her worst enemy. Well maybe she put that way in private, because, here in Cairo, who is going to identify Eydie Gorme?! But, what is she doing here?! She made a real star entrance! But I don't understand why she is not accompanied by her loving husband, the great singer Steve Lawrence! She entered this restaurant followed by an over-the-hill man dressed in a loud, cheap, plaid, polyester suit! In contrast, he was totally out of place since she was impeccably dressed, if not completely tasteful… But what she had on was undoubtedly carefully selected. It was an outfit that said "lunch after a rehearsal" all over it. Could she be in Cairo doing a show? Yeath, probably that's it! That's why she was carrying a makeup case… And judging by what she was already carrying on her face there will not be much left in the case! Better be, because here in Cairo where is she going to find replacements? Her hair was blue-black and shining like the chrome on a 1959 Cadillac…Its shape was round and big, framing perfectly her face in a shoulder length fashion. She was wearing a black skirt and a colorful printed blouse that can be seen from the far side of the Moon and it was unbuttoned "down under" showing an endless cleavage leading to the center of the Earth with two perfect reproductions of the Great Pyramids at 12 noon. To distract from her remarkable frontal architecture, she was wearing two massive hanging gold earrings and her neck encircled by massive gold, Jewish slave chains from before the Biblical Exodus. She was a living spectacle from a *Ringling Brothers* circus.

My eyes were fixed on her since the fraction of a second that she made her unexpected entrance into the Hilton Italian Restaurant. I forgot my childhood songs and everything else and dedicated myself to the contemplation of that one of a kind vision entering the scene in Cairo. I was so absorbed in her contemplation that I failed to mention that following the Polyester Man was an Unremarkable Youngster about 15 years old, faithfully walking behind that circus caravan. And she wanted to be unnoticed?! But, wait a moment! Let's go back to reality! She cannot be Eydie Gorme! Steve Lawrence, her husband was missing! Her entourage was nothing more than two lackluster companions. And they cannot be her staff, because they didn't look the types to be providing enhancement to a frontal, shining star. And, she herself was carrying her makeup case. They entered the restaurant and sat at a table near us, so I had to be discreet with my ocular analysis of that intriguing vision.

Her makeup face was glittering when the waiter arrived at her table—because undoubtedly **SHE** was the main event over her two, gray, supporting characters. By this time she noticed my impertinent observation through her sun glasses and her eyes were fixed on mine while she strongly grabbed her makeup case and put it on the table. That called my attention, but I then realized that she must have felt that I was undressing her with my X-Ray vision and at least she wanted to hold and protect the most precious property she has—and beyond any reasonable doubt—that she was carrying in that makeup case: her face!

My curiosity grew as I saw the impact she was having—she certainly stood out, although Cleopatra she was not. I wanted a closer look, so I got up with the excuse of going to the bathroom in order to pass by her table… She still looked like Eydie Gorme, but with all that extra makeup she cannot be. Even on stage Eydie Gorme would never! Maybe she is an impersonator, who knows. But I'm going to keep my distance just in case. I am a government guest and I cannot get involved in a scandal. So I'll view this as another Egyptian reproduction that I had been seeing since I arrived in this land of desert mirages. After my research, bottom line, this one didn't seem to be Egyptian or Cuban. She looked like she was American. I think I shall call her, whoever she is as: "The Painted Woman" for obvious reasons and her two following companions as: "The Polyester Man" and "The Unremarkable Young-ster." That decided, back at my table, I ate my lunch which I cannot remember what it was with the distraction of the furtive observations of "The Painted Woman."

After lunch we crossed the street to the Cairo Museum to meet with its director Madame Dea Aboughzy. She looks like a little lady who took me to see Queen Hatshepsut in a dream I had previously. Madame Aboughazy was very impressed with my work and she took us to the Chief Curator, Dr. El Nawawee, to get permission to photograph all the sarcophagus lids on display at the museum. They really were great with me in opposition to the treatment I received in art circles in America. Dr. El Nawawee, was nice and understood how important it was for me to see the real sarcophagi in person again. In reality I hadn't seen that many, except during a visit to the British Museum in 1975. When we finished at the museum we walked back to our "Steps of the Toilets" hotel to get ready for our next appointment.

At 6 pm Abulela picked us up to go to the studio of the artist Rushdi Iskandar that we had met at Dr. Morsi's office, the Minister of Higher Education and Chairman of the State Information Agency. Mr.

Iskandar was very nice and we had a very long conversation about his work and mine. Then we left and later I found that Mr. Iskandar wrote a very nice and lengthy article about my work in the Egyptian magazine *My Country*.

From Rushdi Iskandar's studio Abulela drove us to the rotating restaurant *The Tower of Cairo* for dinner. It was located on a tower by the Nile and had a magnificent view of the city. I always enjoy a beautiful view while eating and *The Tower of Cairo* was a promising place to be for dinner! I had already made reservations for 8 pm. Abulela dropped us at the door of the building and he will pick us up later on. We had a very shaky elevator ride to the round restaurant. To our surprise the place was as empty of live souls as a cemetery and it was not rotating. Probably it was too early we thought… The other parties will be arriving in a while. As magic, a waiter materialized out of thin air and ushered us to a table by the window. The view was breathtaking indeed! He gave us the menu and we ordered our meal. After we finished eating our salad, a party of two arrived and were seated at a table nearby. Still the restaurant was not rotating, I thought that other clients would be arriving soon. After the waiter brought the first course I asked him, "When are they going to start rotating the restaurant?

And he nervously replied, "Very soon Sir, very soon," and he left in a hurry. We started eating and some time later we were interrupted by what appeared like a mile-high earthquake of vibrations followed by the sharp shrilling sounds of a motor in need of heavy duty lubrication, followed by jerky tremors on and off. By that time I completely repented of my question to the waiter about the rotation of the restaurant. How can we eat with this jerkiness going on? I thought. It seems to me that the machine that makes the restaurant rotate hasn't been used since the reign of Pharaoh Seti. And the worst of all is that it doesn't seem to be moving by a motor but by animals or human power! I immediately visualized those strange contraptions I had seen by the Nile to lift water, propelled endlessly by cows circling around and around–sometimes by people pedaling for water irrigation…

It was an unforgettable experience, and after all, the maximum customers they had while we were there was six people. Obviously *Cairo-ans* knew something we didn't. Don't start rotating until the customers have their dinners, hah! We paid and left the place in a hurry, got in Abulela's car and felt relieved to stand on solid ground again–well, we were getting used to Cairo's driving style.

Next morning on our way out of the "Steps of the Toilets" hotel they called us from the reception to give us notice that we could stay one more day. I never understood why the hotel was booked the first day we were taken there and now everyday they let us stay one more day… I guess there is no use trying to figure it out. We just have to live one day at a time. It's as inexplicable as the rotation of *The Tower of Cairo* or the existence of "The Painted Woman." [Play the "Tomorrow we have overbooking" jingle here.]

Punctually, Abulela arrived with the Director of Delegations Department, Abdessalam Diab, at 9:30 am, to take us for a "non-tourist" visit to the pyramids of Giza, Sakara and Memphis. I was looking forward to this!

I entered the Great Pyramid of Cheops for the first time in my life! After having entered so many times in dreams, I had to remind myself that this time it's real. That was an emotional experience and I was shaking all over. I could hardly talk. I will never forget that experience which made me an addict. I was going to be inside this pyramid three more times. The last time, I stayed inside for one hour and lay down inside the open sarcophagus in the King's Chamber!

However, in this first visit with Mr. Diab I was kind of distracted because inside was crowded with elderly German tourists, many little, overweight, old ladies with their short, tightly curled gray hair, wearing sandals and white, anemic bobby socks! The most uninspiring beings you can imagine to encounter in such awe inspiring ancient monuments. It was not easy to concentrate being in such tight quarters with this noisy/talkative, anachronically misplaced corps. Hopefully, the power of this great pyramid is greater than theirs. In spite of this negative atmosphere around, it was almost a religious experience if you cover your ears and close your eyes. The penetration to the King's Chamber throughout the Great Gallery was very inclined. Inside were a lot of particles of dust generated by the German sandals, so the air was heavy. I just wondered how those elderlies were going to manage to continue climbing to the top. To my surprise they all got there alive and were able to crawl through the low entrance into the King's Chamber. At the end of the line, Jaums, Mr. Diab and I entered but I wanted to be there until the last of those "EldersHostel" got the hell out of the King's Chamber so I could have some peace and tranquility for a few minutes inside that impressive chamber with its commanding, high, triangular ceiling.

Once the distractions were gone I could appreciated the simplicity and elegance of the black granite walls—not a single carving and an simple, empty, black, open sarcophagus—if in fact that's what it was—resting on the floor in the middle of the back narrow wall of huge blocks, perfectly fitted together. It was something out of this world. I thought that it might have been built by something out of this world too… I walked to the sarcophagus I looked inside… It looks different from my dream. It was empty. *Dolores del Rio* was not inside of it. Not even *Carmelita Pope*!

I heard Mr. Diab's voice announce that we must leave because the next tour will be coming in about 10 minutes. So we left the King's Chamber through the small access entrance in the corner and initiated our descent through the also impressive Great Gallery with a very high ceiling. While descending I thought that perhaps if there was a body inside the sarcophagus in the remote past, it must have been a very small one. But the most unusual thought that came into my mind was that the sarcophagus was a place for transferring our bodies, or the bodies of the ones who built that pyramidal temple and their souls to their place of origin in the universe. Well, so much for those theories, maybe in the future this mystery will be solved. We got to the entrance and exit of the Great Pyramid to face the line of more Germans and their wives tourists in line to enter the pyramid. We walked around them and descended to the ground.

From the base of the pyramid Mr. Diab showed us the Valley Temple, two of the noble tombs–much better than what the Bedouin showed us before and walked us to the mythical and impressive Sphinx. I had some fantasies about the Sphinx based on my previous dreams, but unfortunately, we were not able to get very close to it so I could discover the hidden entrance to its interior with the correct information about who the builders were and the historic period of its construction, according to my dreams. But now, the reason we couldn't get very close–preventing me from the DISCOVERY OF THE CENTURY in 1978, was because a scientific team was probing with its lasers for hidden chambers beneath. If they would have known that I was coming, they would have known to put their lasers aside and let me approach the Sphinx, as in my dreams. And then, they would find the chambers! Well, it was their loss…

After we left the Giza plateau, we got in Abulela's car to drive to the Step Pyramid of Sakara and the temples around it. Also there we visited Unis' Pyramid. This one undoubtedly was built by the ancient Egyptians. It was the opposite of the Great Pyramid of Cheops. Everything inside was covered with carved hieroglyphic writings. It was very Egyptian indeed! From there, we went to visit the site of the old capital of Egypt, Memphis. There were no statues of Elvis anywhere, however, in the small Ramses museum, we saw a magnificent statue, lying down on its back, of the legendary pharaoh in a museum constructed around the statue with a balcony all around so you could observe all the details of the impressive carvings. As I remember, the museum was built to pre-serve and protect the sculpture from the elements and was built around the place where it was unearthed.

After this extraordinary excursion today with Mr. Diab, we left for Cairo. I was able to see everything up close and in person, to study these amazing things for the enhancement of my imagination. Today was indeed a productive and instructive day, just the way it should be, not like the tourist-trap camel ride of last Monday evening. Meanwhile, the next day was the television interview with Dr. Morsi. And I thought to ask Mr. Diab,

"Did Madame tell you about the TV show I'm supposed to do tomorrow?"

"Oh yes yes," he responded, "But she hasn't heard from Dr. Morsi."

"Did she have anything scheduled for tomorrow?" I inquired.

He said, "Because of the pending TV show, she did not plan any-thing in particular. We cannot send you outside Cairo yet because of the same reason. We need to wait until tomorrow to see if we hear from Dr. Morsi…"

Well–I thought–tomorrow is Thursday, and whatever it is, I'll find out tomorrow.

We arrived at the Steps of the Toilets at about four in the afternoon. We climbed the spectacularly noticeable regal steps one more time–for-tunately no one knew who we were in Cairo, except the government officials involved in our visit. We went directly to the restaurant for a late "lunchette." After that we went to our room, still filled with Jaums' clothes here and there. I wondered what the ladies of room service were thinking about that… After that Jaums complained of feeling sick to his stomach…

In the evening however he was better so we went to the Sheraton, which fortunately, like the Hilton, was within walking distance of our refuge at the Steps of the Toilets. So as we made ourselves inconspicuous in our American refuge to avoid eating something that upset our stomachs. And guess who was there having dinner "in the flesh"?! None other than "The Painted Woman!!!" After our first encounter at the Hilton I thought that we were not going to see her again! Small world! As before she was impeccably dressed, coiffed and made up for a great evening to remember. She had a long black chiffon gown with a very low cut front. You could clearly see much of her more than generous and gravity-defying breasts, pumping out from under her jet black necklace. She seemed to recognize me and wasn't pleased to see me. I guess she noticed since our first silent encounter that I noticed her again and she strongly grabbed her priceless makeup case and placed it on a corner of her table. What was she thinking, that I'm going to steal it?! That would be like stealing her face! Imagine if somebody stole her makeup case! Well, that may be a good idea… Without it she would not be able to come out at all! It was the secret of her attractive face…*The Face in a Case* almost the title of a mystery movie!

The Painted Woman was already at the restaurant when we arrived, therefore she left before we finished our meal, passing by my table pretending that she didn't notice me with her face up, very proud of who she was, followed by The Polyester Man and The Unremarkable Youngster. Good bye Painted Woman–knowing we wouldn't see her again, these were once in a lifetime and second in a lifetime opportunities. What a shame since she provided so much appreciated entertainment since our room didn't have a TV. I wondered if they took the wrong flight and they ended up in Cairo, because they didn't look like they would be interested in ancient Egyptian art.

Next morning, we received an early phone call from Madame telling us that Abulela was on his way to pick us up at 9:30 am to take us to the Ministry of Higher Education. So we rushed to get ready very fast, had a Continental Breakfast. Passing by the reception on the way, the lady called us, giving us the good news that we can stay one more day. Whoopee! So we happily romped down the Steps of the Toilets to the street level just as Abulela arrived!

At his office, Mr. Diab was waiting for us while Indira Gandhi was holding the phone repeating the eternal "Allo…Allo…Allo."

Mr. Diab invited us to sit and explained, "Your TV show, scheduled for today, is being postponed for one week."

"OK.," I said, "that's fine with me.

He explained, " That's why we decided to send you out of Cairo now." Opening the middle drawer from his desk, he handed me an envelope and said, "Inside you will find the EgyptAir tickets for Luxor, Aswan and Abu Simbel and your tickets to return to Cairo. You will depart next Saturday. In each of the cities you will be visiting, a government official with a car will be waiting for you at the airport. He will be taking you to the hotels that have been already reserved for you. They will take care of all the excursions to the temples, monuments and archeological sites."

Mr. Diab opened another drawer and gave me a letter written in Arabic and he explained, "This is an official government letter of introduction that you should show at each destination point and carry always with you all the time in case a problem arises. But everything has been arranged and organized, so I don't foresee any problems…You will be back in Cairo with plenty of time for your TV show. So don't worry and enjoy your trip."

Wow! Imagine! I'm sure not even the Painted Woman had such opportunities.

From Mr Diab, the Director of the Delegation Department's office, Abulela drove us to the Cairo Museum, where I was to meet with Dr. Ibrahim El Nawawee, the Chief Curator to authorize me to photograph the sarcophagus lids the next day, Friday. We entered the museum through the staff door on our way to Dr. El Nawawee's office. But I couldn't help noticing that something unusual was going on, on the way to his office. First I thought that two men were kidding around… But then I realized that they were getting more physical than Olivia Newton-John. It looked like a serious fight, a hostile encounter staged like I had seen in thirties and forties serials I had seen when I was little on TV in my country town. I never thought that I would witness something as realistic in person! And the most amazing thing was that while other people were walking by, they were acting like nothing was going on! Since I was a foreign guest I didn't want to get involved either. Well—I thought—probably that kind of battle between those two individuals was a frequent occurrence. So I acted as if nothing was happening and said, "Excuse me gentleman," and passed by them as the other Egyptian employees had done… "When in Rome do as the Romans do."

Inside his office , I didn't make any comments about the pugilistic exhibition I just watched out in the hallway. Dr. El Nawawee, as nice and diligent as usual, made everything possible for the next day of an exciting sarcophagus photo session. He appointed one of his curators to go with me through the museum in order for me not to miss a single one. So everything was set. I seriously think that I would never be accompanied like that in any important museum in the U.S.!

From the Cairo Museum Jaums and I crossed the street to the Hilton cafeteria for lunch. White entering the lobby we had the unexpected surprise of The Painted Woman, followed by her loyal entourage, The Polyester Man and The Unremarkable Youngster. I figured that the first was her husband and the second probably her son! She hesitated for a fraction of a second as she recognized us. I tried this time not to pay her any attention. But I must confess that it was very difficult to resist and not to look at that vision! She looked ravishing and so very well coiffed. I was sure if she fell her hair would prevent her made-up face from touching the ground. Her attention-getting **BRIGHT**—to put it mildly—turquoise afternoon safari outfit appeared tighter than her corset which induced the appearance of the waist of a "15 year old", safely secured by a wide leopard belt. I simply do not know how she can swallow any food! All this impertinent squeezing made her two, anatomical, hot air balloons more inflated than ever, higher than The Tower of Cairo! I never noticed her shoes before because my attention could go no lower than her torso. But this time I decided to peek-a-boo lower and noticed her disco slides with the highest-possible metallic gold heels I had ever witnessed. As usual, of course, she was clutching her inseparable makeup case, a must whatever she goes! I wondered what her name could be… Probably something flashing, like a female character in Sean Connery's James Bond movie *Goldfinger* named "Pussy Galore."

After that anatomically impossible and distracting pre-lunch shock, Abulela picked us up to take us to the studio of the well-known Egyptian artist, Leila Izzet. At least a return to a normal artist! Her residence was located in a very nice and modern area of Cairo with well laid out streets but it wasn't easy for Abulela to find her address. He drove around for quite some time. But I didn't mind, since the area reminded me of an area called *Nuevo Vedado* in La Habana that had a quite array of modern houses. After Abulela stopped in different places for directions, he was able to find her modern villa. As we got out of the car, she immediately opened the door of the fence surrounding her home. I apologized for being late. She was a young woman, dressed in bluejeans and a blue shirt with short, frosted ash blonde hair. She looked very much like an American, but she was Egyptian. She was very nice and friendly and excused herself for not letting us in her villa because it was in the process of remodeling. However we walked from her villa to her studio. Inside it was a modern, bright and spacious place—I thought that she must have some money in order to have such a huge studio. In it she had an enormous collection of her works. Her work was very interesting. I viewed all of it and thought that it would be suitable for the gallery in Washington, D.C. where I was acting as Curator. I talked to her about a possible show there in the future. She was a very pleasant person to be around and I had a good time talking to her. I felt very embarrassed because she spoke better English than I did. After some time we left her studio and Abulela drove us to the Sheraton for us to exchange money and to confirm our Saturday flight to Luxor. From there he took us back to our Steps of the Toilets' hotel to rest and get ready for the evening appointment at six.

Abulela picked us up on time. With him in the car was Mr. Hasan El Sayet, who was an official from the Delegations Department of the Ministry of Higher Education. The reason why he was coming was so I could officially be introduced to the CBS correspondent in Cairo, Mr. Ezz El Din Shawkat, at the leading Egyptian newspaper *Al-Ahram*. In Mr. Shawkat's office, after we were introduced, Mr. El Sayed left and we talked about me and my work. Mr. Shawkat was very charming and relaxed. We also talked about our favorite Egyptian sites. He highly recommended that I not miss the Isis Temple at Philae island, his real favorite. "It's a must!" he enthusiastically said. I made a note of it and a while later he finished his interview and we left. From the *Al-Ahram* newspaper office, Abulela drove us to the Sheraton for dinner.

Later while still in Egypt, I found that the newspaper *Al-Ahram* ran on its front page his article about my work and visit to Egypt with a photograph of two of my Egyptian Sculptured Paintings. That was very good indeed and definitely more than any American newspaper or publication ever did about my work!

At the Sheraton, Jaums and I decided to eat at the lobby coffee shop whose windows overlooked the Nile. We ordered Italian food and we enjoyed the magnificent view. As we were also peacefully enjoying our food, we received the unexpected and surprising visit, followed by the faithfully following entourage of The Polyester Man and The Unremarkable Youngster of none other than The Painted Woman, moving and acting like The Queen of the Nile firmly grabbing in her ivory hand her inseparable makeup case as if it was a defibrillator in case of emergency! I cannot deny that she looks gorgeous entering the scene! She was like a divinity sent from Heaven or Hell. She was wearing a very tight "damnation red" dress that didn't leave anything to the imagination. I frankly don't understand how she can walk and much less sit in a coffee shop with that dress! Her provocative low cut "*decote*" shamely exposed her superhighway cleavage in the middle of dual Himalayan mountains. If her other fixtures were more than enough; she was wearing a necklace and long dangling earrings with diamonds and rubies and matching high heels also in "damnation red". It was obvious that when she saw us and looked exasperated by my presence and she may even suspect that I am following her around. Well, I can think the same about her appearances and timing. But certainly she was improperly dressed for a Coffee Shop! But she continues working very hard to be noticed in Cairo. Unfortunately this time she chose to walk farther from our table and I couldn't continue analyzing this attention seeking, mysterious woman followed by her two mechanically and expressionless supporters. I hope I don't see her again because writing and describing her is very time consuming and distracting from the main purpose of this fantastic trip…

Next morning at 9 o'clock, Abulela took us to Giza to see the smaller Mycerinus pyramid and also to visit the experimental one being built by the Japanese for a TV documentary. I had the idea in my mind that they were building a real pyramid, but what I encountered was a pitiful little thing, barely as high as a two story house! And their construction time window was running out. Actually what they wanted to do, was to build a pyramid following the accepted theoretical methods of the Egyptologists, Archaeologists and Historians…Well, they tried… But they met with failure and in the end and they used a modern crane in order to lift some of the much smaller stones in comparison with the huge ones used at the Cheops' pyramid leaving the Cheops pyramid construction still puzzling.

There I was introduced to the director of the TV show, Mr. Takayoshi Nato, and the director of the project, Mr. Sakuji Yoshimura from the Waseda University in Japan. Both were very helpful and willing to express their amazement about how such a task was undertaken in ancient times. It's a shame that their documentary may never be shown on American TV! After I was allowed to inspect and photograph their unfinished small pyramid, we went to visit Chephren's pyramid, a real Egyptian one.

From the Giza plateau, Abulela drove us back to Cairo and to the Hilton for lunch. I must explain why we ate at these two American hotels. A friend who had been in Egypt told us about "exotic" meats and other foods served in Egyptian restaurants and I don't have the appetite for unusual "exquisite specialties" of any cuisine. Barf! Therefore I stayed safe and secure with good ole American or Italian standards with familiar names and familiar ingredients. I am not adventurous where food is concerned, even though, or maybe because, I don't cook and I don't want to learn. So now you know.

Fortunately The Painted Woman, The Polyester Man and The Unremarkable Youngster were nowhere to be seen, so I could eat in peace. Today was my last day in Cairo before departing tomorrow for Luxor, Aswan and Abu Simbel, so a quiet lunch was a good thing.

After lunch, we walked from the Hilton to the Cairo Museum to meet the Curator Mrs. Shouhair El Sawy, who Dr. Nawawee recommended to guide me to take photographs of all the sarcophagi on display. Inside the museum flash was not allowed and it was very dark with the non-functioning lights and sand covered skylights, so focusing the Leica that my uncle, Rene in New Orleans, gave me, was difficult. We needed something to see to be able to focus, so Jaums would light a match in front of each sarcophagus, I'd focus on the match, he would move away and I would take the picture. It was not an easy task and don't tell anyone that we were lighting matches in the Cairo Museum.

We worked the rest of the afternoon there. It was very important for me to have photos of the sarcophagi since I based my paintings on them. Now I'll be able to see all the details painted on them. This was an unique opportunity!

Before returning to our Steps of the Toilets hotel, we went to the Hilton for dinner. And fortunately we didn't encounter The Painted Woman again. I began to worry that she lost her makeup case and couldn't face the world. Well it removes a lot of distraction for me trying to realistically describe the indescribable. Maybe I'll not be able to see again. Arrivederci!

Saturday morning at 6:15 am Abulela dropped us at Cairo airport, which was already extremely crowded, confusing and noisy like an Egyptian bazaar at midday. After a lot of walking back and forth, here and there, we finally found the right counter. We checked our luggage directly to Luxor and went to the departure gate.

When we arrived at the waiting room of our departure gate, it was already crowded. All the little old German ladies with their elderly German husbands we suffered with days before during our excursion to the Great Pyramid of Cheops, were already sitting there with their tight, little permanent-ed curls, their colorful dresses, cardigans resting on their shoulders, unshaved legs and old ladies sandals and white Bobby socks—mementos from their 1948 haydays and also grabbing with the same strength as The Painted Woman—their menacing, killer handbags which we later found out were their lethal offensive weapons of mass destruction upon entering an overbooked Egyptian airliner.

But to my astounding surprise, in the middle of that collection of very dried Germanic flowers of a bygone era there was a fresh, live sunflower, full of colors and irradiating make-believe beauty, none other than The Painted Woman, in the flesh! What an unexpected surprise in the middle of so much ugliness! And sitting beside that glorious traveling enigmatic princess were her two loyal companions, protecting and escorting her, The Polyester Man and The Unremarkable Youngster. She looks like the sun, the moon and the stars in the middle of so many ugly meteorites with menacing handbags!

There were so many people sitting and standing that she could not see me and I stayed behind a column to be able to observe her without being detected by her or her entourage.

She had vibrant lilac traveling pants and a pale lilac lace blouse, with white boots and white shoulder strapped bag, and a rather widely rimmed hat decorated with lilac silk flowers shading the entire waiting room. She had white and gold jewelry everywhere. Her makeup case luckily was resting on her legs and of course big sunglasses. She was perfectly equipped for a visit to an archeological excavation in The Valley of the Kings across the Nile from Luxor! At the moment that I was pushed by the passing of a very round German "Amazon," I was physically exposed and I noticed that The Painted Woman saw me and promptly turned her face away from me and said something to The Polyester Man…She really hates me, I thought. Or fears me. Maybe she thought that I was trying to undress her with my eyes–which is not far from reality but because of all the items that she always had on it is quite impossible to see inside, except when she had her prodigious pectorals exposed to the elements. In this case, her lace blouse was not transparent enough to view the 8th and 9th wonders of the world. So it was my loss. And I carefully squeezed back into my hiding place in a *Houdini* disappearing act.

After a while a seat was available just across from her, so I almost ran to it. She looked kind or nervous about it and kept talking all the time to The Polyester Man and The Unremarkable Youngster in order to avoid my lacerating eyes. I realized that The Polyester Man must be her husband and probably The Unremarkable Youngster her son. That may explain why both of them have such gray personalities. She didn't want any competition–But who can compete with such attention getting luminary?! Well, undoubtedly we will be going to the same places at the same time. I'll keep seeing her, and perhaps, who knows, we will finally meet on a cordial occasion… Should I say, "I never noticed you before…"

Later, The Unremarkable Youngster got up and left. I was sure he went to the bathroom because when he came back his shirt was neatly tucked inside his gray pants. I thought of The Painted Woman that her bathroom at home must be all in pink with a refreshing pink bidet! It just has to be: as much a must as her traveling makeup case.

About 8:15 am they called our flight and rapidly everybody got up and got ready for the upcoming battle. However, The Painted Woman miraculously managed to be the first to be up and ready! She really had that undefinable star quality.

Then, as the line was forming in front of the gate, somehow she was the first in it too. The guards at the exit gate were going to conduct a second frisk. I wanted to be as close as possible to see her reaction when the guards were passing their electronic devices around her curvaceous body. But I was prevented by the pushing pandemonium around me not only from the Egyptians–apparently accustomed to it in order to get on the often overbooked flights, there were the fast-learners tightly curled gray haired little old German Amazon ladies with their lethal handbags and wrinkled, mortal elbows opening their advancement to the gate. Actually it was survival of the fittest. And this "Amazon" reincarnated menace was engaged in mortal combat for a seat! So, do not get in their way! Their obeying husbands, nearly invisible, just followed dutifully behind. And on this historic battle ground was when I lost sight of The Painted Woman and her two faithful companions. Therefore I couldn't witness her official frisking! The maddening crowd was between us, as her inevitable first class seat awaited.

The ones frisked went outside the terminal and boarded the bus, also crowded-to-the-rim. No doubt her weapon, the constant makeup case, was superior to the tightly curled's elbows thus, putting The Painted Woman on that first bus. Jaums and I were able to squeeze into the second bus before it closed its doors on our behinds. At least the bus had closed windows, thus preventing persistants from climbing in, SOP for the buses on Cairo streets. There were also more buses in line to pick up more passengers. This must be a big plane. But apparently the first bus leading the caravan didn't know the destination, because we kept driving back and forth across the tarmac and stopping in front of planes here and there, while the bus driver carried on a conversations with the pilots until we arrived at the destination planes but, after chatting for a few minutes with the pilot, we drove on as it was the wrong plane. The same scene was repeated until he finally got the right one! We hoped.

In front of a new European very wide and large plane, we got out of the bus we were asked to walk toward the battery of suitcases piled all over the tarmac beside the huge airplane and the same scene of personally identifying the suitcases standing on the hot tarmac was faithfully repeated before they were loaded into the plane cargo area. So we walked around that enormous disarray of luggage to positively identify each piece. I don't know how we managed in the middle of disorganization and so many people to identify ours and the porters started loading them, but in the end we felt secure they were on our flight.

Before each one of us was allowed to board the plane, we had to be checked with another electronic security device. Some sort of a so-called "line" was formed and after a person was OKed, he or she started running like crazy to climb the stairs and get on the plane in order to get a seat! Jaums and I were the last of the "line" to get in. And were able to find a seat because the cabin was huge. Even a window seat!

I found out from one of the stewardesses that this airplane model was not in use in the U.S. yet! I was very apprehensive about flying in an almost experimental airplane. But what could I do after the ordeal

I had been living in the airport this morning and then getting on this plane?! The stewardess assured me that the pilots flying this plane this morning were a Belgian crew, who were teaching the Egyptians pilots how to operate it. Was I more relieved now…? So, I sat and waited for my fate. It was getting very hot inside the plane. The stewardesses were opening the doors for fresh air. Our seats were just beside one of the doors and I could see one of the huge motors. I heard one of the engines being turned on and seconds later dying out. This operation was repeated many times with the same results. It seems obvious to me that they couldn't start the hesitating engine. Probably was an indication of the Egyptian god Osiris not to fly in that plane… The stewardess was standing at the door in silence looking out at the attempts of starting the engine, smiling nervously… I never witnessed that at any previous fights, especially doing so with the airplane doors open!

The time was passing by and it was getting hotter and hotter inside the cabin under the Egyptian sun, and the engines sounded more like an overflowing automobile motor. The nervously smiling stewardesses were now walking down the aisles, trying to calm the impatient passengers. Also, using the restrooms wasn't allowed.

Later on, the captain announced that the fight was being canceled and ordered the passengers to evacuate the airplane, which everybody GLADLY did in a surprisingly orderly way! Before exiting I asked the stewardess if that new airplane was disabled and she replied that the problem was that they realized the Luxor airport didn't have the powerful generator required to start the motors of this new plane. So, once landed it wouldn't be able to take off.

We exited and assembled on the tarmac under the scorching sun and waited for the buses to take us back to the terminal. One of the elderly European gentlemen–probably one of the German husbands of one of the lethal, elderly German ladies– apparently in pain and unable to hold it any longer, walked a few feet from the crowd, unzipped and began urinating on the tarmac in front of the eyes of the scandalized ladies. Eventually the buses arrived and took us back to the same exit gate. We heard the announcement that we will be flying to Luxor on a special flight that was being prepared and they will let us know later on when it will be ready. Then the officials came and ushered us to the coffee shop to get something to eat.

There I looked for the sight of The Painted Woman, but she was not to be seen! But instead I noticed that Judy Collins, or someone looking very much like her, was sitting alone in a booth. I looked at her and she looked at me "across the crowded room" and she smiled.–It was like love at first sight!–And the chemistry touched Jaums also. We both walked to her and asked if we could sit. And she immediately said, "Yes."

And we engaged in a fascinating conversation with that lovely, lonely traveler. Her real name was Nancy. She was Operation Director of a California based travel agency. She was traveling through Egypt now to make contacts and organize a travel package for her agency. The idea was an unusual and exotic camel–my favorite animal!–caravan trip throughout Egypt. With my little experience I already had with a camel, I was not thrilled with the idea. But anyway, I thought it was a romantic idea. And Nancy was a very interesting person and most charming.

We talked as if we had known each other for years. Somehow we felt that we had met previously in time in another existence. Because of the conversation with her, the long tedious waiting in the airport became very pleasant. The time flew by as we got more acquainted... Suddenly, we were interrupted by the announcement that our flight was ready to board. Fortunately, Nancy was going on the same flight, so we have the chance to continue our friendship.

Then we got up and began to walk in the direction of our gate. There we sat together and continued our conversation until the buses arrived. After the buses were there we were called to board then to form a line with the usual pandemonium of the frisk session before leaving the gate. Apparently the majority of the travelers were even more impatient now and we were separated from Nancy by some sort of wild stampede of desperate people running toward the exit gate. Finally Jaums and I got into a bus for the "take 2" of that odyssey to Luxor. Later, the caravan departed, driving through the tarmac from plane to plane like a disoriented butterfly until the right airplane was found!

Again we went through the suitcase identification routine before they were boarded inside the cargo area and the final frisk before allowed inside the plane. The crowd of passengers was getting very tired and irritable, behaving like vicious beasts, pushing each other in order to get in first and to secure a seat on this obviously smaller plane. Will everyone fit? In all this melee we couldn't see Nancy at all. But I finally did see The Painted Woman making her entrance as the first traveler in the airplane. My only explanation was her disarming look! Who would dare to say "no" to her? Very tight behind her was The Polyester Man and The Unremarkable Youngster. But I couldn't see Nancy.

After being squeezed like oranges we survived the pointy elbows, the lethal handbags and the treacherous attacks of the elderly German ladies and out of breath, we finally managed to enter the airplane alive. Then I saw Nancy in the distance but we couldn't sit with her because the other seats around her were taken.

Then the stewardess came out and announced that due to the short notice in getting the airplane ready for this unexpected trip, they didn't have any water aboard or any kind of drinks or food to offer and no one could use the bathrooms during the trip and that we should remain seated during the whole flight. I immediately imagined the compromised prostates of the elderly German passengers urinating from their seats and the urine running down the halls and floors of the airplane. So I advised Jaums to keep his feet up off the floor just in case… This is going to be an interesting experience and a promising adventure.

Finally about 12:30 pm (six hours and 10 minutes after arriving at Cairo airport in the morning) our flight lifted off! Fortunately one hour later our flight arrived in Luxor!!!

The person waiting for Nancy was at the airport and she had to leave in a hurry. Before leaving she said to me, "Don't worry, Luxor is a small town, I will find you."

But the person who was supposed to wait for me wasn't there. So, we sat and waited. Meanwhile, everybody who came with us in the flight, left the small airport which reminded me of the ones in 1940's movies. Later on, a taxi arrived at the entrance of the only terminal. The driver came out and called my name. I got up and walked toward him, introduced myself and Jaums and showed him my presentation letter from the Ministry of Higher Education. The driver apologized, because he was not the right person to be waiting for me. He said that I will be meeting Mohamed Abd El Dayen right away in Luxor. So, we got into the taxi without our suitcases, which for some unknown reason got mixed up with the incoming tour and were shipped with them out of the airport to who knows where… So, we left without our belongings on our *Road to Luxor* without Bob Hope and Dorothy Lamour…

CHAPTER 14

THE KILLER FLIES OF LUXOR

It was around 2 pm and Jaums and I were tired, hungry and thirsty when the taxi stopped in front of a small store in Luxor. I recognized that it was the same store where a terrible murder scene took place in the film *Sphinx*. Our taxi driver said, "Stay, I have to go in," just like in the Robert De Niro film *Taxi Driver* (1976). And he left us inside the taxi and went inside that store. As in the film, the situation was confusing and tense. I sensed something wrong in the air besides the flies buzzing around. There was a fly trying to get inside the taxi, fortunately all the windows were up, so he or she finally gave up and landed on my window glass. At that moment I swear that he or she was looking at me with not the best intentions in its multiple eyes, like in the last scene of the film *The Fly*, that so strongly impressed me as a child in the darkness of a movie house in my country town. Certainly since we entered the town of Luxor I noticed that there were many flies around. Maybe because there were many coaches pulled by horses as taxis like in the city where I was born in Cuba. Could this be an omen?

After some time our taxi driver returned saying, "Mohamed El Dayen is not available now. He said to tell you that he had to leave in a hurry for Cairo." That sounded odd! Then, a young man came out from the same shop walking up to our taxi and after I rolled the window down a tad he said, "Mohamed El Dayen did not have time to get you a hotel." Oh no, again, I thought! And he added, "But I will ride with you in the taxi to look for a hotel." And I said, "Come in, let's go." And wandering we went through the troublesome flies.

I saw the famous Winter Palace down the boulevard by the Nile and asked to be taken there with the hope of finding a room. Finally there, and after the typical long conversations as in Cairo on our first hotel hunt, the conclusion was unanimously reached that no room was available. I was disappointed, because it would have been marvelous to stay in the historic hotel of *Death on the Nile* (1979), almost one year before they made the movie. With my broken heart, we walked among the flies to the nearby Savoy Hotel. From the outside it looked old but interesting. The lobby looked like a set from a 1930 movie. I could visualize *Joan Crawford* coming down the stairs dancing as in the movie *Untamed* (1929). And at this hotel also the ritualistic conversation took place and afterward it was agreed that there was a room for us! Whoopie! However, at that precise instant, the same *Vincent Price* fly landed on my forehead, making me think twice before blindingly taking the room. So, I said, "I would like to see the room first."

That was not a problem with them and an uniformed bellboy proudly took us to see the room. He took us from the lobby through the main entrance facing the boulevard across from the Nile and went on the sidewalk around the block to a different building in the rear, which was infested by more flies than on the main boulevard. Actually that rear building looked like the old stables of the hotel's past glories. With a huge key, the bellboy opened the door of our room to be or not to be…It was a dark, sad, falling–apart dreadful room with two narrow concave beds and what appeared to be grass mattresses and a pitiful would–be bathroom facility. That was the end of the Savoy!

Our discouraging hunt for a decent hotel finally took us to the French owned newer hotel, ETAP. This was a modern, clean and nicely decorated hotel. I was very pleased with the first impression and I was deeply praying to the Egyptian God Trinity of Osiris, Isis and Horus for a vacancy… After the usual long conversation, the young man that accompanied us on this mission said, "I'll see you tomorrow morning at 9 o'clock at the tourism office to organize your plan of visit." So that was an indication that we got a room at the ETAP! He turned around and left. We were jubilant to have a nice place to stay!

Then the bellboy escorted us to the room. I was eager to get there and take a long bath after such a long and difficult day. The room was fantastic, new, modern, clean, with a big, complete and immaculate bathroom, flat beds and also a balcony. And what a view! Serene, peaceful, reassuring… But at the same time an eerie feeling invaded me while I was on the balcony. The view I was seeing for the first time seemed very familiar. I was somehow very much acquainted with the surroundings. I had been in this place before! And to my amazement, I was completely convinced that a point in the distance, much farther than the other side of the Nile, and no bigger than a pinhead, was The Temple of Queen Hatshepsut… After a few minutes of silent contemplation from the balcony, I had tears in my eyes. The Nile was across the boulevard from the balcony and The Valley of The Kings. What a relief and piece of mind. And I went inside the ample room and rested on the comfortable bed… I was happy to be there.

Later, I took a bath and we went out to the main boulevard by the Nile—filled with flies enjoying the horse manure—looking for the restaurant that the hotel bellboy recommended for lunch since the hotel's restaurant was not serving any meals now.

Chez Farouk, which was its name, was a picturesque restaurant, night club, discotheque and what have you. It has a square dancing platform over its dirt floor. Actually, I didn't have an exactly conventional roof, instead it consisted of layers of matchstick mats. Well, after all, a solid roof wasn't that important in rainless Luxor.

Since we arrived at Chez Farouk at the wrong time for lunch, the place was deserted, except for the native flies freely flying around.

I saw a lady in the back who seemed to belong to the place and asked her if they could serve us a meal. And she immediately said, "Yes," and ushered us to a table by a row of windows facing the Nile. The view of the other side of the river, which was the location of The Valley of The Kings and Queen Hatshepsut temples, was magnificent. Soon after the lady brought us the Menu, which consisted of Egyptian plates we didn't know anything about. So we ended up ordering the only thing we were able to identify, "Shish Kabobs…" What else…?! This was going to be our first contact with a typical Egyptian restaurant since we have been eating in American hotels in Cairo. Jaums was very apprehensive about the food and his stomach. But what are we going to do…? We were hungry and there was no McDonalds around for thousands of miles! Well, Doris Day, "Que sera, sera. Whatever will be, will be…"

The lady, who said she was the owner of that multi-purpose business, brought our meal and it was delicious. While eating—to my delight since I love dogs—there was a puppy dog roaming in the restaurant. That was real freedom! Since I came to the U.S. I have always hated the fact that dogs are not allowed in most places, even in rental apartments or houses. I think that dog and pet discrimination is as hideous as discrimination against race and minorities. So, I called the puppy under our table and fed him our leftover Shish Kabobs before the flies got them.

After our late lunch, we walked among the impertinent flies back to the hotel to find that our suitcases were still at large and they may have been lost. That was bad news that I refused to accept. But fortunately we stopped on the way and bought gallabeahs as well as typical head scarves to wrap around our heads like the Egyptians. However, I decided to go to the EgyptAir office at the Winter Palace Hotel and talked to the Manager for him to locate our luggage. He was a very kind man and immediately got some of his people to check with all the tours in

Luxor. Finally by 7 pm that evening our two suitcases were found in two different hotels in Luxor and brought to us. So we changed clothes in his office and he took us in his VW bus to the Luxor Museum where Jaums and I spent the rest of that evening.

Next morning at 9 o'clock we were at the tourism office. The young man of the day before was not there yet, but the two ladies who were there said they were in charge of organizing our visit. After everything was arranged, the young man who was going to be our guide today arrived. His name was Mr. Dissoki Hassin Aly and he took us on a horse coach which is the picturesque visitor's way of transportation into the Luxor and Karnak temples. This coach was identical to the ones they used as taxis in Cardenas, the city where I was born. Maybe the coaches in Cardenas had taken me far beyond the town limits all the way to Luxor. In my dreams. Anyway, our ride was pleasant and evoked many childhood memories. The only problem was the flies bothering us all the time. After a 20 minute ride, we arrived at the spectacular and grandiose Karnak Temple. We disembarked and walked to the entrance of the huge temple complex. As soon as we entered, the swarm of flies ceased following us. It was as if there was something inside the temple that kept them away, or they just knew not to go there. It was a curious phenomenon! Whatever it was, I was very glad to be free of them. The size and height of the columns and walls was a breathtaking experience as well as the height of the obelisks. We wandered freely inside the temples and all of the rooms, nooks and crannies. I was imagining how it would have looked in its heyday, especially with all the bright colors of their wall reliefs. That would have made it even more impressive! It's impossible to imagine the civilization that could create this architecture!

However, walking through the temple and being inside of so many different rooms, from small to huge, I couldn't begin to sense or imagine their function. It all seemed very foreign to me. I couldn't relate to them, only just admire the grandiosity of it. It made me long for a trained archeologist with a deep knowledge of ancient Egypt so these convincingly thoughtful things could have an explanation or at least a theory. But I was just an artist born on a Caribbean island who was attracted to Egypt for as long as I can remember and dared to recreate a notion of what it was. Four hours had passed, too fast, inside that temple… It takes longer! It was just 1:30 pm and we were asked to take a local bus to go back to our hotel. I thought that we could visit the temple another time. It was only 20 minutes from Luxor.

This time we took a falling-apart local bus to go back to the hotel. It was full of local, colorful characters that you would see in the movies. I guessed we were unusual ones and colorful characters to them too. This ride back was an interesting experience! And we got out in front of our hotel in the usual Egyptian way, which was that the bus slows down "a little" and you jump from it while it's still moving… This is another case of "When in Rome do as the Romans do!" In Cuba after the communist revolution and with the overcrowded buses because of lack of transportation due to the shortage of spare parts, jumping from the crowded bus while moving was another "benefit" of the regime. So for me it was just a "deja-vu," but for Jaums was a frightening experience.

After we rested for a while in the hotel we walked to the Luxor Temple which was very close to the ETAP hotel on the way to another restaurant that the bellboy recommended. By the time we arrived at the temple, there was the beginning of a dust storm we had never experienced before–as a matter of fact we didn't even know what was going on and for sure it was going to make our visit even more interesting since we were the only ones crazy enough to be inside that magnificent but smaller temple under such circumstances. But the wind and the dust storm was getting stronger and there was a point that we could hardly see. So we wrapped our heads and faces with the Egyptian scarfs we previously bought at the town bazaar. We wrapped everything but left the eyes exposed as the Egyptian did and put sunglasses to protect the eyes. Looking very much like a heavy fog at home this fog was of dust and I got so we could hardly see where we were going. Then I realized how functional the Egyptian or Arab wrap is for the desert environment. It protects the eyes and allows you to see in such adverse situations. However, Jaums used contact lenses and he was having a lot of problems with his eyes. So we decided to leave The Luxor Temple and go to the restaurant to eat and we walked in the middle of the wind and dust fog and we could hardly see and apparently there was not a single self-respecting Egyptian soul on the boulevard.

We finally managed to reach the restaurant named "Marhaba." Of course it was empty, we were "Crazy Americans", silly enough to be out in this fog of dust. Egyptians know not to go out at all–including the flies!– when there is one of these dust storms. We ordered the only thing we knew "Shish Kabobs" (!) After eating, the dust storm had subsided and we decided to walk back to The Luxor Temple and spent the afternoon there almost alone enjoying that temple for ourselves until it closed for the day. We walked back and we decided to eat again at "Chez Farouk." Guess what? "Shish Kabobs" again…

On the return to our ETAP hotel room we discovered that after we took off the headdresses, we couldn't get a comb through our hair because of the impregnation of the dust! Unlike our fog, their fog leaves a reminder.

Next morning at 8 o'clock we were at the tourism office as scheduled. But no one was there until 15 minutes later. This time another of the ladies we met before was going to be our guide. But at first, I didn't identify her because her hair looked completely different. She explained that because of the dust storm, she was wearing a wig. So that's why since ancient times the women wore wigs and headdresses! Her name was Mrs. Saheir Salah Eldin Mohamed. With her was an older man, who was dressed with the typical gallabeah and headdress. After meeting them we boarded a boat to cross the Nile toward The Valley of The Kings and afterward the Temple of Queen Hatshepsut. On the other side of the Nile, we got into a falling-apart, sand-blasted taxi. It was a surviving 1950's Henry. I love cars and it was an unexpected treat seeing that car again in Egypt and seeing it moving… It trembled and jerked almost as much as it moved forward, but it worked! After a "ride" on a bumpy road we reached the famous valley!

There we visited everything that was open, including of course Tutankhamun's tomb! That was almost like a pilgrimage to the boy king with its legendary "curse". I was hoping that nothing macabre would happen to me, that my representing him so many times in my Egyptian Sculptured Paintings might give me immunity. I hope that based on the ancient Egyptian belief that "talking about the departed is like bringing them back to life again," I certainly modestly contributed with my grain of salt to his immortality. I remained in silence there for quite a long time trying to absorb from such a moving place. From there, following the solemn silence we boarded the Henry again. I didn't ask our guide where we were going next, surrounded by the almost Martian landscape. As we advanced, the area looked familiar to me. At a point in the road, I was feeling chills all over my body. I was very puzzled by that sudden sensation. Then the Henry made a turn around a cliff, and there it was!!! The Deir El Bahari Temple!!! Queen Hatshepsut's electrifying wonder! I felt like crying from the emotion at the sight of that magnificent ancient but modern structure carved in the front side of a monumental stone cliff. I was like a dream, a mirage in the desert against the vibrant turquoise sky. I couldn't utter a word. I only observed in awe like a child would in front of an elephant for the first time in his life. What a sight!

I was amazed when I realized that her temple was right there in the same geographical area as the legendary Valley of The Kings! A fact unknown to me.. But I realized at that instance that that point that I had observed from my room's balcony in Luxor the day we arrived was in fact the Hatshepsut Temple as I had immediately thought. How could I have known that? That balcony was on the opposite side of the Nile and I didn't bring binoculars to Egypt.

While walking toward Hatshepsut Temple, I realized that its straight geometric land and ramps were similar to my favorite architectural style and that something like that could have been designed by me. All of it is just a coincidence since I reject the belief in reincarnation. Because if I had designed, worked or had anything to do with this or other temples in ancient Egypt I should be able discover any hidden place on those structures. But I couldn't. I needed real proof and so far it doesn't exist. I wanted to visit the upper tiers of that temple but I was not allowed to because a Polish restoration crew was working there. I felt incomplete and I left the temple area with a profound sadness within me.

From there we visited The Valley of The Queens, the tombs of The Nobles, The Ramesseum, Madinet Habu and the Colossus of Memnon. All very impressive and spectacular sights that are so much better seen in person than in photographs. Later on that exhausting and emotionally drenching day we crossed the Nile back to Luxor and the flies gave us a **ROYAL** welcome! The flies are such a bothersome problem as the elderly German ladies with their dangerous handbags and lethal pointy elbows at the airports of Egypt. I must point out that another local industry in Luxor is the fabrication of a very artistic utensil designed for the sole purpose of keeping flies away. It's like a magic wand, about a foot long, nicely carved, made of plastic or bone. From its aggressive end hangs a cascade of what appeared to be the tail of a horse, preferably died in white or natural. Walking the streets, you waive the device back and forth in fast strokes like a car windshield wiper. That prevents about 80% of the attacks and will definitely cause carpal tunnel. As a souvenir I keep one as a memento in my library. The good thing is that you don't have to get a license or register it with the U.S. Government and you automatically will have a license to kill flies in Luxor (007).

Unfortunately on our way back to the hotel we encountered a ghost from the past I had completely forgotten. I am sorry that I have to subject you to this again but it seems to be something that I cannot get away from. Since this is a book, I am obliged to recount all incidents related to my trip:

So, in one of Luxor's coaches pulled by a horse who excretes manure on the pavement which attracts flies which suddenly enter the boulevard from another street whose name I am not privy to because I am from out of town, I could not help to notice, sitting in it quite proudly was The Painted Woman, The Polyester Man and The Unremarkable Youngster! The three of them had already purchased and they are now carrying the instrument to keep and kill flies in Luxor that I previously recommended. I have to admit again that she looked ravishing as usual, wearing a feminine orange with white polka dot dress of ruffles and lace with an ample skirt with matching parasol. She looks like a piece of Florida sunshine. A refreshingly delicious prime quality orange, fumigated against the Med-flies. Sitting uncomfortably beside HER was The Polyester Man. In between them was her inseparable makeup case and sitting beside the coachman was The Unremarkable Youngster. Fortunately she didn't notice me since I was on the sidewalk wearing a typical gallabeah, headdress and sunglasses. So to HER I was one, unknown Egyptian on Luxor's boulevard, the (Cuban) Bedouin.

That day we had lunch at ETAP's cafeteria. The food was overpriced and the service was lousy. Afterward we rested and in the evening we ventured around town and discovered the real bazaar where the Egyptians buy. There we bought a few things and went back to the restaurant Marhaba for dinner and we ate our unescapable Shish Kabobs—at least if we died, we will know what killed us… Afterward we took the inescapable ride on a horse powered coach to the ETAP.

Next morning after breakfast, we went to the EgyptAir office to confirm our flight to Asawn tomorrow. Then we walked among the impertinent flies with my local handy-dandy "fly killer" to the legendary Winter Palace for lunch at their restaurant.

To our pleasant surprise we found Nancy sitting in the lobby! She had been staying in a hotel outside Luxor but that same morning, she moved to the Winter Palace. We had lunch together, and thanks to her expertise with the local food we were able to break our inescapable circle of Shish Kabobs and eat something new! And it was "so tasty too!" as Lucille Ball as "Lucy Ricardo" said on her hilarious episode of *I Love Lucy* about the "VITAMEATAVEGAMEN." That afternoon we made a date with Nancy to meet that evening for dinner at the Winter Palace again.

From the restaurant Jaums and I went to the bazaar again to buy two fancy gallabeahs for our special dinner with Nancy and two extras to bring as gifts to friends back home. That afternoon was very hectic at the bazaar, marked by the frantic hustling of the peddlers and the bothersome flies. After about four hours in that confusing foreign environment, I was able to buy the gallabeahs I wanted but I was completely exhausted by the experience and walked in the direction of the ETAP hotel amid a swarm of increasingly aggressive killer flies. I remembered that inside the temples of Karnak and Luxor there were no flies. Apparently there was a limit and they didn't cross that line. I wondered if there was a supernatural force at work in those temples that prevented the entrance of those aggressive killer flies...

Then a big fly landed on my forehead and the swarm that had been following us from the bazaar for quite some time, literally started attacking us. I really was in a panic when I found Jaums. We tried to defend ourselves with the "fly killer" weapon almost to no avail because they were now in bigger numbers. I was feeling a prickling sensation from their legs on my body and their plumose antennae on my face and my eyes and ears and crawling inside my clothes. In the middle of that agony I was able to realize that I was not far from the Luxor temple and I ran like mad toward that sanctuary. As soon as I entered the perimeter of the temple, like magic, they flew away from us. But anyhow, I ran inside the temple to be sure. I didn't know what we should do next unless a sand storm chased them away, since I remembered a few days ago when we had the sand storm, the flies were nowhere to be seen. But I certainly do not have the power to conjure such a natural event. Then I remembered that the end of the Luxor temple was closer to the ETAP hotel and we should walk inside until the end, the next building was a Mosque and then our hotel and we should run as fast as we can to it. So that's the only plan of escape we had. So we advanced until the very end until we saw the Mosque and then ran like hell in the direction of the hotel. As a matter of fact, we never noticed a fly inside the hotel either. So we executed the plan and were able to enter on the ground floor where the shops were located. And in front of us there was a jewelry shop and in its counter I saw some reproductions of jewelry from the XVIII Dynasty during the period of Tutankamen. There were long necklaces with a single hanging amulet for the protection of the mummy during the trip though the Underworld, according to the ancient beliefs. So I immediately had the idea to buy them all for our own protection against the killer flies of Luxor. Still, we need protection tonight for our trip to see Nancy at the Winter Palace and to come back safely to our hotel and also tomorrow morning's trip to Luxor airport for our trip to Aswan. So we went back to our room already wearing all of the jewelry for our protection. When we arrived at our room I carefully sneaked onto the balcony. From it I can see the Mosque and the back of the Karnak Temple beyond and I didn't see a soul on the streets. So no one witnessed what we went through… I guess they all knew to stay away from the flies.

I felt exhausted after the harrowing experiences and fell back into my bed. I was becoming sleepy and decided that it was better that I rest for the dinner with Nancy at the Winter Palace… Then I saw myself inside the temple wandering through the magnificent courtyard of Rameses II, the chapels of Tuthmosis III, the colonnade and courtyard of Amenhotep III, the vestibule, the hypostyle hall, the sanctuary of the secret boat and the sanctuary built during the Ptolemies Dynasty. I was floating as if I was traveling through time and I forgot the unpleasant reality as to why I was confined to that temple. But I stayed in that inner sanctuary in static contemplation for an immeasurable period of time. However, I felt that I was not alone as if I was suspended in time. I felt powerful but a sudden burning presence on my back followed by an urge to turn around and face whatever it was. I did! And there it was! A figure standing, just like a painting, framed by an entrance door. It was an imposing, eerie sensation what I felt from that unexpected apparition, which was emphasized by the luminescence emanating from behind that sight with colors similar to a sunset and in the middle, a black silhouette wearing something that appeared to be a flowing, silky, black gallabeah and what could be seen through the filmy fabric appeared to be the contours of the body of a woman. I walked toward her with trepidation. She began lifting the veil from her face… And I couldn't hide my surprise when I finally saw her complete face exposed and I couldn't help but exclaim, "For all the ancient Egyptian Gods, it's you!" This is the magic moment I have been waiting for since I set foot on this magical land! We finally and officially meet! Then I was going to say, "Hi, my name is," when she stretched her arm, closing my lips with a touch of her heavenly hand. And she took my hand and pulled me out of the sanctuary, dragging me throughout the temple in the direction of an electric exit sign. "But the flies, the flies!!!" I screamed with all my strength. Then, she turned her face to me and didn't say a word. But somehow I knew that she meant "never mind the flies." We ran together and left the temple by an exit I never knew existed near the Muslim Mosque. Outside, the white sandy square behind the Luxor Temple was deserted of people and flies. Then she ceased holding my hand and running ahead of me. I understood immediately. We were in a Muslim country and it was not accepted that she walk in front of me in public. So she was walking beside me and I was very happy about it. And her image dissolved in front of my eyes… The sound of the shower woke me up. I was on my bed in the hotel! I looked at my watch and I realized that after Jaums finishes in the shower I should run and take mine to get ready for dinner with Nancy at the Winter Palace. I think I know who the elusive woman in my dream was.

After my shower I got dressed in my new red gallabeah and head-dress. I also wore the new jewelry I purchased after the return from the Luxor Temple. Jaums was also sporting his new gallabeah and I gave him new jewelry for his protection in case we were subject to another attack from the killer flies. We met Nancy at The Winter Palace. She was very surprised by our "made in Luxor" dressy gallabeahs. We had a fun and charming evening with her. I don't remember what we ate but being with her anything would taste good. We made arrangements so after we get back to Cairo we will meet again. Fortunately we didn't encounter THE PAINTED WOMAN and her two loyal gray compan-ions. I thought she was probably busy tonight selecting her outfit for tomorrow's flight to Aswan and especially busy with her initial coats of makeup for her trip.

Next morning Jaums and I got up at 5:30 am to get ready to go to Luxor airport for the EgyptAir flight to Aswan. At least in 1978 all flights inside Egypt had to be on EgyptAir, I don't know if that contin-ued to the XXI century…

This morning after I woke up, I was feeling sick and I began los-ing my voice. Could it be the flies' sickness? I looked forward to some peace and tranquility in Aswan. We took a taxi to the airport, which we shared with a Modern Art Professor from Germany. He also was a guest of the Egyptian government and he was heading to Aswan too. He was carrying bug spray and a "killer fly" device just like ours and the other tourists were carrying in Luxor. He seems to be well-prepared indeed! Maybe he visited before… I became worried that the flies were going to follow us to Aswan! I cannot imagine being the target of attacks by The Killer Flies of Aswan! Well–I optimistically thought–perhaps to give us a farewell. But, coming back to the reality of this world in upheaval, I added to my previous thought: Or perhaps a massive and bloody attack before leaving town! Who knows, these flies are unpredictable…

We got to the old airport without any trouble. After all the security rites and precautions, we finally boarded the plane at 9:30 am with no incidents and half an hour later we were airborne in route to Aswan… I wondered, what would be waiting for us there?

CHAPTER 15

ESCAPE

I gave a kiss to my mother, to my father, to my aunt and to my uncle. Just a quick kiss and a quick goodbye to all in a low voice, amidst nervous chatter, before entering the gate. What I wanted to do was to go back to them, to stop that painful moment and go back to the security of the past before this horrid political nightmare began.

I shed a single tear, so did my mother as she watched me leave. Her face pressed against the cold glass that separates the world of the people who had to stay from the world of lucky ones who might get to leave this surreal country.

After many hours of sitting in the waiting room beyond the gate, the secret police officials in charge of the airports in Cuba moved us to another room called "the exit door". From there, we would not move again until it was time to board the plane to freedom unless ejected for cause or for no cause. From that room, I was able to see my parents, aunt and uncle in the distance. Their eyes were locked on me.

We, the group of lucky ones who may get to leave that island, sat in "the exit door" without knowing what would happen next. What unusual documents would the authorities demand at the last minute in order to cancel our trip, in order to humiliate us more, and to make us feel even more at their mercy?

The time passed at an agonizingly slow pace. I was getting more and more nervous. My diaphragm was trembling uncontrollably. I tried to comfort myself by thinking: Why be nervous? My situation is different from the rest of the people in this room who are given the hated official government derogatory code name "worms," which identified people who disliked the revolution. The authorities know who they are. They know that they are leaving, never to return. Officially, I am not like them. I am leaving because I am going to study abroad. I am the recipient of two scholarships in Canada with all of the documents to prove it. I am even allowed to carry more belongings than these people. Why should I be nervous?

So, I kept trying to appear relaxed and without any worries, which was the same thing the others were trying to do. However, the authorities should not suspect that what I really wanted was to leave the country for good as badly and for the same reasons as the "worms." Honestly, I was one of them too but the secret police must not know that...

The situation in the room was tense. The silence was excruciating. You worried that the deafening sound of your heartbeat could be heard by everyone in the room. Everyone was trying very hard to look relaxed, so as not to call the attention of the authorities. Any unusual or suspicious behavior could be fatal for our plans to escape that hellhole.

Suddenly, from behind a counter, one of the official secret police in charge began calling out our names, one by one. The tension increased even more. Now I could hear the nervous heavy breathing of the people around me. Like them, I was dying inside, and like them, I forced a serene smile on the tense muscles of my face. The young woman sitting on my right was called and I inconspicuously followed her with my eyes. After she arrived at the counter, the official secret police asked her for something. She opened her purse and started searching. I could not hear what they asked from her. I dare not move and risk attracting the attention of the other officials in the room.

Time seemed to stretch and stretch in there. The minutes on my watch took forever, while in reality, only two hours and fifteen minutes had passed since I entered "the exit door". The young woman returned to her seat beside me. Without looking at her, I whispered, "What did they call you for?" There was silence. Then, pretending to scratch the tip of her nose with her hand covering her lips, she whispered back to me, "He wanted the inventory of my jewelry for verification."

Well, that problem won't happen to me, I thought, comforting myself. I have an "official permission" document allowing me to take what the rest sadly could not.

The old lady sitting on my left whispered to me, "Are you traveling alone?" "Yes," I whispered, covering my lips. I then remembered the warnings that the authorities placed secret police on these flights, so, I elaborated, "I will be in transit in Madrid for a very short time and then will continue to Prague. I have a scholarship there and official permission."

The old lady appeared to be alarmed by my answer and became speechless. I then realized that she was not part of the secret police. In volunteering so much information and mentioning Prague, my answer gave her the impression that I was a proud communist. I felt relieved that she was just another ordinary person who wanted to leave for the same reasons I did, but I then realized that I had made a terrible mistake. I shouldn't have elaborated and mentioned Prague. I was not going to Prague. That was not my destination and the authorities knew it.

Inconsistencies like this could call attention to me and I could be questioned. I cautioned myself to be more careful.

Finally, the official called my name and I walked to the counter. I showed him my passport, my official exit permission, and an official letter requesting considerate treatment from the officials since I was a scholarship recipient. The official quickly glanced through the letter and gave me a look of complete disbelief. My mouth went completely dry and I was frozen with fear. He then shoved the letter into a drawer and told me to sit and wait.

I had entered the gate at six in the morning; it was now nine in the evening and I was still sitting and waiting. I had not eaten anything. I couldn't remember if I had been to the bathroom or if I was too afraid to leave my seat even for that! I had no idea what would happen next or when it would happen. I was physically and psychologically exhausted.

Then, another official, who had replaced the one at the counter, called my name. I promptly went to him. This time it was to verify the inventory of the jewelry I was carrying with me, with the inventory the authorities had performed in my house a week ago. I was not expecting this since I was leaving with a special permission, but I did not say anything to upset the official. I was carrying a Sterling silver identification bracelet I had purchased with my first paycheck, a Russian watch my mother gave me and a pair of cufflinks made in China I had purchased. He double-checked and found that everything was in order. He told me to go back to my seat and wait.

At 10:25 pm, three secret police officials rapidly entered the room. They looked around counting us as if we were cattle. Hatred and suspicion radiated from their eyes. They were smoking cigars that they kept frantically moving around with their lips, filling the room with a putrid stench as they swaggered about looking over each one of us. The mood in the room changed to one of doom. I had heard that they sometimes canceled flights at the last minute. I started trembling with the thought. I hoped they wouldn't notice. Then I noticed others waiting were trembling as well. The room was completely silent except for the sound of the officials' boots on the tile floor. Suddenly one of the three stepped out from the group. He was short and fat, and he said in a very loud authoritarian voice, "You people on this flight are carrying a lot of weight in your suitcases. It is necessary that each of you give up half of your luggage. If not, half of you will have to stay behind."

With the choices given, everyone immediately agreed to the confiscation of half of their few belongings. The three policemen smiled cynically and left the room, very satisfied.

Later we could see the authorities opening individual suitcases and deciding which pieces of clothing were going to be left behind. One more incident of humiliation and inhumanity toward "the worms." These people were leaving everything, their loved ones, their pets, their businesses, their houses, their cars, their money and all of their belongings. What they were carrying in their suitcases was nothing in comparison with what they were leaving behind. The only things the state permitted them were one coat, two suits or dresses, one pair of shoes, three shirts or blouses, two changes of underwear and two pairs of socks or stockings. And now the authorities were confiscating half of that misery. But most of us didn't care. We had already lost everything. For only a chance to live free of totalitarian rule, we would leave our country naked, if necessary. Freedom is vital for the human spirit. It was not there in the suitcases at the state's mercy. But, we were not free yet… And we all watched in silence at the looting.

Just at 11:00 pm, the same three policemen erupted into the room. The same short, fat one with the authoritarian voice announced, "In spite of the reduction in weight, the plane is still overloaded. Therefore, it is necessary for some people to stay behind". They turned and left the room as the tension in the room was increasing.

We all felt the air had been removed from our lungs. We were paralyzed. The faces in the room grew paler. Some of us looked at each other. The atmosphere was charged with anxiety. All of that horrible tension we have been enduring and now this! It was like waiting for our death and it was unbearable. After 17 agonizing hours waiting in that room, no one knew for sure who was finally going to leave! I just wanted it over, to disappear or to wake up from this nightmare, not just for me, but for all the souls trapped inside this gate..

After a while the same despicable official entered the room holding a sheet of paper in his hand. He called the first ones to be left behind. It was an elderly couple. The second ones, a family of three. And then he called my name. That's the end of my escape. That's it. I silently took my coat, my camera and my documents, got up from the seat and walked in the same direction as the others to be left behind. I could see my mother and father in the distance, still waiting behind the glass nervously wondering what was going on. One of the authorities called me to an adjacent room where I was told to sit and wait. I automatically did it without question or hesitation, as a good robot in that society. I sat alone on a chair in the middle of the room with only misery for company. Sad, I no longer had any hope left.

Another official entered the room, walking directly to me. He stood just in front of me. Gathering all of the strength and courage I had left, probably produced by my panic-stricken glands, I decided to play my last card. I have nothing to lose. What could be worse than staying alive but prisoner in that hell?

Using my training as an actor, I "acted" very upset about the whole situation. I choose my words carefully using only revolutionary jargon—political correctness—in order to stress my status as one of them sharing the same ideals, "Comrade, I am a scholarship recipient. I have to be at my destination without delay to attend classes. Comrade, I do not think it is in the best interests of the Revolution for me to lose this scholarship."

"Comrade", he replied quickly, "don't be upset. We have another flight next week."

"Comrade, you don't seem to understand," I said. "I have to be at my destination no later than this week. If not, the scholarship will be lost. Comrade, I have to be on this flight. You must put me on this flight."

"Can you spare some of your belongings?" he asked.

"If it is necessary to leave half of my belongings, that is acceptable with me," I replied, "But Comrade, at the same time, I think that is wrong. Comrade, I am going to a very cold country. Everything I am carrying is absolutely vital."

He was silent after my speech. Desperate but trying to appear calm I added, "Of course, Comrade, if you still think it is necessary, it won't be a problem."

He was still silent as if he was studying me… I had never felt more alone and lost in my entire life. I should have kept my mouth shut about the damned suitcase and let him keep everything! I saw myself in my mind going back home to my bed, to my books, to my paintings. I couldn't go back to an uncertain future of oppression, repression, depression as many people were experiencing while trapped in that asphyxiating environment. He broke into my thoughts by ending his silence. "Don't worry, Comrade," he said. "You will be on this flight."

"Thank you, Comrade," I said in the most grave and conscientious tone I could muster, suppressing the JUBILANT feelings I was having inside. "The Revolution will benefit forever because of your wise decision." I said to complete my political deception of that despicable secret police official.

I took my documents again, got up and walked back to the waiting room, but this time in triumph. I couldn't believe it! It worked! I triumphed as an actor! I had succeeded once more to fool to the authorities! I was able to breathe again. All of this agony will be over soon! I was elated and victorious very deep inside. The great accomplishment of this Revolution was to teach how to pretend how much you love the regime and its leaders! I kept walking toward the waiting room. I saw my mother and father in the distance, and I made a discreet gesture with my head indicating "it was nothing". I sat in the same seat as before but was more assured the nightmare would be over soon..

Half an hour later, the same official who spoke to me came in and announced that the plane was ready to board and that everyone should form a line and, in his most authoritarian voice said "The women and children will leave first."

But then, he called me first! I was number one on his passenger list! I got up and finally stepped out "the exit door". The official took my passport and stamped the coveted exit seal. I turned around for a last look at my mother and father in the distance, still standing with their faces against the glass during the long and excruciating 18 long hours of not knowing the outcome of my escape.

I saw the plane on the tarmac about a block away and walked over to it, but this walk seemed eternal, like in slow motion and I was worrying deep inside that something would happen at the last minute that would prevent my escape. The night was clear and cool. I could see most of the stars. Suddenly I felt relaxed but empty. I walked automatically, knowing deep in my heart that as soon as the plane took off, some sort of window in space would open up and I would be flown to a far away sanctuary that would protect me.

I reached the plane. It was all like a dream. I went inside the cabin. I was afraid I would wake up. No, no, I am quite awake! This is happening. This is really happening. I kept repeating that to myself while walking to my assigned seat. I am living the reality. This is not a dream. I sat down. It was hot inside the plane. Then I became worried that something might go wrong. The authorities might find out that I was leaving because I was hungry for freedom and wanted to escape. No, no, no! I repeated to myself over and over. Nothing will happen. Everything will be alright. The worst is over. In a matter of hours I will be free! I will have control of my life, of my future. I will not be at the mercy of any government or any oppressive political doctrine. I will not be sent to any concentration camp. Everything will be fine. I will be free.

Finally, everyone was inside the plane and in their seats. Everyone was very still, in self imposed silence, also petrified that something will happen in the last minutes and their escape will be canceled. The fear and anxiety of the past hours was reflected in the faces of the passengers around me. The silence inside the cabin was eerie.

The door of the plane was closed with a deep bang. Well, that's it. This is it. This is for real. One by one the motors started. The propellers accelerated rapidly and the whole plane was vibrating. I put my face against the window, putting my hands beside my eyes in order to see out. I was trying to see the terminal building in the distance. Trying to pinpoint my mother and father against the glass of the building for one last glance. But, I couldn't find them. It was too far and there were more than one hundred faces there pressed against the long airport windows, trying in vain to see us.

The airplane started moving slowly. My heart was beating rapidly and I felt a lump in my throat. "Good bye" I said in my mind, and that was my only thought. I felt still completely empty. The plane turned and I was no longer able to see the terminal building. I recline the seat, rest my head and close my eyes. I realized then that I hardly saw my mother and father today. It was a very quick goodbye at the airport. I might never see them again, I thought. Memories of my family, my home, my life went through my mind. But now I am safe. I was surprised when I began to feel somehow relaxed. I was leaving my past, both of my parents and the rest of my family, my dog, Terry, who was my friend and companion since he was about one month old. I loved him very much and I had to say my goodbye to him just a week ago. But his memory will always be with me.

"How do you fasten the seat belt?" whispered the old lady sitting beside me. I told her how to do it while fastening mine. It was still very hot in the cabin. The plane reached the end of the runway and turned again. The propellers began maximum acceleration. I felt the plane wanted to go. The signal to go had not been given yet and the plane was impatient, wanting badly to go and fly away like all of its passengers. The signal was finally given and the plane began to move rapidly picking up speed and we took off! I felt elated, liberated, as if a heavy weight had been removed from my shoulders.

As I looked out of the window, I saw the lights of the airport getting smaller and smaller. I saw the millions of lights of the city of "La Habana". I thought: down below there is a country full of people, trapped in a prison without walls, slaves of new kind of oppressive and totalitarian order, who are not living, but existing inside that nightmare. People who would leave because their country was no longer theirs. They would leave only because redemption cannot be seen in any direction. It is finished. Yes, they would leave sadly, like me, leaving a part of my soul behind knowing Cubans live only in Cuba.

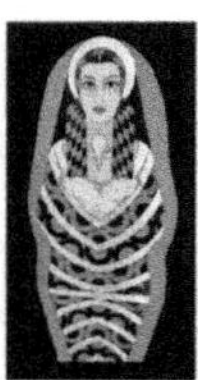

CHAPTER 16

PRISONERS OF AMUN

We touched down at 10:24 am at the Aswan Airport. An official from the government was waiting for us. He ushered us to a black Russian car that I was familiar with from seeing them in Cuba after the communist revolution. The first place the driver took us to see was the Russian-Egyptian monument near the high dam of Aswan. Damn! It was a Russian monument all right, with all the implicit Soviet Bolshevik's bad taste. That's one of the things they have plenty of to offer!

After that, he took us for the customary visit to the Aswan High Dam, which was finished in 1970. Damn! It flooded a big part of the ancient Egyptian historic heritage. But, what do the Soviet Bolsheviks care about history? It was very interesting to see anyway. In my modest, artistic judgment, however, it would never surpass the ancient pyramids and any of the glorious ancient Egyptian architectural feasts from the pharaonic times.

But, having lived inside a Marxist's Paradise, I cannot embrace these samples of communist propaganda from a totalitarian regime that enslaves and oppresses its people causing so much suffering and misery. I am not just a prejudiced or a political fanatic, no. I simply have plenty of reasons, based on personal experiences and knowledge about this unnatural philosophy and the damage they have done to humanity every-where they have grabbed their absolute power. Repeating again what the ancient Egyptian said, "I have lived the past, I know the future." They take away from you everything including the most important and needed gift for humankind: Your Freedom. They cannot fool me! I escaped from the Red Cuckoo's nest...

The name of our guide was Mr. Mohamad Hussein and he was very nice and polite as were all of the Egyptian officials appointed by the government to help us get the most from this extraordinary trip. After he finished with this instructive tour of the famous high dam, a pet project of the late President, Gamal Abdel Nasser, who died in 1970 and was followed by President Anwar Sadat. The official inauguration was in 1971. After our visit was over we got into the sinister black Russian car and he drove us almost to the edge of the huge Lake Nasser.

From there we took a boat to Philae Island to visit the impressive Isis Temple, as Mr. Ezz El Din Shawkat, recommended one evening in his office at the *Al-Ahram* main newspaper in Cairo. The temple was salvaged from inside the waters of Lake Nasser by an UN effort to save this jewel of the Nile. It was, as Mr. Shawkat said, "magnificent." At the time that we were visiting there was an Italian company working there—the same that rescued it from the bottom of Lake Nasser's waters–and now was in charge of its reconstruction and restoration. We were able to see and photograph the placement of one of its big stones on the top of a tall wall by a huge XXth century crane. This was an interesting sight which made me wonder once more how the ancient Egyptians were able to manage the construction of such complicated temples with those heavy stones. They must have been very accomplished peo-ple! Inside the temple we met the Egyptian expert in charge of the restoration and he gave us a complete VIP tour of the outstanding Isis Temple with its marvelous reliefs.

The reliefs here make the stone come alive.

From Philae Island, Mr. Hussein took us to the town of Aswan, where we were supposed to go to *Hotel Paradiso* (1966) with Gina Lollobrigida, Alec Guiness and Robert Morley. The town of Aswan and its geographical location was outstanding, beautiful and charming. It is crossed by the Nile. We were finally out of the Russian Bolshevik black car and got into a beautiful Egyptian barge to cross the Nile to the magnificent Elephantine Island. Mr. Hussein explained to us that he made reservations at the luxurious Oberoi Hotel and that he would be back later to take us to the city in the evening. And he left.

Jaums and I sat in the plush seats of the large barge and we thoroughly enjoyed the spectacular view and the soft and relaxing cruise over the serene waters of the legendary Nile on our way to Elephantine *Island in the Sun* (1957) with James Mason, Joan Fontaine, Harry Belafonte and Dorothy Dandridge…

On the other side, we got out of the barge on the Oberoi Hotel pier. Two bellboys came immediately to carry our luggage to the inside of the hotel. I was very pleased with the looks of the hotel, a tall and shining tower in the bright sunlight and could just about imagine breathtaking views from its rooftop of Aswan and the *Island of Desire* (1953) with Linda Darnell and Tab Hunter. We followed the bellboys through the interesting pier of numerous ascending levels, leading to the staircase to the entrance of the hotel. I was completely convinced that from now on, everything was going to be fine and dandy and as smooth as the barge that took us to this hotel… As soon as we entered the lobby through its golden revolving doors, the lights went out in the hotel… But anyway, I acted as if nothing happened and continued advancing toward the reception desk. However I tripped on the Oriental Carpet and fell flat on the floor. Without losing my cool, I rapidly got up, with the hope that no one noticed *The Fallen Idol* (1949) with Ralph Richardson, Michele Morgan and Bobby Henrey. Not to mention *Fine and Dandy*, the musical (Broadway, 1930).

However, at the reception desk, the employees seemed very much at ease with the lack of electricity and were working normally under candle light. So…the first thing I asked the attendant was, "Does it happen often…?"

"Sir, I beg your pardon," was his surprising reply. So I thought that he didn't understand my accent.

So I repeated, "The lights, the lights," I tried to clarify due to the unusual, obvious circumstance that the lobby was dark and they had candles on the counter.

His insolent reply with a question, "Sir, what's wrong with the lights?"

I wondered if what is happening now is that I am in the middle of one of my surreal dreams and I tried to wake up by shaking my head. But nothing happened. I was in front of the desk and a clerk with a puzzling look reflected on his face…in candlelight. So since I am not dreaming at all, I'll try again with a surreal comment to see if I can get to him, "Oh, there is nothing wrong with the lights. They just simply went off."

He replied, "Oh…you are talking about the electricity…" finally realizing what I had been saying. And I replied, "Yes, 'the electricity'." Does it happen often?"

"Oh yes Sir, constantly." he said.

Well, I see now where the mutual misunderstanding happened. We have different ways to say the same thing… So I will proceed in a different way because I already had reservations in this hotel and I like the looks of it very much. If the "electricity" will not be off for long periods of time, it will be acceptable. For only one day it would not be a big deal… So I proceed to introduce myself to the desk clerk, "My name is Agustin Blazquez. I am a government guest and I have reservations for today."

"Let me check," the clerk said and went looking in his book. Apparently he couldn't find my name in it, because he got another book and was looking in it too. After a while, he was talking to another clerk who joined in the search until yet another third joined, forming a total of three musketeers and I observed that the three of them disappeared to a back office. A while later my first clerk came back to the counter with a flashing smile from ear to ear and said to me, "I'm sorry Sir… but we do not have a reservation for you."

"That couldn't be," I said and suggested, "it has to be here somewhere."

"Sir," he stated, "there is no record of you coming to this hotel."

Then I stated, "I am an Egyptian government guest. The official in charge of taking care of me, Mr. Mohamad Hussein, explained to me that he himself had made a reservation for me in this hotel."

And he replied, "No Sir, he didn't."

"Well, anyway," I said to avoid any further discussion, "Do you have a room for us that we can rent now?"

"No Sir, we are booked, I am sorry." He said.

"Do you have a phone?" I asked him.

"Yes Sir…but…I don't know if it's working…, " he hesitatingly uttered while looking around.

"Well," I said, "get it anyway and call at the government office for foreign visitors and ask for Mr. Mohamad Hussein."

"Yes Sir, I'll do what I can." and he left to search for a phone…

I looked at Jaums and said, "I simply cannot believe this!"

And after a very long wait the clerk came back and said, "I was able to talk to Mr. Hussein. He told me that you must wait for him here." So we sat in the dark lobby waiting for him. After he came, he went to the reception desk to talk to the clerk I was previously talking to see if they could find us a room. But the effort was futile. So he asked us to go back with him to Aswan for another typical hotel hunt in the middle of the tourist season! This was going to be the third wild chase for a room in Egypt! Could this be the last…?

We reversed our previously optimistic trek from the still dark (!) Oberoi hotel lobby to the pier, then on to the barge with its nice pillow seats to leave Elephantine Island, crossing back over the Nile to Aswan. At least we enjoyed the relaxing spectacular view and we didn't have to make reservations for it!!!!!! After all, the Egyptians were going out of their way to be nice and helpful to me, excluding the HOTELS with their elusive reservations. I must consider myself privileged for being here and should take everything for what it is, the adventure of a lifetime and an unforgettable one! Probably it will be better this way. It will be a trip of everlasting memories. It was a pity not to be able to stay in the "electrically challenged" Oberoi. It was a very nice hotel with a spectacular view of Aswan and the Nile. Well, some day, some day…

The detail that is difficult to understand is that so close to the high dam and the hydroelectric facilities, how is it possible that the electric power fails "constantly." (?!). With that constant menace, the Oberoi and other hotels in that area should have very powerful generators.

In Aswan we got in the black Soviet car with Mr. Hussein hunting for hotels. The first one was the historic and famous Old Cataract Hotel of the film *Death on the Nile*. This time they had a room but without a private bath. So that was the end of that. From there we went to other hotels and nothing was available.

Finally Mr. Hussein decided to take another barge—not as nice as the one for the Oberoi—but it was able to cross the Nile reaching the tiny Amun Island which looks like the film *Island of Lost Souls* (1932) with Charles Laughton where the Amun Hotel was located. This time the barge and the pier didn't have "star quality." But it was a very attractive Arabian style older building with domes which was apparently the only construction on that tiny island in 1978, the year of our visit. Apparently all the souls were lost on this island because that was the only building they could still haunt at night… Actually this old historic hotel turned out to be very charming and looked like an oasis in the middle of the Nile surrounded by palm trees and the huge smooth rock boulders that looked like gigantic elephants. That's why the name: Elephantine Island. Between the boulders the water circulates as smooth rapids between those elephantatious boulders. From the pier and before we entered this set from *Arabian Nights* (1942) with Maria Montes, Jon Hall and Sabu, I crossed my fingers for good luck for finding a room…

After the inescapable, ritualistic, lengthy summit at the reception desk, Mr. Hussein came back to us holding the key of a room between his fingers. We were more than happy, ELATED that at least we have a place to stay! Two bell boys helped us with the luggage to the room. I was pleasantly surprised with the large room with a private bathroom and a gigantic terrace for a Fred Astaire-Ginger Rogers dance number, a tango, I'm sure. This incredible terrace allowed a 360 degree view of the spectacular Nile and general landscape and the entire geography of Amun Island. We can see on top of the hills beyond the irrigated gardens of the hotel, the sands of the desert appearing yellow against a sky of dark, dark blue all the way down to the horizon. And, in the distance, almost as a mythical mirage, the domes of the Aga Khan Mausoleum. Probably the terrace occupied one third of the area of the edifice of the hotel. And to literally crown the surprising hotel, the room had a dome ceiling! What else do we need?! Mr. Hussein left for Aswan, but not without making arrangements for a dinner invitation and a visit to the Palace of Culture that evening at six.

By the time we explored the room, the terrace and the outstanding landscape with the bright turquoise-shading-to-midnight sky, we were desperate to take long and relaxing baths in the huge bathtub. But we have a problem filling the tub because of the weak stream coming out of the old faucet. But it was worth the wait. Afterward we sat on the terrace just admiring and absorbing the relaxing surroundings. I cannot recall if it was Jaums or me who made the comment that the terrace of the Amun hotel "was the perfect place to write a book or become a painter." I highly recommend Aswan as "the place to visit" and I made plans in my mind to come back there again. It's a shame that we were scheduled to leave the next day. Well we have to use our time wisely. If I wanted to do some sightseeing we had to take faster showers. "So now let's run to the hotel restaurant for lunch," I said. And we ate Shish Kabobs AGAIN! That's going to be a problem…

After lunch we went to the pier to wait for a barge to take us to Elephantine Island. We sat there for a very long time and the barge never came. That's odd, I thought… We kept seeing many the serene Egyptian fallucas, fishermen's sailboats gliding by in the Nile. I kept signaling to them for a ride, but I was silently ignored. And the barge never materialized. That was very odd… So we decided to go upstairs to the terrace to see if from there we could find a path between the boulders that we could use as a bridge to walk or jump to reach Elephantine Island. From the vantage point of the terrace it seems I found a path jumping through the boulders. So we carefully studied my plan that *From the Terrace* (1960), with Joanne Woodward and Paul Newman, looked feasible and safe. We went downstairs and found the area with the natural bridge I proudly discovered. But when we saw the boulders and other smaller stones of my recently discovered bridge up close, I realized that it was an optical illusion. In reality they were *From Here to Eternity* (1954) with Deborah Kerr, Burt Lancaster, Montgomery Clift, Frank Sinatra and Donna Reed. The stones were much farther from each other than they looked from the terrace, also they were covered by some slippery growth and if we fell on the rapids between them we would be trapped by the river current and I may end up in Cuba, and that was a much too discouraging scenario, to put it mildly. So, we have to do as a dog, put our tails between our legs and abandon my crazy project. So from that moment on, I realized that we have become *Prisoners of Amun* (1978) with Agustin Blazquez and Jaums Sutton which was unceremoniously passed over by the Hollywood elite who never forgave me for the unforgivable sin of having escaped their Marxist island paradise. They are unforgiving, you know…

So we spent the rest of the afternoon exploring the tiny Amun Island for another miracle.

Maybe we'll find a buried treasure or one of the lost souls… But at one point in our search we found a barge. It really looked like a derelict from Cleopatra's times. There were lotus flowers on both ends of the barge, just as you see depicted on the old papyrus. Its paint color decoration was still partially visible. I had another crazy idea in order to reach Elephantine Island, it might work,

I thought…maybe if we push it to the Nile… After all, it looked to be seaworthy, unless it had a hidden hole we can't plug fast enough and it were to sink, it might be a historical loss for Egypt and they may have to spend a lot of money and time to repair it. But I didn't have the heart to do that to Egypt after they have been so supporting and helpful to me. I would rather be a prisoner in Amun Island and stay in our room with that fantastic terrace and its otherworldly, although tantalizing, views. So that was it for another of my crazy ideas. I turned and left Cleopatra's barge behind the bushes where I accidentally found it. That's it, we were marooned. Tonight Mr. Hussein will come for us at 6 pm with a barge somehow at his command to liberate us. I realized that it was almost five already. It's time that we find our way back to the hotel to get ready…

After we dressed for the evening we walked out to our terrace again to enjoy the now new, now late afternoon views with that fantastic turquoise sky, and the afternoon breeze, without doubt a splendid and unforgettable experience. Contemplating the Nile that afternoon, I had the idea that when I return to Cairo I must tell the Chief Curator to send an archeologist to examine that barge. I was interrupted by the phone bell… It was Mr. Hussein apologized for being late since it was about 6:30 pm. That's unusual, he has been very punctual since we arrived in Aswan. But it didn't bother me at all and gave us extra time to enjoy the terrace. He said he will not be able to come in the barge for us. He will just send the barge and wait for us at the Aswan pier. We went down to the hotel pier and in a few minutes the barge came for us and we crossed the Nile to Aswan. Mr. Hussein was there and we walked to the Palace of Culture. On the way there I told him what happened with the barge that never came at the Amun Hotel's pier today. He apologized for not telling me that any time we want to cross the Nile to Aswan or Elephantine Island we have to let the reception desk know and they will call the other side for the barge to come to pick us up. It was so easy and we didn't know! Prisoners were we? Well, as we walked by Aswan Palace of Culture on the way to the restaurant, I realized that its architecture was very similar to my elementary school in my country town in Cuba. After that we walked through a bazaar area to go to a typical Egyptian restaurant. The food was very good and of course was Shish Kabobs…

After dinner we went to the Palace of Culture where Mr. Hussein ushered us to a meeting room where a crowd of local artists and professors were waiting for us and he introduced me as an artist from the U.S. And very soon the photos and slides of my "mummies," were presented to the attendees who were very impressed that somebody in the U.S. was producing new art in the Pharaonic style of ancient Egypt. They said that they had never seen work like mine in Egypt. That unexpected meeting that they organized for me to welcome to the art community in Aswan was very nice and touching for me and of course more satisfying in opposition to America where I was, "treated like dirt." But I know why, because "I escaped from the Red Cuckoo's Nest." Their comments that evening and in other art and Museum circles in Egypt restored my confidence in the validity of my work and I returned to my adopted country–which is MY COUNTRY–with new ideas using the ancient Egyptian style in different ways.

After a meeting concluded, Mr. Hussein took us to the theater inside the Palace of Culture where a Sudanese Folkloric Dance Group presented a show of their typical dances. As I remember, after the first part of the dance presentation, a group of tourists that was visiting Aswan at the same time we were there came to see the dance presentation. Some of the faces were already familiar to me from the airports. Among them the handbags and pointy elbows of lethal old German ladies and their elderly husbands I had suffered from London to Cairo, to Luxor where I spent four days among them and the flies and to Aswan. But little did I know that there was one person I did not expect to see in this cultural evening to share the same location with me. But she was here again to hunt me out of the blue and *Dressed to Kill* (1941) with Lloyd Nolan and Mary Beth Hughes, carrying her inseparable makeup case: THE PAINTED WOMAN. I thought we were done with her in Chapter 13, but she lives on…

She was a walking stoplight at a Hollywood premiere at the Grauman's Chinese Theater at the opening of *King Kong* (1933) with King Kong and Fay Wray. This occasion THE PAINTED WOMAN was a walking carnival more shining and blinding than 12 suns at 12 noon in the middle of the Sahara desert with her long, gold sequined evening gown–hardly the one to be used for a Sudanese Folkloric Dance Group. The theater had to dim the lights because of the excess of multi color lights reflecting on all the interior walls or the theater. Her "super-decote" was so low and the super push-up, was so fearless and pushy that her monumental pair of well done breasts gave the impression of being two Halloween pumpkins on an electrified barbed wire fence. As extra adornments–as if she needed more attention getting utensils, she was dripping in gold and diamond jewelry. The opulence of The Tower of London was just a Salvation Army Store after Christmas Sale in comparison with her dazzling display of physical and material *faux* richness.

Resting over her shoulders, on that dress, she also had the guts and "good taste" to sport a transparent yellow silk stole embroidered with sequins here and there and canary yellow feathers around its perimeter. This has to be the most impressive appearance she has made on this trip so far!!! She is really a vision whatever she goes. And in spite of her peculiar style, she is a person or an entity that has to be seen and she always looks gorgeous! I am sure she can be noticed from Pluto!

Although she was strikingly over-dressed for an evening of folkloric dance, she was probably nearing the end of her trip and was not going to go home without taking an opportunity to use that dress. That many sequins are heavy!

Of course, I have to give credit to her two faithful companions that dare to accompany her out of house or hotel: The Polyester Man and The Unremarkable Youngster. Maybe they take a "Valium" before they set foot out of their safe house.

Then she MAJESTICALLY walked down the middle aisle followed by her two gray companions and took a seat in the middle of a row where nobody else was seated faithfully followed by The Polyester Man on her right and The Unremarkable Youngster on her left–this time carrying her makeup case!

After this interesting evening filled with music, dances, local artists, emotions and unexpected surprise, I was literally exhausted and we walked with Mr. Hussein to the pier and arranged for a barge to take us to The Amun Island Hotel.

Early next morning Mr. Hussein came to pick us up. We took the barge to Aswan and went in his black Soviet car to the airport for our next flight to a new Egyptian destination.

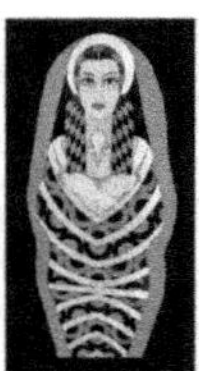

CHAPTER 17

THE FLIGHT OF THE ROOSTER

"Papa Gordo" and "Mama Zoila," that was what I used to call our next door neighbors in the country town of Coliseo, where I lived until I was about 7 years old. Papa Gordo was a general doctor and my doctor. Mama Zoila was his wife. They loved me and I spent a lot of time at their house. It was a very pleasant place to be with very nice furnishings, all a reflection of their warm and wonderful personalities. They had a car, a chauffeur, a cook and two maids. The big front porch of their house was covered by a very thick vine on two sides with white blossoms with a delicious fragrant perfume in the springtime. That's where they kept their 4 door, DeLuxe, two tone green Chevrolet. Papa Gordo was tall, dark and distinguished. Mama Zoila had an immaculate alabaster complexion with red hair. Both were very elegant and culti-vated. She wore diamond rings and earrings and fox or mink coats in the winter over her designer dresses. Her favorite perfume was Shali-mar and I knew when she was around. They had only one son, maybe in high school in South Carolina. He was at his parents house during vacations only, that's why I don't remember him very well. What I do remember of him is that his tutelage gave me my extensive repertoire of "bad words". Unfortunately, I always spoke very clearly so there was no doubt of what I was shouting to others. Apparently my "radio voice" developed at a young age, and I learned that using my voice got results, so, no excuse was valid with me—clear and simple. And I had the necessary repertoire!

My neighbors had money and they would travel abroad every year. My childhood fantasies were nurtured by the colorful and unforgettable stories of their trips. They sent me postcards and brought me mementos from Rome, The Vatican, Paris, Madrid, the U.S., Mexico, etc. They all sounded fascinating to me and I dreamed of traveling to those places someday… When I returned to my home, I was also carrying in my hands something from those fascinating places. In the evenings our neighbors conducted very sophisticated *tertulias* in their family room and sometimes important people, artists and even politicians attended those evenings as well as my mother and father and me. I think I was the only child at some of them. It seemed very natural to me at the time, but looking back now I realize the significance of that unique opportunity that I was exposed to those evenings next door.

Inside the plane, my freedom flight to Spain, I was thinking about them and wondering how many times Papa Gordo and Mama Zoila had taken the same flight to Europe… But after the revolution, they had to abandon the significant world they had built for themselves and others and escape the Marxist hellhole that our country had so rapidly become. They left knowing that they would not be back. So I might be able to see them again in the U.S. where he was working as a doctor in a Hospital in Danvers, Massachusetts…

From my window I was able to still see in the distance the lights of La Habana, but soon they faded away. Some time later I thought of trying to see the lights of the United States, but I couldn't. So, I rested back on my seat. I thought that I was saved. Now there is sea and air between that hell and me.

I finally got my wish to travel and visit some of the places I had heard about from the dear neighbors of my childhood. But this was not the same. I was leaving not for fun. I was not leaving to come back but to get away from a totalitarian nightmare, without illusion and with no foreseeable destiny.

At the time of becoming a Republic in 1902 we lacked a truly valid and honest government. People, patriotism, honesty had all changed, not only in my country, but in the United States as well. There was very little difference between them and us in our daily lives. And in both cases the people were free and independent from the government and if we worked hard we could have a better life and a future. Even the last president of Cuba, Fulgencio Batista, came from a dirt poor family of an interracial marriage and he was elected president defeating Ramon Grau San Martin in the 1940 presidential race under the new 1940 Constitution. He served a four-year term as President of Cuba. Batista was <u>to this day</u> the one and only non-white president of Cuba. In the next presidential elections of 1944, he didn't run. Batista's mistake was his bloodless coup on March 10, 1952, although he led an unparalleled six-year period of advancement and prosperity for Cuba.

But, in 1959, Castro's communist totalitarian regime took advantage of Batista's coup and became the everlasting hurricane that destroys everything, including human beings, animals, nature's environment and an entire culture. Everything the communists touch they ruin. Paraphrasing the Cuban intellectual, Vicente Echerri about Castro's long tenure of power in Cuba, "Batista was a mild flu and Castro a terminal illness."

Castro was nothing else but the bastard son born of the union of his corrupt father with his maid. His father was a Galician soldier who fought against Cuba with the Army of Spain in the 1895 Cuban War of Independence. Later, he switched sides and became a landowner in Biran, in the province of Oriente, Cuba, where he expanded his holdings by moving the fences at night, stealing land from his neighbor, the United Fruit company in nearby Banes. He stole their tractors which he quickly painted a different color to erase the United Fruit Company markings. Castro's father stole tractors and acreage. His son stole a whole island! All of this was witnessed by my friend, the late Barbara Gordon, daughter of the man in charge of the United Fruit Company at that time. But the general population of Cuba knew nothing of this prophetic history of the Castro family.

The so-called "Cuban Revolution" which generated millions of exiles all over the world was concocked via deceptions, lies, prohibitions, the theft of properties of Cubans and Americans, executions, judicial assassinations and other crimes by a gangster at the University of La Habana with self-directed, self serving morals and principles. He probably would have drifted harmlessly into oblivion had it not been for the 1957 New York Times interviews of Herbert Mathews and other liberals and communists in the American media, Hollywood and Academia who created a false bandwagon that he rode to fame and fortune. They all contributed to the total loss of freedom, the suffering, torture and death of people in that now totalitarian Island overcome by a foreign ideology…

In 1958 my mother and I were living in La Habana in my grandmother's home. At Christmas time we went back to the country town, Limonar, where we had moved just before my eighth birthday. In the early morning of January 1st, 1959, from my bedroom I overheard an excited conversation of my mother with our next door neighbor, Anita. I got up and opened the door of my bedroom. I overheard Anita saying that "Batista is gone." However, Anita indicated that "It's not for sure since the radio and TV hasn't confirmed it yet." Then, I heard some noises coming from the street and I hurriedly put some clothes on and ran to the exterior corridor beside the central patio. My dog Terry greeted me and ran with me. I saw Anita and my mother entering through the back entrance of the grocery store where my father was the manager. That January morning was chilly and very clear and beautiful.

The sky didn't have a single cloud. Excited, I went with them through the store and out the front door to the Main Street of the town.

Most of the town people were walking up and down the street. They were all smiling and excited, embracing and greeting each other. I overheard someone saying again that "The whole thing was generated by an unconfirmed rumor."

Then I ran with Terry through the main door of our house and closed the door and ran to the family room and turned on TV and the radio. They kept repeating that "The Cuban people should have patience and behave in a calm manner, because later on, important news will be announced for everybody." Then I ran with Terry to the grocery store and told my mother and father what I had just heard on TV. From the front of the grocery store we could see the people on the street walking anxiously back and forth, waiting for the news to start the celebration. They just wanted peace in light of the pro-Castro terrorist attacks at movie houses, nightclubs and other places where they would set off bombs to keep up the pressure to make Batista resign and leave power. The concern in the street that day was for the violence to stop and for the business of daily life and prosperity to be able to continue.

Then an army jeep from the local military depot in town passed by on Main Street with military officers in their uniforms, in an attempt to keep the crowd under control. The crowd was not completely intimidated by this small-scale effort, but no one screamed anything derogatory since they all were fellow townspeople—everyone knew each other, so some just flashed their victorious smiles at the officials. There was no incident as the jeep continued its silent vigil…

My father left Kiki, an employee of the grocery store, in charge and went with my mother, Terry and me to the family room to watch the unfolding developments on TV. After a while, my father went to the grocery store and decided to close its doors and sent Kiki home, because no one knew what would happen with the agitators of Castro's network in the cities and towns…

When the announcement was finally made on TV and radio, from the family room we heard an incredible sound outside as if the doors of a huge dam suddenly opened! It was the jubilation of the townspeople believing that the terrorism was over and that everything was going back to the normal, relaxed life we were all accustomed to in our small community. No more fear of sudden violence. Security, peace, tranquility and freedom was returning to our community!!!

We all ran to the front door—and this time we opened it all the way—to see the overwhelming demonstrations of happiness and relief! People were kissing and hugging each other and tears of happiness were in the eyes of many. Some were jumping up and down screaming, "We are free again!!!"

Those memories were vividly coming back while in my seat on the old, Cuban Airline's Britannia four-propeller airplane flying to Madrid, Spain. Cuba didn't even have modern passenger jet airplanes in July 1965, thanks to Castro's communist revolution! A jet would take 6 hours from Cuba to Europe and the old Britannia, 18 long, excruciating hours to reconquer the freedom we lost in 1959…

What an irony! In reality we are the ones who would be free again in 18 hours! But the Cuba Airlines stewardess was far from the usual friendly, smiling face. They can't smile at "Worms" who are hated and discriminated against. It goes without saying in that twisted totalitarian system where you have to demonstrate your allegiance to Castro's revolution with everything you have, including the frown on your face. Even though "unofficially," I was one of them, **AT HEART**, I had to deceive them using the "Actor's Studio" Stanislavsky method of acting, even though I hated this "method" in the acting class at the Academy of Dramatic Arts in La Habana, I summoned it to get me through this ordeal.

The stewardess was literally throwing the tray with food on the fold-down trays displaying the appropriate disdain. Maybe they were trying to make up for an amazing misdirection of rations! They were giving us **<u>FILET MIGNON!!!</u>** This is something that I hadn't seen since a trip with my parents and grandmother to the tourist destination of Giron Beach in 1961! There had been much (quiet) talk about the disappearance of this traditional part of Cuban cuisine which had been disappeared by the Revolution from the plates of the regular Cuban people and redirected to the Elite, Diplomats and Foreign Tourists. That "supported the revolution" so was a typical "benefit" of all Marxist-communist regimes where extensive propaganda attempts to make up for the fact that not everybody is equal. Such disappearing acts became extensive after Castro, which led to: "What's the difference between a filet mignon and Jesus Christ? None, because both are talked about but neither can be seen."

I ate it very slowly so I could enjoy it again, not only for the taste but also for its political value. I want to remark that all of the Cubans on that airplane did the same as I did because the cabin was more silent than a cemetery at midnight! No one opened and closed their mouths except to eat, which they did very slowly… Maybe the whole experience lasted longer than waiting in a line in Cuba to see if you can get a very bad roll of toilet paper.

Later on during the flight when the old plane had to do the arch near the very north of the globe, the stewardess, with her best arrogant expression of silent screaming on her face, threw blankets and pillows at us.

I must explain that inside the cabin, mostly filled with Cubans escaping, no one dared to talk to anybody or show their feelings. I don't even remember seeing anybody going to the restroom. Everybody–including me–was petrified that anything said could be used as a reason to be returned to Cuba. And, no one knew who might belong to the dreaded

Castro secret police, known as the G2. So for all these hours that were passing very slowly the cabin was in complete silence. It was eerie. In the emptiness, memories of the past kept coming back to me.

Later in the day on January 1st 1959, my mother walked to Anita's house because the local Telephone Center and switchboard operator was there. My mother called her mother and father's house in La Habana to inquire about the family there. Her family had congregated at their parent's house and they were fine and very happy to hear the promising announcement. But we were not able to return to La Habana because Castro declared a General Strike because he didn't accept the Constitutional Provisional Military Junta left in place to carry out the constitutional process for new elections to select a new president. Castro wanted to take all power by his own declaration based on his loyalists and collaborators as well as his cells that participated in the terrorist attacks throughout the island. So Castro demanded that all transportation was to be used only for his loyalists who were working to dissolve the official Junta, force its members into exile or jail to leave the pathway clear for Castro to take full power of the county. At that point in time most people on the island, out of admiration and ignorance of the 33 year old "liberator," supported the general strike which opened the door for him to grab absolute power.

Later in January 1959 my father was able to get a "safe-conduct" from the new, local pro-Castro officials who took over and began unconstitutionally ruling the town of Limonar. And with that permit my mother and I were able to travel to La Habana. My father stayed in Limonar for a time. I was enrolled in a private school in La Habana, but soon after it was expropriated in the name of the revolution. The owners were a very nice black couple, both professors who had founded the school–before Castro– in a very nice residential area. I liked the school–especially having the benefit of their private bus to pick me up at my grandmother's house. Soon after, the school ceased to exist thanks to the "New Order."

And my parents had to find a public school to continue my high school and use the now increasingly unreliable public transportation.

My mother's father, mother and her younger brother were communist sympathizers at that point, so of course they were elated by Castro taking power. My mother's father had been listening to communist editorialists on their daily radio shows years prior to this political-upheaval in the making. So listening to Castro broadcasting from the Sierra Maestra Mountains and his supporters from elsewhere in Cuba provided an apparently clear and approving foundation for what was coming. My mother's family was very close, always helping each other and they adored their mother and their father, who had two strokes in the past and was retired. They had full respect for their father's opinions and did not contradict him. Thus from the beginning they supported and loved the new revolution fully believing it was a tremendous step forward for Cuba and its citizens. Only one of the sons didn't like the drastic changes that the revolution began to impose on the population, especially the violation and eradication of the 1940 Constitution, which had the most advanced social and labor laws in the Americas. Inside my mother's family you could not say anything bad about Castro's revolution and the facts of the rapid, unconstitutional trials and convictions, executions and incarcerations, could not be discussed inside the family.

Sadly, my mother's father died after a 3rd stroke in early 1959, and he was not able to see his communist dreams come true. But his children—except the one—had to continue to cherish, protect and defend the tragic nightmare that was destroying the nation and sending thousands of Cubans to exile from the beginning of 1959.

Something that history has overlooked—maybe on purpose to benefit Castro—was the fact that Batista, in November 1958, had presidential elections in Cuba and he didn't run. The President elected was Andres Rivero Agüero, and his inauguration was going to be early in 1959. So the fact was that Batista was going to leave power in Cuba voluntarily.

That's why Castro needed to eliminate the Military Junta: to make sure that the constitutional change of power didn't take place. The idea that Castro got rid of Batista is not really true since he was leaving office anyway plus the U.S. State Department had a lot to do with his departure and the interruption of the constitutional process. Read all in the book The Fourth Floor, written by the last U.S. Ambassador to Cuba prior to Castro, Earl T. Smith.

So, we now have the "**NEW & IMPROVED!**" unconstitutionally installed "The Maximum Leader," topping his father, Angel Castro, who stole land and tractors from the United Fruit Company for his own benefit. Now his bastard son, Fidel Castro, was set up to steal a whole island–a whole country. "Like father, like son." Except bigger and better!!!

By 1958, before Castro, Cuba had six or seven TV stations including one channel with all programming in color. Very soon, thanks to the rule of "The Maximum Leader," the wide variety of channels was reduced to only two stations both strictly controlled by Castros' goons and for the sole purpose of supporting the revolution by lying, misinforming and indoctrination of the population. Oh, and to transmit the multi-hour-long speeches of "The Maximum Leader," channeling the styles of his heroes, Hitler and Mussolini. Those speeches were printed by Castro-controlled publications and read at Castro-controlled Unions and Schools. So it was impossible to escape from government propaganda from kindergarten to university. "Shut-up and obey" was the surreal soup we were finding ourselves swimming in, as the Twilight Zone TV show became real.

In Cuba, during the years before Castro, when you purchased a gun it had to be registered with the government. In that first year of 1959, Castro's goons got the registration lists and they knocked on doors at night and demanded the surrender of your gun. It was an easy and efficient way to totally disarm the civilian population.

People were changing in Cuba during the early years of the revolution. Some were captured by the belief of the romantic idea of a revolution and others lived in fear of "The Maximum Leader" regime. As the use of fear tactics spread to more and more of the population, victims of those tactics and their families and some friends began living in fear, while others either believed the propaganda about improvements, or decided they could benefit by apparently accepting the revolution. As the fear tactics spread, everyone was living in fear, even those who, by all appearances, were living as if they believed in the revolution.

A cousin I was very close to while living in La Habana was just 12 years old at the time, but at that young age he was already acting as a pro-Castro, unconditional admirer. Only a few weeks had passed after my mother and I moved from Limonar and he had totally changed. He had become a walking revolutionary slogan machine. He reminded me of the Hitler youth groups I had seen in films about that period in Germany. He proudly told me that on January 1st, 1959, he had joined an angry mob and took to the streets to destroy parking meters, arcades and stone the houses of suspected collaborators of Batista. I did not approve of this type of aggressive behavior and destruction of private property, but he was my little cousin and I liked him after all.

However, from then on, our dreams and interests became further apart. His dream was to attain revolutionary powers and carry a gun. Mine was to become an actor in the theater and films, to be close to "The Virgin…" In the future he attained his dream and I became an actor and finally I met her. I still keep in touch with him however we do not talk about politics. So it's not a complete relationship.

These thoughts about the past preclude me from sleeping on the plane. I find myself thinking that the decor of this Britannia airliner is not in good taste. I can see through my window that it is a clear night. The moon is very bright. It's getting very cool in the cabin now. I wish I could fall asleep. I'm feeling nervous again. I'm thinking that I might have lost some of my documents. I turn my light on and check in all my pockets. Everything is in order. I'm relaxing again and turning the light off. I'm thinking about a second cousin on my father's side, now in Madrid, that I sent a cable to announcing my arrival. I figure it's 6:15 in the morning now in Madrid. No, perhaps it hasn't reached him yet. I hope he gets it. I have no money. I hope there is somebody waiting for me at the airport. Well anyway there are more hours to go to get there. And we have to land at Santa Maria de Azores for refueling. Then continue this flight from Portugal to Madrid. Our arrival there will not be until around 7 pm on Monday. Well no… perhaps… The difference in time has me very confused. I better forget it all and try to sleep. I wish I could fall asleep. I don't understand… I took a sedative at the airport in Cuba before leaving and I still do not feel sleepy. My stomach is trembling again. I have to write to my parents. Yeah, that's a good idea. I turn on the light again, open the folding tray and get my pen. It's my mother's, it has her name engraved on it, she gave it to me. When am I going to see her again? In the beginning she didn't want me to leave. But later on she understood and helped me all the way.

A few years had passed since Castro took control. We were already officially declared as "The first Socialist country in the Americas" and families were successfully divided. Families were not what they used to be. They were separated by politics. My mother's side of the family was unconditionally obfuscated to defend the undefendable–except one of my uncles–the nightmare that we were living. My father's family were in favor of freedom, free enterprise and the democratic principles in our 1940 Constitution. Many of them had already left Cuba for exile in the U.S., including the two children of my uncle Rene who escaped Cuba through a clandestine operation known as Operation Peter Pan. From 1960 to 1962, 14,048 unaccompanied children were sent by their parents to the U.S. This exodus is known as the biggest exodus of unaccompanied children in the Western Hemisphere–of course this is unknown to the American people as a result of the liberal media and Marxist academia censorship.

My dog Terry was on the side of freedom. Dogs dislike oppressive captivity against their own will. That's why they are escape artists. Like me.

After all the incessant, inescapable propaganda and brainwashing going on 24-7, there was a moment that even I accepted the revolution, but not so blindly as others. I even thought that "Socialism" was good. But I understood perfectly that some people disliked living under the New Order and wanted to leave for the U.S. or other countries. Since my childhood as a neighbor of Papa Gordo and Mama Zoila, I understood that traveling or living in other countries does not make someone an enemy, a traitor or a "Worm."

A lot of people, relatives and friends were leaving or thinking about leaving. I always wished them the best and, with some I, kept correspondence which was a **<u>NO NO</u>** in revolutionary circles. I liked the idea that they were going to travel abroad and see wonderful things like my childhood neighbors. All that hatred in the revolutionary air failed to register deep within me.

My little cousin soon joined the "The Union of Young Communists," which was like Hitler's Brownshirts. When he tried to convince me to join, I would tell him, "Look, you may be a soldier of the revolution with your guns, but I'll be one from the stage." I don't have the same desires and you should respect my choices."

"That's inconceivable for the Revolution," he used to say, adding, "Either you are with the Revolution or against the Revolution. The show business world is not regarded as having any value by the Revolution."

A phony comment, because a few years later the only plays and movies being done were in support of the Revolution or "revolutionary principles" as the arts became tools for propaganda, indoctrination and brainwashing of the masses.

As he kept trying to convert me he said, "You should join the revolutionary organizations and go whatever they send you for the benefit of the Revolution."

And I replied, "I don't want to be sent to any place I don't choose. I am a person, a human being, an individual. I want to choose my own destiny. I want to be free."

"You have already chosen your destiny," he said, "and it is not a good one… Don't say to anyone what you just said to me. You may get in grave trouble with the Revolution… I'm your cousin and I will not say anything."

And I inquired, "What's wrong with what I said…?

"I cannot explain it to you," he answered, "obviously, you will not understand."

And I asked him again, "What's wrong with wanting to be free? Isn't that what everybody wanted from this Revolution…? I was free to make my own decisions before 1959."

"Just forget it," he rapidly said, "I will forget that this conversation ever took place."

I was very troubled by my little cousin becoming increasingly hostile toward anybody who is not considered a "revolutionary" and warning me of "grave trouble" for simply expressing my individual opinion. But unfortunately it was not only him. That attitude was growing among the youth being indoctrinated in the government public education system. Private education of all denominations was almost non-existent now or in the process of disappearing. And the new curriculum imposed was political Marxism geared to collectivism and obedience to the dictums of the Revolution. Adults deemed not to be sympathetic were sent to distant "reeducation camps". Even a Castro speech was specifically geared to artists and intellectuals when he said,

"With the Revolution everything, without The Revolution nothing!" So maybe my little cousin was referring to those "reeducation camps" for me because I wanted to be free! But being free is a natural desire of all human beings! This Revolution was eliminating all vestiges of individual freedoms.

But so far I had been very lucky and I kept my ideals to myself and learned how to pretend. That was a phenomenon that was not unique to me. Everybody had to do it in order to survive inside that monstrosity, even those in favor of the Revolution. But I kept my sanity by focusing on my goal to be an actor, in spite of my bad memory. I kept a very low profile to be unnoticed but free in the middle of so many limitations. I was free to a point I could not cross in order not to be found in need of the services of one of the feared reeducation camps in the distant countryside. The horrors of those camps became evident as people who survived them were back home. So it's true, The Revolution was evil and contrary to all decent aspirations of mankind. You have to live and survive inside that political aberration to understand what living in hell is… I watched everything from the outside, like a critical spectator and I felt a profound revulsion for what I saw. The excuse that the "revolutionaries" used was "That's part of the revolutionary process."

The major problem is that the horrors of "the process" systematically impacts everyone, even the sympathizers, whether they realize it or not. And, it never ends. The goal of some sort of utopia doesn't get closer and closer, it gets further and further away.

I learned from friends and from clandestine rumors circulating based on experiences from other victims–that's the way you find out what is really going on inside communist countries, because the government press and TV is not going to present the cruel reality. So very hushed recounts of the repression, arrests, tortures and crimes by the Secret Police, the G2, were rampant. People in Cuba were very afraid of the revolutionary "JUSTICE" arresting thousands of people in the darkness of the night from their own homes. In the beginning I discarded those rumors, but when it affects close friends, you stop and think. A G2 accusation without proof that you were a U.S. CIA Agent will land you in Castro's dungeons without a trial and executed by firing squad. All lawyers became official government lawyers, the only kind allowed, so they always sided with the government. The Revolution always was right and you were always guilty. There was no escape from that reality. The people were terrorized, so the previously very much alive streets of La Habana were filled instead with fear. At night I didn't go out at all. Actually most people who before Castro used to go to restaurants, theaters, night clubs, or to visit friends or relatives instead stayed home with the shades drawn thinking, "This can't last very long".

During those horrible times I was attending classes at night at the Municipal Academy of Dramatic Arts of La Habana. But it was located in a nice area where some elite of The Revolution lived in expropriated mansions and fancy apartments, along with some foreigners and diplomats. One such elite was the opportunist prima ballerina, the famous Alicia Alonso who was given a duplex almost facing the Municipal Academy. Being inside the Academy at night was safe but I didn't venture to other places in the city.

One of the female students at the Municipal Academy was working on a weekly children's radio show on *"Radio Rebelde"* ("Rebel Radio" meaning rebelling against the pre-Castro government and civilization) which was the former radio station *COCO* that was expropriated by The Revolution from its rightful owners and it was renamed as the clandestine radio station of Castro's broadcasts from the Sierra Maestra Mountains: *Radio Rebelde*. Because of being recommended by my fellow student I was hired as one of the regular actors on the show. Finally my little revolutionary cousin was proud of me for working at *Radio Rebelde*! During my few years tenure on children's show as a regular actor, I also wrote two stories in four chapters each that were used on the show. The name of the show was *Jardin Infantil*, "Garden of the Children." After a few years the station canceled the show because they wanted a more political show to indoctrinate children. So the lady who created the show and had it for years, Carmita Garcia Guerra, was fired and went to exile in the U.S. I also participated in some shows on other radio stations.

After four years I graduated and immediately landed the main role in a play based on the Greek comedy of Aristophanes, *Lisistrata*. This play was converted into a musical comedy and the female star was the great actress and singer, Maria de Los Angeles Santana. The play was a great success and got very good reviews. During those times I went only from my home to the theater and vice versa avoiding being out at night. So nothing happened to me.

After that I was offered a third co-starring role in a film about the revolutionary "voluntary teachers" who went to the Sierra Maestra mountains to teach the isolated people on these mountains to read and write. However, this was a ruse because everything in that program was pure and simple communist political indoctrination specifically designed to create supporters of the revolution.

The set of the "voluntary teachers" was constructed according to the typical "communist planification." They think that they can control everything, **EVEN NATURE**! Or maybe they thought nature would change itself to conform to the needs of the revolution. Anyway, they didn't take into consideration that it was the rainy season in the mountains! So we departed by train with the full cast, crew and equipment. To make this long story short, we stayed 30 days and 30 nights and couldn't film anything because it was raining all the time. The name of the area where they built the set is "La Magdalena," named like that indicating that **IT RAINS ALL THE TIME**. So much for the communist *planification*!

So everybody was sent back to La Habana by train which took 16 hours! I didn't want to go through that again, so I went to the capital city of Santiago de Cuba with one of the main actors of the production and we returned by plane. It was a Russian bimotor *Ilyushin* that was an old, vibrating coffee pot but at least the return was just three hours. My father picked us up at the Jose Marti Nacional Airport near La Habana. We descended from the Russian plane still vibrating!!

A new set was built in *El Bosque de La Habana* (*The Woods of La Habana*) and we completed the production there.

I also participated in two other films in small roles. One of them was a co-production with East Germany with an actor that years later did American films and was nominated for an Oscar for Best Supporting Actor, Armin Mueller Stahl.

I also was involved with a theatrical group geared to children as an actor and another group for which I wrote five one act plays that were censored for being critical of the "wonderful" Castro revolution.

It was during this period that one afternoon while walking to the theater where I was rehearsing a play, I saw sitting on a shoe-shine chair in the corner of a bar, one of my old roommates from my first year of High School at the Presbyterian Boarding School and he recognized me immediately after 5 years! He got up from the chair smiling with his right arm extended to me. I don't know exactly why, but I acted as if I had not seen him and continued walking without acknowledging his presence. What a terrible thing I had done! He was always very pleasant and friendly to me at school. After I turned the corner, I took a fast glance at him and there he was like frozen, with his outstretched arm waiting to shake my hand. He was in disbelief of my reaction to seeing him. I really felt extremely bad and wanted to go back to him and apologize and shake his hand. But I was so embarrassed that I could not bring myself to do it. Perhaps it was destiny–I thought–we are not supposed to meet again. So I continued walking to the theater. Now with hindsight, this could have changed what happened to me later on that evening...

After the rehearsal was over in the early evening, I found out from a fellow actor in the play that the Films Institute (*Cinemateca*) was showing a well known French film based on a play in one act by Jean Paul Sartre titled *The Respectful Whore* which was released as a film in 1952. It was directed by Charles Brabant and Marcello Pagliero with Barbara Laage and Ivan Desny.

Sartre's play had been performed on stage in Cuba directed by the famous Cuban director Francisco Morin whom I met later in exile in New York. Sartre was a blind admirer of Castro and he and his wife, Simone de Beauvoir, visited Cuba after 1959 to meet their hero "The Maximum Leader of The Revolution." So the exhibition of that film in Cuba was a big event. After my rehearsal I went to see the movie. When I arrived there the film had already begun and the theater was packed. I checked downstairs in the dark and could not see an empty seat. I went up to the upper balcony which I detested, because in movie theaters I always wanted to sit no farther than the tenth row and in the center, but I had to compromise and sat on the first seat I found available. After a while I was tapped on the shoulder and somebody whispered something I didn't understand. I turned and with a flashlight he was showing me his ID card. I couldn't understand why he was doing that and I couldn't read it well enough to figure out what it was. Then someone joined him and asked me to accompany them to the lobby so they could verify my ID. It was such an odd situation and I had no idea why they picked me. I said, "I'm sorry but I don't have to go anywhere with you." Then one of them said, "Come with us because you are under arrest!" I replied, "Arrest for what?" And he said, "Come with us to the lobby so you can show me your ID and clarify your situation." So, I decided to go down with them to the lobby to resolve the situation and not create a scene in the crowded movie house. There were a lot of people from show business in the movie house who knew who

I was so I was sure it was a misunderstanding and the whole situation would be clarified quickly in the lobby.

Under the light of the lobby I saw that the two men were not older than 20 years old. Standing in the lobby was a bald man in his forties I didn't know and he looked like he was in shock and disbelief of the whole situation. I noticed that there was also a younger man tightly holding him by his arm. But somehow I was confident that the whole situation with me would be over quickly. The young man that was holding me again showed me his ID from the already infamous and dreaded Union of Young Communists which said they were acting as vigilantes inside the movie house. That was not a good sign, I thought to myself. Young communist "vigilantes" must be another of the many specialized, repressive organizations that The Revolution had created to oppress and terrorize the population that I didn't know about. But it confirmed the rumor about the introduction of more and more of these efforts to instill fear. How am I going to get out of this? And I said, "Look comrades, I think you are making an error. I came here to watch a film about a play written by a personal friend of "The Maximum Leader." As you can see on my ID my name is Agustin Blazquez and I am an actor who used to work at Radio Rebelde, the original broadcast station of "The Maximum Leader" when he was at the Sierra Maestra mountains and I participated in films for the government. I also work as an actor at the theater The Basement (*El Sotano*). You can verify this on my ID to prove that I am "a worker of The Revolution."

Then one of them asked me if the older man was with me? "No," I said, "I have never seen him before in my life, I don't know who he is." Then one of the young men said, "Shut up, that's it! Now you pair of SCUM have to go to the office with us!"

I had heard of people experiencing things like this, but just until that exact moment, I was not able to completely believe them. And I thought that would never happen to me! I wasn't involved in anything harmful against this revolution—even though I disliked it because we lost freedom of speech and we were at the mercy of Castro's goons. But what I was experiencing was the true reality of this anti-natural, crooked philosophy. Now I face reality on my own skin. This was not a dream or a fantasy. Actors, singers, artists, poets and intellectuals were suddenly no longer considered "workers." Workers are now the ones who work in the fields, in factories, mines and other heavy jobs. We were just scum. And we have to be eliminated or sent to reeducation camps where Marxism is fed 24-7 to the prisoners in inhumane cells where torture and where death are abundant. Innocent people were in fact victimized, just because they are human beings who happen to be in an industry that is being converted to support Castro's rule.

In the office of the Cinemateca the two young men took my Cinemateca membership card and my official ID card issued by the government that showed I was a productive, working member of this revolutionary paradise. Without the Cinemateca card I would not be able to attend anything there again, but at this point I didn't want to go there any more. But the government ID was required–carry and without it you are a non–person, so these two kids converted me. I realized that there was nothing I could do. There were no constitutional protections for the citizens against this abusive government. Just shut up and obey. I realized it was all over.

From there I was taken to a Police Station where I was shoved onto a bench and the two young accusers went inside to press the charges against me. I sat there wondering what would happen next. Some time later the same two young accusers came out smiling and very satisfied with the success of their mission. I thought, "Perhaps they filled their quota for the night. What kind of people go along with this monstrosity?" The whole situation was so absurd that I started playing with a puppy dog running around the station in order to forget the horrible reality I was living through. Later I needed to go to the restroom and asked permission from one of the policemen around. He was not very pleased with my request but he granted permission and pointed the way.

I went through a door to a dark hallway and at the end of it it was the restroom. On my way there I passed in front of a cell full of people all standing one against each other like sardines and holding their arms up in the air, in complete silence. It was a surreal and chilling thing to see. The restroom was filthy and the stench was almost unbearable. Finally I was able to urinate and get the hell out of there and back to the bench where I had been sitting. I kept insisting to another police-man to let me use the phone to call home. A while later they let me but with the policemen standing just by my side and with the condition that I wouldn't reveal where I was. Fine, anything as long as they let me hear a familiar voice. My mother, very alarmed, answered the phone because I was never late returning home at night. The only thing that I was able to tell her was that I was fine and would be home later due to "a small inconvenience." I was pretty sure she understood because of the unusual tone in my voice. After the police heard "inconvenience," he ordered me to hang up immediately. My mother, hearing that order in the background, suspected what was going on, especially because she knew that things in Cuba were not as before, as well as what The Revolution had done against relatives who were small farmers–their properties were expropriated by the new regime and most of them were leaving Cuba for exile in the U.S.

My mother's brothers in La Habana –except one–were firm believ-ers in "The Maximum Leader," so he could not get a position in the regime, especially in the dreaded Secret Police G2; the others could.

She knew that after the rehearsal I had gone to the *Cinemateca*. She immediately called one of her younger brothers, a firm believer, and together with my father went to the *Cinemateca*. As a member of the Secret Police her brother was able to find out what happened. But they had already transferred me to the dreaded *El Castillo del Principe* (The Prince Castle) built by the Spaniards during colonial times, now used for such things as holding and torturing prisoners. Since I was already there, nothing could be done until the next morning.

Meantime, when I was admitted there as a prisoner, a guard stole from my wallet a silver dollar issued in Cuba in 1953 to honor the 100th anniversary of the birth of the Cuban patriot Jose Marti that my father gave me while we were living in Limonar. Since "The Maximum Leader" expropriated the island from the Cuban people, it was forbidden to possess silver coins from the past nor any U.S. money. Prior to the Revolution the Cuban Peso had the same value as the U.S. dollar, so both currencies had circulated freely on the island. The guard also stole my watch.

The guards conducted me to the second floor of the former castle. I wondered what time it was. It was very dark outside. We arrived at an old, iron door. The guard produced a big key, opened the door and pushed me into a huge, dimly lit dungeon full of prisoners. When the guard left an old man came to me asking, "Why are you here?" I replied, "I don't have the slightest idea. Two guys came out of the blue and detained me and sent me to a police station." The others were repeating, "The same for me…" They did not have any idea why they were there either. Apparently they were all newcomers like me from raids that the G2 Secret Police was conducting in La Habana at night. They came to be known as *"recogidas"*, "collected", referring to the massive apprehension of civilians that the regime suspected of being "Worms" or non-supporters. Some said the G2 knocked on their doors at midnight and said, "Come with us." They were dropped at various police stations and later were taken to this jail. They looked like decent, educated people. One of them was a Jehovah's Witness leader–Castro early on declared war against this religion and its members. The dungeon had no beds. You had to sleep on the very cold, stone floor. One of them took off his jacket and gave it to me so I could use it as a pillow to sleep. So I laid down and closed my eyes but I couldn't sleep thinking about what might happen next…

In the morning there was suddenly a lot of activity on the opposite side from where I was lying on the floor. I noticed that there was an iron gate to an outside terrace and daylight was entering. Then a guard announced that breakfast was on that terrace. So people began to walk toward that door, so I did and returned the jacket to the guy who gave it to me. On my way I passed by the area where the commotion was and I saw why the other guards were making loud comments and laughing. It was because an overweight guard was naked taking a shower and dancing in front of everybody. I kept walking. The terrace was surrounded by a two story high stone wall so we were "safe" inside. I joined the line for breakfast. It was a dirt color liquid and a small piece of old bread. I took it and found a piece of wood on the floor and sat. I drank that dirty water but I couldn't chew the "iron" bread. I overheard other prisoners saying that they were there for no reason and without charges…

Then a guard called my name. All the other prisoners turned toward me. I got up and followed the guard to the opposite side of the room to the door where I entered the night before. He opened that door and asked me to follow him. From there in the daylight I could see a big terrace around the central courtyard of the former castle. We walked downstairs to the same room where I was admitted the night before and they told me that somebody was waiting for me outside. So two other guards conducted me to the main entrance of the castle—still I had no clue what they were going to do with me… Then they opened the door to the exterior and I saw about a third of a block away, a car with the door open. To the side was one of my G2 uncles and my mother and father. And the guard released me to them. After quick greetings, we all got in the car and left the hill where The Prince Castle was located. About 10 blocks away was my grandmother's home. But she didn't know anything about what had happened to me. So we went directly to our home. There my uncle told me that he couldn't expunge my record and that I would have to go to trial…

Very soon after–trials are one of the few speedy and efficient benefits of this putrid totalitarian regime–I had to face the "<u>revolutionary justice</u>." which is nothing else but "INJUSTICE" because all lawyers are regime lawyers who had to agree with all accusations, however bogus; they could only beg for clemency. We now found out first hand that the rumors were true. So my mother, father and my G2 uncle attended. Before the rapid proceeding, I had no alternative than to plead "GUILTY." I'm not sure what the charges were, if I knew at the time, apparently the trauma erased it from my mind along with what happened afterward. The only thing that I remember was that after that I didn't set foot outside without my mother and father day or night! I didn't complain, after that experience I knew it was necessary inside that monstrous regime.

Now you see why I should have acknowledged that friendly high school roommate. Probably after the play rehearsal I would have gotten together with him to sit and talk about what we have done in these five years since we last saw each other rather than going to see that film. And probably my destiny would have been different! By the way, what I saw of this Sartre's film at the Cinemateca was VERY BOOOORING.

I eventually realized why I was apprehended. After the revolution, the youth in Cuba was being castigated for dressing like teenagers. Anything and everything related to The Beatles, rock'n roll, jazz, and American music in general was cause for arrest for charges such as being "Anti-Social". Yes, that was the official charge. Males were prohibited from having long hair or too short, including a trendy French hairstyle that was short. And bluejeans, pants too tight, bell bottoms or pants too short. Girls were also punished for having the latest fashion and mini skirts or short hair. For any "extravagant" way of appearing in public, you could be apprehended on the streets and 100% of accusations were found to be guilty as charged.

The Castro regime created the official "Bureau of the Fashion," to dictate how his subjects should look. MUST look.

In my case the real cause for my apprehension was due to the fact that I was dressed like a French "existentialist," which was the philosophy put forward by Castro's friend and visitor to the island, Monsieur Jean Paul Sartre. That fateful evening, my black shirt, black pants, black shoes and black socks topped off by the forbidden French short haircut did me in. Ironically, although what I had on was particularly appropriate for going to the film of Castro's friend, the developer of the philosophy of Existentialism—which, ironically Castro of course didn't want for his new society—it was now being considered a display that I was dissenting of "The Maximum Leader." As for Sartre's philosophy "frankly my dear, I don't give a damn."

SO NOW YOU KNOW WHY I WAS ARRESTED AND SENT TO JAIL!*!*

Inside the plane I turned off the overhead light and looked outside the window to see the rims of light around the edges of the clouds and the stars. The total silence inside the airplane continued despite the growing number of miles between us and the seven long years of revolution. We were scared even of our shadows and we had perfected politically correct auto-censorship. We learned to survive with two faces. One in a very low voice inside our homes how we feel about the status quo and another on the streets as "supporters of the revolution."

After the horrible experience of my arrest, as the student of the well known soprano Zoila Galvez and baritone Bendoiro during the day, I began my career as a singer. Later I began to create my repertoire, also during the day with the famous composer, Candito Ruiz, who accompanied me on the piano. He made my debut possible at Jim's NightClub in La Habana and I was on two Special TV shows thanks to him.

After that I was put under contract with a theatrical group the government created to present plays in the countryside around La Habana. It was of course in a legitimate revolutionary company that I was sure my little cousin would have approved and even been PROUD of me. What he didn't know was that at that time I detested THE REVOLUTION more than ever because I had more information and first hand experience with the actual "REVOLUTIONARY JUSTICE". But I didn't see my little cousin during that period. He was busy involved in defending the indefensible. Even my mother was afraid of him and asked me not to talk to him anymore!

My days working with that government theatrical company required us to arrive at the big mansion expropriated from its owner at lunch time during the day for a complete lunch cooked by the kitchen staff in the dining room. Then we would rehearse the play. After that we put on our makeup and then were transported in a common Russian truck with improvised seats to the location in the countryside where the presentation was going to take place. When we arrived, after a very bumpy trip, an earlier crew had already created the exterior stage, set, furniture and lights. Our wardrobe was already there and we got dressed in an improvised area. The free presentation was already advertised and the audience of farmers was dragged there, as their attendance was compulsory. And the show must go on…

The first play I did with that company was the translation of a Communist Chinese, political indoctrination play titled *Counter Revolution in the Chinese Village*. It was specifically designed to indoctrinate people with the idea that the capitalist business owners were **EVIL** and the exploited workers were **THE GOOD GUYS** and they **MUST REVOLT AGAINST THE CAPITALISTS' WAYS**. That's what I could get from this political concoction. The only good thing about it was the colorful, classic Chinese costumes of the Chinese capitalists.

One evening the outdoor stage was full of flying insects attracted by the lights and the cast didn't have any other alternative than trying to swat them away. We had to be very careful because in a few instances they went inside the mouths of the main actors. We could not contain our laughter. The actor who played the mayor of the village took decisive action and got his wooden post weapon and quietly began fighting the bugs and smashing them on the floor of the stage as if it was part of the play. Apparently the audience thought that it was! They began laughing out loud, as did, unfortunately, the rest of the cast. The lighting technician lowered the intensity of the lights but the swarm of bugs continued and that was the abrupt end of the awful play while the audience cheered the fun and exciting conclusion! It was much better than the actual play.

Finally, that awful play was removed from our repertoire. And we began rehearsals for the civilized but political play by Irish playwright Sean O'Casey, *Juno and the Paycock* which was directed by the Mexican director Rodolfo Valencia. I was given the role of Charlie Bentham, alternating every other day with another actor. The Charlie Bentham role was much better than my character in the abominable Chinese nightmare.

Every night each actor was transported back to their own homes—I guess the people managing that traveling theatrical company knew in their heart that the government was arresting actors, intellectuals and anybody else in the arts field, so they gave us a lot of protection during those horrible times.

During this time I made contact with many of the female singers of the Opera Company in La Habana who were not far from the head-quarters of the company I was under contract with. One evening two of the sopranos were performing the main and rival leading characters of the Spanish zarzuela *Luisa Fernanda*. An actor friend and I walked the few blocks from the location of my company to the opera house.

I had told him about my horrible experience at the Cinemateca, but apparently he didn't completely believe it. He was working with a very left wing company whose founder and his sister were known as communists since before the revolution. This actor friend was very good friends with the Italian professor of Marxism at his theatrical company, Wanda Garatti. What had happened to me was not what The Revolution or Marxist Communism promised to do, according to his Marxist political indoctrination. Therefore, it couldn't happen. And it couldn't be true. If the revolution arrests someone it has to be for a valid reason.

After the opera we were to get together with our soprano friends to eat at one of the restaurants frequented by the government elite which had much better food and more variety than the others. When the show was over my actor friend and I exited by the front door of the beautiful old theater—this was my first venture out at night. It was a very short walk outside on the sidewalk around to the stage door. About 25 feet before reaching the door…suddenly, out of nowhere, a man stopped us, fashing his official G2 secret police ID and he demanded for us to come with him. Based on my previous experience, I immediately understood what was going to happen next and froze on the spot.

My friend thought it was a joke and said, "Oh come on…get out of here."

And he replied, "You are under arrest!"

My friend said, "You have to be kidding!"

The secret policeman responded with a menacing tone in his voice, "You two better come with me to the police station for identification!"

"We don't have to go to any police station for that." said my friend, adding, "Comrade, I can show you my ID right now." And got his wallet and showed the police his ID card. I did the same proving that I was also an actor working for theatrical companies owned by the revolution.

With the same menacing tone he responded, "You have to go with me." And threatening, "Don't make a scene here! Do not attract anybody's attention!"

My friend inquired, "Listen comrade, can you explain why you are arresting us?

"It's simple, for identification. If you go with me everything will be over soon," he said, trying to convince us.

My friend had not had an experience like this before, so he still thought he could use reason to end the situation, so he explained, "Comrade, we are here to pick up our two friends who are the stars of the zarzuela in this official theater managed by the revolution"–he mentioned their names since both of them were well known–"And we came to pick then up to go to a restaurant for dinner. That's it. That's why we were here walking to the stage door."

With my experience, I was afraid he was making things worse.

The secret policeman didn't give a damn about a reason for our presence on the sidewalk and mechanically replied, "You have to go with me."

My friend responded, "Can you come with us to meet the singers to corroborate what we are doing here?"

"No way," he categorically responded, "You do not go to or call anybody."

Then, in a last effort to make that man reason, he said, "Comrade, listen to me for a moment. I am an official actor and he is another official actor. Both are under contract with companies supported by the National Council of Culture. We are workers. You should not arrest us for no reason. You are making a mistake. We are not 'parasites of society,' we are workers of the revolution, just like you."

And the secret policeman, getting his revolver from under his shirt and pointing it at us, ordered us to go with him.

And my friend asked, "Can you assure us that as soon as we show our IDs at the police station, everything will be clarified?

He replied, "Yes, come on and everything will be over soon."

At that moment Maria, a friend and well known coloratura soprano, with her husband, the conductor of the opera orchestra came out of the stage door and saw us and because we did not walk over to greet her she suspected something was wrong was going on and asked from the distance, "What's the matter with you two? Is something wrong?"

And the policeman pressed the gun against my friend's stomach and threatened him, "Don't you dare to tell her anything! Tell her that there is nothing wrong!

And he had to say to her, "No, Maria. it's nothing. We just have to leave."

He made us turn our backs to her and walk in the opposite direction from the stage door with his revolver in our backs...

The plane was going through some turbulence, jumping and vibrating. I had never been on a big passenger plane like the four propeller Britannia and was surprised at the ratling and jumping like this. Are we going to crash?

My previous plane trip was in a bimotor Russian Ilyushin which felt like riding an old coffee pot.

Prior to that, as a kid, I flew in a Piper Cub used to deliver milk in the countryside near the town of Coliseo. Suddenly during that flight, the right door opened while up in the air and my father had to put his arm outside to pull the door closed! I must have been 5 years old and I still remember that sudden scary incident! My mother, watching from the ground, was very upset. The pilot could have been a character from a movie. He would land his Piper in agricultural fields around the area. The pilot of this milk delivery "enterprise" had to cease and desist his risky deliveries because one time some of the fairly big metal milk containers fell from the plane onto the roof of a house.

We heard the voice of Britannia's pilot announcing the turbulence and advising us to remain in our seats and lock our seatbelts. But we were all silent in our seats afraid to move. The only ones up and about were the nasty stewardesses. Let's see if this turbulence is over... And I kept thinking about some traumatic events of my life that finally made me make the decision to fly away from that hellhole, and it was a bonafide hellhole…

While we were walking toward the police station my friend was still trying to convince the secret police that he was making a mistake with us. As we walked we left the beautiful, ornate building where the theater was located behind us. Located across from La Habana's central park, the correct name of the building was "Centro Gallego" which was built around an old theater named "Teatro Tacon, built in 1838 with 2,750 seats. In 1914 the new building, designed by Belgian architect Paul Belau, built by Purdy and Henderson Engineers, was built around the existing theater which was remodeled and later renamed "Gran Teatro Nacional". The 1914 building was paid for by immigrants from Galicia, Spain.

After the revolution this theater was renamed "Garcia Lorca" to honor poet and writer Federico Garcia Lorca who died during Spain's Civil War on August 19, 1936. After the revolution, it became the new location for Operas and Zarzuelas.

Forced to walk away from our dinner date with the opera singers in that previously very much illuminated and lively area of La Habana, now it was dark and without a single soul around. It was eerie. I remember that before the revolution that area was full of restaurants and live music, places with orchestras and people dancing, taking and singing. But now that was over and it was becoming known as a place not to walk and laugh.

Certainly it was not late. It was about 9 pm when we were conducted to a police station for simply nothing in particular. That loneliness of empty streets was because Castro wanted to eliminate the famous nightlife of La Habana and was conducting raids to apprehend people that were on the streets after 8 pm. It was inconceivable that a "worker" would be on the streets after 8 pm during the six day work week. I learned about that from my G2 uncles and other people who were victims of these raids, but my friend refused to take seriously what I had learned. On the one hand I understood my story was impossible for him to accept, while on the other I was concerned that his insisting would only make things worse for both of us.

As we walked I could see the changes–everything was gone, even the shadows of what it had been. This is what "The Maximum Leader" had accomplished! This is what his revolution has done to all of us! I felt a deep, loud and desperate scream deep within myself.

After a few more blocks, we arrived at the police station. We entered and just as we stepped in the secret G2 policeman pushed us against the counter and shouted, "Here are two more!" And he turned away in a hurry and left. I guess by saying "two more" of his arrest quota for the evening!

The friend still couldn't believe what was happening! He turned to face the officer behind the counter. He said, "He just brought us here for identification, that's what he assured us," and got his ID out and put it on the counter, "See? Here you are… This is my actor work ID. This is from the theater company where I work everyday." He said to me, "Show yours…show yours! So they can see who you are, too!"

Based on what I learned during my preview experience at the Cinemateca, I knew that the official government ID is of no use in this case, but I got it out of my wallet and put it on the counter. "You see comrade…? Are you satisfied we are just workers? Can we go now?" That was my friend.

And the officer at the counter said, "Stick your IDs in your ass holes!" He called over another officer nearby and said, "Hey you! Come here and take these two inside!"

This other officer came promptly and pushed us through a door into a dark hallway. In it he opened a second door and said, "Get in here!" and pushed us into a very dark room where I could hardly see and he slammed the door behind us. It was pitch black, hot and oppressive. I could hardly move but felt a lot of bodies around me. Obviously that cell was packed to capacity. After a while my eyes got used to the dark and I was able to see the silhouette of way too many people all standing with their arms raised. With a lot of effort I was able to raise my two arms like the others. I guess this was a way to save some space. It was like being in a horror nightmare. You heard the breathing of the other prisoners and the almost whispered sound of voices saying that they were detained on the streets or picked up by the G2 goons from inside their houses. And some others said that they were asleep in their own beds when they were taken. I kept my head up so in order to breathe. This was a scene in a horror film. I thought, is this what Castro's revolution and the socialists and communists involved in it call "Social Justice?!"

I thought of my uncles involved in this monstrosity, too. How come they are participating in this violation of human rights? It was getting very hot there and I was wondering what they were going to do with us. I heard my friend apprehended with me, crying and repeating, "I cannot believe this. It has to be a mistake. I cannot believe this, it must be a mistake!" And I whispered to him, "Now do you believe me?" His attitude and refusal to accept that the Castro regime was ordering these raids to terrorize and silence the population bothered me. Actually I was the victim of this second horrible experience. He refused to acknowledge this reality after Castro took control of the whole island.

I suppose that explains why people the world over don't believe these horrors. Even as it was happening to him my friend couldn't believe it.

This was not a positive change for Cuba and as time passes it seems it's still getting worse. If you didn't like Batista, there were options. You could leave the country freely with all of your property. Your homes and businesses were not expropriated and they didn't punish the relatives you left behind. But now with his repressive machine trained and equipped by Russia and Bulgaria, the G2 and the block by block Committees for the Defense of the Revolution spying on each city block all over the island, it is impossible to move a finger without being discovered. We are doomed.

I hope that my friend will learn once and for all what Castro has done. So I whispered to him, "Calm down. You will not go very far like that. You have to be calm in order to survive this situation."

I was thinking: since I would not be arriving home at the usual time, my parents would suspect that something was wrong and would be able to do something…The only thing to do is to wait. I whispered my thoughts to my friend. Then, a guy beside me whispered something that I didn't understand.

I whispered to him to repeat and he said, "Where did they pick you up?"

"Close to the stage door of the *Garcia Lorca Theater*," I replied.

"Yeah, I was leaving that theater too when I was detained. Many people in the cell were leaving that theater when they were detained, too. Obviously they were detaining a lot of people there tonight. Some of my friends were detained around that area." he explained and I thought, that's why that usually bustling area was so empty.

Then I asked him, "Do you know what they did to them?"

"The same, they were sent to this police station and later were transferred to a place in *La Habana Vieja* (Old La Habana) where they were photographed with a number on their chest and were released later on after agreeing to sign a confession. Tell your friend that there is no use in being hysterical or trying to make any sense of this senseless repression…Is he a supporter of the revolution?" he asked.

"Yeah…kind of," I answered

And he stated, "He will not be for long after this experience…He'll see, he'll see…"

The friend asked me about the whispered conversation with the other detainee. I whispered back to him what he said. Then I heard somebody in the cell asking in a loud voice, "Does anybody know what they are going to do with us?"

And somebody in the cell loudly exclaimed, "Send us to a farm with all the faggots!" and a few seconds we heard a voice exclaiming, "God damn you, I'm not a faggot!"

Most people in the cell made some 'shushing' sounds and somebody else added, "Do not create any scandal… We are all in the same boat. We can all be punished! You know how these criminal goons are! And silence again returned to the cell.

I don't know how long we had been standing here, but I was getting very tired and restless. I do not know how I would be able to keep my arms up in the air. I was feeling muscular pains. Then the door of the cell was opened and more people were squeezed in. These goons are worse than any wild animal on this planet! I overheard someone crying in the background and the door opened again. I could not imagine more people squeezed in here! But this time the goons of the G2 in charge of this cruelty were ordering a group of the prisoners to move out in an orderly manner. Fortunately my friend and I were in this "lucky" group.

So, followed by the G2 goons carrying machine guns pointed at us, we were rushed into a paddy wagon parked just outside the entrance of the police station. For a few seconds we were able to breathe some welcoming fresh air. Outside, because of the street lights I was able to see that there were a great number of blacks among the prisoners. We were loaded like sardines inside the wagon. It was extremely hot inside and I was quickly drenched with perspiration. Once our group was squeezed in by a G2 goon who was having a lot of problems closing the doors of the paddy wagon as if we were not human beings. This was one more example of the much heralded "revolutionary justice" in the press and the two TV government channels that we were allowed to watch on our island paradise. After that the "comfortable" paddy wagon left the "friendly" neighborhood police station.

In our group inside the revolutionary delightful paddy wagon in route to our next violation of human rights, were a disproportionate number of blacks—certainly "black lives matter" a lot to these communist goons.

There was also a very distinguished and educated older man who said, during our ride to our next opportunity to serve The Revolution, "I am a teacher. I am not 'scum,' The G2 broke into my own home when I was in bed sleeping. I do not know why. I am an old black man. Never in my entire life, have I ever been subjected to degrading treatment like this. In my own country!"

Another person in the group replied, "Well, now you will learn what this revolution has been all about from the beginning."

And a black man beside me added, "Now we are slaves again."

"Amen," someone else said.

The rest of the trip to the unknown was in silence until the paddy wagon stopped. The doors were opened from the outside and another group of G2 goons with machine guns was ready and waiting for us to get out. I recognized the place where we were. I had passed by that old colonial building before. It was in a narrow street of the older section of La Habana. I think it was an old Catholic school that was expropriated from the Catholic church. This old and quaint side of the city flourished from its foundation by Don Diego Velazquez in 1515 until the end of the 19th century. It was filled with historical, architectural treasures including beautiful colonial homes. And in one of them we were being rushed at machine gun point. And more paddy wagons arrived throughout this long, dark night. Now this house was dark and dreadful. It wasn't beautiful any longer. A few single low-watt light bulbs were hanging from long wires from the high ceilings, probably the chandeliers were removed and distributed among the revolutionary government ruling elite and relatives and lovers. These insufficient lights contributed to the gloomy atmosphere of doom.

We entered the former school through the original front carriage entrance. And from there we were conducted through the ample corridors surrounding the huge central patio and we were surprised to see at least a thousand prisoners standing in a big line around the four sides of the corridor around the patio. They "the victims tonight's catch." waiting to be photographed for the revolution's new plan of oppression. I saw one group being conducted to one of the rooms of the ground floor of happier times, now converted into an ample cell. Our group was not the first being shoved in a room. Fortunately we were still able to move around there and went to a corner and sat on the floor. I asked a guy sitting nearby, "How long have you been here?"

"I don't know. I just don't know. I have lost track of time… I wish the earth would open and swallow me now." was his answer. As I waited for the next step of this ordeal, I thought that by this time my parents would be asking the same G2 uncle who got me out of prison before to again find out where I was and use his influence to get me out of this new nightmare. I thought of the stories of the atrocities I had heard and terrible tortures the G2 is using now against the population. It was so bad that it was very difficult to accept that something so brutal was taking place in Cuba and that the rest of the free world was so silent about it. Perhaps Cubans are considered expendable and they only care about the false myth of Castro and his revolution as perpetrated by the media. This revolution had become an out of hand monstrosity that was eating every one, one way or another and new ways every day…

Fortunately the turbulence in our plane is gone and we are sailing smoothly to our final liberation through a clear night under a bright moon. Even the air inside the plane feels clean and fresh. The middle aged couple sitting beside me continues their silence and I'm not wanting to start a conversation not knowing where it will take me. I heard her crying very discreetly from time to time during this trip. I am wondering what her or their story is. Who and what they had to leave behind in order to leave Cuba. Maybe I'll never know or when we finally land in Madrid, I'll be able to talk to them or see them again without fear. They appear to be very nice. I kept my light off so it would not bother her. I wanted to talk and tell my story, but to whom?

This Cuban nightmare lasted so long and destroyed so many lives… I am sure my parents are very happy that I finally left that horrible existence. Actually, after my second apprehension, they realized that it was best for me to leave all that behind and go to a place where I would be really free and could attain my goals and be happy. But we didn't know if we would ever see each other again. Leaving that regime was a nightmare of major proportions where you have to go to extremes and concoct your escape. It depends on so many variants and takes so many risks. I am now partially liberated in a plane taking me to Spain and I am still scared to death, insecure, unable to trust anyone and not truly free because I am still inside a Cuban airline and until I set foot on the land of Spain, I cannot consider myself free.

While still sitting on the floor of that former Catholic school converted into a repression center in the hands of the dreaded G2, I remember very well, even though I was a child, that since Batista's 1952 bloodless coup, the opposition to what he did was formed in Cuba. There were newspapers and magazines criticizing him as well as radio and TV editorials.

There were even well known TV comedians such as Tito Hernandez, who imitated Batista, poking fun at him. I remember it on a New Year's Eve 1958 TV special. At that time my mother and I were visiting my father in the country town of Limonar and we watched the TV special in our family room. The special was titled something about the "missing page" which was alluding to the missing chapter of Batista's story.

It was clearer than water that it was implying that the last page of Batista tenure in Cuba was still missing and the population still didn't know when and how it would end. But we soon found out because in November of 1958 there were elections and a new president was elected to be inaugurated in early 1959. So the Batista era was over.

I was a child and I was able to easily figure out the symbolic message on that comedy TV special. The show was live and it was not censored. But with Castro, the situation was drastically different. And it was clear what you were allowed to say or not to say. "The Maximum Leader" was untouchable!

After "The Maximum Leader" was installed in total control and the 1940 Cuba's Constitution was abolished, no one on radio, TV or even in editorial cartoons could poke fun or even hint anything but praise. Comedians disappeared from all Castro's controlled media–better to have no humor than take a chance. Comedians in Castro's Cuba were canceled and they went into exile.

Since Castro became the owner of the whole island, freedom of speech disappeared. Also in the way of Communism, parents lost their authority over their children's education. Political indoctrination began in kindergarten and continued through university as the government set the curriculum, all of which was geared to creating followers. It was inescapable as everything became political. It was "inconceivable" for the revolution that a Cuban citizen was not a supporter of the revolution. And the punishments for the people disaffected with what was going on in Cuba were as cruel as during the Inquisition in the Dark Ages. Fear became a staple of life under Castro's boots. And Cubans were forced out of fear to attend political rallies and to cheer and applaud their own oppressors. A totally surreal situation!

Sitting on the floor of this former Catholic School, waiting without knowing what will happen next is like sitting on a bed of nails. I cannot stop thinking about the past, the before and after of the drastic change from a pursuit of happiness, prosperous country to this tragedy forced on us. However, I have no idea what will happen from this point on. But there is something I am now sure of: I wanted with all my heart to leave this twisted prison island. I do not know when and how. But I will be leaving. My future cannot be trying to survive inside this hellhole.

I moved closer to my friend and I told him some of my thoughts about leaving. But in the middle of his "eye opening" experience, he, with the Marxist indoctrination he received at his theatrical company, kept thinking that the whole thing we were involved in was a painful "part of the revolutionary process," as the Marxist communists say to justify every atrocity.

Sure, Marxist indoctrination does wonders with the human mind, I thought to myself and didn't say any more to him. He optimistically said to me, "This will be corrected when the right authorities learn about it." I bit my tongue and thought to myself, "Nothing happens in Cuba without the direct knowledge of Fidel Castro." Actually this communist revolution wanted to change the total makeup of our society and they firmly believe in "The ends justifies the means." They don't feel guilty for their actions and most certainly they know what they are doing. People living in such deep, complete fear are afraid to even complain.

So the G2 goons came out and directed us to enter one of the rooms facing the corridor and the central patio. We were moved like cattle and soon the room was filled. From there I heard the screams of people obviously being tortured some place in that former school for nuns. After a while another G2 goon entered the room. And there was a deadly silence. One of them shouted, "Get up, you bunch of scum and faggots and follow me!" We ended up at the central patio where there were many G2 goons with their machine guns pointed at us and one little humpback man about 4 feet tall with a piercing, high pitched voice–he looked like the evil character in a horror movie–who was put in charge of keeping us in line. Somebody whispered to me, that he was the vicious brother of a Cuban rumbera who immigrated to Mexico at the end of the 1940s and became a popular rumbera in films and who still lives in Mexico and now he was ordering us to join the line to be photographed.

After a long time standing there listening to the insults and obscenities directed to us by the vicious, little humpbacked creature the line began to move. This horrid scene reminded me of the films I had seen of the Nazi Holocaust and the Jews forming lines in the concentration camps. As I moved toward the front of the line I was able to see the process inside a cabin. The photos were front and profile headshots with a number on the chest. Apparently this was the prelude of a master plan…

After they took my photos I was rushed to the second floor through what had been the formal, grand, white marble staircase of that old colonial mansion. On the second floor was where the G2 goons were creating a file with your name and photo. It was a big bureaucratic operation and it was being conducted efficiently. They had to process all the catches of the night before the crack of dawn! After all it was a secret operation conducted under the darkness of the night. This big rectangular room was filled with at least about 50 desks with two chairs each and brightly lit by fluorescent tubes. One of the chairs was for the G2 goon and the other for the guilty victim. And this room was filled with victims in silence with fear reflected on their faces. I read the time on my watch, it was 2:38 am.

I turned to a black man standing beside me and whispered, "Do you have any idea what they force you to sign?

He whispered back in my ear, "A friend of mine who was caught a week ago told me that he didn't read the form, because the official said that it was a formality and as soon as he signs, he will be free to leave. And he did and left… In my case I don't care what it says, I'll sign whatever is necessary to get the hell out of here…"

A G2 goon who apparently overheard whispering, turned in our direction loudly shouted, "Shut up you all God damn mother fuckers! It is forbidden to speak here! The next whispering I hear I will dump you all in the cells again!" With that menace in perspective, everybody froze and stayed as still as they possibly could.

From time to time the G2 goons were bringing bags filled with forms as they called us one by one. It was 4:15 am and I kept thinking about how my mother and father were worrying without news from me…

Near 5 am, they called me and my friend to be processed. The G2 goon asked me for my ID and I gave it to him and he carefully copied all the information. He proceeded to ask me for information about my parents. I told him that my dead grandfather had been a member of the Communist Party since the 1920s and my mother, as the administrator of a factory, was a member of the ORI to see if these credentials could help my case. But the G2 goon ordered me to shut up!

(The ORI, founded after Castro in 1959, was nothing more than Castro's own communist party in disguise. My mother was forced to join the ORI, or she would be fired from her job.)

Then he asked me where I was arrested. And I briefly explained everything. But in the end I said that it was a mistake because I have a job and I was no "parasite of society." Then the G2 goon stopped and looked at me with an expression of profound hatred and shouted out loud "Son of a bitch I told you to shut up!!! You answer just what I ask you and do just what I tell you! Now you sign this document at once!!!" And they energetically placed the document in front of me to see. I glanced at it and I saw my photographs attached on top and tried to read the text as fast as I could, but I couldn't read and assimilate much, but certain words jumped out at me: "scum," "antisocial" and "parasite of society." And the despicable-disgusting-repulsive G2 goon shouted loudly at me again, I told you to sign it now!!! If you don't do it, you are going back to the cell and no one will be able to get you out of here!!! Sign and you'll be free. Don't sign and you'll stay, it's that simple."

I had already made my decision to get out of that diabolical island of Dr. Castro, so I gladly signed under duress and I will jump out of that evil cuckoo's nest and <u>let's see if you can catch me!</u>

The diabolical G2 goon smiled, proud of his victory and quickly removed that false document from the desk with his bloody hand. Then he ordered me to get up and exit the room which I gladly did to abandon that hell and what they put me through without valid reason. I did not commit a crime. They are the ones committing crimes against the people of Cuba. Before exiting I turned and saw my friend sitting at a desk with his face turned to me. He was holding the pen in his hand with a question reflected on his face that I was easily able to interpret as a question, "Did you sign this?" I responded with a subtle downward movement of my face and turned away. Another G2 goon conducted me out of that inferno all the way to the carriage entrance where he pushed me out to the dark old street where I would be temporarily free, because I would not be truly free until I was thousands of miles away in another country.

Alone on the dark, lonely and deserted street I felt insecure, now with the worry of being apprehended again. I didn't know where to turn. There were no public phones in sight and there was no public transportation. In the dark I could not even read my watch. I assumed that fairly soon it would be dawn. I walked a little bit and I decided to turn right at a corner without knowing where that street would take me. I was exhausted and emotionally drained after what I went through, so I decided to sit on the curb and rest for a while and I noticed about a block away what seemed to be the silhouette of a person walking in my direction. I was concerned that it was another G2 goon and froze. But I got up and hid behind a column as the person was approaching. I was able to distinguish some familiar characteristics until it was about six feet from the column that I was hiding…I was my fellow-victim friend who was looking for me! We got oriented and began to walk in the middle of the street in the direction of his home that was closer than mine.

Eventually we got to a public phone that was working! I called my parents, they were up and ready and my G2 uncle goon was with them waiting for news from me.

What happened during our mysterious disappearance at the hands to the G2 goons goes as follows:

Sarita, one of the sopranos we were going to have dinner with, when she realized that we were not at the Stage Door as planned, called my friend's mother inquiring what happened that her son and I hadn't shown up.

His mother told her that he left early for the theater and that I was to join him there, confirming our plan.

Knowing that Maria, a famous coloratura soprano, had left the theater earlier before her, Sarita decided to call her to see if she had seen us at the stage door. On the phone Maria told her that she saw us not far from the stage door with a man that she didn't know. She was surprised that we didn't go to talk to her as usual and seeing us in what looked to her an odd circumstance.

(That was when we were apprehended). And she asked us if "There was something wrong?" But we replied that there was nothing wrong. And she left with her husband–conductor of the opera orchestra.

Sarita again phoned my friend's mother and told her that we had been seen not far from the stage door with an unknown person. Although Sarita was aware that people were being apprehended around the theater, she didn't tell my friend's mother on the phone because she also knew the government was listening to phone calls–and because she didn't want to worry her.

My friend's mother called my mother and told her.

My mother called her G2 brother-goon who immediately went to my mother and father's home. My mother's brother already knew about these raids at night and he knew that those files with the photos were being prepared to call those people later on to be sent to concentration and labor camps that were built in the distant province of Camagüey. These camps were the brainchild of Che Guevara with the total approval of "The Maximum Leader." He knew that the people who were arrested and signed the paper agreeing to the accusation of scum and parasites of society would end up there. The only thing he could do was to try to retrieve the paper he knew I would have been given to sign.

I must say again that my mother's family was very close and supportive of each other. In spite of each family member's total belief in the revolution, if another member got into trouble with the system, they would take risks to help them. Now that all the uncles have died, I can reveal this fact

I can also now reveal that as the long years of that abominable revolution passed, they knew that they were fed lies and misinformation from the beginning. They wasted their lives protecting and defending the undefendable. They also knew that if they had tried to withdraw from their supportive stance, the penalty would most likely be permanent.

The next day, my G2 uncle came to my parents to tell them that he couldn't retrieve my folder because it had already moved to the next department where he didn't have jurisdiction or access and advised that the best way to avoid being sent to a concentration camp was to leave Cuba. So, the problem was to invent a way to leave, because, unlike before the revolution, now permission to leave the country was required and given only to people the government thought were in support of the revolution or in last instances to the "Worms" to expropriate more properties. Somehow, I had to come up with a plan…

I thought that I could go back to the theatrical group as my friend and fellow actor was able to continue working in his. But to my surprise my contract with my theatrical company was canceled immediately. Also, I was fired from my weekly children's radio program after four years. So, I was what you cannot be in the "workers paradise," an <u>unemployed</u>. I was now a bonafide "lumpenproletariat," the derogatory title given to a person that didn't have a job in their twisted communist jargon.

My G2 uncle's advice was that since my IDs were taken and destroyed I would need to get a new one because being on the street with no ID was cause for apprehension. Since I wouldn't be able to get permission from the government to work, I should quickly enroll in a school and get a student ID in order to be under the radar for a while. What subject I studied wasn't important. The problem was that the choices were very limited to the Cuban youth at that time. You cannot study what you want. You have to study only what the government makes available, according to its immediate needs.

So I went looking for a school so I could get a student ID. I enrolled in the Business Administration School of Commerce, a public school, of course, where they teach you to be an Accountant and Planner within the state controlled business limitations of communist countries. Specialized training for accounting and other business functions is needed in communist countries since the practices are so different. I learned in the school that the Planners control the amount of products on the shelves of grocery stores and all the rest, in order to ensure that production is geared only to the number of citizens. This is one of the causes for shortages that keep the population busy much of the time waiting in lines for their turn to buy something that is often gone by the time they reach their turn. It also means that in the stores for the government elite, diplomats, foreigners and tourists, they have special stores, everything is plentiful.

So I am in a public school studying something my brain doesn't relate to trying to be completely unnoticed, rarely talking or socializing with anyone. I am The Invisible Student. But, unfortunately, a fellow student, a girl, looking at a three year old magazine in her home, saw an article about the Greek musical play I did after graduating from the Academy of Dramatic Arts. It's a review, complementary of me, with photos of me, in costume, that became somewhat famous in La Habana. The girl had the idea to bring the magazine to school to show to her schoolmates. I am invisibly seated at my school desk and I am hearing in the background some girly-giggles. After a while, I turn to see what the commotion is all about. I see a group of teenage girls and boys standing around where the girl is sitting holding up the magazine. I cannot imagine what the fuss was all about. Now the girls are pointing at me and showing me the article. Suddenly, I am no longer invisible. My cover is blown. I am doomed! My life is over.

From that unexpected moment on I became the focal point of the class. They all are wanting to be my friend, talk to me and the worst of all, they are coming to me for advice as if I am some sort of a male version of "Miss Manners" in the Washington Post!–As if I know anything! They look at me with reverence, as if I am somebody worldly–not only the girls but the boys are coming to me to tell me their problems with their girlfriends! Even the intimate (and dangerous) confession of a guy in the class who is confessing that he is gay!!!!! And that his boyfriend abandoned him and how he was suffering . . . What can I say?! They are confessing everything to me as if I am a Catholic priest… I just listen to their stories and hardly say anything. Fortunately, one day I left Cuba and I disappeared from the school without saying goodbye to my admirers. I hope that they have finally learned to live without me.

My father was driving me to school every day so I wouldn't be easy prey on the street. I also enrolled in France's La Alliance Francaise to learn French in case I could find a scholarship in Paris. This foreign institution in Cuba gave me another student ID. Also, an actress friend whose sister lived in Montreal suggested I go to the Embassy of Canada and look in their library for schools that issue scholarships to foreign students. Yes, I am now a bonafide student! But I hated school and studying, but anything to keep me from being apprehended again as I concoct my escape from that horrible, oppressive and repressive country.

Meanwhile, my actor friend who was apprehended with me took his case to the communist sister of the communist director of his communist theatrical company. The sister was a famous radio, TV and film actress and a militant in favor of the Cuban communist system but had defended other actors apprehended by The Revolution. She elevated the case of my friend to the Cuban Communist Party itself which discussed his case in one of their meetings. The answer she received from her fellow SOB higher-echelon elites of the party about this obvious mistake was that, "There was nothing to do about the existence of his record and eventually he would be sent to work at a 'farm' in the province of Camagüey."

So his Marxist beliefs betrayed him, as well as the "powerful" communist sister of the communist founder of that theatrical company, as well the Communist Party of Cuba whose General Secretary was "The Maximum Leader." And this "farm" project was the twisted brainchild of the sociopath (and so beloved worldwide–to this day!) "Che" (Ernesto Guevara), baptized by his victims as "The Butcher of La Cabana Fortress" for his crimes and countless executions. So my friend's ruling was absolute and cannot be changed. So much for working in that system.

However, for this actor friend, the situation of leaving Cuba was easier than mine, because for some unknowable reason he was still under contract with this communist theatrical company and had the support of the communist director and sister. And during 1964 and 1965 these nighttime raids increased a lot and were affecting many Cuban intellectuals, writers, directors, actors, musicians, dancers, singers and artists and anybody connected with the arts. Also on the increase was a clandestine exodus of talent under the guise of traveling abroad with scholarships to increase the educations of the revolution's comrades that actually provided permanent escape from Castro's "social justice". These thousands of escapees drained Cuba of very capable, talented and freethinking people that could question Castro's revolution. So this was a tacit outlet to get rid of an opposition that would cause him problems in the future.

So the sister of the founder of his theatrical company helped him join this exit outlet. It's ironic: a communist actress helping other actors and talent to escape the communist system that she promoted…He ultimately accomplished his unlikely exit via the East German commercial cargo vessel Freiligraph from the Port of Matanzas to East Germany. From there he crossed to West Germany I don't know how, finally arriving in Paris where he got a job in a hotel as a chambermaid in 1965.

Finally, in La Habana, on my own, I was able to get two scholarships. One was to study a summer course at Banff School of Fine Arts in Alberta, Canada. The director of the School was Senator Donald Cameron in Ottawa. This was a complete scholarship including room and board. The Second was at The Conservatory of Music and Dramatic Arts of Montreal. This second one was for education only. Having the scholarships, the next <u>MAJOR</u> problem was to get "The Official Exit Permit" from the Cuban Government, the Transit Visa from Mexico and the Canadian Visa. Piece of cake! Or *Flan de Leche*.

So, I went with my mother, and her Party ID card, to the National Council of Culture who was in charge of everything related to the arts after the revolution. Actually, I didn't have the right to be there because I was canceled from the theatrical company where I had been under contract. But at that time there were no computers to research current information, so they didn't know that I didn't belong there. The director of the Council was Comrade Amanecer Dotta, a communist from Uruguay who came to Cuba to help Castro's revolution to impose Marxist Communism in Cuba with thousands of other "useful fools" from all over the world including Americans from the U.S. After talking to him he referred me to Comrade Corona.

This Council is the only one that can give the coveted Exit Permit to official intellectuals, artists, etc. in Cuba. The comrade in charge to request this "SALVO CONDUCT" to allow me to leave that hellhole was Comrade Corona. I showed him the papers of my two scholarships in Canada and pretended to be as comrade as he was and that I would come back to teach all the techniques I will learn to other comrades for the benefit of THE REVOLUTION. That was the most revolting acting job that I forced myself to play! Comrade Corona knew the date I had to be in Alberta, for my first scholarship and the other date to begin at the conservatory in Montreal. But over our multiple visits to his office he kept delaying my permit and the dates were getting closer. Then at one of our visits the Comrade secretary of Conrade Corona said that he was traveling and she didn't know when he would be back. My mother opened her wallet and got her Party ID, slapped it firmly on the counter and the secretary of the traveling comrade was speechless and very impressed and my mother energetically requested that we <u>will</u> get the exit permit so I <u>will</u> get to Canada on time! The secretary, facing the energic request of a party member, said she would get the exit permit as soon as possible, perhaps the next day and she will call when it's ready to be picked up. And without saying anything else that could jeopardize the situation, we left. Everything in our bodies was trembling! We couldn't even talk!

Next morning the Comrade secretary called very jovially to ask us to come to pick up the permit!!! So we went. Now with that permit authorized us to go to the Cuban Airline office to buy the ticket! The easiest and most economical way to fly to Canada was changing planes in Mexico. But there's a problem. Mexico dislikes the United States since the Mexican-American War that ended with The Guadalupe Hidalgo Treaty of 1848, when a lot of territory went to the U.S. so their attitude in general has been anti-U.S. And since Castro was a fervent U.S. hater with the declared goal to destroy it, Mexico had been a close friend and ally of Castro. In general, Mexico has been denying asylum or visas to Cubans leaving Cuba to make things more difficult for them. In my case it was just a Transit Visa to change planes only. And with two scholarships in Canada, why would I want to stay in Mexico?! But, no dice, no visa.

So my only option was from La Habana to Madrid, change to Canadian Pacific airlines to fly to Montreal and then on to Alberta. So thanks to Mexico, we had to spend a lot more money!

So I had to get the visa to travel to the land of my ancestors and from there to Montreal. An exchange of money was required because the Cuban government did not allow the Cuban airline to sell tickets for Cuban pesos. Instead foreign money had to be used so that the Cuban government ends up with foreign money which was much more valuable to them. Plus it made it more difficult for the Worms leaving Cuba. Actually my ordeal to get out of Cuba and get situated in another country required multiple, complex, clandestine exchanges of money. For the airline, we made the exchange through an Egyptian diplomat in Cuba. So there you have it! Egypt came to my rescue for the first time! There is another connection with the land of the Pharaohs! Now, the next problem was to be able to make a Cuban airline reservation to Spain soon enough so that I could use the scholarship at the Banff School in Alberta.

Another thing that I had against me was my age. Now for the first time in our history. Cuba had compulsory military service. No male age 15 to 17 was allowed to leave Cuba. How am I going to overcome that new hurdle?

I had all the papers for the scholarships in Canada. My father arranged to send me his car with a driver to take me to the Embassy of Canada for the visa I needed.

Canada was another nation that, like Mexico, had very good relations with Castro's revolution. However, they were not very kind at the Embassy and quickly got rid of me saying that the papers I received from both schools were not specific enough. So I went directly to a friend who spoke English to ask him to call both schools in Canada. He talked to them and they sent me other letters to satisfy the demands for the Student Visa. So, more delay... Eventually I returned to the Canadian Embassy with both letters. Then the Consul told me—for the first time—that the visa had to be requested by the schools in Canada!

I ran back to the friend's house so he could call again to Alberta to talk with the Director of Banff School, the Senator. But he was not in Alberta that day, but in Ottawa. So my friend called the Canadian Senate in Ottawa to talk to the Senator. The Embassy of Canada would not deny the request from an active Senator!!! The Senator was out to lunch but he knew about my request for the visa.

We needed to call him back, but at this point we had made several phone calls abroad from the friend's house. This may be suspicious to the regime which listens to all phone calls. I do not need any extra problems with our paranoid revolutionary regime. The revolution could accuse me of being a "counter revolutionary" or "a CIA Agent." Those two were the worst possible charges that anybody could be accused of at that time. It doesn't matter if they have any actual proof. If the regime accuses you, you are GUILTY! So I decided to bring my friend to my house and make the call mid afternoon. This time he was able to talk to the Senator and explained the new situation with their Embassy in La Habana. The Senator was extremely kind and understanding and replied that he will do everything in order to get the Student Visa for me. I was elated!!!

After my friend left, I decided as a "good luck charm" to hang a calendar behind the main door and circle in red the day I would have to be at the Banff School in Alberta, which was <u>July 5, 1965</u>, and cross in black the days left for me in the hellhole. And I focused my attention on that calendar. Every day in the morning I counted the days left to achieve my goal.

Finally I was given a passport, which was also an ordeal to obtain from the regime and my parents had to hire a lawyer to handle all the new bureaucratic hurdles imposed by the regime to obtain that simple document. I was extremely happy with that document in my hands as another sign for my upcoming departure.

After more phone calls and escorted trips to the Embassy of Canada in my father's car–and now with a valid passport–finally the Embassy of Canada called me to stamp the Student Visa on my passport! Another goal accomplished! It was unreal what a simple stamp can do for you when you live inside a communist regime. The most insignificant things in life are elevated to great heights. Everything becomes a matter of life or death!

The only people who knew that I was leaving Cuba with two scholarships to study in Canada was the Embassy of Canada, the two schools in Canada, the two officials and the secretary of one of them, at the Council of Culture, the lawyer that got my passport, and the sister of an actress friend who lived in Montreal and my mother and father. No one else knew. These kinds of things you learn to keep private in totalitarian countries–anyone who knows about it could even secretly decide to go against you, report you, and it's over. So the fewer the better even though that means you won't be able to say that forever goodbye to ones you love.

And, anyway, the outcome of all this escape stuff, realistically, is still in the air. Something can happen at any time and it's over. My mother, father and I were tense and living in fear. The fact that I was asking for an official Exit Permit put a permanent stigma on the government records of my family.

Nazi Germany was on our minds, after all, fear is a tool of all totalitarian regimes. Lenin realized he needed fear to keep the masses from taking away his power when he applied Marxism in Russia in 1917. In Germany, they called themselves "National Socialists" but they also needed fear. Castro literally studied the masters, so: Ditto Castro.

All of these, Marxism, Communism, Facism need fear because they go against nature and are contrary to the aspirations of human beings of being free. They are contrary to nature's concept of family: a mother and father produce and care for offspring. Even most animals and birds live in such families: nature's system for survival. In all places on our planet where one of the totalitarian systems has been used, basic human concepts like family get in the way, and fear is used to force the people to accept what is contrary to nature. Since the beginning, Castro's Cuba has needed help from the outside in order to survive, along with a suppressed population living in fear. Thus, the wall around these countries is to prevent people from leaving, not to prevent people from coming in from other countries, as happens in capitalist countries where people can prosper and are free from government interference in their private lives and their future.

My goal to be in Banff School of Fine Arts in Alberta, Canada on July 5 when the classes began came and went and nothing was moving! I was still trapped. I began to feel Castro-claustrophobia. I couldn't breathe the polluted revolutionary air… I was asphyxiating inside the suffocating, unhealthy environment of malicious inescapable propaganda and revolutionary slogans to indoctrinate the masses 24-7. It was inescapable on radio and TV. Some people not able to leave the country became alcoholics and others were committing suicide to escape the inescapable. For students, summer became the glorious opportunity for "volunteer work" on far off agricultural fields with dangerous living conditions. Somehow they approved a medical certificate that fortunately exempted me so I could be home working on my escape. My free time was spent listening to a set of old records of an English course from The National School in Los Angeles, California. It belonged to a brother of my mother who, years before the revolution, went to the United States and had lived in Santa Monica, California.

During this impasse I was desperate and decided to add another good luck charm to the calendar behind the main door. I decided to pack my suitcase and place it on the floor behind the door. This brilliant and desperate idea was very practical indeed. Every time that someone knocked on the door, either my mother, my father or I had to run and hide it so no one would suspect that anyone was leaving. But it was somehow satisfying.

My frustration and anxiety grew so I was ready to do anything to escape my captivity even briefly no matter how bizarre an opportunity was! One afternoon my mother and I went to visit an older black woman named "Lucrezia" whose name my mother overheard in a conversation of two of her employees at the factory where she was an administrator.

She heard that that lady had accomplished miracles to solve the bad situation of an employee, and she immediately thought about mine which was also hers and my father's. My mother casually asked that employee and asked for "Lucrezia"'s address and phone number to give to a "friend." My mother didn't give me more details because she knew I otherwise would not want to go.

We arrived at "Lucrezia's" the next day, were invited into her modest home. I looked around and quickly realized that she practiced "Santeria." This was a religion brought by the African slaves when they were taken to Cuba in the 15th century. In my modest opinion the best thing that the slaves brought to Cuba was their complex rhythms that were incorporated into such things as the European Minuet and eventually into the roots of nearly all Cuban music giving it such a rich foundation that it spread from Cuba to the rest of the Americas and beyond.

But in my modest opinion, the practices of Santeria handicaped believers by distracting from spiritually positive beliefs and deeds thereby hampering their success. Everything had to be consulted and complexly ritualized rather than using initiative. I had no faith and little tolerance for Santeria.

Back to "Lucrezia", she was a short, petite lady who spoke with a weak voice and a saintly aspect. She was modestly dressed; her home impeccably clean. She was very low key, peaceful, sweet and friendly but looking at the altar in her living room, she clearly practiced Santeria. So I understood why my mother–in a last ditch effort–brought me to the "miraculous "Lucrezia". My future in Cuba was looking bleak and everything seemed to be paralyzed. I had done everything I could but I was frozen in time and space.

Well, no matter how bizarre this last ditch effort becomes, I am desperate enough to participate. I was subjected, by this sweet lady, to the most "god-awful" ceremony I had ever seen or experienced!!! This frail, sweet and totally inoffensive little lady came in with a poor, innocent and unsuspecting rooster and in front of my horrorized eyes cut his neck–I hate even the thought of killing innocent animals–to spill his blood on the floor around me while the poor innocent animal was having convulsions and rubbed the rooster it that condition all over my body… I can't believe I am even writing this…while I was desperately thinking "Just to leave Cuba! Just to leave Cuba!" I kept repeating inside my mind and feeling <u>SO SORRY</u> for that poor, innocent rooster. I was sure that he was feeling excruciating pain… I closed my eyes and I was glad when it was over. I wanted to disappear from that room and forget what I had to go through… I heard the sweet voice of the tiny and skinny "Lucrezia"' almost whispering to me very seriously, saying in my ear, "Now all the doors will be wide open to you and you'll be leaving soon."

I thought to myself, "I never thought that a rooster had so much power!"

My mother paid "Lucrezia" for her work and we left. I could not talk any more that day, I was literally crushed by that experience and by what I saw. I wanted to get the whole thing out of my mind.

The next day The Royal Bank of Canada cable transference for the total of my flight from La Habana to Madrid arrived in Cuba and now we can make the Cuban Airline reservation for the first leg of my trip because for the flight from Madrid to Canada the money was transferred by the Royal Bank of Canada also in Canadian dollars to the Canadian Pacific office in Madrid.

For a change there was exciting news thanks to the chain of many things, maybe including "Lucrezia".

So my father drove us to the Cuban Airline and I officially got a seat reservation for July 18, 1965. At that point I didn't know if I would be accepted at the school in Banff, because I would miss the first day of classes on July 5. Arriving the same day was an official government letter from The National Council of Culture addressed to the Department of Foreign Cultural Relations (even though I was no longer a part of the Cultural Council since my contract with the theatrical company was canceled months earlier). This letter included a list of all the items I requested to carry to Canada, a privilege given only to officials employed by The National Council of Culture. So what they were allowing to carry was much more than a regular citizen was allowed to carry abroad. This letter was signed July 13, 1965, I decided to keep that important letter so people will see the limited freedoms a citizen has in a communist country.

Suddenly everything was moving very fast, as in a dream. My excitement prevented me from falling asleep at night because now staying in Cuba was a matter of a few days and hours. I could not stop my mind from thinking about all that had happened these last months…

I'll be extremely tired when we land in Madrid. It was not so cold inside the cabin now. I opened my eyes. There was some light coming through the edge of my closed window shade. I got up a little in my seat and looked around the cabin. Most passengers seem to be sleeping. I wondered if in fact they, like me, were reliving their last days in Cuba…I wanted to open my window shade, but I didn't want to disturb the couple sitting beside me or the peace reigning inside the plane, so I relaxed and closed my eyes again…

My last five days in Cuba were emotionally draining. I had to get used to distancing myself from sentimental material things that had been around me since my childhood. I'll never see those items again. I couldn't do anything with my possessions. Everything I made and owned was itemized inside my house in an official inventory made by a G2 goon from the Ministry of the Interior (which was the secret police). From my paintings and other collectibles through to my last pair of socks were on that inventory. We could not decide that any of my belongings should go to someone in the family. If I don't return to Cuba, they will take all of the items on the inventory for the mighty regime. It's very frustrating that there is an official robbery of your property but nothing can be done about it. We don't have any rights. So we have to shut up and obey. That's life on the "Island Paradise."

The only items the regime would not include in the inventory were personal photos, papers and newspaper clippings. A few days before my departure I began reviewing my accumulation of such items and everything I don't want the goons to have, I destroyed. It was sad to see all those mementos gone from my life. The only memories they couldn't control are the ones inside my mind.

No one in my mother's family knew about my trip. For them to know was risky for me and for them especially, since, unfortunately, most of them were G2 and their duty would have been to stop my sneaky escape from the hands of the ogre. It's better for them not to know. Eventually they realized it was the best for me. Deep in their hearts they knew as everybody else, in what terrible trap they had fallen. So I didn't see any of them before leaving, not even my only living grandmother. The only ones who could be trusted were a brother of my father who had already sent his 9 year old son and 7 year old daughter, unaccompanied, out of Cuba through Operation Peter Pan and a sister of my father. Both were aware of the evil of Castro's revolution and were getting ready to leave to reunite with their children in the U.S. They were all elated that I was leaving!

Of course, if trusting my own family was dangerous under Communism, trusting old friends and acquaintances was out of the question. I couldn't say goodbye to anybody, except one, my dear and best loyal friend for the last 13 years: Terry, my dog who grew up with me. My father had already taken Terry from our house to the mill where he was an administrator because there was more country where he could run and play than around our home with so much traffic. So I was deprived of his wonderful company at home. One afternoon I went to the mill with my father so I could spend that last time alone with Terry, talking and playing with my dearest friend. It was extremely sad and difficult to say goodbye forever. I hugged him and cried a lot. He was surprised because he was used to seeing me happy, playing and laughing with him. And this time I was sad and crying. He looked at me with a very serious look, trying to understand what was happening to me. I stayed hugging and kissing him all afternoon, until my father's working day at the mill was over. I had to say my final goodbye knowing that I would not see him again.

I entered the car and we drove away and Terry ran behind the car for a few blocks until he realized that he couldn't catch us and he stopped and walked back to the mill with his tail down.

I will never forget him and he will always be in a special place in my heart.

Even though I was forced by a hideous political system to close a chapter of my life, it had an unfinished touch that gave me a bitter flavor that was going to be difficult to erase for a long time. If I was escaping because I committed a crime, my feelings would have been different. But I was escaping from a new society in which my only crime–just like the Jews in Nazi Germany–was "to exist."

I heard the announcement that the plane was going to land for refueling on one of the islands of the Azores archipelago belonging to Portugal named *Santa Maria de Azores*. I opened my eyes again, opened the shade of the window to look out. It was getting dark and what I could see was the Atlantic ocean below all around. The other passengers were also opening their window shades. And you can feel we were descending slowly. The lights were turned on inside the cabin. Very soon we will be landing on a free land, however that was not our final destination and we were still inside a Cuban Airliner under their jurisdiction and had another leg to go. So the passengers continued their silence without any demonstration of excitement. We all still had the fear that if we were to do or say something that could be interpreted as suspicious, we could be delivered back to Cuba…

The descent to Santa Maria de Azores continued slowly and in an almost religious silence inside the cabin. The Captain announced that we would be there for only half an hour. And that we could go out to the small airport building. After landing in our first free soil after seven years under "The Maximum Leader" and hours flying to the Azores archipelago, everyone went out in silence, anxious to breathe the fresh, unoppressive air of a different country. On this land people were not oppressed at the whim of a totalitarian regime. The air was fresh, clean and invigorating.

I had a very particular feeling of being liberated, as if a very heavy weight had been removed from my shoulders as I walked out from that Cuban plane and walked toward the small airport building in a foreign land. I Thought about my childhood dreams inspired by the travel stories of my neighbors Papa Gordo and Mama Zoila during my early childhood.

Inside the airport building we all wandered around in silence, admiring consumer goods in the shops that had already disappeared from Cuba since the revolution. Some of those items I had even forgotten that they existed! Now I know for sure that they are still available. None of us could buy anything because we were not allowed to carry any money—even me with my official special permission from the National Council of Culture! So we all stared at the windows like poor children at Christmas windows.

In the small restaurant of the airport I noticed a uniformed U.S. Marine and I was very afraid of him. Once Castro took power in Cuba he made a point to portray the U.S. military as hard core criminals, and being bombarded by the indoctrination 24-7 of the last seven years which made me believe that the American soldiers were very dangerous and the Russians were the good guys. It took me some time to realize that it was simply misinformation.

Communism normally accuses the <u>other</u> side of the crimes <u>they</u> commit! It is a system of lies and deceptions. So, after seeing the U.S. Marine, I turned around and went back to the plane. I will have to overcome some things in order to liberate myself from my seven-year past in a lying hellhole!

After about three and a half more hours to our final destination of Madrid, back inside the cabin of an obsolete Cuban airline was the same oppressive silence again as if we were in Cuba. I thought, "How different this trip would have been aboard a Spanish Iberia Airline jet plane!" But, our landing in Madrid will initiate a new chapter in our lives!

"Thank you rooster, for the gift of this flight!!"

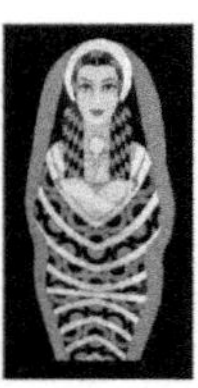

CHAPTER 18

NEFERTARY HOTEL

From the airplane's window, I was able to see the famous Abu Simbel temple on its new higher location facing Lake Nasser. What a wonderful sight!

It was a marvelous gesture of the pilot to tilt the plane that way in order for us to see that extraordinary view. I managed to take two photos of it! One from the distance, while approaching, and the other while passing by. Lake Nasser which looks huge and of a beautiful deep turquoise blue, reflecting the spectacular cloudless sky… What a view!!!

We began descending fast and at 1:12 pm, we touched down in Abu Simbel.

A gentleman from the government was waiting at the small airport in a Russian version of a Jeep–they copied our cars like China does with so many American products. It's more economical for them because they don't have to spend much on research and development. They are "so nice" you know…! They love us to DEATH!

The official introduced himself as Sabery A. Lteif Hassan, giving us a polite welcome. That airport seems to be in the middle of nowhere. The only thing around was a vast flat desert as far as the eye could see. Not a single *McDonalds* in sight. It was like being the first people on the planet Mars. On all our airplane trips throughout Egypt, the desert looks like Mars.

Jaums and I jumped aboard the open Russian Jeep and along with our two suitcases off we went at "light speed," the Jeep zoomed leaving a trail of dust behind us on the very bumpy so-called road. We had to hold <u>very tight</u> to whatever we could grab of the interior of the Jeep to avoid being ejected into the desert. We kept an eye on our bouncing suitcases. Sometimes over big bumps in the road, all four wheels were "airborne." It was like in the movie *At War With The Army* (1950) Dean Martin and Jerry Lewis.

At 1:45 pm—after we survived the worst part of Mr. Saberry A. Lteif Hassan's Jeep ride—fortunately he slowed down and turned at what looked distinctly like an artificial hill, driving on around to the front where we found just in front of us, the spectacular Abu Simbel Temples in all their wondrous glory. Actually the temples were going to be under water, covered by Lake Nasser, the lake that formed once the Aswan High Dam was built. Through an international effort these temples were cut in pieces and transported to higher ground and surrounded by an artificial hill looking much like the original position of the temples that were carved into a mountainside of rock. The solar alignment was maintained so that the sun would still penetrate to the innermost statues every February 22 and October 22. I cannot find words to describe the enormous beauty and serenity of this ancient Egyptian marvel. It is something to experience with your own eyes and presence there. The golden color of the stone and sand against the bright turquoise sky without a single cloud and the surreal Martian-scape around Lake Nasser contribute to the mystic air of the site.

White concentrated on the contemplation of this wonder, a bus loaded with visitors arrived. I was forcing myself to ignore the distraction of the colorful and improperly dressed tourists, raping these ancient relics of the Egyptian past. I must overcome this anachronistic intrusion.

I would have liked to have a Pharaoh's whip in my hand as in Cecil B. DeMille's early Hollywood films, energetically beginning to whip those tourists out of the sight! **Cut!**

All of a sudden, I felt a strong presence behind me… There was something burning the back of my neck as if I was being blasted by the waves of radioactivity of a nuclear explosion. I turned to find out what was producing that weird, inappropriate sensation…And to my chagrin…Again!!! She appears again!!! The Painted Woman here, in the flesh, AGAIN!!! She alone had the power to destroy, however momentarily, my enjoyment of contemplating these temples in peace! And to make her presence even more strident, she was dressed in an out-of-place red safari outfit with her usual ample *decollete* of voluminous, hot-air balloons pushed up all the way to the North Pole. Only her makeup case was as constant an *accoutremente*. And assisted by her wide, zebra belt squeezing everything above the waist upwards, in deference to the curvaceous presentation below, of the rear end of a 1959 Cadillac El Dorado Convertible. Topping it all off was a zebra hat completing the inevitable matching hat–belt set. Oh, her long scarf, wafting in the desert breeze, reached all the way to the border with Sudan. Moving about, I don't know how she could walk on the sand and desert rubble in those shiny black high-heel boots, mysteriously devoid of even a hint of desert dust. And this time looking kind-of embarrassed, was her constant entourage of The Polyester Man and The Unremarkable Youngster. Despite all of this, I instantly looked away so as to minimize the distraction from my concentration as she tried so hard to disturb my peace.

But this time she looked at me, and I turned my face away, even though I had the slightest curiosity of the mystery of that unusual traveler. What in the hell was she doing in Egypt?! It would have been more justifiable in the Frederick's of Hollywood Parade.

Coming back to reality, we spent most of that day inside and outside of the Great Temple of Ramses II and the also spectacular Small Temple of Hathor and Nefertari located just beside. Because our guide Mr. Saberry A. Lteif Hassan, gave us the VIP tour of both temples and the interior of the artificial hill constructed that looks like a gigantic set for the finale of a James Bond production. After we finished the tour at our leisure, we sat on a grassy area in front of the temples and enjoyed the magnificent view with Mr. Saberry A. Lteif Hassan.

Then back to Mr. Saberry A. Lteif Hassan's Russian Jeep for a ride to the hotel where we were to spend the night and rest up for our flight the next day back to Cairo.

Again at Mr. Saberry A. Lteif Hassan's light-speed, jumping all over with our suitcases, the short drive to The Nefertari Hotel. During the trip we saw, way in the distance, The Lighthouse of Alexandria!!! Oh no, I made a mistake, it was The Painted Woman, apparently in the middle of the desert, near the setting sun, getting into the tourists' bus to return to the plane at the Abu Simbel airport. *Bon voyage.*

In our case, fortunately we and our suitcases all survived the driving style of Mr. Saberry A. Lteif Hassan to our next destination, leaving our traditional trail of dust: *The Nefertary Hotel.* This hotel was in the middle of Desert Nowhere. From the outside the hotel looks like a 90 degree angled, one floor, very long hotel perhaps built when the foreigners were involved in the salvage and reconstruction of the temples almost around the corner, in the 1960s AD. Actually, it resembled a huge motel, but without the parking lot and not a single vehicle in sight, rather lovely with its mariage-like gardens, surrounded by an infinite desert. Mr. Saberry A. Lteif Hassan helped us with the suitcases into the nice, spacious lobby with a huge dining room. Then, Mr. Saberry A. Lteif Hassan, turning toward us said, "You will spend the rest of the day and night here. Tomorrow morning before 9 am, I will be back to take you to the airport for your flight back to Cairo, so, I'm leaving now, have a good rest of the day and night here." And Mr. Saberry A. Lteif Hassan turned around, walked rapidly and jumped in the Russian Jeep, and at light-speed our Mr. Saberry A. Lteif Hassan promptly disappeared in a trail of dust in the desert. Fade to black.

The grand *Nefertary Hotel* was grandly empty, save the owner of the hotel who managed the desk and two servers, all dressed in the typical Egyptian gallabeah and turbans. Doris Day and Rock Hudson were nowhere to be seen. Everything was very clean, organized and well decorated in the 1960's AD style. I asked at what time they usually serve dinner and Mr. Desk replied, "At any time you want." Since it looks like an American Motel, I asked him if they have a swimming pool. He replied "Yes," pointing to the outside. Then, he called the servers, Mr. Short and Mr. Tall, to take our suitcases and to go with us to our room. Through the lobby and on to the corridor to our room, we couldn't see a single guest anywhere. Not even Henry Kissinger with his towel on his way to the pool. The hotel was very long, as was the hallway where the rooms are located. Fortunately our room was the first one at the beginning and we didn't have to walk much, so we arrived very soon at our appointed room. Mr. Short proudly showed me the key and after having a lot of problems unlocking the door, finally did and very ceremoniously held the door open for us and we entered. It was dark. He turned the lights of the room which were very dim and we noticed that on the wall opposite to the door, a rectangular window closed by a shade and a door to a patio. I knew by opening the shade we would get the near-the-equator sun streaming in. The room had two beds and a private bath. I opened the door to inspect. It was clean, with the traditional appliances including a tub and shower. So for one night in the middle of the desert it was quite nice. I was relieved. Mr. Short and Mr. Tall, proudly standing by looked like they escaped from a French Moroccan comedy. Their efforts to welcome us with sophistication were quite splendid as they left the room smiling. I proceeded to open the shade to see the view of what promised to be a beautiful and exotic Egyptian desert. In fact it was magnificent with elevations in the distance and the distinctive Martian coloration. I thought we were going to sit out there and relax facing the enormity of this background. Then I looked down expecting to see lounge chairs… But none were there and I noticed that the floor had what appeared to be a thick black carpet, maybe to be sat on? But I notice a jerky movement in the carpet. That unexpected movement on the carpet made me concentrate my eyes on the phenomenon I witnessed. Suddenly I realized what I was watching! There were thousands of what appeared to be locusts camping on our patio for an 18 year reunion today, just today! So much for the romantic idea of sitting there to enjoy the view! I was never going to open that door again! Imagine if they enter the room?!

A swimming pool in the desert sounded interesting, so we walked through the grand lobby and out in the direction Mr. Front Desk had indicated to the pool. Well, out to look for the pool. As we walked, we found ourselves at the perimeter of the property where the irrigation ended and the desert began…with the Mr. Short and Mr. Tall following us. Queue Moroccan walking music. Were they there to make sure we were not doing something we shouldn't or to make sure nothing happened to us? Almost as far as we could walk without ending up in the desert, we found a rectangular concrete construction that could eventually be called a "swimming pool." Not a drop of water–perhaps the hot sun of the desert took the refreshing liquid…

Back to the room, I decided to take a shower. It was getting late and we wanted to go to the hotel's restaurant for lunch. So I went to the bathroom carrying my soap, my shampoo, conditioner and my hair dryer for a nice, refreshing shower. I got inside the tub and got the water running and used my soap and shampoo and applied the conditioner. But I noticed that the volume of water was dwindling and becoming like drops of morning dew. I closed the faucet immediately thinking that the force of the water would recuperate and I could properly rinse off everything. After a while hoping for the miracle of water in the desert before the products all over me dried out! But the miracle never materialized. In a life and death panic, I called Jaums to find a glass or any other empty container in the room! He had no idea what for… Well, I had looked inside the toilet tank and it was filled with water. So with a container I would be able to extract the water with it and rinse my head and body. So he found a small glass.

With it I began the task of extracting the water from the toilet tank. When I successfully accomplished my great idea born from panic, I got my hair dryer, plugged in the electric outlet and turned it on… In the second it started running, we heard like an explosion in the distance and the power went off! Both Mr. Short and Mr. Tall quickly appeared inside the room with candles; so quickly that they must have done the drill many times before. I not only blew the fuses not only in our room but in the entire Nefertary Hotel!!! Apparently in that hotel you cannot plug a hair dryer which is a limitation for our 20th century civilization! No hair dryers in the 1960s, AD. So I came out of the bathroom wearing a Gallabeah I bought in Luxor and sat very upset on my bed which immediately collapsed to the floor!!!

Mr. Short and Mr. Tall left the room—probably laughing at the situation that a crazy American guest of the Egyptian government had created for himself in The Nefertary Hotel in the middle of the desert near the sacred temples in Abu Simbel of Ramses and his wife Nefertary. I was very embarrassed of all the problems I had caused so far in this tranquil part of Egypt.

After the electricity was restored in the entire hotel, we decided to go to dinner in the huge restaurant of the hotel, if they would let us in. I wore the Gallabeah and a turban since I really couldn't completely remove the shampoo and conditioner, I couldn't get a comb through my hair.

We were hungry and headed to the restaurant. When we exited our room we found both Mr. Short and Mr. Tall standing guard–one at each side of the door. I mentioned "the restaurant." Both smiling from ear to ear, they conducted us very excitedly through the door to the lobby in the direction of the restaurant passing by the reception desk and what looked like a freshly decorated cocktail lounge ready for Rosemary Clooney to sing a few tunes, on to the huge dining room for hundreds of hungry guests, full of empty tables. And no guests. The ceiling was very high and was surrounded by floor to ceiling windows facing an endless desert. The windows had expensive draperies. This dining room was open to a lounge area with many comfortable looking upholstered chairs and coffee tables. My conclusion was that this hotel was built with great expectations… But so far we had the impression that we are the only guests in The Nefertary Hotel, Abu Simbel, 83616, Egypt, 1978 AD.

And with that impression after this tour through the extensive facilities, we were seated at a table in the middle of the dining room of Las-Vegas-in-Abu-Simbel, by Mr. Short and Mr. Tall.

Mr. Short automatically quickly disappeared through a side door. I thought, "I hope he is not going to the desert to hunt for desertkill to serve us…" Mr. Tall presented us with the menus while staying close to take the order. The menu, even though written in English, was probably of Egyptian-Nubian cuisine because geographically, we were very close to the border with Sudan. Of course, coming from Silver Spring, Maryland, we didn't recognize anything and we are not ready to experiment. I had heard stories of people eating snakes, crocodiles, monkeys, elephants and even insects… But I don't have a refined taste enough for those "exquisite delights," and so I reject those foreign "appetizing" barfy plates. Jaums is not willing to *mangiare* those plates either. I decided to ask Mr. Tall… And he quickly decided to bring Mr. Front Desk who spoke English.

Mr. Tall came back promptly with Mr. Front Desk. He decided to sit at the table to eat with us. He recommended that we order something that "you haven't been eating in Egypt," that was called "Shish Kabobs." I cringed deep inside. While we waited for it to be prepared, the Mr. Front Desk explained to us that he had bought the hotel not very long ago and he recently added the cocktail lounge. He seemed not very satisfied with its decor. However, I reassured him that, as a visitor, the Nubian decor was proper for that area and in reality was very attractive. But I could not resist the temptation to ask him in lieu of his empty hotel, "Do you really have any need for it…?"

"Oh yes of course!" he said.

And I asked, "How often do you have entertainment in the lounge?"

"Oh, we have entertainment every night, " he categorically stated and added, "We are all booked, you know." On weekends? Every February 22 and October 22?

Well, I thought, maybe the rest of the guests will appear in the evening…Who knows…My impression may be wrong, this is Egypt and this is the most southern area and almost at the border with Sudan and the customs may be different, even Mr. Short and Mr. Tall looked more like black Africans than Egyptians. And he continued talking to us about his hotel and his unhappiness with the lobby and the dining room decor and since he knew I was an artist, he asked me for advice. Since this hotel was in a very lonely area—really in the the middle of the desert—and the closest and only attraction was the Abu Simbel temples that can easily be visited in a few hours and the tour group visits consisted of flying in to the nearby small airport a short bus ride to the temples, visit the temples, get back on the bus, return to the airport, back on the same plane that lifts off for another destination in Egypt, I do not see the need for an extensive facility like The Nefertary Hotel. See? One quick round trip. There was nothing else around but a vast desert, spectacular, but a desert that can be very dangerous for people without knowledge of how to survive in it. And no McDonalds.

So, that explained why we really were the only guests. The group of tourists we saw at Abu Simbel came on the same plane with us and left without a trace. No hotel room needed, no Rosemary Clooney, no swimming pool, no dinner in a vast dining room. So my reply was, "If I were you, I would not spend a lot of money on this hotel…However, you should consider painting it in a better color. The walls need to be repainted because the paint is noticeably peeling in some areas."

"Yes, I know, but what about the furniture?"

"Well…" I replied, "I would come up with a better arrangement. The placement of the chairs and coffee tables should be done in a more functional way. All the chairs piled against the windows is not right. They should be arranged in conversational groups with some of them facing the windows so your guests can enjoy the spectacular view of the desert. The walls in that area should be painted of a color matching the upholstered chairs, creating a more harmonious environment, more inviting and relaxing."

"Oh yes, you are right, and I never liked the color of the walls of the lounge anyway." He said.

Then I added, "You must be sure that all the beds in the room are properly put together. Earlier, when I sat on mine, it collapsed on the floor. And see if you can fix the water and electricity problems. By the way, the swimming pool in the back of the hotel doesn't have water."

"And talk to the tour companies about having some groups spend the night."

After our inescapable diet of "Shish Kabob," Jaums and I went back to our room and Mr. Front Desk kept on talking about the refurbishing of his hotel, so he walked with us to the front porch entrance of the hotel and he sat beside me in one of the porch chairs and continued the discussion. So I told him that everything can be solved with a little imagination and to illustrate what I meant I told him that I was going back to my room to get some photos of my home to show him as samples. "Yes, yes," he exclaimed with a glint of excitement reflected in his eyes and asked me, "Would you help me move the furniture around this afternoon?"

"Yes, of course I'll help you."

"All right," was his excited reply and added "I will wait right here for you!"

I rushed to my room, got the photographs and came back immediately to the porch where we were sitting and he was gone. There was not a living soul around. Finally, I saw Mr. Short walking around the front of the hotel and I asked him for Mr. Front Desk. He indicated that he didn't know where he was but he would look for him. And I sat in the same chair waiting. After a while, back in our room, I saw a torso out the window calling me. There he was, his white gallabeah wafting against the turquoise sky, matching white hat shading his face, calling out to me, "I'm sorry it's time for my nap. I'll see you this evening!"

I decided a nap was a good idea, and lay down very carefully on my bed.

After I woke up and before sunset, we decided to go outside and walk around the perimeter of the hotel to see the desert sunset. As soon as we stepped out of the front of the hotel, both Mr. Short and Mr. Tall appeared and began to follow us, at a distance of 15 feet as before, but this time they were each carrying a long cane. After we walked around the hotel. We decided to observe the sunset from the Abu Simbel temples about two blocks from the hotel. We thought that was the best place to observe from and we would be able to see Lake Nasser and the rough mountains on the far side resembling a Martian landscape.

Suddenly, we were hearing a lot of howls similar to wolves. I looked around and saw in the distance what appeared to be packs of wild dogs grouping around the Nefertari Hotel. I stopped walking immediately. I love dogs but they looked closer to the jackal, the Egyptian god of the dead, Anubis, and they looked ferocious! The cane-bearers, watching, kept smiling all the time, maybe amused by our unexpected exploratory trip. We decided to walk back to the hotel just in case… The surroundings, with the colors of the sun lowering on the horizon made the sand ever deepening in reds and golds as in the photos of Mars' surface. After the sun was completely gone and the first stars slightly appeared in the darkening sky, I turned and walked to our seeming protectors to ask them why they were behind us again. And they indicated that there were a lot of wild dogs around and they were protecting us from being attacked. "Wild dogs…? "Yes Sir!" That was a bit scary but they were watching out for us. We walked faster toward the security of the hotel. We went inside and to our room to get ready for an early dinner since Mr. Saberry A. Lteif Hassan will be coming the next morning before 9 in his Russian Jeep to take us to the airport to go back to Cairo.

We were not going to risk taking another shower in this Nefertary Hotel, so we changed from our desert adventure clothes to our dinner-at-the-Nefertary-Hotel dress, curious how it would fare beside that of the other adventurers in this southernmost outpost of Egypt, circa 1978. I was wishing that it would turn out to be a lively, colorful occasion. We arrived at the dining room and the same Mr. Short and Mr. Tall ushered us, apparently as the only employees of the Nefertary Hotel, to a table and near the one and only other occupied table! We waved "Hello" and not knowing if this couple wanted to talk to us or not and hoping our wave was a proper international one. Certainly we would enjoy conversation on our last night at the Nefertary Hotel. The couple responded appropriately enough for us to move to a table next to theirs, saying "Hello!" The young man looking perplexed with the menu in hand asked, "Do you know what's in these dishes on the menu?" And the young woman said, "We do not know what to order."

"We had the same problem for lunch" I answered.

"Were you here this afternoon?!" the young woman seemed surprised.

"After visiting Abu Simbel temples, we arrived here maybe near 3 pm," I replied.

"Ohhhh," the young man exclaimed.

And we all introduced ourselves. They were a young married couple from Ireland… Patrick and Colleen–what else?!

"You must be the other two guests in this hotel!" Patrick said

"How do you know?" Jaums asked.

"We asked after we arrived at this long hotel this morning," Colleen answered. "You know, we were very curious. We haven't seen anybody except the two servants and the owner…We thought that we were the only ones."

Then I said, "You are the only two guests we have seen. So we thought we were the only ones! Today at lunch time the owner told me that the hotel was all booked, full, you know!"

"Really!" Colleen exclaimed.

"Jaums and I were expecting to meet the rest of the guests tonight. He also told me that they have entertainment in the cocktail lounge every night."

"Oh yes," Patrick said, "noticed the drums, the speakers and the microphone."

"Probably there are some tours that will be arriving all at once," Jaums added.

"How long are you going to be here?" Patrick asked.

I answered, "Jaums and I will be leaving for Cairo tomorrow morning before nine."

Patrick said, "We are going to be here a full week."

"A week?!," I could not help but exclaim, "What are you going to do here for a full week?!"

"We didn't have much money when we got married," Colleen explained, "so we worked and put some money together to come here. We dreamed of spending our honeymoon in Abu Simbel."

"I see…" I said while the smiling now-waiters appeared to get our orders.

And Patrick asked us again, "Do you recommend anything in particular?"

"Well, you cannot get 'fish and chips,' I said. "I or we can recommend the same dish I had for lunch and likely the same we will be ordering again now, Shish Kabobs. We have been mainly eating that for about three weeks since we arrived in Egypt and we are still alive to tell you the story. I swear that after we leave Egypt, I'll never eat that again in my life!

Then Patrick and Colleen invited us to sit at their table, which we did without hesitation.

While waiting for our order, Patrick commented, "You know, this hotel is funny. This evening, when I plugged in my electric shaver…"

"Were you able to shave?!" Jaums interrupted laughing.

"Nooo…I could not!" he said, "as soon as I plugged it, I blew the fuses!"

Realizing what happened, I exclaimed, "Oh no! We must have done it at the same time when I turned on my hair dryer!!"

"What?! Patrick asked.

"Yes, that was it!" I explained, "See…when I turned on my hair dryer, the electricity went off in the entire hotel… Apparently we cannot correct two electrical appliances at the same time. It's too much for the hotel electrical system to handle! How can they handle it when all the rooms of this hotel are full?!"

"Oh, and I thought that it was because of me!" said Patrick, very much relieved.

We all had a good laugh!

During the course of our Shish Kabob meal, we talked about my official invitation to Egypt, some of our amusing adventures, and my paintings. But no other guests arrived at the huge dining room of the

Nefertary Hotel. Much after nine o'clock Patrick said; "Well gentlemen, we must go now, we have to go and visit a person who lives in a nearby village."

Curious, I asked, "What village?" I haven't seen any sign of civilization around this hotel and it's pitch black outside this hotel.

Patrick said, "We have a little map a friend back in Ireland gave us showing the location of the village where the person lives."

I said, "Patrick and Colleen," you cannot venture at night outside this hotel. Not only is it amazingly dark, there are packs of wild and hungry jackals roaming in the desert out there. If you wait until tomorrow in the daylight, it will be safer.

Colleen said, "We have a flashlight…It will be kind of a romantic adventure."

"The desert at night can be very dangerous, especially for people not accustomed to the environment," I said.

Patrick said, "The animals will be afraid of the flashlight! Don't worry we'll manage. We will see you later and they left for their room to get their backpacks and their flashlight for their *Journey Beneath the Desert* (1963) with Haya Harareet and Rad Fulton.

Jaums and I decided to sit at the entrance porch and admire the gorgeous wild sky that because of the lack of light pollution was filled with "billions and billions of stars" as the late *Carl Sagan* used to say about the universe. We could clearly see part of our own *Milky Way galaxy* transversely cutting the void of our horizon. The stars were clearer and brighter than we are accustomed to see in the skies over the U.S. cities. I remembered seeing the same spectacle of lights in the countryside when I was a child in Cuba. The night was cold and you could hear the jackal Anubis howling in the distance…

Exiting the Nefertary Hotel through the main door were Patrick and Colleen. This Irish couple was going to finally live their romantic adventure into the pitch black desert. They were properly attired in their obviously new khaki explorer outfits. Their only defensive weapon was a simple two-battery flashlight.

In a last effort to change their *Dangerous Mission* (1953) with Victor Mature, Piper Laurie and William Bendix, I said again, "Why don't you stay here tonight and try to find the village tomorrow, in the daylight?"

Colleen smiling replied, "We planned it this way. Don't worry, we'll see you tomorrow morning at breakfast."

And then they vanished along with the trace of their flashlight into the pitch dark night under the magnificent starry sky of the desert, becoming an easy prey. Almost giving themselves to the jackals, the wild dogs of the desert who can see in the dark. I thought that I shouldn't be thinking that way and wished them with all my heart the best of luck in their expedition to the uncharted surface of Mars.

We stayed seated there for quite some time in silence enjoying the multitude of stars in a black velvet sky and relaxing before going to bed. There was not a sign of anybody, just the howling of jackals far away. Later on we went to our room, got our suitcases ready for the next morning and I checked the sturdiness of my repaired bed before I carefully got in to sleep.

But I was unable to sleep thinking about the Irish couple… I was awake, and didn't hear their footsteps in the hallway coming back to their room… In the morning I got up and dressed with a black gallabeah I had bought in Luxor and wrapped my head with a black and white Saudi scarf–also bought in Luxor–because since we arrived to the Nefertary Hotel, I was not able to properly bathe or wash my hair. Fortunately in the dry desert climate there is no perspiration.

Also Jaums got up after me and he said that he didn't sleep well either. I asked if he had heard footsteps in the hallway. He said he had not so we went to the dining room in all its grandeur breakfast, I asked, but no one had seen the Irish couple since the prior evening.

We were there until 8:20 AM and nothing. So we went back to

our room to bring our suitcases to the lobby and wait for Mr. Sabery A. Lteif Hassan. I inquired again of Messrs Short and Tall as well as Mr. Desk, still nothing. There were no phones in the rooms, so we got the number and knocked on the door and got no answer.

Well, there is nothing else we could do. I repeated in my mind that I told them twice last night "not to go to the desert at night." It was their own choice.

Then I couldn't remove the film in my mind, running over, of two little Irish skeletons, abandoned in the desert with a flashlight nearby moving back and forth by the wind…

At 8:52 AM, I saw a dust storm outside the Nefertary Hotel… Oh, it was the Russian version of the jeep of Mr. Sabery A. Lteif Hassan arriving, just as he said, "Before 9:00 AM, our pick up time for our ride back to the airport." The Messrs Short and Tall carried our suitcases to the jeep. The owner of the Nefertary Hotel came out to say goodbye to us–perhaps with tears in his eyes since we were the only two guests in his grand hotel because his other two guests, there for a full week's stay, may have been eaten by the jackals in the desert the night before…

We jumped in the Jeep and since we were acquainted with the driving style of Mr. Sabery A. Lteif Hassan, we immediately grabbed the familiar inside fixtures to avoid being ejected into the desert because in an instant we will accelerate to light-speed… And there we went, leaving a trail of dust rising above the so-called "road." We kept looking around during the fast trip to the airport to see if we could see the Irish Couple or the Village where they should have found the "recommended" person…But nothing, just sand and rocks in the treacherous endless desert as far as the eyes can see.

Somehow I was feeling sad not been able to see the temples of Abu Simbel again as I felt equally sad leaving Aswan, Luxor, Karnak, the Valley of the Kings, Queen Hatshepsut's Temple and the other magnificent historic monuments—that I had seen during this fast-moving three weeks in Egypt.

At the light-speed of Mr. Sabery A. Lteif Hassan, we and our trail of dust reached the airport at 9:02 and 9:03 AM—just a 7 minute trip! I thought of *Albert Einstein's Theory of Relativity* and I figured out that at the speed we were moving in the last seven minutes, the Nefertary Hotel would be gone by now. It would have become one more grain of sand in the vastness of the desert. I hoped that Abu Simbel would still be there because I was planning to come back some day.

Mr. Sabery A. Lteif Hassan, rapidly and efficiently helped us with the luggage and said "good bye" in a hurry since he had to take care of other people that morning…leaving a trail of dust at the speed of light. And he disappeared into the desert.

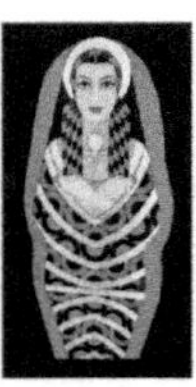

CHAPTER 19

UNVEILING THE PAINTED WOMAN

We went to the counter of the small airport of Abu Simbel to verify our flight number and checked our suitcases directly to our destination, Cairo. The attendant advised us that we should take the 10 am direct flight to Cairo instead of stopping in Aswan. Based on our experience we had with lost suitcases, the direct way was better for us. We had to wait less than an hour, so we wandered around the small airport and to the terrace overlooking the empty runway.

From there I heard the attendant calling us back to the counter. Then he told us that our flight wasn't going to leave at 10 am but at 11 am because it was rescheduled. Well, what can we do, but to sit and wait an extra hour. This time we decided to walk to the waiting room. Then, I heard a voice calling, "Sir! Sir!"

I turned and saw the same attendant behind the counter was pointing to me. So, I got up and went back to the counter and he said, "Sir," he said, "They just informed me that your flight will be stopping in Aswan, and may have to change planes there." Egypt Air had become Reschedule Air.

Well what can I say? But with the change of planes there could be a confusion with the suitcases. So I didn't have any choice and replied that it was OK with me. And said, "Thank you very much for letting me know that in advance." But I was glad about that stop because that was another chance to see a such a beautiful geographical location from the air. I walked back to the waiting area and told Jaums about this 3rd change of plan by Egypt Air.

After a while I noticed the attendant walking in the direction where I was sitting. "Oh no, what is it now," I thought to myself.

"Excuse me Sir,"he said, "We are planning to send your luggage direct to Cairo. I finally got the labels…" and he proudly showed them to me. And I replied "Oh yes, yes, thank you. <u>But, make sure</u> you write clearly on them 'Cairo' to be sure that the employees do not ship them to other locations. We had a bad experience before with our suitcases in Luxor and they were sent to the wrong place."

"Oh yes Sir, yes!" He said and went back to the counter.

Well, after I thought the whole thing over for a while, I realized that checking our luggage direct to Cairo was not a good idea either because I had heard from different sources that luggage gets lost more often when they are checked directly to a later stop, so checking it to Cairo was not a good idea. So, I got up, and this time it was me who went to the counter and said to the attendant: "Since we have to change planes in Aswan, I think it will be safer for us to pick up the luggage in Aswan…" Interrupting me the attendant said, "Oh, wait a minute Sir, I'm going to check something"… And he walked to the small office in the back of the counter. I overheard a lot of conversation in Arabic…Later on he came back to the counter and said, "Sir…they said that you don't have to change planes."

I was speechless for a moment not knowing what to say until I recuperated from the surprise and responded,"That's fine…In this case, yes, check our luggage directly to Cairo. But be very sure that it says <u>Cairo</u>, very clear on the label, <u>OK</u>?"

He said, "Yes Sir!"

I turned around and as I was walking to my seat in the waiting room hoping that this was the last time I would have to talk to that attendant, when I heard the sound of a landing airplane and changed my direction toward the outside terrace. Jaums saw me and got up and walked outside, too. We both thought that it was our plane that was landing. Now it was very hot and the sun was very glary, even with my sunglasses.

So we went inside the waiting room and sat in other seats that allowed us to see the passengers disembarking the plane and walking across the tarmac and entering the small terminal. That flight seemed to be completely full because of the amount of people coming out of the plane and being ushered in a straight line through the main door into buses, just like cattle.

I saw a familiar face in the crowd. It was Nancy! What a small world! I got up and went to her. She was very surprised and pleased to see us there. We hugged and kissed. But she didn't know how long she was going to stay in Abu Simbel. And she said, "I'll probably be in Cairo next Tuesday. "Please Agustin, go to the Sheraton Hotel and leave a note for me as soon as you know in your hotel in Cairo. I want to get in touch with you again." I said "Yes, I'll meet you there and we will go to dinner together in the place you select." She replied, "The Meridian Hotel, it's beautiful there." I said, "OK." And she said, "I'll have to run. I'll see you there," while leaving in a hurry among a large group of people. I couldn't see if she got into a bus or what. She just vanished… There was a mystery and enchantment around Nancy that made her a fascinating person to be with.

After all the waiting buses were loaded, the caravan promptly departed, leaving a trail of desert dust in the distance… I wondered if this is what the owner of the Nefertary Hotel told me when he said that his hotel was booked…

Well…it's now 11:01 AM and there is no sign of our plane leaving. If in fact that is our plane.

By 11:15 some people with suitcases began arriving at the airport.

With the corner of my eye I saw the attendant taking our suitcases and placing them on the ground terrace outside the terminal. I assumed it would be loaded into the plane. At least that's a good sign. Then other attendants joined the effort taking more luggage to the terrace. So, we decided to go out there to avoid more confusion and to avoid our luggage being shipped to Timbuktu. Also with the thought in mind that since we were the first arriving at the airport this morning, we should be the first boarding that plane so we could avoid the usual stampede. Most of the other passengers arriving also had that in mind and we have plenty of experience on boarding airplanes there.

Then, Jaums, ponting at the waiting airplane on the tarmac said, "For sure, this must be our plane."

I said, "But apparently it looks like that is going to be almost empty. There are not too many people here and this is a big airplane."

"Good!" Jaums exclaimed, ``I'm tired of those crowded fights that we have been involved in where people behave like wild beasts in order to get in and get a seat."

And I reminded him, "Especially the old, gray-haired old German ladies with their lethal pointy elbows and handbags, However, probably more people will board in Aswan."

"I'm sure," said Jaums. And at that very moment a lot of people begin arriving on the terrace out of who knows where. We haven't seen any signs of civilization but the airport, the Nefertary Hotel and the Abu Simbel temples.

"Where are those people coming from?!" I exclaimed in disbelief.

Jaums, highly discouraged, said, "Maybe from buses outside." But we cannot see the entrance door or the road outside of the airport due to the large and disorganized crowd behind us.

I said very discouraged too, "Oh no… and I was looking forward to a peaceful boarding."

In a flash, the crowd filled the terrace and the interior of the small airport, and the anxious pushing to get into the plane to secure a seat began with the force equivalent to a *Tsunami*. We have been in that situation since we arrived in Egypt. I was getting sick and tired of this apparently inescapable and unavoidable experience. Very soon we were pushed with our suitcases onto the runway. All the people there kept moving their suitcases forward and pushing each other along the way.

The attendant knew that Jaums and I had been the first to arrive in the airport for the flight back to Cairo and had indicated to us that we would be the first to board the plane. Then a while later he came back carrying the electronic searching device and he used it first on us and he personally sent us carrying all our luggage walking across the tarmac toward the plane. As soon as we were released from the electronic device, the attendant searched the next and so forth. So very soon while on our way to the plane, we kept seeing people running like mad ostriches passing by and getting in front so they would be the first to enter and get a seat in the plane. We couldn't run because our luggage was too heavy and "the runners" were not carrying any. Nevertheless, this is going to be another "survival of the fittest." So we at least walked as fast as we could in spite of the burden of our luggage to get a seat… We didn't have any alternative than to join the wild crowd of desperados. Finally before climbing the staircase to the plane we gave our luggage to the porters in charge of loading them inside the cargo area. Then we had to pass another check with the electronic device in the line to enter the plane. Of course we were not at the front, we lost our place because of the pushy crowd, even pushing each other again in an uncontrollable frenzy to board the damn plane…

Fortunately, the same attendant from the counter came running to us and cleared our road to place us as the first in line again! However this was short lived as other wild characters pushed us aside and got into the plane first. But who cares now, we were the second. What is inexcusable is the violent way they pushed us away.

The plane was big enough and empty so we got to our seats on the first row after the pilot's cabin, but one of the seats was broken since the back didn't stay up in the sitting position.

The seats behind were empty and we decided to sit there. We checked and they were in perfect condition. And very soon the aisles will be overcrowded by an enormous number of wild beasts, even women had to fight each other for their equal-opportunity survival. So now, sitting in my seat, I closed my eyes to forget this shameful episode where human beings became like rabid animals fighting each other. I wanted to escape what I just witnessed.

Later, Jaums touched me on my shoulder and woke me up from my kind-of "trance" I induced on myself in order to forget this experience and said, "Look, look… Look who just entered the plane…," I slowly opened my eyes and looked at him and said, "Why did you wake me up? I need to rest and sleep if possible." And he said, "I just want you to get up from your seat and look back in the aisle." Feeling exhausted I got up and looked back… and said, "Oh no, The Painted Woman again!!! Where did she come from?! While Jaums began to laugh at the coincidence of that woman appearing whatever we had gone on this trip, I collapsed in my seat and evading the new situation, I fell into a much needed deep sleep.

When I woke up we were already in the air. I was kind of confused and it took me some time to locate myself. Then vaguely remember something about The Painted Woman inside the plane. I asked Jaums if I had been dreaming.

"No," he said, "She is here on this plane with her makeup case, The Polyester Man and The Unremarkable Youngster." I saw her and I decided to go to the bathroom just to take a closer look at her. She looks very put together as usual. But when she entered this plane I noticed that she was very upset, maybe about the stampede to board the plane.

"All right, when I am completely awake I will go and pass by her seat to observe. I hope she doesn't recognize me," I said.

When I was completely recuperated from my nap, I got up and walked to the bathroom with the objective to observe her very well. However, I couldn't help but notice that the aisle in her direction was already lined with aging gentlemen. Therefore walking by her was fortunately very slow, allowing me and the others to look at her for a longer time. The first thing I noticed was the sky blue low cut *decollete* pullover, remarking even more her celestial pair of helium balloons inflated to the maximum and waiting for a pin to explode and provoke a wind storm that deviated this plane right to heaven without consulting Saint Peter. As once before she was adorned with American Indian turquoise and a white, wide brim straw hat and a navy scarf around her alabaster neck as a subtle call of the wild to the sailors of submarines anchored in the Port of New Orleans.

Just as I got to my seat, I found two feisty little old ladies standing in the aisle pointing at us indicating something about our seats in Italian. They were demanding that our seats belonged to them. We had no comprehension of their claim because they was no reserved sitting in any of the planes that flew in, out and about Egypt. The seats are just decided by the customary stampede of passengers. I wondered, how was it possible that these two little old Italian ladies in Egypt were acting that way with somebody dressed with a black gallabeah, a Saudi headdress, beard and dark sunglasses, like me. For them I should have looked like a Saudi. And you don't mess with Saudis! After all, they weren't in their own country. But they continued carrying on… Then one of the male stewards on the plane, the same one we had seen in all our previous flights inside Egypt and who knew who we were, came and said to me, "Excuse me Sir. What the ladies are saying is that you are sitting in their seats."

"I beg your pardon. I understand what they are saying, Italian is not far from Spanish. These seats were available quite some time ago when we boarded this flight at Abu Simbel airport. There were no reserved seats in any of the flights I have been taking in Egypt. Those two ladies were not sitting here when we entered this plane. The seats were empty."

He replied, "Sir, they are claiming that they were sitting here and that you took their seats."

"This is absurd…There was no one sitting here," I said. "Where were these two ladies inside this plane? They just materialized? This is totally absurd!"

The steward turned to the ladies and explained the situation in Italian. Then the ladies made a big fuss about it. The Steward turned to Jaums and said, "Sir…They are saying that they will not seat anywhere but their seats. They are demanding for you both to leave their seats."

I said, "This is ridiculous. They should be returned to where they were sitting or hiding before. I am sure this plane would not be able to take off with these two ladies standing in the aisle or hiding in the restrooms."

The steward replied, " I know Sir…But, they are threatening me that if you don't leave their seats, they will remain standing in the aisle. We have to take off soon and that's against the regulations…"

My Spanish blood was getting very hot and circulating very fast throughout my Cuban body and I was getting real upset about the absurdity of this situation! I went over the fact that we had been sitting in the seats since the beginning of boarding and anyway, there is no such thing as reserved seats on these flights. The steward tried to calm me down by saying, "Sir…don't get upset."

I gave him the detailed explanation he seemed to want.

"All right Sir," he said, "I'll do my best to convince them to sit in some other place." Then he began speaking in Italian to the old Italian monsters. But they were screaming and yelling back at the poor

Egyptian steward. By that time, Kitty, a tall statuesque–much improved version of Goldie Hawn–and who was a tour hostess we had met days ago in Luxor, hearing the commotion, came and asked me, "Agustin, what happened?"

"Kitty," I explained, "These Italian ladies wanted for us to give them our seats. You know perfectly that here there is not such a thing as a reserved seat. We simply were here first."

"You are totally right Agustin," she stated, "but <u>unfortunately</u> they are on my tour…I just found out from another steward that they are causing a problem, but, I beg you, please, get up, let them sit in your seats so they will shut up and this plane can take off. I promise you that I'll find you a seat. If not, I will sit you on my lap!"

"OK Kitty. Only for you!" I replied, and turning to Jaums I said, "Come on, lets go…" We got up and left our seats to these Italian so-called ladies. But I was very upset and fuming like a Cuban dragon when I passed by the now victorious-acting little devils, I could not resist the temptation to tell them in a hushed tone of voice avoiding to create a scandal, and even if they would not understand me, "I can see why Italy sent you away!"

That must have been a comical situation for the mainly European tourists to see what appeared to be a Saudi, insulting a pair of Italian women in a hushed voice, in English with a Spanish accent. So Jaums and I went to the seats Kitty found for us. And we passed by The Painted Woman, The Polyester Man and The Unremarkable Youngster–but this time because we were upset, we didn't pay attention to her.

Then we overheard another commotion inside this doomed flight–that hadn't taken off yet and was still waiting for the Italian Devils and us to take a seat.

Suddenly, I heard the loud voice of a woman screaming vulgar insults in Spanish but with the typical sound of an uneducated Cuban woman from a falling-apart old tenement in the old section of La

Habana. I hadn't heard those sounds and the particular way of delivering them since those dramatic presentations recreating real crimes of passion on the afternoon radio shows of my youth in the small country town where I grew up.

I turned my head toward the front of the plane where that loud voice seemed to be coming from. What I saw was outstandingly shocking indeed!!!

From behind I saw the wide brim of the white hat of The Painted Woman making convulsive moves back and forth while her shoulders in her light blue sweater were shaking almost as rhythmically as is done in popular Cuban music. Those shoulder movements became traditional after the arrival of the Africans in the sixteenth century and their gift of rhythm that became an integral part of Cuba's new popular music which later extended throughout the Americas. But those shoulder movements celebrating the rhythm can also can be viewed as vulgar in other circumstances. The evolution that originated from the mix of the minuet with the African percussion rhythms insisted on these movements that became part of being a Cuban.

So, how can I, even imagine, that the impressive and regal looking Painted Woman knew about such a detail and had the ability to imitate those things!!! And even displaying the ability to use that particular vulgar vernacular that was ringing through the plane to my ears? As a matter of fact, this is the first time I was to hear her voice! She was always silent and dignified. But this surprising revelation doesn't paint a pretty picture. Could she be a former Cuban Rumba Dancer? But I had met a famous one who made films in the late 40s and into the 50s in person in Miami and she was very sweet, dignified and refined. Not a single hint of vulgarity. Certainly The Painted Woman dresses very flashy and calls so much attention all the time, but she seemed to be very reserved and always escorted quietly by The Polyester Man and The Unremarkable Youngster. So I was shocked to hear her shouts and wondered at whom they were directed. She was still seated with her two faithful companions and her inseparable makeup case… This was one more mystery of our own mystic queen of the Nile with her pair of floating pontoons still undiscovered by the Mexican film director, Juan Orol*. From that moment on, I forgot the decrepit Italian devils and was concentrating on this, this extraordinary revelation…

I had better sit so this airplane can finally begin her flight to Cairo… Finally our plane was airborne to another unknown adventure of our Egyptian journey. Below is just desert and no hint of the village that the Irish couple went to visit last night. I hope that Patrick and Colleen are still alive.

Kitty gave me a seat beside her; Jaums is in a different row. Turning to Kitty, I asked, "Who is that Painted Woman?" And she immediately understood who I was asking about and she broke up laughing. After she recuperated from my question, she said, "You are too much! Well, she is married to a prominent Architect from Chicago.

"Really," I said, "but he doesn't look like one! I told her of his moniker, the "The Polyester Man." And Kitty burst out laughing again and said, "You are really something!"

I said, "To me he looks more like a used car salesman on TV."

I told her of their choreography: FIRST & ALWAYS her, second, The Polyester Man, that I assumed was her husband, and third and per-fectly aligned The Unremarkable Youngster, perhaps her plain teenaged son.

"Kitty said while laughing, "Yes, you are so right!!! They always walk in a line and she is always up front!!!"

I asked Kitty, "Did you notice that she always carries her makeup case wherever she goes?"

––––––––––––––––––

* *Juan Orol, known as the "Involuntary Surrealist", was a founder of "Film Noir" and "Film Rumbera".*

"Yes, yes and yes!" Kitty said laughing.

In the window seat beside me was sitting an overweight, six-footer with Richard Wagner's little Valkyrie mustache, short, gray hair, unshaved legs and the standard-issue sandals with white bobby socks. She occupied all the space in her seat and her fat was crawling to my seat and and on her lap, her lethal handbag–Valentino: and here she comes…

Kitty told me what was going on with the two old Italian ladies. She said, "Our tour left Aswan this morning for two hours of sightseeing at Abu Simbel. There, the plane was going to wait for us and take us back to Cairo. I told everybody to leave their hand luggage inside the plane and under their seats. Except 'your friend, The Painted Woman… Everybody left their hand luggage, but she insisted on carrying her makeup case which she takes whatever she goes. But the two conniving little old sneaky ladies stayed behind. The seats where these ladies were sitting broke. So after the rest of the passengers left the plane, these conniving 'ladies' moved their luggage to the next seats behind which were the seats you took when you first entered the plane and you didn't notice their things under the seats because you assumed that the plane was empty because the first seats were disabled and you rightfully– logically took the seats behind. You were right! And these 'ladies' Were the ones who caused the problems."

I said, "Now you see. Don't ever trust innocent looking Italian little old ladies because they are not and probably are from Sicily…"

"I know," Kitty said, "but your 'Painted Woman' who always insists on being the first one in the front row, also lost hers and had to sit in the back. And that was unacceptable for her! So that's why she was so upset and saying things in Spanish that we could not understand."

"Thank you so much Kitty, now this absurdity we experienced has a logical understandable explanation. In relation to The Painted Woman and her sacred makeup case that she has to carry always is because inside that case is her face…And she, without any doubt, is the traveling Queen of the Nile and she must always 'save face.'"

Kitty said laughing, " You are very funny, Agustin! You have made all of this very amusing. It's really funny now!"

"Actually The Painted Woman tried to negotiate with the conniving Italian 'ladies' for the front seats. But, they were so adamant and refused." Kitty explained that these Italians didn't speak English, "so that's why 'your friend' exploded in Spanish! Probably she thought the Italians would understand from her Spanish how upset she was at them. Oh, I'll be glad to get to Cairo to get over with this tour!!!"

Isn't that something! Finally, because of this incident, provoked by two Italian witches, unveiled, to a point, the mystery of The Painted Woman!!! And finally, a connection was established between her and me, I thought.

But also–perhaps–it is a coincidence that after Egypt we had already planned to stay a week in Italy…

Kitty and I continued chatting until it was time to land in Aswan. There we stayed for over thirty minutes. But no one dared to move from their seats… If the Italians had ventured out of the plane, I could have taken a photograph of The Painted Woman switching their hand luggage far from HER seat… But they knew better! And no more incidents happened with them that afternoon.

CHAPTER 20

CINNAMON SKIN

I felt calm. The cool afternoon breeze was caressing my face. It was peaceful up there. Then, I remembered… and images from my past were coming to my mind like a film… And I was right here in this old movie house named *Gardel,* honoring the name of a very famous tango singer and movie idol in the 1920s and 30s, not only in Argentina but in the rest of the Americas, Carlos Gardel. But then, four years ago, the exterior was painted in a dark gray color and its architectural style–if any–was some sort of rough cement facade simulating a middle age fortress…

It's located on the corner of a lively but run-down section of *La Habana* where thousands made their daily bus transfer to other buses to go to their jobs in the mornings and in the afternoon to come back home. The traffic of vehicles was very heavy at that intersection, consequently, the smell was of burned gasoline as it was polluted by the engines' exhaust fumes in a city with many automobiles and other forms of transportation in the early 1950s.

The Gardel theater, paradoxically specialized in showing *"La creme de la creme"* of the worst Mexican movies made at that time. Movies that only desperados would venture to see and some other movies equally untouchable. The Gardel always had a double feature of two differ-

317

ent movies daily. The interesting detail was that between movies they had live variety shows–that bore not the slightest resemblance to New York's Radio City Music Hall shows. These shows were much below 3rd rate…This "movie & theater" was an equal opportunity enterprise presenting singers and rumba dancers commonly called "*Rumberas*" with holes in their net stockings and feathers missing from their headdresses. Cheap ladies rejected from *The Gong Show* and in dire economic need. Some of them were of dubious reputation and others notorious in La Habana for other endeavors not having anything to do with <u>The Arts</u>. Well, not <u>The Fine Arts</u>. They also presented tango and bolero singers with their bra straps fastened with rusty safety pins in the back of their run-down gowns and as they moved on the small stage sometimes you could see sequins falling to the stage floor. The official orchestra of the Gardel had four musicians; none were conservatory trained. Sometimes one of the "musicians" was drunk. They had magicians with raggedy tuxedos and instead of rabbits from their hats, they extracted rats in their very obvious tricks. And some kinds of circus acts that often ended up in accidents. That was part of the thrill to be in the audience at the Gardel, because you never knew what was going to happen. The audience went there paying 50 cents for two movies and a show, and were getting their money's worth watching and sometimes even participating in the shows. Actually it was a lot of fun for the uneducated customers of the Gardel. There are audiences for everything in life, believe it or not. Poor Carlos Gardel, busy even in death, very busy turning in his grave. I don't think he was "resting in peace" once the Gardel opened in *La Habana*.

Most of the time the Gardel was nearly jam-packed. Of course, the kind of audience that used to go there was mostly men and they all looked like hard-core criminals and outlaws and I never understood what they were doing there–what they were looking for… Out of sheer curiosity, one afternoon I decided to go there to see what it was all about. What was the fascination? And there, one afternoon, I saw her…

I bought my ticket and entered the lobby of the Gardel for the first time in my life. I was eighteen years old then. The lobby was square and of a medium size. The walls were papered with hundreds of old posters from Mexican and some American films like the original 1933 one of *King Kong* and some Roy Rogers and Dale Evans westerns. Those looked out of place where Mexican films were the speciality of the house. All were stained by the passing of time, but who knows? They might be covering cracks in the walls. There was an old ceiling fan slowly revolving… In the back of the lobby, in the middle, was the door to the movie house. By the door, sitting on a stool, having a nap was the old black man who took the tickets. I walked slowly so as not to wake him up and I slipped my ticket through the container slot and went through the door.

I could hear the piano, the maracas and the bongos of a live orchestra, so the show must be on… I moved the ragged wine colored curtain and entered the orchestra seating area. The air was hot, smokey and the smell of the room created a surrealistic atmosphere. It really was a new world…

On stage, lit by a single spotlight, was a woman. A singer, since she was wearing a long, black, sequined, strapless gown. It was very tight under her knees, where it opened like a trumpet bell or a very low tutu. The orchestra started playing the introduction of a popular tune of the time, the song "Cinnamon Skin".

Then, the woman on stage moved her hips and shoulders provocatively, and was walking at the rhythm of the bongos. The fact was that when she moved her hip to the right, the upper, strapless part of her gown went to the left and vice versa was disconcerting to me. I wondered how she was able to do it. Eighteen years old, I was.

I walked down the aisle and when she started singing, I sat immediately on the first seat I found on the aisle… I watched her… The right side of her face, viewed from my seat, which in reality was her left side, was magnificent. I never had seen any other face more beautiful than hers. But the other side was hidden. I wondered who that mysterious woman was, who, at the same time, was so voluptuous and sexually inciting with half of her face covered by her dark hair… Could her hair be parted like that and falling over half of her face be her trademark..? Was she hiding a secret..?

The way she was singing, saying the lyrics, word by word, giving an intention, to every sound, and movement, was like a slow masturbation. Her lips slowly opened and closed sensually. She was a singing vagina. Her single presence on stage was exerting animal feelings within me. I was feeling an extraordinary desire to run to her and hold her in my arms very tight and kiss those inviting lips…

But the audience around me was behaving so wildly! They were doing all kinds of suggestive gestures at her, throwing lascivious kisses and disgustingly libidinous movements with their tongues at her. And the poor woman, while singing, she seemed to be suffering in silence on stage at the harassment from the vicious audience. Why don't they exercise some restraint like I did and let her finish her song with dignity? However, that was too much to expect from this vulgar mob of desperados.

And one of them shouted, "Hey you! Why don't you show the other side of your face?"

The mob started laughing while another despicable individual, looking very much like a moron, sood up and yelled at her, "Did rats eat your face darling?"

And the laughter of the cruel mob increased…

I was ashamed. That was too much. I saw the contraction of the muscles on the gorgeous left side of her face, produced by her intense pain and suffering… –How cruel.., how cruel they are!– Suddenly, she stopped singing and was going to leave the stage when she realized that she was going to faint. Then, she desperately got hold of the curtains of the fly gallery to her left in order not to fall, but it was too late. She was fainting and falling… and with her, part of the curtain, which was torn apart by her pull. She fell onto her back, and when she landed on the wooden floor of the stage, it produced an incredible banging noise, which was accentuated by the acoustics of the place. Part of the torn curtain fell on top of her body, covering her completely, and in its fall, left a trail of dust that showed clearly in the stage lights and quickly blew all over the stage.

It was a pathetic sight and I decided that I had to do something! I must break through my fears! I got up from my seat, ran through the aisle, jumped onto the stage and ran to her! I rapidly removed the dusty curtain from her, and there she was… all covered in brown dust, her face, her hair, her gown, but one of her hands was desperately keeping her hair over the hidden right side of her face… She was very upset… I thought that I should call for a doctor in the house. But, would it be possible for a doctor to be among this mob of degenerates? I'll try.

"Please, she needs a doctor! Is there a doctor in the house?"

There was a momentary silence, and then, a middle aged man, dressed in a white suit who was nervously zipping his fly, got up and ran to the stage…

He immediately picked her up in his arms. –Damn! I could have done that!– I thought, upset at myself. And he said, "Let's take her to her dressing room."

"I don't know where her dressing room is!" I replied.

I ran backstage and asked an old man standing by one of the entrances. He pointed to a filthy door in a dark corner. I ran back to the doctor and said, "It's in the back! Follow me!"

And he followed me while the orchestra was starting another tune and a magician was starting his act.

"The show must go on," the old man said to us as we passed by him, completely oblivious to the fact that the poor singer was scorned by the disgusting audience on that very stage, causing her to faint.

–What kind of place is this?– I kept thinking. Then, we got in front of the filthy door, but there was no name, not a single cardboard star covered with chocolate kiss foil paper pasted with chewing gum as I had seen in the worst Mexican films. The only writing on the door, besides the incessantly obscene drawings of explicit sexual scenes and parts, was the word "ladies" with a question mark. How insulting and degrading it must have been for that poor woman to have to walk through that door! And I decided that I had to get her out of that place somehow, even if I have to sell my soul to the devil!

"Is <u>this</u> your dressing room?" the doctor, incredulous, asked her, still being carried in his arms.

She slightly opened her eyes, well, eye, of long eyelashes full of dust, looked at the door and, still holding her hair over the right side of her face, she said, "Yes it is. But please cover your nose before going in."

The doctor and I looked at each other completely confused by her advice, and apparently we both thought the same thing, that because of the shock she had suffered she was not in full control of her mind and did not know what she was talking about. Disregarding her advice, I pushed the door open and we went in… And immediately, the doctor and I comprehended the full extent of her profound advice. The room was filled with a putrid urine and other human droppings stench. We both automatically covered our noses, consequently, she fell from the doctor's arms… Fortunately, she fell on a dilapidated chaise lounge that, even though it broke down, falling apart on the floor by the weight of her body, protected her with its broken springs, from impact on the tile floor. The main cushion of the chaise lounge burst open and the stench room was suddenly filled with little feathers mixed with more dust that was getting into our eyes, nostrils and the inside of our mouths.

"Hey..! What is going on here..?" shouted somebody with a parrot-sounding voice coming from the back of the room, but from some-body we couldn't see.

"It's nothing..! It's me, Esperanzita! I just fainted!"

So now I know her name! Esperanzita.., Her name is "Hope"! It sounded heavenly and full of hope for me, I thought.

And she added to the other person in the dark, "Cachita.., there are two gentlemen here!"

"Gentlemen..?!!" incredulously exclaimed the parrot-voice, laughing afterward and adding: "Gentlemen are an endangered species here, darling..!" and continued laughing.

"Yes, two gentlemen! I am serious!" replied Esperanzita.

Then we heard a toilet flushing in the background, but not wanting to swallow its load, it was making an excruciating noise. A while later, a door, fastened by only one hinge, was painstakingly opened.., and a short, very plump ugly young woman came out, smiling without a single tooth while pulling up her yellowish bloomers… And with her unpleasant parrot-sounding voice, she exclaimed as she got rid of the newspaper folded under her armpit: "Oh my God, Esperanzita.., What happened?! What are you doing lying down in that position..? Well.., I shouldn't ask… With these two gentlemen… It's not my business…"

Then I bent over to help Esperanzita, who was extending one of her hands for me to get her up from the chase lounge wreckage. Her other hand was still keeping her hair in place over the right side of her face. And when she was up, she said to me with profound gratitude: "Oh, thank you… Let me introduce myself first.., my name is Esperanzita Maria Magdalena Delores Suibiaur Echemendia. But my friends call me Esperanzita… Nice meeting you both…"

I was going to say something to her, but the doctor cut me off by saying to her: "Nice meeting you, Esperanzita," while he took her left arm to kiss her hand.

Esperanzita looked at me with great surprise and, pulling her hand away, she said to the doctor: "Wait.., let me remove the dust first," blowing air from her sensuous lips, she got rid of the dust and graciously extended her hand to the doctor, who deposited a long smoochy kiss. Then, she gave me her hand and I kissed it with great pleasure… Perhaps too much, too obvious, too soon… And while still holding her hand against my lips, she lifted the arch of her perfect left eyebrow while giving an indescribable gesture by hollowing her left cheek and pronouncing forward her inviting lips, making her round, high, left cheekbone appear more splendid than ever, under the unflattering brown dust which still covered most of her face. And that particular gesture ended in a sparkling smile while she retired her hand from my lips…

Then, I proudly said: "It is the most extraordinary pleasure for me to make your acquaintance."

"Oh, come on..!" commented that hideous creature with the parrot voice named Cachita to spoil the flavor of the moment.

And the doctor interrupted by saying: "By the way, my name is Victor Manual Villareal Monteagundo del Pozo.., and now Esperanzita, how are you feeling..?"

"Better.., better..," she bitterly said, and turning and looking at me, with a languid voice, she asked me: "You forgot to tell me your name."

"I'm sorry," I said, "My name is Juan… Just Juan Valdes."

"He must be an orphan from the Beneficence orphanage!" the disgusting Cachita exclaimed, making that assumption because all of the orphans there were given the last name "Valdes".

–I could have strangled her on the spot!– But, Esperanzita was looking at me expecting an answer. I remained silent and lowered my eyes to the floor.

And she apparently understood the actual truth.

But, to my surprise, she asked me: "Are you the coffee picker..?"

I immediately responded: "Oh, no, no. Nothing like that… I am just the audience. I mean, your audience. I am your admirer!"

And the doctor, interrupting, asked her: "Esperanzita, I am here because you fainted on stage. I want to know how you are feeling now?"

She responded: "Better, thank you, doctor."

Then he said with an unwholesome smile drawn on his thin lips:

"Please, call me Victor."

–Dirty old man!– I thought to myself.

And Esperanzita repeated: "Thank you, Victor…"

"Call me 'Juan'," interrupting, I immediately said.

"Thank you Ju-an," she provocatively pronounced my name.

–Oh my God..! I'm going to melt…– I commented deep inside myself.

And then, Cachita, twinkling one of her tiny, fat, little eyes at Esperanzita, gave her uncalled-for advice: "A doctor and an orphan… I hope you make the right choices this time, darling. Well…, gentlemen.., if you excuse me, I have to go do my number, darlings. I have to leave…" and thank god, she left!

"What kind of number does she do?" I asked Esperanzita.

And very matter-of-fact she replied: "She breaks wind on stage."

I could have killed myself. –I shouldn't have asked! It figures..! Such a vulgar individual!–

"Esperanzita," the doctor said, "What were your symptoms before you fainted?"

She turned very grave and said: "Pain, doctor. A big pain. A great pain."

"Where did you feel the pain?" he asked her.

"In my chest, doctor," she answered, "very deep within my chest."

Then the damn doctor placed his lustful hands all over his luscious chest, unmercifully, as if he was kneading bread dough with her baby soft cinnamon skin. And he said, "Breathe deeply," while he placed one of his ears on her chest…

–"Oh, how much I envied him that moment…–

"You are tickling me, Victor," nervously laughing, Experanzita said, "you know.., my chest is very sensitive… You have a hairy ear."

"I'm sorry," he said, "now relax and breathe deeply again..," and finally removing his ear from her chest, he said: "Well, I cannot hear anything unusual from your heart. Nothing out of the ordinary. It seems perfectly normal. Have you had this pain before?"

"Oh, yes, doctor," she answered.

"Call me 'Victor'", he insisted.

"Yes, Victor," she replied, "yes…always, all my life. Ever since I was a tiny little girl,,," and she broke down into tears.

Black tears were coming out uncontrollably from her left eye, running down her cheek. The doctor got his expensive handkerchief from his jacket and offered it to her. And I instead, did not even have an old piece of Kleenex in my pocket to offer her…

"Calm, calm down, Esperanzita," the doctor said, "I am your friend and I am here to help you."

"Me, too! Me, too!" I frantically added to point out that I should not be excluded. Then the doctor turned his face at me and gave me a derogatory look in conjunction with an insulting gesture indicating for me to shut up. I felt completely impotent, not sexually, but physically. I was unable to do what a man ought to do in a situation like this, break his neck. No, I had to control myself, after all, he was the only hope of helping the sweet Esperanzita with her painful illness.

"Yes.., Victor and Juan," she graciously put it. "I have carried this pain all my life. It is a horrible stigma. It is something that is present all the time. I cannot erase it. I can not forget it. And this evening.., was the worst."

What happened this evening that made it worse?" inquired the doctor.

And, very excited, she said: "They were screaming and yelling tonight..."

"I noticed that," the doctor said.

"Me, too!" I interrupted and added: "Oh boy,,, was I upset!"

"Yes," she said, still very excited, "but tonight they yelled something that touched me deeply... Something that killed me and completely destroyed me."

And the doctor asked her: "But what is it my dear Esperanzita?"

–Son of a bitch! She is not your "dear"!– I furiously thought to myself.

Then she answered: "They yelled something that was true, that was my truth. They yelled..."

And, remembering the incident with the audience, I realized that it was the last yell that made her faint. It was after that despicable individual looking very much like a moron shouted..., and automatically, I repeated that unforgettable line: "Did rats eat your face, darling?"

Very much surprised, Esperanzita looked at me and said: "Do you remember?"

"How can I forget such an uncalled-for insult?" I replied.

Then gravely, she said: "That uncalled-for insult, is the truth. My truth," and she started crying controllably again... She blew her nose a few times after she calmed down.

We stayed there in silence, waiting for her to compose herself again and to continue her story. But, by this time, I was suspecting that the way she had her hair, covering the right half of her face, was not a gimmick, but her stigmatic truth.

And she finally continued: "While I was an innocent, tiny, little girl, my parents died and I did not have any family. An elderly woman took care of me. She was very poor. We used to live in a shack.., and improvised cardboard, palm tree wood, grass and tin roof shack... It was horrible. Every time it rained, it had to be rebuilt. Oh, it was horrible, it was horrible! The shack was located on the infamous 'Donkey's Hill'... The old lady was a professional beggar... Sometimes she took me with her to the steps of the Sacred Heart of Jesus church and we stayed there begging all day until late in the evening. But other times she used to leave me alone in the shack. It happened one day that I was left there. That day, she left me earlier than usual. It was still dark outside. It was during daylight saving time, you know. After she left, I stayed in my bed which consisted of a beaten up old wooden cod fish box with old newspapers and dry grass as a mattress... There were a lot of rats around there... Many babies there had been completely eaten by them in the past. I had heard the stories... but I thought that it would never happen to me... That day, I fell asleep after she left.., a wet feeling on my face and a painful burning sensation woke me up. I put my hands on my face and it hurt and I noticed with my fingers the shattered flesh and blood all over... I screamed and ran out! Some neighbors came to my rescue... They kept screaming and yelling around me: "The rats ate her face, the rats ate her face!" and she broke down crying again.

The doctor and I were in silence. I was feeling very sorry for that wonderful, sweet woman, full of youth and dazzling beauty, carrying that horrible stigma from her past. And then, at that point, I made a firm commitment to help and take care of her from now on. I will do something to get her out of this horrible theater environment and clean her wounds.

"Were you taken to a doctor then?" the doctor inquired.

And she responded: "Yes... The neighbors took me to the closest first aid house."

"What did they do.., do you remember?" the doctor asked her.

"First," she responded, "the doctor there cleaned and disinfected my shattered face. It was so painful, it was so painful! I'll never forget that pain! Then, he salvaged what he could and stitched the rest the best he could. He put bandages all over my face and gave me rabies and tetanus shots. I'll never forget the rabies shots either, twenty one shots around my navel in addition to the pain I was going through. He said that it was all he was able to do for me. The next step would be to send me to a plastic surgeon… But I could not even dream of that."

"How old were you then," the doctor asked her.

"Nine," she replied while breaking down crying again.

Then, the doctor solemnly said: "You know my dear Esperanzita… I think destiny has placed us together. I think I can help you."

"How, Victor?" she inquired, "how?!"

And with the same solemn tone in his voice he stated: "Because I am a plastic surgeon."

Suddenly, a loud and strong, emotional music shook the room! The three of us looked at each other in a state of utter confusion. –But anyway,– I thought, – so what! It is not of any importance, the source of the musical fanfare! The important thing was the incredible and surprising news!–

"A plastic surgeon?!" she exclaimed in disbelief.

"A plastic surgeon?!" I could not help repeating, knowing that this particular fact was going to place him in a more prominent place in sweet Esperanzita's heart.

"Yes, a plastic surgeon," he stated again with profound conviction.

Esperanzita looked at him now as her savior and I at my heart out with envy. He had a lot to offer her. But, I have so little.., just my honest, abstract desire to help,

Yes, Esperanzita, my darling," the doctor said, drooling dirty-old-man saliva from the edges of his mouth with thin lips outstretched by a perverted smile.

–Damn! Son of a bitch!–

And he continued, saying: "I might be able to operate on you and restore the original beauty to your marked face."

"Oh, doctor..," she exclaimed, deeply moved.

"Call me 'Victor', remember.., your Victor," he pointed out.

And she said: "Oh, Victor, my Victor.., thank you, thank you!"

"Now, I would like to examine your face," he added.

Then the expression on her face became very serious. For a few seconds, she did not know exactly what to do, and, turning her face to me, almost begging, she said: "Please Juan.., not you. I don't want for you to see. I don't want to upset you."

"Oh, no you can't," I immediately said, interrupting her. I don't care how your right side looks… I like you unconditionally."

"Anyway," she added, "I don't want for you to see. You should respect my decision."

"Yes, I will. Whatever you say," I said while turning my body facing the toilet room door where that hideous wind-breaker, Cachita, made her entrance pulling up her yellowish bloomers… –I'll never forget that spectacle!– The horrible stench coming through that half opened door that was making me nauseous.., but, I kept my promise not to look back… There was a silence in the room. I assumed that Esperanzita was getting ready to uncover her truth… And then I heard: "Uuggghhhhhh" (splash), followed by Esperanzita's surprised but contained scream, and I decided to turn around to find out what was going on. And I saw the doctor finishing to vomit a viscose, bubbling liquid all over Esperanzita's lap while she was abruptly standing up and jumping back to avoid more of his unwelcome vomit. But, I couldn't see her face, because she had already covered the right side of it with her hair again.

And the doctor, very apologetic, said: "I am so sorry Esperanzita… I didn't know it was going to be that revolting…"

"Oh, gee, thanks." she said.

Cleaning around his mouth and chin, the doctor said: "In all the years that I have been in my profession, I have never seen anything quite like this."

"Now you know what I have been going through," sweet Esperanzita said.

"Yes," he said, "I know very well now."

With profound anxiety reflected in the tone of her voice, she asked him: "Do you think… you'll be able to do something for me..?"

After a silence, he said: "Well.., I'll try and do my best. It's going to take a long time, perhaps a few operations…"

"Thank you, thank you, my Victor," she said almost crying, "at least now, there is hope for me. I can look forward to it."

Then, I got a dirty, raggedy motel towel I found on the floor beside the stained, corner sink, opened the faucet, got it slightly wet and went to Esperanzita and I started to clean the doctor's vomit from her black, sequined gown.

While I was doing this, she asked the doctor: "And… how can I pay you back, Victor..?"

There was a silence hanging in the room after her question, and I turned to him with the same question projected on my face. Then, I saw reflected on his dirty-old-man face a lustful glint and the appearance of a corrupt smile, filled with sexual connotations galore. That made me extremely upset. And without wasting any time, I immediately got up, stood protectively beside Esperanzita, and putting my arm around her splendid shoulders, I shouted at the disgusting doctor: "There will be nothing like that! You are not going to take advantage of this extraordinary woman! I will protect and defend her from dirty rats like you!" Realizing the connection of the last thing I mentioned, I said to her:

"Oops…, I'm sorry."

Then lifting his left eyebrow, the doctor said to me: "Then, how is she going to pay for it?"

And Esperanzita, turning her face to me, seriously asked me: "Yes, Juan…, how am I going to pay him back?"

Committing myself, but without knowing exactly what the solution would be, I said: "I'll do anything. I will provide. I will come up with the money!"

"Oh, really..?!" the doctor said sarcastically and remarked: "You poor penniless orphan!" Then he laughed and added: "My fees are very high. How are you going to pay..?!"

"Never mind," I told him, "I will get the money! I will pay you until the last penny! You fix her face and I will pay for it!?

"But Juan, how can I pay you back..?" Esperanzita asked me.

And I answered her by saying: "Don't worry. You already have."

"Very well," said the doctor, "I want to see her tomorrow morning in my office," and he got one of his cards and put it in front of my face. I took it, and then he said: "Now, if you excuse me, I have to leave" and he walked back to the door and opened it. From there, he turned directly toward Esperanzita, smiled suggestively and winking his wrinkled mundane eye, he said to her: "I will see you tomorrow."

He finally left and I was glad to be alone with her. I had already made up my mind. I was going to do everything in order to get her to the operating table, even if I had to rob a bank.

Next morning, I met Esperanzita in the popular downtown meeting place at the intersection of the streets Galiano and San Rafael. I started early and she arrived half an hour late. I saw her coming down San Rafael... According to my criteria, she was dressed just too provocatively. She was wearing a high neck red angora sweater that made her breasts look like two launching rockets aiming for heaven, a very tight black satin skirt, opened in the back above her knees, remarking her definitively voluptuous contours, a red crocodile ankle-strap pair of spike heeled sandals with matching handbag hanging from her right shoulder. Her hair was like the night before on stage: it was parted on the left side and neatly falling in a cascade over the stigmatic right side of her face.

When she walked, her rounded hips bounced from east to west at an unsettling speed. And I could swear that I kept hearing the sound of drums with each movement… I did not say anything about my disapproval of her choice of clothes for going to see the perverted doctor, because, after all, she was in show business and these people always have the tendency to dress on the wild side of the spectrum. So, I was sure that she dressed like that normally and not especially for this occasion.

But, what was upsetting to me was the fact that every time a male passed by, walking or from a vehicle, he had to shout a compliment to her generous beauty. I felt very jealous, furious and impotent inside. I would have liked to hit each and every one who dared to say something offensive to her. And what they were shouting from all directions was very offensive at the time! But, I couldn't, –how could I? There were hundreds going crazy over her looks!– So, I just had to control myself and get used to this kind of wild behavior around that gorgeous tropical Venus. Fortunately, the bus that will take us to the medical center arrived soon and we took it.

In the bus there were all sorts of comments from the male passengers about her beauty and even the conductor refused to accept her fare, exclaiming: "Honey.., how can I charge you..? For you, it's always free!"

–That was disgusting!– And he even ushered her to a seat. I sat very quietly beside her and he took my fare. –Well, after all,– I thought, – It's not that bad. I saved eight cents for her fare, and now every penny counts.–

In the modern and fully air-conditioned medical center, I had to wait outside the office as Esperanzita requested. Apparently, she did not want to take any risk of me seeing her marked face. She was inside for a long time. And during all that time, I overheard all kinds of strange squeaking sounds, as if made by the springs of an old couch. Also, I overheard a lot of moaning and heavy breathing coming out from the doctor's office. –It must have been very painful for her,– I thought, and

I wanted so badly to get in to find out what was going on inside and be able to help her.., but I promised her to wait.

After about three hours, she came out, fixing her hair and smiling with a satisfied expression on the left side of her face. She explained to me that the doctor had already started the preoperative procedures that very morning inside his office and that the next day, she was going to be admitted at the center for the operation two days later. She was extremely happy about it. Also, she mentioned that everything was going to cost five thousand pesos…just to begin with.

Very apologetic, she said: "There may be more expenses later on, you know."

My heart jumped in my chest! And I thought: —Where in the hell was I going to get that kind of money?— However, I said to her: "That will be alright," I did not want to let her down and I will not! —But, damn it! Why does it have to be that much! Well,— I said to myself, —I will pay somehow. I promised her. Anyway, a man has to do what a man has to do.—

By the next day, I got the money, never mind how and from whom, and she was admitted to the medical center. She was extremely excited. It was all worthwhile for her beautiful smile and that unforgettable kiss that she deposited on my forehead.

I went with her to her private room in the center. That same day, they will first start running the preoperative tests, so she went to the bathroom to change her tight, navy blue velvet afternoon street dress, embroidered with rhinestones and pearls, to a comfortable hospital garment.

When she came out, I was completely knocked out by the sight of what she was wearing… a black lace see-through nightgown! I gulped audibly. I was able to see everything of her Venusian body, except her nipples and pubic area, because they were hidden by an embroidered, black sequined heart with a red tassel on each of the three crucial points!

The next day, I went to see her again. She was very happy to see me and she kissed my forehead again… It was difficult accepting this kind of innocent kiss while she was lying in bed wearing a skin-color, see-through negligee, with red brassiere, bikini panties and black garter belt and stockings… –But that's the way she was– I was sure she did not mean anything… However, I found a few boxes of rubbers scattered throughout the room. That made me very confused, and I just wondered how they got there. But, of course, I did not ask her. And… very carefully, in a way she would not notice, I disposed of them in the trash.

Then she told me that Cachita, her only female friend, was going to be there the next morning for the operation… –What could I say..?– I hated the guts of that hideous, toothless woman from the very first time I saw her coming out of the toilet like a pile of shit! But, sweet Esperanzita liked her so much that… I'll have to accept her company.

Next morning, while I was walking in the hallway toward her room, I saw three young interns I had never seen before, coming out of her room in a hurry. As I pushed open the door and entered, I caught her naked, lying on the bed. It happened in a flash, because, as soon as she recognized me, she prudishly covered herself with the bed sheet. I blushed. Then, she kissed me on the forehead again and explained to me that the interns just came to prepare her for the operation. Nevertheless, it sounded unusual to me that for a face operation she had to be stripped completely… But that is what she said. Apparently I was not totally informed about plastic surgery. Then the hideous Cachita entered the room flashing a toothless smile that could have scared the hell out of King Kong.

After sitting there for a while, trying to talk to sweet Esperanzita, but being constantly interrupted by Cachita's foul mouth with her crappy stories, two male nurses came to place Esperanzita on the gurney to take her to the operating room.

I followed them until the entrance, and just before they took her in, I closed my fist and slightly hit her on her left cheek while I told her "I'll see you later."

Then turning her face, she kissed my fist. That was the first time she kissed another part of my anatomy besides my forehead.

The nurses pushed the gurney away and she disappeared behind the swinging doors. Only Cachita and I were left in the hallway, and I decided to go to the waiting room to watch the *Howdy Doody Show* with Clarabell and Buffalo Bob. Cachita followed me there and sat beside me.

The waiting room was not very big. There were a lot of people sitting here, consequently, it was kind of stuffy. After a short while sitting in the room, the hideous Cachita started breaking wind… –Oh God! How embarrassing and disgusting!!!– And she was putting an innocent expression on her fat face, so the people in the room thought it was me and they were giving me incriminating looks. Then I decided to get up and left the room, going to the hallway. But the damn Cacchita followed me there with her nauseous stink. I didn't know what to do in order to get rid of her company, and I started walking as fast as I could through the hallway until I saw the men's room and I immediately went in. I went to take a booth and sat there the rest of the time. –She is a plague!

After ten hours, the operation was over. Later on, after leaving the recovery room I saw Esperanzita again, but she was sleeping, unconscious in her room. Her whole face and head were totally bandaged, like the invisible man. There were only slits for her eyes, nose and mouth. She then mumbled something. I couldn't understand anything. But the hideous Cachita, with her parrot-voice, told me that she wanted to make *oui-oui* and she ordered me out of the room. So I left the room and I also left the medical center since there was nothing for me to do there.

The next morning, when I went back to see Esperanzita, Cachita was already in the room and it stank like skunk, but sweet Esperanzita was sleeping and I could not talk to her that day either. However, I was able to talk to the doctor. He told me that he was able to do some corrections on her face, but that he would need to perform at least three more operations in order to complete the total facial reconstruction. He indicated that the cost will continue escalating and that I should provide more money. Well, I was determined to get all the money she would need, no matter what.

The third day after the operation, when I walked into the room in the morning, she opened her eyes and recognized me. That was the first time I saw the pupil in the iris of her right eye. It was only a shiny black pupil through the bandage slit, but I felt an extraordinary emotion. And, she held my hand very tight.

After a few more days, she was up and herself again. One afternoon, when I arrived, she received me wearing a long, see-through black lace robe with matching underwear. Also, she was wearing a long, black wig on top of her bandages, rhinestone dark glasses and the mouth slit was painted, simulating her sensuous lips in a bright orchid-red. She looked just heavenly!

A month later, another operation took place. After it, she bore the same type of concealing bandages. So, there was no way for me to see the progress, so I just had to trust what the doctor was doing.

After a month and a half more, the next operation was performed. It was the same thing, her face and head were totally covered by bandages.

Then, almost a month later, the fourth and final operation, according to the doctor, took place. She came out with the same type of bandages as before; I was getting impatient! I have been deprived of seeing her face, even just the left side, for almost four months.

Esperanzita was also getting very impatient and curious to see what was under all of those bandages. But at least we know that this was the last operation and the bandages would be removed in four more weeks. There was nothing to do but wait.

The thing that made the waiting unbearable for me was the constant presence of the hideous Cachita, her foul stench and her foul mouth… And by that time, she had appointed herself as Esperanzita's personal nurse. She even dressed in white! –She was gross!– Her very tight bloomer-lines on her jiggling jellyfish buns were painstakingly showing through her cheap white nylon nurse's uniform.

Finally, finally, the day of the removal of the bandages arrived. It was the day before Christmas Eve of 1953.

I woke up that morning nervous and excited like a child around those holidays. I got dressed in a hurry and ran to the medical center.

As usual, the hideous Cachita was there first. She was fixing sweet Esperanzita's wig on top of her bandages. That morning, Esperanzita was wearing a vivid red and feather robe with matching underwear and garter belt. She had on cinnamon-skin-colored stockings and gold spike heel slippers with red feather pom poms on the front.

I walked to her and held both of her hands. I asked her: "How are you feeling today..?

And she responded: "Nervous. Very nervous. Worried, very worried. Curious, very curious."

Then, the hideous Cachita, interrupting, spoiling that sublime moment, said: "She has been having diarrhea this morning, darling, you know… She has been sitting on the toilet, shitting black and green stuff all morning… She had shit all over, even on her panties! The pair she has on is the second one she has been wearing this morning! If she shits again and gets it on those panties, there will not be any others to match the robe. I told her that I'm going to stick a cork in her ass hole!"

"I get the picture! I get the picture, Cachita! Say no more!" I said interrupting, in order to stop that disgusting, filthy talk from that hideous creature. Deep inside me, I implored to God: −Why don't you take her with you, please..!−

The doctor, followed by a few nurses, entered the room. And then, I prayed hard and deep within myself that Cachita would not repeat the same story in front of the doctor and nurses… Apparently God listened to me, because she didn't. −Thank you God! Thank you!−

One of the nurses was carrying a revolving stool and the other one a mirror, which she hung on the wall over of the sink, because, prior to that moment, all mirrors had been removed from the room.

The doctor walked to her and solemnly said: "My darling.., the big moment has arrived… The moment of truth!"

Esperanzita walked to him and embraced him. And he took advantage of that innocent, sweet woman by squeezing her against him and touching her all over with his dirty-old-man hands.

His despicable actions burned me up, and while pulling them apart, I exclaimed: "OK, OK, doctor! That's enough! Remove her bandages and that's it!"

"Oh yes, Victor," Esperanzita, almost crying, begged, "I'm dying to see my face. I cannot wait any longer!"

"Yeah, yeah…, before she shits on her painties again!" added the hideous Cachita.

"Very well… Sit down on the stool, my child," the doctor said, placing the stool in front of the window.

Immediately, Esperanzita sat on it. Cachita then took off the wig and the rhinestone dark glasses… One of the nurses handed the doctor a pair of bandage scissors. He made some cuts in the bandages and got a loose strip. Then, he started pulling on it, while Esperanzita, on the revolving stool, started spinning around. And he kept pulling and pulling… The seconds and minutes seemed to go on forever, while the sweet Esperanzita was spinning faster and faster. She looked just like a spinning ice skating ballerina so fast I couldn't see her face that was beginning to come out from under her bandages. Finally, he finished pulling the last of the strip of bandage and the stool slowed down until it stopped revolving. But Esparanzita's face was facing the window and I still could not see! Then, the doctor put his hands on her shoulders and turned her to face him. However, he was in my way and I still couldn't see!

He examined her face for a while… and said: "Remarkable… Only just one thing. Just one thing…"

Then, he moved away… and I was able to see her face in all its splendor.–It was gorgeous! Gorgeous, gorgeous, gorgeous!!!– Her cinnamon skin complexion was as smooth as… baby's skin. Not a single mark or scar. –Perfect! Simple perfection!– The finish of her complexion looked like a Max Factor Pan-Cake makeup advertisement. Her rounded, high cheekbones were glimmering in a bright and glossy pink. Her sensuous lips were of a rich and shiny RED. Her sparkling black eyes were beautifully lined in black, with an opalescent blue eyeshadow, disappearing at the edge of her eyes, in the direction of her delicately arched eyebrows. Her velvety eyelashes were thick, long and curled, pointing at the only place you could go after seeing that face: heaven. Her black, luscious hair was perfectly styled, falling in cascades around her face and over her shoulders. She was the epitome of a gloriously finished and polished movie star. And utterly confused, I asked myself: –How in the hell did she manage to accomplish all that under those bandages?!– It was a mystery for me. Perhaps, something that I'll never know… However, there was only one thing… Just one thing…

And Esperanzita, looking at my eyes, anxiously asked me: "How do I look?! How do I look?!"

"Unbelievable," I replied, "unbelievably beautiful.., but… There is just one thing… Just one thing I cannot comprehend…"

"What is it, what is it?!" she anxiously asked again.

And Cachita said, "Yeah..,Yeah.., there is jus' one ting..," and turning to the doctor she impatiently inquired: "yeah, doctor.., what in the hell is that thing?! What in the hell is that thing that looks like a fly and keeps changing places on her face?!"

"What is it?! Tell me, what is it, please!" Esperansita desperately inquired of all of us.

"Well, my child," said the doctor, "my darling Esperanzita. Everything is perfect. Everything worked out as planned. Your face turned out extremely beautiful. There is not a single imperfection… But only one thing, just one thing I could not foresee.., and I could not correct it now."

And, frantic!, the sweet Esperanzita shouted at the doctor: "But, what is it, damn it!"

"Well..," he responded, "it is a beauty mark."

Then, very much puzzled, she asked him: "What's wrong with it?" and said: "A beauty mark is a beauty mark."

"Yes, my child," he said, "but the beauty mark you just got.., it is what we scientifically call: a jumping beauty mark."

Very confused, Esperanzita asked: "A jumping beauty mark?!"

"Yes, my darling," he said, "it is a beauty mark that does not stay in one place… It keeps jumping like a butterfly from one place to another on your cheek.., and in a few seconds it might be on your chin or on your forehead, or in your…"

And Esperanzita, very happy and excited, interrupted him saying: "Oh doctor, my dear Victor.., what a relief! That was just what I always wanted to have.., a jumping beauty mark!"

"Well.., you never know what turns people on!" the doctor commented.

"Now please," she said, "let me walk to the mirror and see myself, and she stood up.

We all moved aside and let her walk to the mirror… But before she was in front of it and seeing her reflection, she turned her gorgeous face with her newly jumping beauty mark away from the mirror, as if she was afraid to see her face, after all… Then she took a deep breath, arched and lifted her left eyebrow, repeating that indescribable gesture she performed for me in her dressing room almost five months ago, but this time, hollowing both of her cheeks, and pronouncing forward her inviting lips, making her round cheekbones appear stunningly attractive. And with that magnificent expression on her face, she slowly turned to the mirror… When she finally saw her reflection, her expression changed to that of astonishing surprise that left her completely speechless for a long while… And, after she regained control, she indulged herself with the contemplation of her own divine image.

And then, she said "You know… I like it very much. And the jumping beauty mark is what I always wanted to have in my dreams and fantasies. I feel now that my dream came true," and turning her face away from her narcissist contemplation, she said to the doctor, "Victor.., my Victor. You have done an extraordinary deed. I don't know if I'll ever be able to completely pay you for this."

"You know very well what to do and how to do it," said the doctor with a suggestive tone in his dirty-old-man voice.

I immediately interrupted saying : "Don't worry, Esperanzita. I have paid him until the last penny he requested. You don't owe him anything! As a matter of fact, after today, I don't want to see him around anymore."

After the doctor and the nurses left the room, Esperanzita ran back to see herself in the mirror, and engaged in her narcissist contemplation again. This, I very well understood, because anybody who looks like her has plenty of reasons to do so.

I sat in a corner of the room, waiting for her to dedicate some time to me. Meanwhile Cachita was getting Esperanzita's suitcase ready.

After she filled herself with the beauty of her reflection, she turned her face in my direction. Then she started looking at me in a different way than had done in the past. It was an electrifying look, long and suggestive. She also gave me a Delilah smile… Nervously, from my seat, I returned a smile to her. And then.., slowly, moving her enticing hips, she walked back to her bed and reclined on it like "The Dressed Maja" of Goya… She gave a look to Cachita, and she promptly left the room smiling. She signaled to me to get close to her bed, which I did. Then, she made me sit beside her and started breathing unusually heavily. And she said: "You know Juan… I owe everything to you. You have made me feel very happy again. Now I am what I always wanted to be. And even, as a bonus, I got a jumping beauty mark. And all, thanks to you. I want to make you happy, too. You can have anything, buy anything from me. Just ask.., and it'll be yours. I am yours…"

Just her presence on that bed, and hearing her talking like that, made me completely excited! −But no!− I said to myself, −I can not take advantage of this sweet and innocent woman!− And I nervously tried to control myself, avoiding for her to notice the source of my involuntary carnal excitement. I did not want to offend her at all. No! I wanted to do things the right way! I wanted to be a complete gentleman. −Oh no…− she placed one of her angelical hands on my left leg! So, I got up immediately from the bed and walked to the window.

"Juan.., what happened to you?" she asked.

"Nothing." I answered, "I just was hot. I mean cold, cold!"

"Don't you like me..?" she asked.

"Oh yes, I do, I do.," I responded and explained: "But I have other plans, other interests…"

And she interrupted asking: "Are you queer..?"

"Oh no, no!" Nothing like that! Heaven forbid!" I replied stating:

"I am very much a man. But I am a gentleman, too. I don't want to spoil anything."

"It will not be spoiled." she said.

I have other plans," I repeated while turning around to face her, and filling myself with courage I said: "I want to marry you."

Very much surprised, she exclaimed: "Marry me?!"

"Yes, I want to marry you," I stated.

Then she exclaimed" That cannot be! That cannot be!"

"Why not..? Don't you love me?" I inquired.

"Yes, I do love you." She said, "You have an important place in my heart."

Then," I ask her, "why don't you want to marry me?"

She paused, and very dramatically stated: "Because.., I am a mulatto!"

Suddenly, strong, loud music shook the room! Just like the one I heard before in her dressing room the night I met her. Just like that night, I was not able to determine its source… But, never mind!

"So what," I stated, "I don't care if you are a mulatto! After all, I am not that fair skinned either. Remember that I am an orphan and I don't know anything about my real parents. I could be a mulatto, too."

"How could you be?!" she exclaimed.

And I said: "If that is the only reason why you don't want to marry me.., you shouldn't care, because I simply don't."

Then, she relaxed and said with a sweet tone in her voice: "You are very kind and sweet… But, see..? I care. I will not marry anything but a proven mulatto," and turning very serious, she stated: "That's final."

–Oh no…– I'm sorry, I deeply said to myself, –there is no hope for me to honestly love this extraordinary woman… But probably she will change her mind as the time passes by and I can prove to her more and more my unlimited love. But, how can I prove to her that I could be a mulatto?

In silence, she got up from the bed and walked back to the mirror. In front of it, she engaged in the contemplation of her image. Then Cachita opened the door and came into the room, asking an indecent question that only such a hideous individual with that rotten mind would do: "Hey… did you finish?! That was a quickie!"

There was silence in the room. Neither sweet Esperanzita nor myself answered. So, Cachita went to finish packing the suitcase, while Esperanzita was still looking at herself in the mirror. But this time she was smiling, and looked as if the wheel of her innocent mind was spinning at one hundred kilometers per second. Something that was making her very happy and excited was crossing her mind…

Finally, she said, very excited: "Now that I can show my entire face and move my hair freely, Not worrying about hiding anything at all I can be what I wanted to be in my fantasies…"

And, silly me, I asked her: "What is what you always wanted to be?"

Turning her gorgeous face to me, she answered: "I always have dreamed to be a Rumbera!"

Completely scandalized because of my Catholic upbringing at the orphanage, and not giving credit to my ears for what I just thought I heard, I could not help but exclaim: "A Rumbera..?!"

"Yes! A Rumbera!" she exclaimed and said: "Now I can dance and move freely without being afraid..," then, she lifted both of her arms and pulled up her hair with both hands while moving her hips frantically and her shoulders as Rumberas used to do…

I ran to her, trying to stop those abominable movements, and in my desperation I said: "Oh.., no, no Esperanzita, please! A Rumbera, no!"

"Why not?!" shouted the hideous Cachita at me with her parrot voice while shaking both of her fat arms in the air, questioning me in that vulgar Cuban way.

And I said "Because.., a Rumbera is not… nice… Everybody knows what Rumberas do!

Then, that hideous creature asked me, shouting in a grotesque way, that only could be visualized in a Buñuel film: "And what does a Rumbera do that she doesn't?"

I ignored the innuendo coming from such a low and repulsive creature. Anyway, whatever I would say, she would not have any comprehension in her retarded, amoebic brain. I would have loved to kill her on the spot, stepping on her like a crawling insect. But, because of sweet Esperanzita, who was still dancing in front of the mirror, I could not do it. By this time she had removed her robe and was dancing in just her revealing underwear, so I begged her: "Please.., a Rumbera, no, please I beg you…"

"Yes, yes, yes..," she said, "I want to be a Rumbera. My jumping beauty mark will be my trademark… And I'm going to call myself on the stage, like the song I used to sing: 'Cinnamon Skin'… Making it clear to everybody that I am a mulatto… I can see myself dancing on stage… and, I'm going to be the best!"

And a Rumbera she became, against my will. I suffered a lot in silence while the sweet Esperanzita and the hideous Cachita were having a ball planning her debut on stage… But, I was madly in love with her, so much.., that I finally accepted her decision to be a Rumbera. After all, I shouldn't be prejudiced. She might become the first decent Rumbera in history…

Her debut was in the Gardel movie house, this same one where I met her at one of the fifty cent shows between movies. The place was jam packed with a herd of screaming, vulgar people, who came to see the new Rumbera that was heavily promoted with posters designed by Cachita all throughout La Habana.

When she finally came out on the stage that evening, the wild herd roared and cheered her. Of course, she came out half naked! I had never seen any other Rumbera wear so little while in fact she had so much! Almost nothing was left to the imagination in that Cachita-designed costume! The whole thing was like a riot. The obscenities shouted by the mob were hard to believe… Then the orchestra started playing the popular rumba "*Oyeme Cachita*" (Listen to me Cachita) and sweet Esperanzita began to move… The movements were… just… unbelievable! –How could a human being be moving like that?!– And she made the mob shut up. They were watching her as if in a religious silence, with their lustful eyes jumping out of their faces and drooling saliva all over… I wondered if appeasing the rioting mobs was her real mission on earth (?)… Then, in that case, I should not interfere with her divine ministry, and let her be, it's bigger than me.

She was indeed a rhythmic, tropical hurricane, and as such, "Cinnamon Skin" took La Habana by storm!

And with that swirling frenzy, we went from theater to theater, from cabaret to cabaret, from night club to night club… except television, because the Minister of Communication made a special law forbidding her on that medium, alleging as the only reason: her suggestive and scandalous movements. However, he did not hesitate to be her friend and give her a house as a gift.

The sweet Esperanzita was very excited with her brand new house by the Almendares River. That was going to be the first time she was going to live in a house, since prior to that, she was living in a room with an old Chinese man as her roommate in the same phalanstery where Cancita used to live in Luyano Heights. So, Esperanzita wanted to furnish and decorate her house by herself.

The house was a beautiful two story Spanish style villa, with a big, tiled central patio, two car garage and front garden with an iron fence all around. Esperanzita, who always was very much gifted with colors, had the red roof villa painted all in chartreuse on the outside, with all its doors and windows in violet and its trimmings in orange. I was very proud, it certainly looked stunning.

The interior of the house was all painted in flamingo, her favorite color. Most of the furniture was upholstered in vinyl, imitating tiger, zebra and leopard skin. But, she cleverly had it all covered with clear plastic slips to protect the vinyl.

Even though the house had indirect fluorescent lights in all the rooms, she had crystal chandeliers installed everywhere. And to protect them from dust and spider webs, she covered them with cellophane paper fastened with a red felt ribbon tied to the ceiling chain.

All the rooms were her masterful creation. But, the one that she really went out of her way, was her own bedroom. Of course, that was the room where she spent most of her time, because she needed a lot of rest due to her extenuating rumba movements. This room was very big and it was in the shape of a horseshoe. On the rounded side, she had a round hot pink velvet bed with heavy upholstered headboard simulating a Spanish galleon. Esperanzita named her bed "La Santa Maria", like Christopher Columbus' decked ship. So, La Santa Maria was on a one-step high platform which covered that end of the semicircular wall. The floor on this platform was covered with a wall-to-wall marine blue carpet simulating the ocean, with printed sea horses, dolphins, barracudas, mermaids, mermans and seaweed, all in vividly realistic colors. In the semicircular niche around the bed, the walls were hand painted by a muralist in a panoramic seascape with more galleons in the distance and exotic islands with beaches full of coconut trees with exotic birds. Also, there were a lot of seagulls flying across the sky. The ceiling on top of the bed was covered by a huge beveled mirror, from which a trapeze was hanging. Esperanzita said that she needed it because every morning she did exercises to keep in shape. On each side of the bed, Diana rain swag lamps were hanging from the ceiling. At each side of the bed there were four Doric columns; between each one, electric floor candelabras, fashioned as Caribbean Indians holding the candle-foot for the candlesticks. On the left side of the bed, she had a pinball machine with the Jim of the Jungle game.

One step down from the platform, in the other half of her bedroom, the carpet was sand color and was printed with beach motifs, such as different kinds of sea shells, starfish and driftwood. The walls in this area were papered in a futuristic version of hundreds of banana trees over a flamingo background. In this area, she had an early American sitting room set, upholstered with leopard vinyl and clear plastic vinyl slipcovers with purple velvet pillows on the sofa. This set was completely accessorized with all sorts of Mediterranean and Polynesian knick knacks and an early American water wheel floor lamp. This set was gracefully placed in a diagonal position in front of the French doors accessing the balcony overlooking the fountain of the central patio. These doors were covered by draperies, in a beautiful bright yellow with jellyfish prints in silver gray and navy blue.

Across from this private sitting room she had a chaise lounge, which was upholstered in orange crushed velvet with its clear plastic slip. On it, she had placed a lot of small pillows in different shades of green and red. At its side, there was a heavily ornated bronze table with some of her collection of Geisha and Spanish dancer dolls.

Beside the chaise lounge, was her long makeup table with its three-way mirror and chair. The legs of this table were a pair of golden peacocks. The chair was supported by another peacock, whose outstretched tail formed the back rest. At the left of this table, there was a complete fish tank with a breathtaking three-dimensional Shangri-la background scenery that glowed in the dark.

On the opposite wall facing the semicircular niche where the Santa Maria was, Esperanzita had a Gothic fireplace installed. It had real wood inside, but the fire was simulated by a red flickering light. Over the mantle was a beautiful altar dedicated to the virgin saint of Cuba, who was the virgin of the waters, that is why she cleverly carried that theme all over the room. This virgin was called: The Charity of The Copper. And a few months earlier, Esperanzita, who, according to the Afro-Cuban religion, was the daughter of this virgin, through special ceremonial rites was converted into a saint. Because of my Catholic upbringing I did not approve of this, but that was what she wanted, and I went along.

The image of the virgin in the altar was lavishly dressed with a white robe, embroidered with a lot of pearls and aquamarines. On top of it was a sky blue velvet cape in a richly embroidered metallic gold ribbon. She had real black human hair, in the same fashion Esperanzita had hers. The virgin's complexion was like hers, cinnamon, since she was supposed to be a mulatto, too. She had a gold crown full of pearls and a magnificent golden halo of stars. In her right hand, she was holding a gold cross and in her left, she was holding baby Jesus. She was standing on an early moon over the troubled ocean, looking after three shipwreck survivors who were praying to her in their lifeboat.

The image of the virgin was encased inside a gold leafed renaissance urn. As a detail of Esperanzita's good taste, she placed around the urn a blinking multi-colored Christmas garland, which was lit 24 hours a day as a tribute to the miraculous virgin.

The ceiling in this area of her bedroom was painted by the same muralist simulating the sky at sunset with different species of native Cuban birds flying across it.

In general, her bedroom was like a magical vision that made me feel at ease every time I had the opportunity to visit it. Esperanzita had such a graceful sense of harmony and colors… She was really talented, and made me feel proud of being part of her life, in spite of the fact that she was a Rumbera.

She also put "her touch" on the garden of the house. This used to be planted with an unusual variety of roses, but she had all of the roses pulled out and she planted hundreds of sunflowers instead. —It was beautiful!— Then she had installed five seahorse bird baths painted to glow in the dark. Also, she had a dozen pink flamingos, and a flower bed that was a carriage being pulled by a donkey. Perhaps with her marvelous touch, she wanted to make the statement that she did not forget her past childhood, when she used to live on the infamous Donkey Hill.

However, the only thing I thought runed her statement was the fact that Cachita planted flowers of her choice in the carriage. But coming from that untasteful and hideous creature, the flowers that she selected — of course — were the flowers that everybody used to call in Cuba, because of their foul stench, "Flor de Peo" (Break Wind Flower). That was an unforgivable choice! But, somehow, this struck the sweet Esperanzita funny, so it was left untouched. I guess I have to learn to like it, too.

In the middle of all her success and money she had been attaining as a Rumbera, I tried to hide my adverse feelings about it. But Esperanzita was not dumb. She knew in the deepest of her heart that I had never completely approved of it. So, as time was passing by, she was getting cooler with me.

Cachita, however, became more and more important. She was her friend, confidant, secretary, manager, agent… you name it, Cachita was it! But me, the only thing left for me was chauffeur of her new Kaiser limousine, given to her by the Minister of Transportation.

I never fully understood that friendship. Sweet Esperanzita told me one day that the Minister had a terrible marriage and that his wicked wife was making him suffer a lot. That was why, she said, he came to visit her every night to cry his unhappiness on her shoulders and that she was some sort of psychiatrist for him. —She really was a nice human being!—

She let me stay in her house. I used to sleep in the garage on a canvas folding army cot. The garage was just under her bedroom. At night,

I used to hear a lot of vibrations and noises coming from her room above while the Minister of Transportation was visiting her. I felt sorry for that man, too. He cried very hard!

One evening the vibrations and noises abruptly stopped earlier than usual. A while later, I heard a fast knocking at the door of the garage. I got up in a hurry and opened the door.., and there she was, Esperanzita, wearing a brief, black nighty, exposed 'till her buns! She appeared to be hysterical. She asked me to go with her to her bedroom because something had happened to the Minister. I put on my pants and followed her upstairs.

And there he was, the old man, completely naked, lying on her bed. Very much surprised, I asked her: "What is he doing naked on your bed?"

"Oh..," she replied, "he was.., showing me the marks of his wife's whip."

I could not see any visible marks.., but I believed my sweet Esperanzita. Then, I put my ear over his heart and I noticed that it was not beating.

Then she said: "I think he is dead."

"I should say..," I replied.

"We have to get rid of the body! We have to get him out of here!" she said. "What are people going to think about me..?!"

"Yes, that's true," I answered, "but wait.., let me be sure he is completely dead. He might have fainted, you know..," then I felt his pulse and I did not notice any. I tried again to listen for his heart, but nothing. And I said: "He's dead all right." I looked at her and asked: "Where do you want me to take him?"

And she answered: "Take him to Jaimantia beach and throw him there… The police might think that he died while skinny-dipping."

"That's a good idea!" I exclaimed. Then I carried him to his own car, drove to the beach, threw him in the ocean and walked back to Espiranzita's garage.

After the Minister was gone, other men kept coming at night to visit Esperanzita, and the vibrations and noises were repeated every night. –She really was trying to help people with emotional problems!– I thought.

During that time, she was making a lot of money. More than she ever dreamed to have or to know what to do with. Then she decided to reconstruct the Gardel movie house, because, she said, it was the only place that gave her a chance when she started in show business.

So, one of her evening friends, who happened to be an architect, based on Esperanzita's ideas designed a new look for the Gardel without changing the castle concept of it. What she wanted was to change the dark gray, austere, rough-cemented facade simulating a middle-age fortress and convert it into a Walt Disney Sleepy Beauty castle, with a lot of high towers, pointed roofs and multicolored flags. In front she insisted on having a garden with a fountain and a bench overlooking it. She wanted to call that bench: "The Lover's Bench". –She was so thoughtful.., never forgetting the most minimal detail!– The final renderings really looked like a Disney creation. I was very much satisfied as she was. I was totally convinced that it was going to be a beautiful place after it was finished.

But then, a police detective who was assigned to the investigation of the unusual circumstances of the death of the Minister of Transportation, came in one afternoon to question the sweet Esperanzita. Fortunately, as she told me later on, he also became her friend because he was a terribly unhappy man. And from then on, he was coming to visit her every night, looking for her psychological advice, too. And the investigation about the minister's death was soon forgotten.

The reconstruction project of the Gardel started very soon. Also, Esperanzita became the psychological counselor of almost all one hundred construction workers hired for it. Every night around the central patio and all along the walkway to the garage, there was a line of them waiting to go up to her room to release their psychological tensions and receive her expert advice.

Cachita, as enterprising as usual, opened a vending stand in the central patio selling them beer and rubbers–this last item, I never understood why. So, the construction workers usually ended up getting drunk and being very noisy, disturbing me in my sleep in the garage.

Also, the vibrations and noises coming from the sweet Esperanzita's bedroom became unbearable. –Those construction workers–they really have deep troubles!– But, one evening, I overheard a conversation between two of them that were standing, waiting in line, just outside the garage door......... And it was then that I started realizing what was going on......... I fell on the floor on my knees and cried a long time in the solitude of the garage, while covering my ears in order not to hear those vibrations and noises coming from above, which now had an infuriating meaning. I was disappointed and very upset at her. I felt jealous of everybody.., because everybody was having her except me. I was even preserving my virginity for her! She owed everything to me! Because of my single-handed effort, she got her face fixed! I have more rights than anybody else to go to bed with her. –To hell with my principles: To hell with being a gentleman! I just got to fuck her too!!–

I got up and dressed in a rush, got out of the garage and pushed the crowd of construction workers out of the house. Then I ran upstairs to her room, and with my foot, I pushed the door open...

There was a naked construction worker lying on her bed with his legs wide open while she was suspended by her legs from the trapeze, with her naked torso hanging down, and her huge tits resting on his legs while sucking his dick! Surprised by my unexpected interruption, the man got up and ran out of the room, while she, totally unashamed, veered in the trapeze as a circus star would do and adopted the sitting position on it.

Then she defiantly said to me: "How dare you enter my room when I am comforting a friend!"

"I just realized what is going on here and who you are…" I said brokenhearted.

"Ohhh.., you just realized that…" she said while starting to swing on the trapeze.

"Yes, I happened to open my eyes," I sadly said.

"It certainly took you a while..," she added while swinging faster, "four years living under the same roof and you just realized that… Not very smart, Juan. Not very smart, indeed."

And I responded: "All these years I have been crazy for you… loving and idolizing you… Love is blind… you know..?"

"Very blind in your case," she sarcastically said.

"You lied to me all the time and I believed you," I said.

"But what could I have said to you..? You were so naive… "How could I have said to you that I was going to bed with everybody in town..?" After she said that, she paused, stopped swinging on the trapeze, and asked me: "And now.., what do you want? I have more business to do this evening. The Gardel has to be finished and I have to pay for it."

"There is no one waiting for your services," I stated, "I threw every-one out onto the street."

And reproducing her very own indescribable personal gesture with her face, involving the lifting and arching of her left eyebrow, hollowing her cheeks which emphasized her magnificent high cheekbones and pronouncing her sensuous lips, she said: "How are you planning to pay them? I don't think they want your pretty ass."

"I'm not planning to pay for anything anymore," I stated, "it is you who has to pay. You owe me something. And I came to collect my payment, too."

"After all this time..?!" she exclaimed.

"Yes," I stated with profound conviction.

And she laughed as I never heard her laugh before. She was sounding like a real witch… Then she said: "No.., now is too late. Your time was over more than four years ago, when I proposed to you on the hospital bed.., and you turned me down."

"I wanted to marry you then!" I clearly pointed out.

"That was your chance and you lost it!" she replied, "you can not fuck me now!"

Very upset, I shouted at her: "I can and I will, even if I have to rape you! Don't forget that I am a man!"

And she laughed at me. My blood was circulating very fast and all of a sudden I felt as if all of it rushed to my head, blinding my senses. Then, I jumped on the bed and pushed her down from the trapeze, forcibly untangling her legs from it and placing her on the bed while she kept uncontrollably laughing and then saying: "If you rape me… it will not be the same… I will be lying here like a corpse… It will not be the same… I will not be doing the numbers that made me famous and the best paid whore in town… You are not a professional rapist… You will not get a kink out of it… You will be fucking a dead cunt!" and she continued laughing, while lying on the bed completely naked and relaxed with her legs wide open.

Then I decided that it wasn't worth it after all doing it under these horrible conditions. I could not rape that woman who meant so much to me in the past. I felt deeply hurt and my real feelings were all mixed up. So, I got up from the bed and decided to leave forever, although I felt that I still loved her.

"Yes, get out.., you are finished!" she shouted at me.

And just at that instant, I heard the orchestrated introduction of a ballad inside my confused mind. I had never sung before, but, never mind, I turned to her bed, fell on my knees at the foot of the bed and when I heard the right chord, I broke into song:

> I, remember when
> You, said you'll be true.
> Please, come back again
> This lonely heart, needs you.
> When, I hear your name
> Now, it's not the same.
> For, I'm sad and blue
> My lonely heart, needs you.
> All my lonely broken heart it's behind some foolish pride,
> I won't let it!
> Life, is nothing without you and no one else will do.
> Darling can you see?
> This lonely heart needs you.
> I'm sad and blue.
> Let's start, I need you!
> This lonely heart, needs you.

During the musical bridge, Experanzita, who was already sitting on her bed watching my surprising performance, got up and walked very slowly, completely naked, toward me. In the dim red light of the room, I was able to see for the first time her voluptuous body for more than a flash, as I had always seen it in the past. It was a magnificent moving sculpture, wrapped in that inciting cinnamon skin. I was still on my knees looking up at her divine breasts crowned by her splendid face. She was looking at me in a different way from before. She seemed to be moved. And when I heard my chord, I started singing again:

All my lonely broken heart it's behind some foolish pride.
I won't let it!
Life, is nothing without you and no one else will do.
Darling, can you see?
This lonely heart needs you.
I'm sad and blue,
Let's start, I need you!
This lonely heart, needs youuuuuuuuuuuuuuuu.

When the mysterious orchestration ceased, I was still on my knees looking at her… Then she placed her hands on my shoulders, and exercising a slight pressure around my arms, she made me stand up in front of her and she hugged me as I had never been hugged before. I felt her whole body, warm and vibrating with emotion squeezed against mine. I reciprocated her warm reception with the extraordinary desire that I had been accumulating for her through all of these long and frustrating years. Then, she kissed me like a lioness. With a wild animal desire that I have only experienced once before, when Mother Teresita caught me by surprise in one of the orphanage confessional booths when I was in my teens. But Esperanzita's was a longer kiss. It was a superior one. This kiss, I had dreamed about, because I loved and desired this woman… Mother Teresita was old, wrinkled and had a prickly mustache.. Esperansita's was an unforgettable kiss.., and I closed my eyes and enjoyed every second of it. When she finished, I was literally out of breath and out of commission.

Then, she pulled me to the left side of her bed, slowly removed my open shirt, unbuckled my belt, unbuttoned my pants, unzipped the fly and pulled my pants down to the floor. I got my feet out from the legs of my pants. And then, very slowly.., she started to remove my shorts. Pulling them down little by little… creating a frenzy of various voluptuous sensations that were driving me to an uncontrollable sexual madness. I knew that my virginity was on the verge of being violated forever… –Oh…, what a marvelous way of giving it away…– The lights in the room automatically got dimmer and the only thing I was able to see were the artificial flames of the fireplace that somehow seemed to be getting stronger and redder on that August night.–Ooohhh– When my penis was totally exposed just in front of her face, she stopped pulling my shorts down, her heavy breathing ceased…, and she left a profound silence which was interrupted by her saying: "Oh no… You are uncircumcised…"

"So what..?" I said, "what's wrong..?"

And she said: "Listen, Juan.., honey… I don't dig that. I am strictly kosher."

"It's not my fault. The nuns in the orphanage did not practice circumcision," I explained to her.

"I'm sorry, honey..," she said, "it's a very nice dick indeed.., but, not for me."

Then I said: "Oh.., come on.., can't you make an exception? You can't leave me like this…"

"I'm sorry, it's not my fault either," she stated, "you should have taken care of it already. And now, if you please, you can leave the room.

There was nothing else for me to do there. Obviously, she was turned off by that fact. So.., I pulled up my shorts, grabbed my pants and shirt from the floor and, highly depressed at my failure to please that woman, left the room. While walking out the door, I saw standing there, watching the whole thing from the darkness of the hallway, wearing only her cheap underwear, the hideous Cachita. Her presence there burned me up and made me feel worse. But, I completely ignored her, passing by her in silence, walking down the hallway… Then, I heard from behind me: "Pssssss… Pssssss Darling, darling!" I stopped walking and turned around. Then, she approached tiptoeing in a hurry, and very hushed she said: "You know, darling, I don't care about your problem… I am a very good sucker," and opened her toothless mouth, pointed to its inside with her fat index finger and licking her thin lips with her slimy tongue.

It was a revolting sight coming from that immoral, hideous creature. My blood became very hot and rushed to my head in an instant, that was how upset her disgusting solicitation made me feel. And, I said to her: "You know? There is something that I have always wanted to tell you ever since I had the enormous disgrace of meeting you and that is: <u>FUCK OFF!!!</u>" And I turned my back and walked down the stairs.

In the front garden of the house, I put on my pants, my shirt, and went out to the street and started walking away… I didn't know exactly where to go and what to do, but I kept walking. I could not believe that I was twenty-three years old and I was still a virgin! And all because of my love for that woman. I didn't want to continue being a virgin, but, I didn't want to lose it with anybody but her. Then, in my confusion, I remembered that I had seen a house somewhere around that had a sign about a rabbi. So, I decided to go around and look for it. And, I started running like crazy until I finally found it. I ran to its door and knocked loudly many times until I saw the lights inside being turned on.

A while later, somebody owned the visor and an old man's voice inquired: "What happened? What do you want?"

"I want to come in and talk to you," I responded.

"What for..? It's very late…" he said then asked me: "Can you come back tomorrow?"

"No." I categorically stated, "it has to be now!"

"What is what you want?" the old man inquired.

And I said: "please.., let me come in."

"Not until you tell me what your problem is," he said.

OK, OK..," I replied, " I need help… Are you a rabbi?"

"Yes, I am," he answered and asked: "What kind of help do you need?"

Then I said: "I need a circumcision."

"What's the hurry..?!" he exclaimed, almost laughing. "You can bring your son tomorrow."

"It isn't for my son… It is for me," I said, ashamed of myself.

"Come back tomorrow," he said again.

"No, no, please.., now. I need it now…" I said begging to him, "I'll give you anything for it. I'll give you one hundred pesos!"

"Tomorrow morning," he stated.

"I'll give you two hundred… Two hundred and fifty..," I stated.

"Listen..," he said, "it is very late now."

"Three hundred," I continued.

And he exclaimed: "You are in a rush!!"

Then I stated: "Five hundred!"

"In advance!" he pointed out.

"Yes! I'll give them to you now!" I stated.

And, opening the door, he said: "Come in my son."

I was inside and immediately gave him the money, which he counted three times. And afterward he said: "I'll do it on the kitchen table… The kitchen is at the end of the hall, follow me please. But don't make any noises. I don't want the children to wake up."

And I followed him in silence to the kitchen. There, he said "Take your pants and shorts off and get on the table. I'm going to get the instruments.., cotton, bandages and ether.., I'll be back," and he left the room.

I stripped from my waist down and got on the table. A while later, he came back carrying a tray with everything he needed for the procedure.

Then, he warned me: "You know.., It's going to be very painful… There will be no anesthetic but the ether…"

And I said: "Don't worry. I am a man. I am not intimidated by pain."

"Well, it's a very sensitive area," he said, "It's going to hurt a lot. You will not be able to wear your shorts or pants for a few days...."

"Can I stay here..?" I asked him and immediately added: "I'll pay you extra for it."

He paused, and then he said: "Yeah.., I don't see why not. It can be arranged."

"Thank you I'd appreciate it," I said, while he got a hold of my penis.

"Ugh..! he exclaimed. "It sure stinks! That's the reason for the circumcision.., the stink…"

I felt something cool on it.., perhaps he was putting the ether on it…

After a while, he said: "Now that I have cleaned it and disinfected it, the next thing I'll be doing will be cutting… Be brave."

"Of course," I said.

He got a little knife which he showed me, and then, he proceeded to cut…

The pain was unbearable, and I screamed: "Aaaaaaaaahhhhhhhh!!!"

I must have fainted, because the next thing I remember was the rabbi waking me up and a burning sensation coming from my penis…

"Hey, hey.., wake up… Come on, wake up..It's over..," he kept saying. And then he asked me: "What do you want to do with your foreskin..? May I give it to the dogs?"

And I said while opening my eyes: "ohh.., ohh.., ohh.., no, no … I want to save it.., I want to save it…"

"All right, he said, "I can put it in a jar with alcohol. Sentimental reasons?"

"Yes, yes..," I replied: "I want to show it to somebody… Thank you."

I spent a little over a week at the rabbi's house until I was able to wear my shorts and pants without discomfort. And then, one afternoon, I left, carrying the jar with my foreskin in my hand. I walked back to

Esperanzita's house. I was determined to show her what I had done for her, one more thing in order to gain her favor.

But, she wasn't there. The only one in the house was a handsome, blond, young fellow who was basking in the sun in the central patio, wearing just his undershorts. He said that Esperanzita had given him a job as her chauffeur and that she went shopping on Galiano Street for new clothes for him. I left the house in a rush, got into a taxi and went to that shopping area to look for her.

There, I walked up and down like crazy looking for her. It was very difficult, since that area was always very crowded, but I didn't lose hope of finding her somehow.

Finally, when I was across the street from the Century department store, I saw her crossing the street carrying a lot of packages. I stopped, and from my sidewalk I called her: "Esperanzita.., Esperanzita..! It's me, Juan!"

She heard me, stopped in the middle of the street and turned in my direction. Then, smiling, I waved with my left hand while with the other I showed her the jar with my foreskin in alcohol. When our eyes locked together, I felt as if we were the only people around, and then, excitedly, I exclaimed at her "Esperanzita.., I got a circumcision and I've got the foreskin with me in this little jar to prove it to you."

She looked completely perplexed from my statement, and she seemed to want to disappear. Then, I noticed the perplexity of the crowd around me and I realized what I had just said that everyone around had heard. Everybody was looking at me in complete disbelief. I felt extremely embarrassed standing there, in the middle of the sidewalk, holding up with my right hand, the revealing jar. Esperanzita was para-lyzed in the middle of the street, very much confused, realizing what I had done and what I had floating in alcohol in the jar, was in fact, my foreskin. Suddenly, the expression on her face changed from surprise to embarrassment and displeasure about the existence of the jar, and she made a gesture with her mouth and tongue indicating revulsion. Then, she lifted her left eyebrow, hollowed her cheeks and pronounced her lips, giving me a highly derogatory look.., and she turned her back to me and started walking away. However, after one or two steps, a streetcar unexpectedly showed up from the right, appearing just behind a bus at that very instant, hitting and launching her and her boxes into the air in what seemed to my senses, in shock, like a film in slow motion…

–Oh my God!!!– Her body landed about 20 feet away, just on top of the streetcar rails while another streetcar, which appeared from the left was passing by, and two of its wheels rolled over her, severing her body in two halves at the waist… –Oh no!!!– What a horribly grotesque sight, seeing her body divided like that on the pavement, with her guts, and blood all over the place. For a moment I was frozen by the gruesome spectacle. But my love overcame me and prevailed over the situation, so I desperately ran over to her and tried to put her two halves together. –Oh.., there are no words to describe the bloody mess!– Frustrated because of the impossibility of my attempts, I just turned to her torso.., and then.., she opened her eyes and looked at me. I confidently tried to smile in order to comfort her, and I said, "Oh… it's nothing… a few stitches here and there and you'll be like new again…" and I showed her the little jar with my foreskin.

And she said: "You really love me.., don't you?"

"Oh, yes I do, I do," I said almost in a frenzy.

"I think I'm going to die," she said.

"No, No, please, don't say that," I desperately said, "you are going to live, you are going to live, live, live!!!"

Then, trying to smile at me she said: "I'll try… Just for you… But if I don't, I want for you to have something that I have been carrying close to my heart.., all my life…"

"What is it, what is it?" I interrupted her.

"It is something that belonged to my mother who I never met," she said.

"Where is it..? Please tell me…" I inquired.

"You will keep it forever.., do you promise?" she asked?

Yes, I do. I'll do anything for you." I responded.

"I know," she said, sounding profoundly convinced, "It is on my chest, on my left side close to my heart… You take it now. I want to see with my own eyes that you have it."

Then I opened her blouse in a hurry and I didn't see anything but her black lace brassiere…

And she added, "It is under my left breast."

I tore open the brassiere, leaving her divine cinnamon breasts exposed to the hot tropical afternoon sun while the crowd of people around made all kinds of comments about their divinity and even a little old lady shouted at me: "Pervert!" I disregarded her comments and I got hold of that enormous and lucious left breast for the first time in my life, and I carefully lifted. Under it, I was able to see a small manila envelope taped with a bandaid to her baby cinnamon skin. Then I pulled it away…

And she mumbled in agotic pain: "Oh, shit! That hurt!"

"But I have it, now I have it! I exclaimed.

Then she said: "Please, if I die.., you keep it with you forever…"

Just at that time, the ambulance arrived and two paramedics came rushing out from it with the stretcher… They threw her torso on it and also her lower part. However, the torso was facing up, but the other was facing down… Then I turned over the bottom part in the position that it should be, placing them as close together as I could… I helped them to pick it up and place all of her guts on the stretcher, too. I kept picking up everything around that belonged to her body, in case that they were able to sew her together again. I did not want anything of her to be left behind on the hot asphalt pavement for the ants to eat. Her guts were sacred to me.

Before they put the stretcher inside the ambulance, I gave her a kiss on her forehead and I put on her chest the jar with my foreskin, and I said to her: "This is for you to have."

"Oh, gee, thank you..," she said almost in a whisper.

They rushed in and closed the doors of the ambulance in my face and I was left behind, alone in the middle of the street, surrounded by hundreds of curious pedestrians. —God.., I had forgotten to ask them where they would be taking her!— So.., I decided to run behind the ambulance to follow them…

I ran and ran.., until the ambulance reached the same medical center where she was operated on years before.

They took her out in a rush to the emergency entrance. I ran beside the stretcher, holding her right hand.. A few doctors and nurses ran toward us and cleared the way into the emergency room, where they dumped her two selves and guts on an emergency table.

Then, the same plastic surgeon doctor who reconstructed her face years earlier, Dr. Victor Manuel Villareal Monteagudo del Posa, quickly entered the room. Even though I disliked that dirty, old man, I felt relieved, because he was able to save her face before, and perhaps he would be able to save her severed body. He immediately recognized me.., and her.

He approached the table, felt her pulse and said: "It's a miracle that she is still alive."

And he opened her beautiful black eyes and looking at him, she mumbled: "Victor, my Victor…"

I interrupted her saying: "Don't talk, don't talk.., save your strength," and turning to the doctor, I begged him "Please, doctor, save her! Save her life! Please.., don't let her die! I'll pay you anything you want… Please doctor, please…"

"Very well," he responded, "I won't promise you anything… I'll do my best and pray for a miracle this time," and he said to the other doctors and nurses in the room: "Let's take her to the operating room."

While they were moving the gurney in the direction of the operating room, I walked beside, holding her right hand again. Her jumping beauty mark was still changing places on her face, but now at a very slow rate. Just before entering the room, I closed my fist and slightly hit her on her left cheek.., then, she opened her eyes and looked at me, and I told her: "I'll see you later."

And she, turning her face kissed my fist. Then, they rushed her inside, disappearing behind the swinging doors. I was left there alone in that antiseptic, long hallway. –God, please make her live!!!– I implored deep inside me. And I decided to rush to the chapel and pray for her. While going there, I kept frantically repeating in my mind: –live, live, live..!

In the small chapel, I ran to the altar and kneeled in front of the image of the virgin The Charity of The Copper, to whom she was so devoted. And I prayed and begged for her like I had never done in my entire life. While I was doing that, in my mind, I kept hearing Esperanzita's heartbeats and seeing the respiratory balloon in the operating room being inflated and deflated with her breathing. I could not remove that agonizing imagery from my brain. It was a real, excruciating torment and I broke down crying out loud… After a while, there was a silence. Everything was gone from my mind. No more heartbeat. Nor more balloon. I opened my eyes and looked up to the image of the virgin and I, begging, repeated at her: "Oh, please.., my sweet virgin.., my little virgin Charity of The Copper.., make a miracle, save her please! Please! Please..!"

Then I heard the sound of footsteps approaching behind me and I turned around to see who it was. And there, at the entrance, was the doctor, full of blood…

He solemnly walked to me and said: "Juan… She is gone."

And filled with a profound pain, I screamed: "Oh no, God!!!"

"Her beauty mark stopped jumping..," the doctor said, "and she was gone… We tried the jumper cables to no avail… Well.., we did everything we could."

"I guess that's it..," I said, "it's over.., all over."

Yes, that's it," He said and after a pause, he added: "I did not sew her together… I thought you might be saving some money by putting her in a small coffin."

"Oh gee, thank you doctor," I sarcastically said, "you are very thoughtful in moments like this."

And he replied: "You spent a lot of money on her. You have to think about practical things, too."

I walked out of the chapel in silence, with my broken heart and I left the medical center.

I walked and cried a long time throughout the wooded residential streets of the Vedado development where the center was located. I felt devastated. I did not know what to do with my life. —Is it possible to have a life without Esperanzita?— I reached my hand in the pocket of my pants for the little manila envelope she had asked me to keep. I kissed it and held it very tight to my chest and against my heart. That was the only material thing I have from her. I deeply cherished that she confided it to me… I wondered what was inside that little envelope… Then, I decided to open it to share that secret from her. Carefully, I opened it. Inside I found something that looked like a flat semicircular piece wrapped in toilet paper. I unwrapped it, and found what looked like half of a medallion. I turned it around to see the other side.., and then, it looked familiar to me. I had seen this before. I know this medallion!

Suddenly, loud music shook the street, making my heart jump in my chest. —I know this medallion!— I exclaimed to myself again. And immediately, I got my wallet from my back pocket and looked inside. I have carried, since my childhood, half of a medallion with me always. That was the only thing that my real mother left with me when she abandoned me in a basket at the entrance of the orphanage… Mine was wrapped, too, but in a Little Orphan Annie comic strip. So, I got it and unwrapped it in a hurry. −Yes! It was the same!− Then, I placed it against the other half that Espranzita gave me, and they matched perfectly, until the last crack and imperfection. Now, it was one complete medallion: −So.., that means that Espranzita's half also belonged to my mother! And that Esperanzita's mother and mine were one in the same!−

Suddenly, the same loud music that shook the street before sounded again. But this time one hundred percent louder, making everything around vibrate like an earthquake, and with such force that the mangos and coconuts were falling from the trees all around me.

And then, I realized the terrible truth! −Actually, Esperanzita was my sister!− And I have loved her and desired her not as a sister but as a woman! I was going to commit incest with my very own sister… −Oh God.., how low can I get?!− I felt a horrible repulsion about my own self. I started going mad. I felt an urgent desire to terminate my life, and I started running like crazy without any destiny… I let my legs guide me to wherever they wanted to take me. And I let myself go like a possessed wild beast… I ran until I was out of energy and fell on the sidewalk, passed out.

When I woke up I recognized the place where I was.., just a block away from the Gardel movie house. I got up and walked to it. I saw its new fairytale facade designed by Esperanzita, with its tall tower, pointy roofs and multicolored flags happily agitated in the wind, completely oblivious of my terrible tragedy.

I walked by the iron fence, went though the new entrance gate, and slowly climbed the three steps to the entrance esplanade. To the right, I saw the fountain with the lover's bench that Esperanzita insisted on having there. And behind that intimate setting, as part of the facade, there it was, the tallest of all the towers.

I went into the lobby and bought a ticket to get in. They were showing a movie from Spain that was extremely popular, its name was *The Last Couplet*. From grade "Z" Mexican films, they switched to good Spanish ones.

Standing by the door with his new uniform, was the same black man, but he was not sleeping on his stool, he was standing now, very proud of his look. I gave him my ticket and went in to the now air conditioned house. I turned to the right and climbed the staircase to the upper balcony.

From there, I looked for the stairs that would take me to the high tower. I finally found it and started climbing to the top. When I arrived at the very top, I felt calm. I felt the cool breeze of the late afternoon on my face. It was peaceful up there…

I knew what I wanted. I know how to accomplish it. It was just a matter of seconds in order to consummate my wish of finishing with my hopeless existence. I approached the long rectangular opening serving as a window and stepped on it. I looked up to the brightly colored sunset sky. I looked down to the lover's bench on the ground. I made the signal of the cross, took my last breath and jumped…

While I was falling I saw Cachita coming out of the movie house, pigging out on a quart of coconut ice cream and just taking a seat on the lover's bench. −Oh no…− Then I realized that I was going to fall on top of her!!! −It's going to be a big mess mixed with coconut ice cream and everything! God.., that was not what I had planned..! Well.., perhaps, that is what He has planned for me, killing two birds with the same shot… But on the other hand, landing on top of Cachita was not my priority. Is this perhaps my punishment..? Well, I certainly can not do anything about it now…

And while my life was rushing to a smashing end… I kept hearing in my mind the tune of the song "Cinnamon Skin"…

"Agustin.., Agustin.., wake up," Jaums said.

"Ooohhh.., oh," I said very much confused while opening my eyes.

"We are landing in Cairo in a minute…" Jaums added.

"Ooohhh… yeah.." I said, feeling the descending sensation of the plane, "Oh Jaums.. I was having a dream. An incredible dream..," and I laughed, amused at the whole thing and said to Jaums: "You know..? The Painted Woman was the main character. But at the same time, she did not look like her. She looked like Sarita Montiel…Oh it was gross and funny at the same time… I'll tell you about when we arrive in Cairo."

NOTE

Seeing many of the Mexican films of the late 1940's and 50's during my childhood left unforgettable memories which have become scars, leaving their marks forever, deep within me. As the Alvaro Carrillo song "The Lie," very popular in the era said:

> *'Cause we carry scars in the souls*
> *Impossible to erase.*

CHAPTER 21

THE EMBASSY

After we got our luggage, Abulela, our good and efficient chauffeur, found us in the super-crowded Cairo airport, and he drove us to the Rehab (short for "rehabilitation", as Nancy commented later on) Hotel. This hotel was OK. The room was decent and it had a long, hallway of a bathroom, with the peculiarity of a shower in the middle of the way to the toilet. So, if you wanted to use the toilet while someone was taking a shower, you have to cross through it and get wet. It was really unusual. In fact, an architectural feast that would have made the ancient pyramid builders turn in their secret graves.

The first thing I did was to take a shower. I had to remove all of the goo from my hair from my previous day's shower attempt at the Nefertary Hotel. After I finished with my shower, I had to clean and somehow get the water off of that bathroom—the shower did not have anything on the floor to contain the water.

After that, I called John Van Deerlin at the American University and was able to get in touch with him. He offered to pick us up that afternoon at the Kentucky Fried Chicken a few blocks from our hotel, and take us for sightseeing around the city.

With him, we visited the City of the Dead, the old Cairo cemetery where, due to poverty, overcrowding and housing shortages, a lot of poor people live. Actually, the City of the Dead was the City of the Living. However, it was an interesting experience.

Later on, we ate in a picturesque restaurant with a lot of cats and monkeys freeling moving among the customers. From there, we went to the Khan El Kalily bazaar because I had to buy two pieces of luggage to replace the ones damaged during our trips throughout Egypt. I got two leather shoulder bags for a reasonable price and John drove us back to the hotel.

From the hotel room I called our guide, Madame, the Egyptian Olga Gillot, to find out the date of the television show that the Chairman of the State Information Agency was preparing for me. But Madame said that she hadn't heard from him yet about the project and she told me that next morning at 9:30 she and Abulela would pick us up at the hotel.

Jaums and I got up early to take showers and get ready. But.., there was a problem with the hot water and the pressure of it. So, we had to take ice cold, misty showers.

Sharp on time, as usual, they came and took us to the Ministry of Higher Education, where Mr. Abdessalm Diab, the Director of Delegations Department, informed me that after today, my official invitation was over and that we would be on our own. Today, they had scheduled for me to visit the Papyrus Institute, where they will give us a VIP tour. So, after we finished in Mr. Diab's office, Madame and Abulela took us there. It was a very interesting place to visit and just by the Nile, in the Giza area, with a nice and relaxing view of Cairo on the opposite bank. They gave me several sheets of papyrus made there that I later used to make a collection of "Papyrus Fragment" paintings.

At 12:30 pm, Abulela picked us up and drove to the Shepheard's Hotel, where I left a note for Nancy with our new Cairo address, as we had agreed in Abu Simbel, so she can get in touch with us on her return to Cairo. Then, he took us to the Hilton for lunch.

In the lobby of the Hilton, on our way to the coffee shop, we saw

Kitty again. This time, she was involved with another little old ladies' tour to Alexandria. I would have liked to go, but I could not move out of Cairo because of the pending television show. But, she was in a rush and we couldn't talk much.

After lunch, we walked to the Cairo Museum shop, since I wanted to buy some reproductions, but as usual, they were getting ready to close and did not let us in. So…, we decided to go shopping for shoes. However, we were unsuccessful, due to the fact that all of the shoes we were able to find were of abominable designs. The Great Cairo Mystery puzzled us: each time we were near the downtown shopping area, a "shopping guide" appeared to assist us. What made it a mystery was that each time it was the same gentleman.

Late in the afternoon, we went back to the Hilton for dinner. While walking through the lobby, I received the surprise of seeing again The Painted Woman, clutching her makeup case, and being followed by The Polyester Man and The Unremarkable Youngster. She was impeccably dressed in a red gauze evening gown. It was low cut and with her remarkable pair of rounded breasts pumping out resembling two inmates trying to jump out of the walls of Sing-Sing, Song-Song or Sung-Sung. Her neck and chest were infected by diamonds and pearls galore, as well as her arms. She looked dazzling, I guess.., as the temple of King Solomon would have looked in antiquity. However, she gave me a highly irritated look while passing in front of me. I stopped and turned around to see her Rumbera walk.., and she vanished, like a dream, in the crowded lobby… I never saw her again. –Sigh…–

Next morning at 9:15, Abulela came to the hotel to take us to the Fine Arts Institute of Helwan University to see the artist Mandouh Ammar. He was going to accompany us to see the boat under reconstruction at the base of Cheops' pyramid. But, he could not go. Nevertheless, he wrote a personal letter addressed to the man in charge of the project, for him to give us a VIP tour. While in Mr. Ammar's office, the Dean of the University, who had become fond of me and my work, invited us for dinner at his Heliopolis flat next Thursday. He also told me that he had talked with the Minister of Information about the arrangement of an exhibition of sixty Egyptian art works in conjunction with my next showing at a Washington, D.C. gallery.

I was extremely pleased, because that was what I wanted to do. I was glad to know that it was going to be OK with the Egyptian Government, since that was my own idea. He said the ministry will be taking care of all of the shipping and crating arrangements. We left the office about 11:30 and since Abulela was already gone, we took a regular taxi to the pyramids at Giza.

At the base of the great pyramid, we went to the office of the project. The secretary of the gentleman we were referred to told us to sit while she took the introduction letter to him.

After a long wait, she came back and without any excuse, she said that did not want to see us today and she recommended that we come back the next day to see him then. I was disappointed after coming all the way down to Giza for nothing. So, I got up and left that office in a hurry. However, since we were there anyway, I decided to go back inside Cheops' pyramid again. So, we went in and stayed inside for a long time.

From the pyramid, we crossed the highway and went to the Mena House Hotel for lunch overlooking the magnificent pyramids of Giza. After lunch, we decided to spend the rest of the afternoon wandering around the pyramids.

While walking nearby some strange ruins around the base of the great pyramid, my talisman fell to the ground. First I thought that its chain had broken. But no, the chain was intact and perfectly secured around my neck. —Probably the pendant broke,— I thought and I experienced an eerie feeling of *deja-vu*. Then I kneeled in the sandy ground, got the talisman and carefully examined it. To my surprise, as well as Jaums', the talisman was intact, too. We could not understand what had happened. We were extremely puzzled... Suddenly, I remembered that about a year earlier, a friend did some research with me about reincarnation. It suggested that I had lived in two periods of the Egyptian pharaonic times and in my second life, I met with a violent death at the age of eleven... I wondered if the mysterious fall of my pyramid talisman had something to do with it–something I should pursue... Jaums said that the whole thing was very intriguing and that I should investigate further on the spot where the pyramidal talisman fell.

I stayed on my knees, asking to a supreme being for guidance and help. Immediately I started feeling chills. The lady friend told me that on such occasions these chills were signs of confirmation. And I had the feeling, at that point, that my past history was there, buried under the ground... I felt more confirmation chills...

Automatically, I started digging in the sandy soil with my hands, just like a dog would do. Jaums joined me. We dug and dug and very soon started finding what looked like fragments of obsidian stones and pottery... And I started thinking: –How would I react if I really find a coffin with a mummy..?– I got scared about the whole thing and we stopped digging. Besides, there were some Egyptians and tourists around observing what we were doing.

We decided to wait until they were gone to continue digging. But, after they left the area, it was getting dark and chilly and I decided to quit. Anyway, if we would find something, what were we going to do with it..? So, I put some of the small obsidian stones inside my pyramid talisman and took with me some of the pottery fragments, and we left the area, kind of sad and frustrated.. But, I certainly did not want to go further. Perhaps, another time...

Finally, the next day, I was able to meet with the Chairman of the State information agency in his office. He apologized for not being able to get in touch with me sooner, but he had been very busy, he said. And he had not had time at all to prepare the television show. I was glad to know that it was over, so I did not have to worry about being accessible in Cairo. However, our reservation at the Rehab Hotel was expiring on Wednesday and we would have to vacate our room. So, he would have to give us a recommendation letter in order to get into another hotel. But then, he said that he and noted newspaper man Abdul Selin, who had written a very good article about me in the most widely circulated magazine in Egypt, were going to get us a flat where we could stay until we leave the country the next Friday. And then, he asked us to come back the next day to his office for the final arrangements. So, we still have things pending and we could not take any tours outside Cairo yet.

From his office, we walked to the Shepheard's Hotel for lunch. From there, I decided to visit the nearby Abdine Palace listed as a museum in my Egyptian guidebook.

We walked to the Abdine Palace and as we were trying to enter, an armed guard told us that it was not a museum any longer and that it was now President Sadat's residence! —No wonder everybody looked at us as crazy when we so normally entered through the main door!

So, late that afternoon, we finally managed to get a taxi with a driver willing to take us back to our hotel for a reasonable price. —Abulela, how much I miss you!— I kept thinking, because the taxi drivers we had to deal with after my official invitation was over, were a herd of outlaws without any scruples whatsoever. They thought that all foreigners were dripping with money and refusing to use their meters, demanding the most outrageous amount of money. And if you do not agree to their demands, they'd rather go empty or carry a low-rate-paying Egyptian than a foreigner. Consequently, the transportation in Cairo without Abulela was almost an impossibility and became unbearable, making us feel something I never thought I was going to feel about Egypt, I wanted to get the hell out of there. However I couldn't because my flight reservation was not until Friday and could not be changed. Also, our hotel reservation for my next destination was not until that day. And, since we would be arriving in Rome during Easter week, the whole city was already booked. We were marooned.

Back in the hotel, we went to the coffee shop for dinner. But, even though the sign at its entrance said "24 Hour Service", they refused to serve us because we didn't belong to any tour group. We ended up eating in a cat-smelling restaurant.

Next morning, we rushed to the same coffee shop for breakfast, but made sure that time we mixed with the tour group in order to get served.

After breakfast, we went back to the office of the Chairman of the State Information Agency. There we met Mr. Abdul Selin who said the only thing he was able to get us was a flat for seventy five pounds a day and that was an outrageous amount of money for us, so his other alternative was to give us a letter of introduction and send us to the Press Information Office located in the Egyptian National Television building, for help finding a hotel.

With the letter in our hands, we left for the Press Office. There, and after a lot of red tape, going from one office to another, finally a gentleman took care of us. He had to write another letter requesting a room for us in a second class hotel without a private bath.

"Well," Jaums commented, "at least it will be for only two days."

We finally took another taxi, —our third that day!— I told the taxi driver: "To the Khan El Khalily Hotel, please." which was the name in the letter referring us.

Apparently the taxi driver did not know how to find the hotel because was driving around in circles and kept asking pedestrians and traffic policemen for the hotel.

After a while, he stopped the car and said: "It's here!"

We paid and got out in a crowded square. And after the taxi left, we could not find any trace of the Khan El Khalily Hotel. We kept wandering around…, and asking a lot of questions, we finally managed to find the elusive hotel.

It was a fairly big ten floor building that seemed to have been built during the very late fifties or beginning of the sixties and was left untouched since then.

At the reception desk in the long and narrow rectangular lobby we presented our introduction letter. After the ritual conference among several employees with more and more joining in on the simultaneous talking about who knows what, the attendant came back to the desk and said that he will be able to give us a room just beside the bathroom. So I felt very much/somewhat relieved that at least we found a place to live since the next morning we had to vacate the Rehab Hotel.

We were tired of dealing with the taxi drivers, so we decided to walk back to the Cairo Museum and later on have lunch at the Hilton. There we again ate at the Italian restaurant where I saw The Painted Woman for the first time. I sure missed her!

After lunch, we went to an interesting shop across from the American Embassy to try to establish contacts to import some of their unusual items to the gallery I was associated with in Washington, D.C. but to no avail. I found the merchants there impossible to deal with.

That shop was just behind the Shepheard's Hotel, so we dropped by to inquire about Nancy. However, she was not back yet so I left a note with our new address.

From the hotel, we crossed the boulevard and sat by the Nile to watch the beautiful sunset while a dead donkey passed by, floating on the historic Nile current. –Simply flabbergasting.

Later on, we decided to get a taxi back to our hotel… After more than three hours of frustrated intentions, we didn't have any other alternative than to walk back to the hotel, which, by the way, was not very far from the center of Cairo.

After walking about an hour, we stopped at a Wimpy's for dinner, six blocks from our hotel, since I did not want to face the cat-smelling restaurant of the night before. But, the food at Wimpy's was not very good.

As soon as we finished, we started walking on the boulevard toward the hotel and I discovered that in one of the houses to our left. was the Embassy of Cuba. It was a one story house that reminded me of a modern house in Cuba built during the fifties. Many similar houses were converted into something else after the Revolution. It was always sad for me seeing a place that was originally intended as a home to no longer be one.

The house had a medium-sized fence, but walking along the sidewalk, I was able to see the yard and the front door, which was wide open. From where I was passing by I could hear Cubans inside talking to each other. They were speaking with that horrible accent that I had begun to notice from the people coming out of Cuba now. The whole thing made me sad and brought back memories…

The son of Papa Gordo and Mama Zoila, who taught me all of the colorful language I could ever need, sadly, when he grew up, developed mental illness, schizophrenia. They had a very difficult time with him and his unusual personalities. Although when he was all right, he was very charming.

Around the mid fifties, he married a well known singer. But it didn't last very long–he sold her belongings and disappeared. From then on he got involved in all kinds of problems. Finally, Papa Gordo and Mama Zoila were able to place him in a mental hospital for treatment. He was receiving electroshock therapy.

One day he escaped from the hospital and no one knew where he went. For his mother and father it was a very difficult time because he was their only child and they loved him very dearly.

In January of 1959, when the revolution army was marching to La Habana, to take over power as Fidel Castro wanted, they found out that their son had become one of the higher ranking Commanders of the revolutionary armed forces. He escaped a mental institution to join Fidel Castro's army in the mountains!

Handsome and bearded, he became a well known Commander. He was appointed by the new revolutionary government as the Chief of the Motorcycle Patrol. Very shortly after he was in that position, he was accused of killing a man. That was really nothing unusual in the new Fidel Castro Cuba: from the very beginning they started to annihilate everyone who stepped in the way of the revolution.

But, the revolution was in need of a scape-goat to publicly set an example of how honest they were. Besides, Fidels's brother, Raul, did not have a very good relationship with the handsome Commander. So, he immediately was placed in jail to be tried later in a public trial from which he was going to be found guilty and sentenced to die or stay in jail.

Papa Gordo and Mama Zoila were using all of their influence to try to stop that masquerade trial. They knew their son was mentally ill and his place was in a mental institution.

But they couldn't get any help for their son from any of their important friends, so one day, Mama Zoila was able to get to Fidel Castro in the lobby of the Hilton Hotel in La Havana. In front of everyone there she explained who she was and begged him to have mercy because her son was in fact crazy and she had his medical record of his illness. But Fidel couldn't care less about it, and feeling with his fingers the gray mink stole Mama Zoila was wearing he replied: "Well, that's the kind of thing your son does... He does those things."

There was a trial, a famous one, however very short as was characteristic of the new revolutionary trials as was the fact that the result was already decided. He was found guilty. Fortunately, he was not sentenced to death, instead he got thirty years in the infamous jail in La Cabana.

Papa Gordo and Mama Zoila, who still had some important friends during those confusing times, managed to plan an escape for their son from that super secure prison. And one day, they all escaped from the island together. Even though in those early days I supported the revolution, I was very glad that they all were able to escape for good.

Also during the first year of the revolution, another famous and popular Commander disappeared in a mysterious airplane crash the wreckage of which was never found. His name was Camilo Cienfuegos.

There were a lot of rumors around that he did not share the same communist ideas as Fidel and his brother, Raul. Camilo represented a different kind of order, one that everyone was expecting from the revolution.

So, one day, the government-controlled radio and television announced that the small Cessna he was flying had failed to land at the appointed time and place. A huge and very well publicized search was launched throughout the alleged route of the flight. Even Fidel Castro himself was aboard one of the big planes looking for the beloved Commander Camilo.

The search was extensively covered by the media, so we all sat dutifully with eyes glued to the television screen, watching the whole thing. But nothing was ever found. Fidel Castro's plane finally landed and he came out very sad and embraced Camilo's parents at a military base in La Habana, confirming the fact of his disappearance. You could clearly see the sorry reflected on Fidel's face for the loss of our beloved Camilo, and we all cried at the moving scene in front of our sets. Everybody believed the story about the plane crash and monuments, schools and institutions were named for the martyr Camilio.

Five years later, 1965, after I left Cuba and while living in Paris, I found out accidentially in a conversation with a person very close to Fidel Castro, who had defected, that actually Commander Camilo Cienfuegos was killed in a discussion with Raul Castro inside the Presidential Palace in La Habana. This reporter claimed to be there when it happened.

This revelation was a shocking surprise for me. I had believed the story about Camlio's plane crash without question. —Well,— I thought, —this was something else to add to the enormous list of crimes committed in Cuba after the Castro communist revolution took place. Why wasn't Raul Castro brought out to face a trial, as years before, the Revolution did this with Papa Gordo and Mama Zoila's son..?— Actually it was very obvious to me why.

Then, a year later in Madrid, while talking to another defector from Cuba, I learned another detail which indirectly corroborated the revelation of Paris. But this other story was from a reporter who was in the same plane with Fidel Castro when he supposedly was looking for the wreckage of Camilio's plane. This person told me, without knowing about what I had learned in Paris, that Fidel's attitude during the search flight was puzzling, because during all the hours of searching, he never bothered to look out the windows, except for photographs. And that Fidel was very amused all the time, smoking his cigars and telling jokes.

However, the most amazing thing was the fact that when the plane finally landed at the military base where Camilo's parents, the television cameras and reporters were, and Fidel Castro was going to exit and face the media and the whole nation, his attitude completely changed. He automatically became grave and sad, almost running to embrace Camilo's anxious parents. At that time this reporter thought that he was watching the best performance actor in the world!

After the reporter finished that revealing story, I recounted what I had learned in Paris. We both reached the same conclusion that something very sinister was behind Camilo's disappearance. —It was very convenient for the Castro brothers at that time, clearing the path for their plans by eliminating the Camilo Cienfuegos obstacle!—

—What a frustrating feeling to know that in reality the people who live outside the communist world completely ignore what Communism is all about! And when they are warned, they don't believe. Apparently, no one is allowed to know that they want to take over the world to impose a totalitarian system where everybody loses their freedom and become slaves. No one is allowed to know that they are murderous killers. Only we, the victims, the lucky ones who escaped know. But, no one listens or is allowed to listen to us, because "they" have undermined the foundation of our democracy and our civilization... And one day perhaps we all are going to be in ruins, like the ruins of Egypt...–

NOTE

The best defense the people of the world have against cancerous communism is to be well informed, to know the truth, because they prey on the ignorance and naivety of entire countries.

CHAPTER 22

CHICHO

In my hotel room I miraculously got a telephone line and was able to get through to the Dean of the Faculty of Fine Arts of the University of Helwan. I was calling to cancel the dinner engagement at his home the next evening. I explained what had happened to us that day and our frustrating inability to get taxis to take us back and forth to the hotel and that I didn't want to face that situation again. I told him: "I've just about had it with the taxi drivers in Cairo. And tomorrow is going to be another disgrace trying to get a taxi at anything but an exorbitant rate to get us to the new hotel."

But he insisted that I should go to his house and that he would pick us up in the evening and after dinner, he would drive us back to the hotel. –Well, that was very kind of him,– so I accepted.

So we got our suitcases ready for the move to the Khan El Khalily Hotel. –What a waste,– I thought, –We came back to Cairo to do a television show and to take tours to other places and because of uncertainties, we couldn't do anything!–

I was not sleepy when I finally went to bed. I was just lying there while my mind was rolling with more memories…

It was back in March, 1963 that I was contacted by the Cuban Institute of Art and Cinematographic Industry to do a film. This was going

385

to be the fifth time that I would be working with them, but this time it was a better role with a sixty day contract to film mainly on location in the Sierra Maestra Mountains located in the province of Oriente.

I wanted to visit those mountains since it was the birthplace of the revolution. This would be a golden opportunity. Besides, they would pay me one thousand pesos for two months, which was almost a one year salary for an average worker. So I quit my five peso-a-night theater play job to go to the mountains.

The whole cast and crew left La Habana by bus one afternoon for our sixteen hour trip to Oriente. Most of the cast were very attractive young women in their teens and early twenties. The film was about a force of voluntary teachers that went to the Sierra Maestra to teach reading and writing to the peasants who lived there in isolation. Actually, the screenplay was an adaptation from a novel that had won the first prize in a literary contest in 1961. I had never read the novel until I got involved with this film, but I liked the script better. It gravitated, as usual, around the revolution theme. However, it sounded interesting because of the contradictions the main female character, Elena, had with the new revolutionary environment.

I knew of the main actress of the film, we had studied in the same acting school. She graduated before me since she was a senior when I started. I had little contact with her in school, she was much older and did not have much of a charismatic personality. You had to accept her or not. However, her un-femininity was a quality that always bothered me about her when she was on stage, since I kept noticing that she was trying very hard to act like a feminine young woman. But for me, the end result was like watching John Wayne in drag, which was disturbing to say the least.

Who she really was under her stage personality I knew mostly from others who had met her or worked with her and in general, she was not very well liked. My initial reaction to her, that chemical reaction you experience when you meet someone for the first time, was that somehow I disliked her.

I think the feeling was mutual, because we were never able to look each other in the eye. We both turned our faces away in order to avoid even minimal eye contact. Unfortunately, I had to do some scenes with her… but in the plot we were not supposed to like each other, so that was good, we wouldn't have to pretend much.

After a longer than expected trip we finally arrived at the Camilo Cienfuegos Childrens School located on the outskirts of the Sierra Maestra mountains. We had to sleep there that night. However, there were no facilities, so I had to sleep on the hard, cold tile floor using a piece of cardboard as a mattress.

Next morning after breakfast our whole group was loaded into Russian flat-bed trucks to start the ascent to our destination, a few thousand feet up the mountain. The ascent was slow and risky. On more than one occasion the trucks seemed to be losing control and nearly went off the abysmal cliffs… The girls kept hysterically screaming and behaving like hens. But I found the experience a lot of fun.

After a few hours, we reached the top. It was a plateau called The Mines of Cold, because it was alway cold up there. We were supposed to stay there for a few days to film some exteriors around the area and later on to continue climbing to the site where the set of the voluntary teachers' camp had been built.

We stayed in the Mines of Cold in a huge army-type barrack which had a wall in the middle dividing the male from the female quarters. The division did not reach all the way to the metal ceiling, but it was high enough to assure separation. However, the female quarters were on the side with the bathroom facilities. The males had to go to a nearby barrack, still under construction and use the roofless bathroom there.

The facilities were really the pits. I had never seen anything as horrible before in all my years in Cuba. And in a place as cold as it was, the shower only had ice water with almost no pressure at all, which made the daily shower that Cubans were so much accustomed to, a real pain in the neck and everywhere else.

After a few days, I got to film a scene with one of the young actresses. We had been in the same acting class. The scene came out all right in just the three required takes.

Later that same day, I had another scene with the main female character of the film, Elena. We had to look at each other for the first time. –Oh boy.., it wasn't easy!– Europa, the name of the actress (bitch), did not have a good attitude toward me and she was kind of nasty during the filming. When she had to give me her lines off camera for my close ups, she was really vicious. I was young and inexperienced then and easily overcome by her strong G.I. Joe personality. She really made me feel very bad which completely disturbed my concentration. Consequently, I did not perform well in those scenes, kept forgetting my lines and making mistakes. And the worst thing was that I could not complain about her because she was the damn star of the film.

Finally, after many more takes than usual, my job was over for the day. I was very upset with myself because of my inability to overcome her poisonous presence.

A few nights later I was called to do a scene that was not in the script. The director of the film decided to add a typical campfire scene to the plot. I had to participate in it as a master of ceremonies. I was very glad that Europa was not involved in the scene with me.

The director gave me my lines to memorize. The setting was around a big campfire with hundreds of volunteer teachers from the real camp of The Mines of Cold, plus other extras from our own crew, so there were a lot of spectators.

After the lights were finally set and we were getting ready to start shooting.., there she came. And she stood between the camera and the director. She was looking at me with a diabolical smile on her face waiting for me to trip, to forget my lines again and make a fool of myself. And, as usual, the forces of evil are always the strongest. She made me very nervous and confused. After the "action" command was given by the director, I forgot my lines and kept switching the text around. –Damnit!–

"And now at this fire camp…"

"Cut!" said the director. "No, no, Agustin.., it's 'camp-fire'."

"OK, I know," I said, "I'm sorry…"

"Action!"

"And… campfire… now..?"

"Cut!" he said. "No…, 'and now at this campfire, in honor of comrade Elena."

"I'm sorry," I repeated, very apologetic, "I know, I know.., I know my lines."

"Action!"

"And now, at this campfire.., in honor of……. Elena!"

"Cut!" he said again and explained: "'Comrade Elena…' Ok, let's do it again. Action!"

"And now.., at this campfire.., Elena, the comrade Elena."

"Cut!" and he said: "OK, Agustin, listen: 'And now, at this campfire, in honor of comrade Elena, Marili is going to sing *The Big Rounded Moon*…' It's very simple… Then the camera will dolly to Marili. OK…? Let's do it again. Action!"

"And now, at this campfire.., in honor of.., comrade Marili, Elena is going to sing…"

"Cut..! It's not Elena, it's Marili… Again. Action!"

"And now.., Marili is going to sing…"

"Cut! You forgot about Elena. Let's do it right this time. Action!"

"And now, at this Elena's campfire…"

"Cut!" and he said to me again: "Agustin.., you know your lines well, I know. Come on.., relax. There's nothing to it. It's very simple, you know it. Let's do it once more. Silence! Action! Now you say it!"

And.., on.., and.., on making every possible wrong combination of words until I finally said: "And.., now! In honor of comrade Elena.., Marili is going to sing The Big Rounded Moon!"

"Cut!" the director shouted jubilant, "print it! Print it! Print it! That's all for you tonight, Agustin."

I was so embarrassed that I just wanted to die on the spot. And there she was.., the triumphant bitch! Having the best time of her life while I was being humiliated in front of hundreds of people and my fellow workers of the cast and crew. I left the location in a hurry and went back to the barrack. I felt so bad that I couldn't stay there and watch Marili perform her song. I liked Marili. She was very cute.

That damn bitch did it on purpose! She did not have any business being there, even though she was playing the role of Elena. At least for my take! She was just a bitch, like I thought! A goddamn son of a bitch as I had repeatedly heard from others! But.., I felt worse about myself for letting her bother me like that. And I wondered.., what could I do to overcome that?

Fortunately, in subsequent days, I did not have to do any individual scenes, just generals in which I happened to be in the background, so I was safe. However, my scene at the campfire became a classic and made me the laughingstock for the cast and crew. All kinds of embarrassing wild jokes started to circulate about my twisting of the lines. I always had a sense of humor and some of them were really funny indeed and I ended up laughing, too.

It was during that time that I became very friendly with the other female co-star of the film who was young, beautiful and feminine. She disliked the bitch, too. —Well, actually, she hated her even more than I did— so, we became friends.

She had to do a lot of scenes with the bitch, so, what I decided to do was go to watch all of her scenes. After each cut, I would talk to my friend and obviously congratulate her for her performance, completely ignoring the presence of the bitch.

I would say to her: "Carmen you were terrific! Your acting is outstanding! There is only you and no one else when you are in front of the camera!"

My comments made the bitch completely furious. And that was my revenge.

After we finished at the Mines of Cold, we continued the climbing to the camp set built higher in the mountains, in a place called La Magdalena, named for the fact that it rained there most of the time–Magdalena was associated with tears, so rain.

After a few hours of traveling by foot we reached the set where we will complete all of the remaining location shots of the film. The set was an improvised voluntary teachers' camp as were built in 1961. There was nothing extraordinary about it except that it was totally real with a breathtaking view of the Sierra Maestra mountains.

The males this time were staying in a separate barrack from the females. But the barrack was just an accurate and literal definition of the word "pits". It sure made our previous accommodation look like the presidential suite at the Waldorf Astoria! The beds were burlap hammocks. Just what we needed to assure a full night's rest! –Very thoughtful indeed!– The bathroom facilities.., whatever they were, were discouraging.

The next day they filmed a crucial and emotional scene between Carmen and the bitch. I went to watch, of course, to congratulate Carmen.

The day after that, it started raining and never stopped for the next two weeks! That was very thoughtful of the production indeed to build a set in a place where it rains so often. We could not do anything. So our days passed by, slowly, between the barracks and the dining room, where we met for breakfast, lunch and dinner.

The meals were unbearable due to the scarcity of food that the revolution was bringing to the whole island. We had our own provisions of food and a cook, and in accordance with our rank, we supposedly had more and better food. However, it was all awful, in spite of our cook's skills. I could not even imagine what in the hell the other people stationed in the Mines of Cold were eating! I started losing weight and I certainly didn't need to lose any.

Because of the constant rain it became very muddy. So, after the long two weeks in limbo, the production staff decided to go back to the Mines of Cold and wait to see if the rain subsided.

So, one morning, we were given the order to pack everything because we were leaving the camp. Each one of us, carrying our own luggage, started descending by foot, trying to keep our balance on the soft and slippery slopes, our boots sinking into the mud up to our ankles.

All the technical equipment had to be left behind because it was too heavy to carry and no truck was able to safely transport anything.

After a few hours of walking, we finally arrived in one piece to The Mines of Cold, drenched and muddy as a doggie happily rolling around in a mud puddle, but we were not so happy. There, in our same, but now luxurious looking, barrack, where we had to wait and see…

This time the barrack beside ours was occupied by the cast and crew of another film, a Russian-Cuban production also being filmed in the mountains. –Well, at least there would be new people to meet and talk to in order to pass the boring times,– I thought.

The Mines of Cold was a fairly big plateau surrounded by some higher hills–a valley on top of a hill. There was a big camp with a lot of barracks housing the new breed of teachers that the revolution was creating. Also, there were some military installations around, but we were not allowed to venture in the direction of those tactic points, so we never knew for sure what was being hidden there. There were a lot of military personnel around, however, we were not allowed to get close to them either. There was also a helicopter landing site at a higher point and a microwave station and some sort of small medical center that looked like it was built in the late 1950's, according to its architectural style.

The barracks for the male teacher/students were distantly separated from the females. They were not allowed to meet at all, except during classes. They could not even wander around each other's campgrounds. That was part of the new morality between the sexes imposed by the revolution. Sometimes, we saw a group of male teachers passing by our barrack, always supervised and in a military formation, toward their daily classes. In the distance, we could observe the female teachers, in the same fashion, marching to their classes. We just looked at each other in silence through the imposed barrier. How strange this new culture seemed.

Even when our group would go to the collective dining room of the camp, we were placed in a separate section with a wall in between so we could not mix with them. We also had the privilege of eating a different menu prepared by our own cook. I guess.., they should not see that we were getting better food.

That was why the Russian-Cuban production crew was a welcome addition. But, there was only one Cuban actor in the cast, the rest were Russian and the technical crew. It was not easy to be alone with any of them. For some reason they were not very friendly, except Sacha, the still photographer, who was friendly with me and we would talk a lot about photography. Sadly, the presence of the Russian-Cuban film project was not really a diversion for us and we went back to socializing among ourselves again.

I was very much liked by most of the girls in our production and I made a lot of friends but we could not venture very far from the barrack because that was not well regarded with the new morality. So we stayed inside the barrack.

The bitch apparently did not like this fact since she wanted all of the attention of girls for herself.

For me a lot of disturbing things started happening. There were some very hushed rumors (the only way they can circulate in a communist country) about the bitch's inclination for some of the girls in the cast...

Two of the girls in the film who were the example of femininity became very close to the bitch and somehow, they became kind-of butch. Then another of my girl friends, who was a gorgeous, sweet and fragile looking maiden from a fairytale, came to me one day and in strict confidence told me: "You know Agustin... Since I met Europa... my life has changed."

She continued: "She has talked to me a lot in the last few days, and now I am learning about myself. I think I finally know myself..."

"Oh.., really..?" I commented, just to be polite with her but scared to death about her revelation might be.

"Yes," she said very excited, "now I know who I am. I was so confused during all these years... But now I know and it's marvelous!"

Little by little, step by step, the bitch got a few more converted. Fortunately there were some incorruptible nymphomaniacs in the cast who had read Isadora Duncan and the bitch was not able to change them.

It was during that time that an unusual character appeared in the barrack to add some real diversion to our frustrating wait. It was called "Chicho" and apparently it was a he, Chicho was an elusive ghost who started appearing at night in the female side of the barrack.

Upon his first appearance, in the middle of the night, we were awakened by hysterical female screams coming from the other side of the dividing wall. The lights were immediately turned on. All of the males got up, grabbed a coat and ran outside the barrack to investigate what had happened.

Most of the girls were standing in a group outside the barrack, wrapped in their blankets and bed sheets, while others were running out crying and screaming hysterically.

After the commotion was over, well.., not completely over but calmed down a little, I was able to find out what had happened. The story was that the metal army beds on their side of the barrack were shaken and strange sounds and voices were heard, setting in motion a mass hysteria among the girls.

The makeup and wardrobe women, who were much older and very much respected by the crew, insisted that it was not only hysteria and that something unusual was going on in their side of the barrack at night.

The next night, a similar incident happened, but this time before everybody went to bed. The girls and the women of the crew were really frightened. Some of the girls claimed to have seen a ghost-like figure walking in the middle aisle in between the row of beds.

Finally, later on that night, they all went back to bed wearing their clothes in case they had to flee the barack again in panic. I found the whole thing very amusing.

The next day, most of the girls placed their beds close to each other, seeking reassurance of their own presence as a kind of protection for the evening to come. That day there were a lot of jokes circulating among the male cast and crew about the ghost, who was baptized with the name "Chicho."

However, on our side of the barrack nothing was going on. We would not see or hear anything unusual. By the middle of the day, the director got the male cast and crew together in a meeting and asked us not to joke or scare the girls about Chicho any more because they were really frightened. He said a very reliable woman who was part of the crew had told him what they were experiencing was real because she also had seen the ghost and heard the creepy noises. We all went along with the director and avoided the subject.

That evening we stayed up until late at night since the girls did want to go to their side of the barrack. Finally they formed a group and all-went inside at once jumping into their beds with their clothes on. The lights were kept on until they all relaxed and some fell asleep… Then, later on the lights were turned off.

After some time, another hysterical commotion took place and the girls ran out of their barrack because Chicho had appeared again. The director had a meeting with them outside the barrack convincing the girls to go back inside and telling them that they would keep the lights on all night. That's the way the girls spent the rest of the night.

Next morning the director tried to find another barrack for the girls but there were no other facilities available in the area. We talked to the Russian crew who was living in the barrack next to ours to see if there would be a chance to place the girls there, but they didn't want to switch.

Well.., that afternoon, a black girl from the cast, who claimed to have some spiritual powers because of her knowledge of an African religion, in an effort to get rid of Chicho's presence, got together with the director, the producer, the bitch, Carmen and the women from the crew in something I called a "Seance in the Afternoon". This black girl went into a trance…

Later on, I found out through Carmen the outcome of the seance: Chicho was a black slave from Congo, Africa. He had lived in a place nearby early in the previous century. Something that belonged to him was buried under the side of the barrack occupied now by the girls, and he was going around to protect and defend his property from the intruders. —So that was it!—

In the seance, they tried to convince his spirit that he was already dead and that he should leave the place, the earth, so he can go to a higher level, heaven, but his spirit was very adamant and wanted his property back.

What Chicho wanted was a practical impossibility due to the cement slab floor. And anyway, how was a spirit going to take with it a material thing if in fact he found it..? So, what they all decided to do was to perform some sort of exorcism ceremony to get rid of Chicho's spirit. They did something that Carmen could not explain to me, and now, the only thing to do was to wait for the coming night to see if they were successful… or not.

Nevertheless, there were a lot of rumors circulating privately about Chicho. One that I heard through one of the bitch-proof girls from the cast was that Chicho, in fact, was none other than Europa… She told me that a malicious tongue from the cast had told her that Europa wrapped herself in her bed sheet in order to wander from bed to bed molesting the girls.

That indeed was a very interesting rumor and very much in character. But after a self-satisfying internal laugh I dismissed the rumor knowing that in accordance with the new morality, if she had been suspected of such an act, with homosexuality one of the whose things in the eyes of the revolution, that would have meant her total annihilation… And the bitch was not dumb at all since she had managed to survive in that society, and was the star of an important production.

That afternoon, all of the girls were outside their barracks. They didn't dare to step inside. They were just at the entrance of ours. The atmosphere was tense and I could not resist the temptation of playing a joke so they all could laugh about this whole thing and relax. So, I discreetly walked out from the group and went to the back of the barrack where the females' bathroom facilities were. That room had two open windows, kind of high up, so you could not see inside. They were for light and ventilation. On the ground I found a dry coconut.., and that gave me an idea. So.., I got two soft drink caps and attached them to it as a pair of eyes, got a seed for a nose, drew lips with a white chalky piece of limestone, placed a cigar butt between the lips with a nail and put some dry grass on top as hair. The result was a very funny looking face, obviously poorly made of a coconut, nothing else. I just wanted some humor, that was all. I carefully placed the face on the window sill, looking into the bathroom.

I quickly left and mixed with the group in front of the barrack.

After a time, I got engaged in a conversation with one of the girls and I completely forgot about the coconut face when all of a sudden, a loud and terrified scream interrupted us. We all ran to the side of the barrack where the door of the female dorm was to find out what was going on this time.

When we arrived, we saw the wardrobe woman, who was in her late forties, coming out of the door in a panic, screaming with her arms up in the air and the most terrified expression I have ever seen outside a movie screen.

She went on screaming: "Aaaaaahhhhhh..! He was there! He was walking toward me with a knife in his hand to kill me!!! I saw him, I saw him!!!"

"Calm down! Calm Down!' the director was saying to her while the Russians from the next barrack were coming out to see what the new commotion was about. But they had no understanding about what in the hell was going on.

"Aahh.., I saw him!" she exclaimed hysterically while bursting into tears repeating: "He wanted to kill me, he wanted to kill me..!"

–Well..,– I thought, –she must have an overactive imagination! I just put a coconut face in there… I don't know where she got the idea of a knife (?) But.., I'd better go and remove my coconut face! I don't want to get in trouble!– So, discreetly, I went back, got the coconut face down and threw it down the cliff to a valley many thousands of feet down the side of the mountain.

There was a big crowd around that poor frightened woman. The director was giving her water and calming her down. I certainly wondered what in reality took place... −Could it have been my coconut that triggered the situation! Could it have been Chicho in fact trying to scare the hell out of her..?−

I guess I'll never know since Chicho appeared again that evening and continued doing so for as long as we were there. Not even the presence of Che Guevara, who came to the camp one afternoon to pay us a visit, made Chicho go away.

Very soon after, unable to go back to the set in La Magdalena because of the rains, the director and producer decided that it was time to go back to La Habana. There, they will construct a similar set so we can finish shooting the rest of the film there. Everyone was very glad to go back home, especially the poor sleepless girls!

We came down the mountain in trucks and we were to proceed to La Habana by bus. I was not feeling very good for the long trip, so, along with another actor, who had the supporting role, we were excused and allowed to remain in the capital of that province, the city of Santiago de Cuba, in order to catch next morning's flight to La Habana.

Finally home I kept feeling bad and went to the doctor who ran tests. The result was that I had contracted viral hepatitis, as most of the people in Cuba were having then. I had to go to the hospital for two weeks and another couple of weeks resting at home... After all, I was lucky because a black girl member of the cast of the film came back pregnant!

When I was better, I had to go to the studio. They paid me five hundred pesos extra because of the extra time I had to stay in the mountains. That was very nice. But neither the director or the producer had any idea when they would be able to continue shooting the film.

All depended on the construction of the set. We all had to stand by.

I went back to my weekly radio show and started rehearsing a musical play. One evening after a rehearsal, I went to the Cinemateca (Film Institute) where they were showing a film I wanted to see… And a very unpleasant incident happened to me which opened my eyes and made me realize what the revolution we were having in Cuba actually was. After that, I was not the same.

A few months later, the studio called me back for two more weeks of shooting. In the mountains, my hair had grown longer than usual and the exposure to the sun had lightened it. But because of the incident, and following my relative's advice, I had cut my hair very short. Physically, I was not the same either because of losing weight on the mountain diet as well as having hepatitis. The makeup department decided to make me a wig to match my hair the way it was in the earlier takes. I was glad, because I didn't have time to let my hair grow again and long hair, in the eyes of the revolution meant that you were a parasite of society.

Very soon I went back to the set which was built in a wooded area of La Habana by the Almendares river. It was very good and it was pleasant to know that every evening after the shooting was over, I was able to go home. Word was beginning to get around more and more that it was risky to be out, so being on set became a sanctuary. I was driven to the set each morning in my father's car by a driver who picked me up and took me back home.

Even my father's sister and brother, who hated the revolution, came to visit me on the set. They disliked the militant uniform that I was wearing in the film. I didn't tell them anything.., but I was beginning to hate it all deep inside of me even though being in the movie was a big stride forward for my career.

There were a few more scenes for me to film with the bitch. She was bitching, as usual, but somehow I managed to get through them all in the three required takes. Nevertheless, the revolutionary jargon of the dialog became increasingly difficult for me to repeat. I really had to force myself in order to say those lines that my character, a revolutionary slogan robot, had to say. —Well…, that is what acting is all about!—

After my two weeks were over, the shooting for my role was finished.

At the end of the year, 1963, I had to go back to the studios for my dubbing session. Then, I had to face two unpleasant items again: the bitch and the dialogue. But there is always a good side, and that was the fact that the new dubbing facilities were located in the same television studios where five years earlier I had met the Virgin in person for the first time… And after all, I was there again because of her.

CHAPTER 23

MEETING THE VIRGIN

In July of 1965, while in transit to Canada, I stopped for two days in Madrid and very soon I found myself on the street where she lived. While I was outside looking at the building, I kept singing in my mind the song "On the Street Where You Live", but in Spanish, from an album of the Mexican production of *My Fair Lady* with Manolo Fabregas, who played the role of the doctor in her anthological 1953 film *Cinnamon Skin*.

I didn't see her then. But I knew that sometime, someday and somehow, we would meet.

I left for Canada but three months later I went back to Europe to live in Paris. While living here, a lady there bought me tickets to travel to Madrid for Christmas. So, I went.

I liked it there so much that I went back to Paris to get my things and moved to Madrid. I wanted to be close to The Virgin.

The only thing that I was prepared to be in life was an actor, so I went into show business.

After just a few weeks I started working in Spanish television. I worked there for four or five days a week which enabled me to get some income to survive. I did not have to worry about paying rent for a while because another lovely and generous lady who looked a lot like the French actress Michele Morgan, offered me one of her apartments to live in without any strings attached. I had been lucky so far after leaving Cuba.

A friend of my mother's left Cuba and came to Madrid bringing me a verbal message from my mother that, just one week after I left there, she received a telegram from the Cuban government requesting my presence so they could send me, finally, to one of the dreaded "farms", –I had left just in time!– I thought, –what a difference between being at the mercy of a communist state and being really free!

In Spain, I felt very happy and very much free. All throughout my prior life in Cuba I always heard that Francisco Franco was a fascist dictator and, much more after the revolution in Cuba with the controlled media and huge propaganda machine discrediting all governments and political systems which are not communist. But, living in Spain I realized that if the same atmosphere of relaxation, peace and individual freedom I was experiencing in Franco's 1966 Spain had existed in Cuba, I wouldn't have left.

A contradiction I found in Franco's fascist government was, and it particularly called my attention, that I saw on display and for sale in many bookstores through Madrid, books about Marxism-Leninism and "The Capital" by Karl Marx (?!). So his version of "fascism" was not afraid of books, unlike Castro's Cuba.

Besides working as an extra and acting in one or two line roles in it seemed like hundreds of soap operas, dramas, comedies, musical shows, series and movies for television, in which I had the opportunity to work with important and admired actors, singers and personalities, I started rehearsing the Bertolt Brecht epic play, *Mother Courage and Her Children*, in the Fine Arts theater, under the direction of a very well regarded Spanish director. I had already seen the play and others of Brecht in Cuba, so I was familiar with the style.

In it, I got the role of a soldier who happened to sing a song in the play. I disliked the music of my song very much. I spent long hours alone with the musical director learning that horrible music—if at least they would have let me make an arrangement and change the tempo I would have managed… but not as it was written!

But, fortunately, the play in general was not coming out very well, so the director decided to stop rehearsing for a month to get new ideas. —I was so glad!

When rehearsals of that boring play started again, they didn't call me and I was glad. Anyway, I hated Brecht, I hated the play and I hated my song.

The person I really wanted to work with was The Virgin and for one reason or another it never happened. It was during that time that she was making a new film titled The Lost Woman, but even this time I was in Spain, I was unable to get any connection to the production.

Before starting that film and then after it was completed, she was never in Madrid. She was always traveling in Spain and other European countries or engaged in artistic tours in America, so I could not see her.

I developed and executed all sorts of schemes in order to get into her new flat in Spain Square, facing the Don Quixote statue. (She was born in La Mancha, like the famous gentleman.) But everything I did to meet the woman From La Mancha resulted in failure. I was only able to meet the doorman and her personal maid and they didn't have any pull. It was very frustrating! We were so close and yet so far at the same time…

In addition to my show business activities, I started painting again and had placed some of my new op-art works in two galleries in Madrid. And my lady protector organized a show of my paintings. The opening was attended by two princesses, a couple of retired army generals and society people. I got notes in the press and my photograph with one of the Spanish princesses was published.

—Poor princess.., she seemed to be very nice and sweet.., kind of gone, though, but nice.– Actually she was old and ugly as hell. I felt sorry for her. She was not what you think of when you think of a princess. Deep in her heart she must have felt bad about it.

She wore a lot of makeup over her wrinkled face, curls, hats, black velvet and rich lace dresses adorned with ribbons, sequins and feathers, plus pounds of pearls, diamonds and massive gold jewelry. –But nothing helped. She looked like a Halloween witch, the poor but sweet and rich princess.

One evening, my rich lady protector took me out to an exclusive Russian restaurant with the Spanish and an Italian princess who was a very sweet lady indeed. –What a paradox!– I don't know why in the hell I mentioned in the conversation that I used to sing in Cuba.., because they made me get up and sing a song for them…–I have never been so embarrassed in my life!

Another evening she took me out again with the same group of princesses, and this time to a discotheque. I danced with my protector and her secretary but not with the princesses since they both were too old to dance.

I was very grateful to my protector. She was a very nice lady and a beautiful person of refined feelings, but I wasn't ready for those princesses. I had a terrible time saying "Your Royal Highness" every time I had to talk to them –why doesn't she introduce me to The Virgin..? For her I am totally ready!

Later on, in addition to my television and theater work, I became a dress designer. With the help of the mother of a friend of mine who had just arrived from Cuba, we opened a business toward rich ladies. The idea was I would sketch five exclusive designs for each customer, she would choose one of them and we would execute it exclusively for her.

My friend's mother was a highly skilled, haute couture seamstress, so the dresses were impeccably made. They could be literally worn inside out. But she was slow as hell and such a perfectionist, she was never satisfied with the help of other full or part time seamstresses we could find. We were able to get out just two dresses a month. I could not help since I didn't have any idea how to sew. I just knew what to design that was best to complement the virtues or hide the imperfections of the customers.

Through the enthusiastic American Women's Club of Madrid and its monthly magazine publication, plus articles published in other Spanish magazines about my fashion designs, we got a clientele of very nice ladies, most of them were American, in a good economic position. They all loved the exclusive design idea and the masterful execution of the confections. Some of them would order more than one dress. It was a shame that we could not get more dresses out.

Slowly but surely, we were adding this extra source of income, but then my protector needed the apartment for her sister who was separating from her husband and we had to move out. We rented a flat in a nice area of Madrid and most of the business income went to pay the rent, the utilities and a maid we had to hire to clean the big flat.

Meanwhile, my efforts to contact The Virgin continued, this time not as a one or two line actor, but as a dress designer with some credentials because of the articles in the press. This lead to a brand new scheme: she liked to wear very revealing, low cut dresses, exhibiting to the world this additional divine quality in order to perform her miracles, I designed a *bande* of the biggest, widest, lowest and most indecent low cut dresses I could possibly imagine. They may not have been designed to be…practical…but they were definitely designed to attract her attention. I sent them all to her with the proposal that we will do any of them for free. –The only purpose so that I could have the pleasure of meeting her.– But nothing.., I never heard from her.

Next, in my desperation, I did a painting specially for her, and I took it to her top floor flat, appropriately near heaven…

"Oh, she just left," said her maid, "didn't you see her in the elevator..?"

And before she could finish, I ran down the ten flights to find, upon reaching the lobby, that I was too late. She had just gotten into a car with her husband and left... −Dammit!− So I went back inside the lobby, got into the elevator filled with her delicious perfume, and I pushed the tenth floor button...

Just at her door again, I rang the bell and her maid opened it.

"I didn't catch her," I said, "do you know when she will be back..?"

"No," she replied, "she went out to dinner with her husband and I have no idea..."

"Ohhh..," she said, "you can leave that with me. I'll show it to her when she returns. I don't know if she would accept it as a gift... Come back tomorrow afternoon to talk to her."

−I couldn't believe what she just said!− And I said: "Oh yes, I will. Thank you very much." And I left.

I could hardly sleep that night. Tomorrow perhaps will be the great day! I will finally meet The Virgin... −I guess I will kneel in front of her, I'll say a prayer.., and perhaps, perhaps, she will bless me with her smile, a touch. A kiss...

That day I took a long bath with aromatic salts, put on my best underwear, my best shirt and suit, a silk Christan Dior tie, and my super-deluxe pair of shoes that a rich lady bought for me in Paris. Well *The Best of Everything*, (1959) with Hope Lange, Suzy Parker, Joan Crawford and Louis Jourdan!− I also poured on a gallon of the French eau de cologne Habit Rouge de Guerlain on me. −Not overdone at all... I just didn't want to be forgotten.−

I went downstairs, got into a taxi and proudly gave her address.

In less than half an hour, I found myself in her building's front entrance.

"Where are you going now?" asked the doorman who knew me perfectly well.

"I'm going to see Sarita Montiel," I said, sounding very sure of myself.

"She is not there," he stated.

"Oh..," I said, but she has an appointment with me."

"She is not there," he replied.

"Her maid told me…"

And interrupting me: "She is still not there."

"How come?!" I inquired, very much confused.

"I don't know," he replied.

Then I said: "Listen.., I am the internationally known Cuban artist and designer Agustin Blazquez…"

"I have seen you around here," he said, interrupting my speech.

And I categorically said: "Yes. Yesterday I left a painting for Miss Montiel because she is dying to have one of my paintings. But she was not here. So, her maid asked me. She asked me. She was the one who asked me to come back here today in the afternoon to talk to Miss Montiel."

"But neither Miss Montiel nor her maid are here now," he said categorically. "The only person in her flat now is her mother, but she is deaf. So.., why don't you wait around until her maid comes back."

"OK, I will," and I stayed around for some time until I saw the familiar maid coming back to the building carrying a bag of groceries. She recognized me immediately from a distance and smiled at me. I walked toward her and offered to carry her bag… I thought if I did that, she would let me go inside her flat and I would be able to see the kitchen where the food for The Virgin was prepared… –Oh, this was a golden opportunity!– I had never been able to cross the threshold of the front door of her flat. But that damned clever maid knew better and declined my offer! So, she asked me to enter the building in the front, because she would be going through the service entrance. And then, she would meet me at the front door of the tenth floor flat.

Since the doorman saw me talking to The Virgin's maid, he let me in without any hassle. So, I got into the already familiar elevator, pushed the familiar button and got to the heavenly floor with its small waiting room outside the door of her flat. It was now MY waiting room, I decided.

After some time, the door opened.., but instead of the maid, there appeared a gorgeous woman inside the frame of it. My heart jumped in my chest! That was a very young woman and she looked like The Virgin! For a few seconds I thought that was it! She was The Virgin in the flesh and I was totally speechless!

And she said: "Hi.., I am Sarita's niece… Are you the artist?"

Coming out of my temporary trance, being awakened by the fact that she was not The Virgin at all but her gorgeous niece, I mumbled:

"Ohhh.., yes.., I think I was…"

"My aunt saw your painting," she said with her sweet young voice.

"Yes..?" I said realizing that The Virgin was also an aunt and that she had an earthly family.

"Yes," she replied," she said that it is very nice."

"Oh, thank you."

"She liked it".

"Good, good," I said, containing the excitement I was feeling inside. Then she said: "But, she cannot use it."

"What's wrong..?" I inquired.

"Nothing," she replied, "there is nothing wrong with it. It's just that it doesn't suit her decor. Recently she purchased some paintings from Brazil for her living room and your painting would not blend…."

"Ohhh…"

"She is not here now, " she said very apologetically.

"I know," I replied with deep sorrow.

And she said: "She asked me to give you back your painting… Now if you please, I'm going to the closet to get your painting…"

"I can get it for you," I said to see if she would let me cross that door for the first time, but she knew better…

"No, that's not necessary," she said, graciously declining my offer, "wait here."

And she walked back through one of the doors leading to that foyer. I was left alone outside the open door and I was able to observe the room all upholstered in kelly green suede with its classic Castilian furniture and 17th century Spanish paintings and expensive knicknacks. How much I wanted to enter that room and to stand on its plush kelly green carpet!

But, she quickly came back with my painting and said: "She said that you were very kind and that she was sorry she did not have the right place for it."

"OK.., thank you… Goodbye."

"Goodbye."

And the door was closed one more time.

Every morning, around five thirty, when I had to go to the Spanish television studios to tape a show, I passed in front of her building and I looked at the window of her bedroom. The light was always off. But, one day, at that early hour, the light was on. Of course, that was the day of the premiere of her latest film The Lost Woman and I wondered: — What in the hell is she doing up so early..?! She should be getting her beauty sleep!— Well, one thing I was completely sure of that day and that was that at least I would be seeing her for the first time in eight years since seeing her in person in Cuba.

It was terrible that I had to go to the television studios to tape a show that specific day. However, I would make sure that I would be out of there and back in Madrid no later than twelve noon to buy the ticket for the eight o'clock premiere.

At the studios, I got into the makeup department by six and got my wardrobe for the day's shooting. Then I had to sit and wait for the taping to start.

It was much after ten and there were no signs as to when the taping would start. I decided that if by 11:15 nothing had happened, I would sneak out of the studio. I was not doing anything important that day and no one would notice my absence.

At the appointed time still nothing was happening, so I walked out and went to the dressing room, changed my clothes and sneaked out through a back door and got into a bus back to Madrid.

By twelve, when I arrived at the movie theater on the main street of downtown Madrid, the tickets were almost gone. I got a seat in the back of the upper tier. So, my only possibility of seeing her up close was to get to the theater early that evening and stand in the lobby.

At seven o'clock that evening I arrived at the theater and the place, to my surprise, was already completely packed to more than its capacity. Apparently everyone in Madrid had the same idea as mine. It was a huge human wave. You could not even pass by the wide sidewalk in front of the theater. Everyone wanted to see her. Everyone wanted to see her up close to see if that incredibly beautiful woman was real or not.

I managed to blend into that enormous crowd and squeezed into the lobby, standing by the main door where she would be entering. And I waited, trying very hard to keep my post in the middle of that pushy crowd that was getting hysterical and out of control with the perspective of seeing that woman, the most famous in Spain, their idol, the biggest movie star Spain had ever had.

Around eight some of the other stars of the film and other show business stars and personalities started arriving. There was some excitement, yes, but nothing comparable to what happened around 8:30 when The Virgin finally arrived in the front of the theater in a limousine escorted by two huge policemen. That human wave became wild and hysterical, overcome by her charm and beauty. I had never been in the middle of a situation like that and I was frightened for her and for myself. The screaming was unbelievable. I never heard anything like that before. I found myself in the middle of an out of control riot! The floor to ceiling glass doors and windows at the entrance of the magnificent theater converted into a movie house, were suddenly shattered to pieces by the pressure of the crowd. It was really dangerous to be there! I tried to move away to safer ground but I could not move a fraction of an inch. And then, through the crowd I finally saw her coming with the two policemen who were protecting her on each side and almost holding and lifting her from the ground by her arms. Even in that tense and horrible situation, she looked like a divine apparition. She looked like a virgin! She was The Virgin, surrounded by uncountable rays of light emanating from her beautiful face! –What a sight!– The policemen were struggling with the crowd in order to get her inside the lobby and inside the theater, managing to keep her alive and in one piece, except that she lost one of her crystal shoes, like Cinderella. –What a lucky person, the one who got her shoe!– And then, she passed about three feet from me and I saw the fear in her gorgeous eyes and I heard her screaming: "Please… please.., don't do that, you all are going to kill me..!"

I felt very bad for her, knowing how frightened she was and seeing how easy it would have been to damage her. –What a frightening experience!

However, seeing her again, the last time was 1958, was like magic for me. And watching her latest film with her sitting in a box in that big theater was another magical experience… The audience was completely wild. They applauded and cheered at all of her lines, songs, close ups, changes of costumes or hairdos… –It was really funny!– I laughed a lot about how campy the whole thing was, however, highly enjoyable. She was really a unique phenomenon!

After the film was over, when I was leaving the theater and to my surprise, I saw the actor Manolo Fabragas, who played the role of the doctor in her film *Cinnamon Skin*. —What a small world..!— I thought, and I should have gone and told him how traumatic it was for me to see that film in my childhood and that I enjoyed his singing very much in his version of *My Fair Lady*.

Back to reality, I received a scholarship to continue my acting studies at the well known Studio Theater of Madrid. I went to classes in the afternoon as my activities in television and dress designing allowed.

I was in the same class with a young and beautiful movie actress named Ana Belen. She was under an exclusive contract with a film company that was developing scripts for her. She also sang. I was fond of her, but one day, I asked her if she had seen The Virgin in person at the movie studios.

She replies: "Yes, I have seen her many times at the studios."

Very excited, I asked her: "How is she in reality..? How does she look..?"

"Well…" she responded, "she is not very tall…"

That remark bothered me, because in fact she was not short. She was an average height for a woman.., and coming from a Spanish woman, who happened to be not very tall, that was not a very well founded remark.

And she added: "Besides.., her hair, due to constant teasing, is in very bad condition."

—That was a poisonous remark, too!— I had seen her a few weeks earlier at the premiere of her latest film and her hair was impeccable.., and I thought to myself: —How dare you desecrate the Virgin?!— Well.., that was the end of Ana Belen. I never talked to her again!

With the Studio Theater company I got a role in a play to substitute an actor who was leaving the cast. The play was running in a theater that for some reason I thought was the same one The Virgin died on at the end of her 1957 film *The Last Couplet*. Just being on the same stage where I thought she sang the couplet "Nena" before she died, was an extraordinary thrill for me. And believe it or not, my role in the play on that stage had to do with death.

Well, the play was endlessly-boring, over three hours long–the Cervantes' tragedy *Numancia*. Ana Belen was the female star of the play and one of the actors had to deliver a never ending monologue while I was lying on the stage. I had to do a lot of convulsions, going to a temporary pseudo-resurrection trance and as Lazarus in the Bible, get up and walk… Just what an average corpse normally does. –The kind of role I always dreamed of playing!– As a matter of fact, my role had a lot of lines to say but for some reason unknown to me, the director, who claimed to have a different conception of the play, switched the lines to the other actor, making his already long monologue twice as long and booooring. That did not bother me at all because by that time I had developed adverse feelings for live theater due to my bad memory, so the less I had to say, the better for me. Many evenings I was tempted to fall asleep while the other actor was delivering his endless monologue, but my professional sense opposed my real desires and won out. My justification for being there as an actor was: being on the same stage where the last scene of The Virgin's film took place and to collect the one thousand and fifty much needed pesetas per week to add to my income. –I guess that was enough for an actor of my caliber… Anyway, what did I become an actor for?

The only night that I remained in the theater after finishing my death scene and waited for the final curtain was on my opening night, because in the theater opening night is important, no matter how small your part.

–I must never forget: there are no small parts, only small actors.– However, after the second performance, as soon as I finished my dead scene, I went to my dressing room, changed my clothes from the dead person to an alive one and got the hell out of the theater. And I did that every night.

But, one evening, after I arrived at my dressing room and was getting dressed in my white corpse costume, one of my fellow actors sharing the dressing room told me; "Do you know who came to see the play yesterday and also came backstage to say hello to everybody..?"

"No. Who?" I asked.

"Of course you don't," he said, "you always leave after you finish your scene."

"Well.., who was here?" I asked again.

"Your favorite," he responded.

"Who?"

"One guess..," he said, smiling with a devilish glint in his eyes.

And I, very puzzled, said: "I don't know."

"Sara Montiel!"

Having a fit, I exclaimed: "Ooooohhh..damn! Why in the hell didn't you tell me she was in the audience..?!"

"I thought you knew," was his answer.

"Oh, no, I didn't, damnit!" I said very upset at him, "you know I'm always on the moon! Oh no! That was my chance to see and talk to her..! Do you think I would have left if I had known she was here..?!"

And he said: "You know... she was really nice... She came backstage after the show and talked to everybody for a long time... She looked gorgeous!"

"Oh, damn! Don't tell me, don't tell me!" I exclaimed at him, very upset at myself for not staying until the last curtain as everyone else did.

And he continued: "But the other actors said that she did not watch the play at all... They said that she was sitting in a box just by the stage and she spent the whole time looking at herself in her compact mirror, retouching her makeup and hair..."

"Well..," I responded. "If she did, she was right! This play is an end-lessly boring play… Poor innocent woman sitting through the whole thing! I would have done the same thing if I was her! But.., don't you ever do that anymore! From now on, no matter who is in the audience, you tell me. Don't assume I know anything! You just come and tell me. I'll never forgive you for this…"

"OK, Stanislavski!" he replied.

"To hell with that God damn Russian!" I exclaimed.

I was extremely upset at myself for missing that unique opportunity. –Imagine..,– I thought, –on stage, during my dead scene, I would have twinkled my eyes at her.., added more dramatic convulsions to my trance.., and in my resurrection, I would have gotten up and staggered toward her box like in the movie *The Mummy* (1931) with Boris and everybody else, and accidentally, I could have fallen on her lap….. Oh.., what an evening of real good acting was missed!–

It was during that year, 1967, that my mother miraculously was able to escape from Cuba. It was thanks to a carefully planned scheme involving a letter to her that I was dying. She knew it wasn't true, but it was her claim to get permission to "visit" me and never return to Cuba. The "See you tomorrow!" to her mother was a lie that haunted her for the rest of her life. But she was out. My father, however, had to stay behind in need of a scheme of his own. My mother, who knew how to sew, began helping with the business.

One day after the movie theater riot, I saw a poster near my home announcing a benefit gala to collect money for poor children. There were a lot of Spanish stars in the gala in order to attract an audience and, among them, there she was: The Virgin. It was a rare opportunity to see her on stage in Madrid, since during those times she was strictly a movie star, appearing on stage mainly in America. So, immediately I got tickets.

The theater was full, as usually happened when she appeared, because everyone wanted to see the Virgin performing her miracles. There was a lot of anxiety in the audience waiting for her to appear. Finally, at the end of the first part, she came out and sang two songs. But even though she looked gorgeous, she was a little overweight. During those times, she was having problems with that.

During the intermission, most of the stars of the gala went to the box where Franco's wife was, in order to give her their personal donations of money for the cause she was heading. Mrs. Franco's box was not far from where I was sitting and I saw The Virgin there. I ran to the hallway so I could get close to the entrance of the box to see her when she left, but there were so many people trying to see The Virgin to receive her blessings that I could not get anywhere.

Then, in the middle of 1967 I left Spain and went to live in the U.S. I was very sad to leave Spain. I was leaving a lot of things behind, like my mother, who had to wait for her visa to join me in America and the sadness of living there for a year and a half and accomplishing a lot, except for my goal to meet The Virgin.

However, The Virgin would come to the U.S. with regularity, but always for concerts in Miami. That was too far and expensive for me to travel there to see her. So, I kept looking for her films as they came to town in the Spanish language movie houses.

The Sara Montiel films were not examples of cinematographic art. They were very campy, but I found them extremely amusing. However, the important thing was that she was there and I enjoyed seeing her no matter what she was doing.

Her films were all the same. The only changes were the sets, costumes, hairdos and makeup and the songs. Most of them happened in the 19th century or beginning of the 20th, referring to her films made in Spain since 1957, her prior films were different.

For me, because of her particular style that she found that worked for her, she was some sort of Mae West without the verbal innuendos and of course, with her own mannerisms, since Mae West's films were intended to be comedies and Miss Montiel's were intended to be dramas that resulted in being comedies. As with Mae West, Sara Montiel always played the same role. Miss Montiel's role was always a chanteuse who happens to be very decent regardless of her very low cut gowns, always and forever, 24 hours a day and night. She always gets into a romantic triangle with an older man who gives her everything and a young and handsome man who she really loves. Most of the time she dies or becomes a nun in the end... –When that was the only way to solve the crazy plot.

Her acting, even though very professional, was not the best. Actually, it was probably perfect for the contrived plots and, anyway, nobody cared because she had, as Mae West did, an unmistakable style, plus her extraordinary charm, beauty and that star quality that made her stand out no matter what she was doing. –But anyway.., how could you act those roles in those films!!– So.., she filled all the gaps with a lot of feathers, sequins and a beauty mark that kept changing places on her face with each take. –Very clever indeed! Because with the suspense created by not knowing where the beauty mark would land next, you kept watching!– And anyway people were not paying to see her films, they were paying to see HER.

However, prior to her enormous success with her classic film *The Last Couplet*, the other films I had seen of hers convinced me that besides her beauty and star quality she had acting talent, it was just not fully developed and stayed behind on her road to stardom.

One of the things I enjoyed the most about her was her singing abilities, because I find, in my opinion, that she gives meaning to each word in the lyrics and when she sings a song, I am able to understand what was going on. Besides, I love the sound of her voice. It always delivers extraordinary pleasure and excitement hearing her melodious, grave voice. But apparently she not only touched me with her singing, but everybody else as well. All of a sudden, in a 1957 infected with rock'n' roll music, she revived the "couplet", which was a style of song that flourished during the early years of the 20th century. Being a film of nostalgia for that frivolous and sentimental period, one anticipated that *The Last Couplet* would not make it in our increasingly Americanized society. But it did, and everyone, including the younger generation, was touched by her spin on that era and the charm of the Spanish star, Sarita Montiel. So, Elvis was pushed slightly aside and Sarita became an international Queen.

Well, despite what Sara Montiel, The Virgin, meant for me, I was not blinded by her. I knew artistically who she was. At the same time I knew that she was the only one who for some mysterious reason was ringing my bell and exercising an enormous attraction, making me do wild, crazy things that I would not do for anyone else. —Were we related in another life..?"

My father was finally able to leave Cuba in 1970 after spending six months in a forced labor camp. That was his ticket out. He left through Spain where he had to stay for quite a while until he received the visa to come to the U.S.

I liked Spain very much and I wanted to go back for a visit but that opportunity did not come until 1975. I was going to be staying four days in Madrid as part of the trip, so I decided that I should do something in order to meet The Virgin… What I couldn't accomplish in a year and a half, maybe I could in four days.

Somehow, in the middle of the night, the idea about a screenplay came clearly to my mind. I had written before: two stories for children that were broadcast on my radio show in Cuba back in the very early sixties. And a monologue and five plays in one act and a few adaptations of various plays, but I had never written a screenplay. However, I felt inspired by the Virgin!

So I wrote a musical comedy which I titled *Cougar of the Wild West*, which I copyrighted. The action happened in California in the days of the Gold Rush, and it was a parody of her films from 1944 to date and a take-off on her performing style. I wanted to do it this way because I knew she had a good understanding of comedy. I also designed all of her costumes and hairdos to include them in the script. I really had a lot of fun writing the screenplay.

My plan was to contact her while I was in Madrid, somehow, and give her the script… But the whole thing was like a dream.., and I kept on thinking: –Four days! I decided to take the screenplay with me on my trip and as Doris Day would say: "Que sera, sera… Whatever will be will be."

On April 11, 1975, after checking into my hotel in Madrid I decided to call The Virgin's friend and neighbor, the actor Vincente Parra, because I didn't have The Virgin's number.

Vincente was not home, but the lady who answered the phone was his aunt. I told her, scheming as usual: "My name is Agustin Blazquez. I came from the United States and I have a screenplay for Miss Sara Montiel…"

"Ooohhh.., Sarita just left here," she said, sounding very much impressed. "You can call her at home, she is there now."

"Oh, but you know..," I said taking maximum advantage of the opportunity, "I lost her number on the plane, that is why I am calling your home…"

"Oh, I'll give you the number..," she replied and she did.

–I could not believe it!!!– After I wrote it down, I thanked her and quickly hung up the phone. And.., with my index finger trembling with emotion, I managed to dial the forbidden numerical combination that will open the gates of heaven…

"Hello?"

A sweet and delightfully melodious voice answered the phone. That sound was the familiar voice of the person I have adored since my childhood. That was the unmistakable sound of the voice of the most famous woman in Spain and Latin America. There she was, the woman of La Mancha, the Virgin of Criptana! That voice that had made miracles resurrecting the couplet, returning the hearing to the deaf, speech to the mute and the eyesight to the blind! There she was, for real. That magic silver screen illusion that I have known so well for the past twenty four years. But at the same time I could not say "Hello Virgin" or "Hello Sara", because even though we had met in the darkness of the movie houses, we had not officially met…yet. It was painful for me to pretend that I didn't know that voice, and had to lie to her by saying: "Yes.., I would like to talk to Miss Sara Montiel."

"Who is calling, please?" she asked.

"My name is..," I answered while realizing that I had momentarily forgotten my own name, "…Agustin, Agustin Blazquez… I came from the United States and I have a screenplay for her."

"What kind of screenplay?" she asked me.

"It is a musical comedy," I answered.

"I am Sara Montiel," she said to me. Me!

"What a pleasure!" I exclaimed. And we talked… and we talked… She even sang to me. I explained what the script was all about. She was very sweet, kind and seemed to be very much interested in it. Then she asked me if I could drop the script by her flat that same afternoon, because she wanted to read it and later on discuss it with me.

I ran that afternoon to her building overlooking the Don Quixote statue. The doorman was the same one I had met eight years earlier, but he did not recognize me. The Virgin had already left word that I was going to pass by that afternoon to leave something for her, so he was waiting for me. I gave him the script and left, leaving the still unconquered building behind me.

Even though I had jet-lag and I needed to sleep, I was unable to, so, because of my excitement thinking that she was reading something

I had written and typed with my very own sinner hands. Thinking and worrying as to how she would react to the script that was actually a parody of her films, she might hate me forever for it… If she didn't have a sense of humor, she might be outraged by it. Well.., so, back to Doris Day, this time in the late night rerun:

> "Que sera, sera…"
> Whatever will be, will be…
> The future's not ours to see…
> Que sera, sera…

Two days later, when I called her back, as she asked, she answered the phone again: "Hello?"

"Sara, it's me, Agustin," I said, –How much I have always wanted to say that! She already knew who I was! I was a part of her! I was a part of her life! Not a big part.., but at least something, a name, a person who exists no longer in the loneliness of a movie house…

She told me that she enjoyed the script very much, that it was funny and that she particularly thought that one of my ideas using one of her old songs for a specific effect in the background was hilarious. –I was very much relieved knowing that she understood the humor and did not find it irreverent!

Nevertheless, she told me that due to the financial problems the Spanish film industry was going through, a production like the one I was proposing, a very expensive one, would not be possible. She was right: I had the same concern. The sets and musical numbers were very elaborate. She also added that my script was very much Hollywood and that her audiences might not be able to catch many of the jokes, and by changing the script, the comical situations might get lost. –She was right again.

Then she said that she wanted to meet me and asked me to go to her flat the next evening.

So another sleepless night was on the way…

On Sunday, April 13, 1975, I went on a sightseeing tour all morning and part of the afternoon. Then, back at the hotel I took a shower and got ready for the exciting evening ahead.

I took a taxi from my hotel door to her building at Spain Square… The doorman was expecting me and he opened the door for me. As things were progressing so well, I started suspecting that I was having a dream. One of those very realistic and colorful ones I so often had… –But no.., this time it seemed to be that it is really happening.– The lobby of the building looked different from the way I remembered. – Apparently it had been redecorated.– Then, I reached the elevator, opened its door, went in and pushed the button with its magic number ten… And the slow ascension to heaven began. –The elevator looked the same as I remembered, but I still was not believing what was happening to me and I was afraid, because I could wake up at any time and discover that this whole thing was just a dream.– The elevator stopped and I went out to the familiar waiting room. –The doors of the just two flats on that floor were different! They were not as I remembered. One of them was walnut color and the other was painted in off-white and was carefully antiqued. Could I be on the wrong floor..?– I got into the elevator again… –No. This is the tenth floor…– I felt completely disoriented. –Her door used to be at the right of the elevator when you were exiting it.., but now the color of that door was different…– So, I decided that somehow, because of my nerves, I was confused and that her door was to the left. And I went to the walnut door and knocked and knocked.., and no one came to the door. Then, I decided to knock on the off-white door… After a short while, a tall gentleman opened the door. I recognized him immediately! He was her impresario and fiance! Then I knew that I was in the right place!

"Are you Agustin?" he asked.

"Yes."

"Come in, Sara is waiting for you."

And for the first time following many unsuccessful tries, I was allowed, even invited, to cross that threshold and enter the foyer!!! –It was completely different from what I remembered. It was not kelly green any more and did not have Castilian furniture or fifteenth century Spanish paintings…– Apparently it had been redecorated and I liked the prior look much better. –But, never mind!– The fact that I was finally stepping on The Virgin's heaven and no matter how many clouds or cherubim I find in my path, the ultimate result will be: the apparition of her divine presence!

He asked me to follow him through a complicated maze of hallways to the right and to the left and to the right and to the left. And I was praying not to wake up, at least not now.., not until I have the pleasure of seeing her in her very own environment and meeting her. –Please, please, please, keep dreaming, keep going!!!– The hallways were decorated with a lot of her photographs, paintings, drawings and caricatures of her and other mementos of her long career. Finally, at the end of the last hallway and to the left, we entered a room that was the living room.

I was very much familiar with this room which I had seen in a lot of magazine articles. But nothing in it was as I remembered. The colors were different and everything was rearranged. I liked it better the way it used to be. Her off-white grand piano was now down below, while before it was on the two step up platform by the huge windows facing the big balcony overlooking the show-covered tops of the Sierra of Guadarrama mountains in the distant background. I sat on one of the sofas facing the platform and the windows in the front. That sofa used to be upholstered in a rich gold silky fabric and now it was white leather. I liked it better the way it was before.

Her miniature poodle, Lady, also familiar, came running and jumped on my lap. That was good, I like dogs. And this one was a special one, Lady was the Virgin's dog. So.., I petted her.

On the platform, which started about thirteen feet in front of the sofa where I was sitting, I saw her easel with her oil colors and brushes. Apparently, the Virgin had been painting earlier in the afternoon, taking advantage of the light of that bright room. I had read that she painted and I should have gotten up, walked to the easel to see what she was painting. But, somehow, my legs were not feeling very strong enough at that time to venture walking up there.

Her impresario sat on the other sofa, placed at a right angle to the one I was sitting on. He said that she will be out shortly. And I thought to myself: —She'd better hurry up before I wake up.— But coming back to the reality of the situation, if in fact I was living in a reality, I was worried.., because I did not know what to expect when she finally walked through the door… After I left Spain in 1967, she made four more films. However, she had gone through difficult periods of her sentimental and love lives and her mother, who she adored and who lived with her, had died. She had gained and lost weight many times. Nevertheless, in her last film, made around 1974, she looked great again, but in certain scenes she looked kind of old. And in our last telephone conversation, she sweetly told me that the years had passed and that she was not the same anymore, perhaps worrying that I would be disappointed when I saw her in person up close in her home.

She was forty seven years old, which is not that old, but for a beauty queen of her caliber, the years are crucial. I was really scared to death about what I was going to find when she finally entered that room, if I don't wake up before. —It's a shame that I had never met her during her prime in the middle fifties or early sixties.— Our overdue date was going to be a lot of years later… I was worrying if I was going to stop loving her after seeing her completely natural at home. –Could that destroy the magic illusion of the screen..?–

Then.., entering the room very fast and wearing a simple, long brown dress, there she was… The Virgin at last!!!!!!! That's got to be the most desired and longer awaited moment in my life! The Virgin appeared to me! She was a palpable reality!. She looked as gorgeous as the adored screen image! And the only thing that I was able to do when she entered was stand up and announce to the room in my best radio voice, as if no one knew who she was: "SA-RA MON-TIEL!"

Apparently she loved it, because she smiled. She was not a letdown. She was graceful, kind, simple and sweet. She sat like a great lady on a chair beside the sofa where I was sitting and very close to me.

We talked about the script. I wanted to tell her a lot of things but I really couldn't–I wanted to let her lead the conversation. She asked me to let her keep one of the dress designs I had drawn for the presentation of the screenplay, since she liked it a lot and wanted to have it made. And she asked me to autograph my design and to dedicate it to her, which I did with enormous pleasure.

Before I left her home that evening, she gave me two photographs of herself which she dedicated to me. And she asked me to write another script for her, having in mind the economic limitations of the Spanish film industry and her audience.

"Sure, I will. I will think about it,: I told her. "I'll send it to you when it is ready. And it will be yours, as my gift. I don't want anything for it. If it could be a vehicle for you, you may have it."

And she said: "You are very kind, thank you. Oh.., one thing. I want to let you know that I like to choose my songs myself."

"OK, I understand," I said. "I didn't know that."

"Write something simple that takes place now and that will not require very many sets. The important thing is the idea."

When our visit was over she walked me to the door. But before I left her temple, I told her something I felt I should say, since I sensed that her film career might be over, at least for the moment: "Sara, you are a very important movie star. The most important famous Spain ever had. There was no one like you in the past and I doubt very much that in the future something as unique as you will come along. You are a valuable person. Don't let yourself fall."

And she said: "I won't. When I can no longer do films any longer the way I want, I will not make any more."

And I left on a cloud… But it was not a dream. Our meeting was for real.

NOTES

I wrote and sent to her the second screenplay in August of 1975. On September 6 of the same year, I saw her again at a concert at the Avery Fisher Hall in the Lincoln Center in New York. I met her in her dressing room after the show.

I have made a total of four paintings of her including one Egyptian-style painting. [Editor's note: The latter painting is on the cover and spine of this book] One of the paintings I gave to her.

As of this writing, eight years later, she has not made any more films. However, she presents herself in musical theatrical extravaganzas throughout Spain, such as her last one "Dona Sara of La Mancha". Also at concerts in other European countries, Latin America, Miami, Los Angeles and New York. She adopted a daughter from Brazil and later on, married her impresario. She also may be adopting a son from Brazil. She recorded album number 50 and a festival of her films was held in Paris.

Her movie magic is preserved in films from 1944 to 1974.

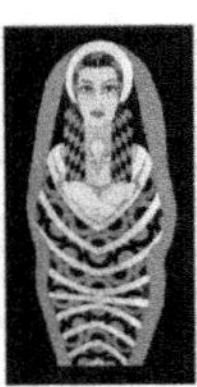

CHAPTER 24

ARRIVEDERCI KHAN EL KHALILY

I got up and took a shower. –Probably my last one,– I thought, since I had no idea how the Khan El Khalily Hotel bathroom would be. The shower was like a drizzle and very cold. After my first shower in that hotel, we never had hot water again.

We had breakfast in the coffee shop by again mixing with a tour group in order to get served. After that, we went back to the room to get our suitcases to move to our next hotel. While in the room the telephone rang. It was from the reception desk announcing that Abulela, our official chauffeur, was there to pick us up. –That was good news! Probably that is a good omen,– I thought. We were not expecting to see him any more. I wondered how he found us. It was great news and will make our move so much easier than trying to *haute haggle* a fair fare.

Good Abulela took us to our new hotel. We got the key to our room, which was on the tenth floor. I liked that since, for sure, we will have a very nice view of the old citadel. The bellboys came for our luggage and ushered us into the tiny four person elevator, which even had an operator! The elevator was in a near fatal state of disrepair, without one of its original pair of front doors. Its single twenty-five watt bulb was hanging loose from an old and greasy electrical cord from the broken light fixture and it swayed like a pendulum. The elevator operator managed to manually close the doors and the elevator made an excruciating noise in its attempt to ascend. After a few jerks and vibrations, it started moving up,,, though hesitatingly. But the worst thing was that the elevator was not going up straight, –no,– instead it was leaning to the left and moving at the pace of an ancient Egyptian turtle. It was a complete experience of suspense not knowing if we were going to reach the tenth floor alive. –Why,– I asked myself in desperation, –this time I get the tenth floor when I always and invariably get no higher than the third..?!

After very long minutes, we miraculously arrived at our destination alive. Well, I was not quite sure yet, –because the elevator operatior could not get the doors open. After a while, he was able to force the doors to open and Jaums and I got out as fast as we could from that contraption.

The bellboys plus the elevator operator (?!) ushered us down a long and dilapidated hallway to our room, which happened to be at the very end. Just beside the door of the room was the bathroom door, which the elevator operator proudly opened, inviting us to see its contents… –Well, the stench coming out was enough.., but out of my damn curiosity, I looked in… Ugh, what a sight!– It was filthy and the toilet was overflowing with human excrement, commonly known the world over as shit. I knew at that very instant that for the next two days I will not be using the facilities. Period!

Then one of the bellboys tried to open the door of the room, but he could not and he gave the key to the other bellboy, who couldn't either. The elevator operator took the key and tried to open the door without any luck. It was becoming obvious that they gave us the wrong key. He asked us to wait and went to some place along the hallway.

A while later, he came back with another set of keys and finally opened the door… The room was awful, as I already expected judging by everything else I had already seen in that hotel. It had two personal beds and an unusual sink, which later on proved to be very useful since we couldn't use the bathroom. —Well, at this point, what could we do?— I thought, —We could not leave Egypt because we did not have airline reservations until two days later. And at our next destination, Rome, we didn't have reservations until Friday evening, and what we were able to get in Rome was very difficult to obtain because of the Easter holidays, so, if we arrive there ahead of time, we will have no choice but to sleep on the Spanish steps, because of my heritage. Oh.., we were stuck in Cairo… I guess we have to make the best of these two last days.

After we got installed in the room, we went down, using the staircase, to the hotel's restaurant for lunch. The place was very icky. The tablecloth was very carefully ironed over droppings of rice and food. —Very inviting indeed.— But I was hungry, tired and very far from the Hilton, Sheraton or any other foreign hotel, so we ate.

In order to get out of that hotel after lunch we decided to go to visit the Islam Museum, —if we could find it.— And yes, we found it, but it was closed. Then we walked to the Cairo Museum and stayed there until it was time to go to dinner at the Hilton.

After dinner, we went to the Shepheard's Hotel to try to find out about Nancy, but nothing yet, so we walked to the Meridian Hotel, where we were supposed to eat with Nancy, —if we ever meet again…— From the Meridian, we went to the American University to see John Van Deerlin after classes to say goodbye. We saw him and he gave us a few things to take as a present to a mutual friend in Washington, D.C.

After that, we walked back to the Khan El Khalily Hotel and we climbed up the stairs to our tenth floor room.

Next morning, we didn't want to face the icky restaurant again so we ordered breakfast in the room. A while later, room service delivered our two trays with the complete breakfast, including two big, brown, live roaches on them as an extra bonus. Jaums got his orange juice glass, turned it over and trapped them both inside. And we sat to eat the appetizing breakfasts.

Just when we started eating, apparently a maid came to fix the overflowing toilet in the bathroom so conveniently located just outside our door. We could clearly hear the sound of the plunger: squish, squish, squish. Ugh…

The floor of the bathroom was one inch higher than the floor of our room, so if the unthinkable happens, everything will run under our door and into our room. In my mind I just pictured a disaster movie, like *Towering Inferno*, (1974) Steve McQueen and Paul Newman. But, instead of being trapped by fire, we were going to be trapped by shit!

As the squishing continued we got cotton for our ears, removed our shoes from the floor and stayed on our beds to eat our breakfasts. –It was an unforgettable experience!!–

To get out of there, we ventured to the bazaar to find gifts to take to friends at home, but didn't find anything

Back at the hotel we had a note from Nancy, called her and had one final, short get together with her as she was in a hurry having to do with her travel business. We had a quick dessert with her at the Hilton where I finally drank the Egyptian water for the first time in front of the amazed eyes of Nancy and Jaums. That was the last time we saw Nancy. I hope she had many happy off-the-beaten-path trips throughout Egypt.

We went back to our hotel and took difficult towel baths from the sink in our room and dressed for our dinner at the Dean's home. I wore a suit. It was the first time after 3 weeks of carrying it around, so I used it.

The Dean, Dr. Shohdy, arrived a little late to pick us up at the hotel because he couldn't find it. He came with a friend who was driving a second car. I rode with Dr. Shohdy and Jaums rode with the other gentleman who was the well known Egyptian artist Sami Rafi, who among other things, designed the pyramid monument of the Unknown Soldier in Cairo, and where President Anwar Sadat was buried.

On the way to Dr. Shohdy's home, we stopped at the monument for a tour and Mr. Rafi explained to us a lot of details about the impressive structure and its construction. It is 32 meters high, half of Mycerinus' pyramid, the smallest of the ones at the famous Giza plateau. It is a very impressive monument and the pyramid shape was the perfect choice for it.

From there we went to Dr. Shohody's flat in Heliopolis. He had not said anything, in order to surprise me, but his wife was Spanish from Barcelona. She spoke a little Spanish, so did he. They were very nice people and both very good artists. The dinner she served for us… homemade Shish Kebabs, the best we had in Egypt!

Later on that evening, Mr. Rafi took us back to the hotel, but before, he stopped at his small penthouse apartment overlooking the pyramids of Giza in the distance. There he showed us more of his works and how he developed the idea of the monument he designed. Mr. Sami Rafi indeed was a very talented man. What an honor to meet him.

We really had a good time that evening, our last in Cairo.

The next day, at 12:05 pm, Abulela, bless him, came to take us to the airport for our flight to Rome, and we gladly said: "Arrivederci Khan El Ehalily!"

The good Abulela had brought two cans of orange juice which we drank in the car while he drove us very fast through those chaotic streets of Cairo, deftly using only the gas pedal and horn.

Everything was passing by my eyes very fast. I felt a lump in my throat. I was very sad to be leaving Cairo. I had already forgotten all of the inconveniences due to lack of communication and disorganization, not from our hosts or driver, but from the country as a whole, during the three weeks we were there.

I had tears in my eyes thinking that I was leaving Egypt and I didn't know when I was going to come back. The time went flying by very fast. It seemed to be only yesterday that I arrived here… And now, my dream was reaching the end. Only my memories, good and bad, will remain. But it was all worth it! It was an experience that I will cherish the rest of my life! And I felt immensely grateful to all of them, the Egyptians, for their kindness in inviting me to see their country, to witness the Egypt of today and that marvelous civilization that flourished by the Nile, thousands of years ago.

Silver Spring, Maryland, U.S.A.
Monday, February 28, 1983

NOTE

The aftermath inspiration derived from this extraordinary trip will take many years to be seen. I do not know if I will be able to accomplish all of it in my lifetime.
Already new "mummies" and other paintings have resulted. But the best is still to come.

Thank you Egypt!

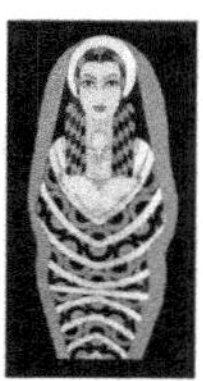

ACKNOWLEDGEMENTS

I want to thank the following institutions and individuals because without their help the realization of this book would not have been possible. Most of them were truly inspirational for me.

The Cultural and Educational Bureau of the Egyptian Embassy, Washington, D.C., especially: Dr. A. Maufouz, Dr. Ezzeldin Ali Mostafa and Dr. Ahmed Azzam.

The Press and Information Bureau of the Egyptian Embassy, Washington, D.C., especially: Mr. Mohamed Hakki and Mr. Ahmed M. Abushadi.

His Excellency Dr. Ashraf Ghobal, Ambassador of the Arab Republic of Egypt, Washington, D.C.

The Ministry of Higher Education, Cairo, Egypt, especially: His Excellency the Minister, Mr. Abdessalam Diab, Mr. Hassan El Sayed, Ms. Indira Ghandi, Madame Ahlam and Mr. Abulela, driver extraordinaire.

The Cairo Museum, especially: Dr. Dea Aboughzi, Director; Dr. Ibrahim El Nawawee, Chief Curator and staff curators.

The State Information Agency, Cairo, Egypt, especially: Dr. Morsi Saad Eddin, Chairman, and staff.

Professor, Dr. Abbas H. Shoudy, Dean of the Faculty of Fine Arts, University of Helwan and Mrs. Shoudy, Cairo, Egypt.

Mr. Sami Rafi, artist, Cairo, Egypt.

Ms. Leila Izzet, artist, Cairo, Egypt.

Mr. Rushdi Iskandar, President of the National Society of Fine Arts, artist and art critic, Cairo, Egypt.

Mr. Abdul Mounaan Selim and Mr. Ez-El-Din Shawkat, reporters, Cairo, Egypt.

The bedouin at the pyramids, the owner of the camel and the owner of the tourist-trap shop, Giza, Egypt.

The reception lady at the Tonsi Hotel and staff, Cairo, Egypt.

Professor John Van Deerlin, American University, Cairo, Egypt.

The Painted Woman, everywhere in Egypt, her make-up case, The Polyester Man and The Unremarkable Youngster.

Ms. Nancy Woolward, friend/artist/traveler, planet Earth.

The staff of the Tourism Office, Luxor, Egypt.

Egypt Air office in Luxor, Egypt, especially Mr. M. Samy, Manager.

Chez Farouk and Marhaba restaurants in Luxor, Egypt.

ETAP Hotel and staff, Luxor Egypt.

Mr. Mohamed Hussein, my guide in Aswan, Egypt.

Mr. Sammy Farog, Resident Archeologist of the Isis Temple, Philae Island, Egypt.

The reception attendant at the Oberoi Hotel, Elephantine Island, Egypt.

Amun Hotel and staff, Amun Island, Egypt.

Kitty, tour hostess, Luxor, Aswan, Abu Simbel, Cairo, Egypt.

Mr. Sabery A. Litief Hassan and his Russian jeep, my guide in Abu Simbel, Egypt.

The keepers of the Ramses II and Nefertari temples, Abu Simbel, Egypt.

Nefertary Hotel and the three member staff, Abu Simbel, Egypt.

Patrick and Colleen (R.I.P.), Irish honeymooners, Abu Simbel, Egypt.

The wild dogs of the desert, Abu Simbel, Egypt.

The tour of little old ladies of Germany to Cairo, Luxor, Aswan, Abu Simbel, Egypt.

Rehab Hotel and staff, especially its "Open 24 Hours" coffee shop, Cairo, Egypt.

The Egyptian taxi drivers, Cairo, Egypt.

Mr. M. Hamzawy, Head of Public and External Relations of Egyptian Television, Cairo, Egypt.

The staff of the Press Information Office, Cairo, Egypt.

The staff of Egypt Air throughout Egypt.

The restaurants and coffee shops of the Hilton, Sheraton, Mena House and Shepheard's Hotels, Cairo, Egypt.

The Tower of Cairo restaurant and its revolving machinery, Cairo, Egypt.

Queen Hatshepsut, Egypt.

Queen Tiy, Egypt.

Akhenaten and Nefertiti, Egypt.

The entire of the people of Egypt, present and past.

Telephone, Correspondence and Bibliography Section of the Library of Congress, Washington, D.C. U.S.A.

Language and Literature Division of the Martin Luther King Memorial Library, Washington, D.C., U.S.A

Mr. James W. Sutton, Silver Spring, Maryland, U.S.A

Mrs. Julia Sales "Pookie", Silver Spring, Maryland, U.S.A.

All schools, institutions, art galleries, visual and performing artists, people and friends I have known and worked with in Cuba, Canada, France, Spain and the U.S.A.

Papa Gordo, Mama Zoila, my mother, my father, Terry and family. They all contributed in one way or many other ways to my formation, therefore, this book.

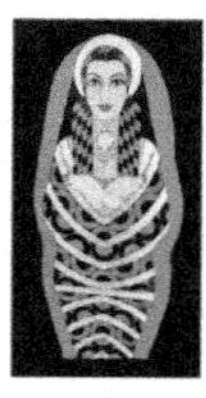

BIBLIOGRAPHY

Alejandra M., *I Want You for Myself*, Ladislao Vajda, Spain, 1944.

Montiel, S., *The Wedding Started*, Rafaello Materazzo, Spain, 1944.

Montiel, S., *Five Little Wolves*, Ladislao Vajda, Spain, 1945.

Montiel, S., *Bamboo*, Jose Luis Saenz de Heredia, Spain, 1945.

Montiel, S., *The Boyfriend Left Her*, Julio Salvador, Spain, 1945.

Montiel, S., *The Clipper Passenger*, Gonzalo Delgras, Spain, 1945.

Montiel, S., *For the Grand Prix*, Pierre Caron, Spain, 1946.

Montiel, S., *Mariona Rebull*, Jose Luis Saenz de Heredia, Spain, 1946.

Montiel, S., *Confidence*, Jeronimo Mihura, Spain, 1947.

Montiel, S., *Don Quijote of La Mancha*, Rafael Gil, Spain 1947.

Montiel, S., *Alhucemas*, Jose Lopez Rubio, Spain, 1947.

Montiel, S., *Confused Lives*, Jeronimo Mihura, Spain, 1947.

Montiel, S., *Madness of Love*, Juan de Orduna, Spain, 1948.

Montiel, S., *A Lot of Ripe Cereal*, Jose Luis Saenz de Heredia, Spain, 1948.

Montiel, S., *Trifles*, Juan de Orduna, Spain 1949.

Montiel, S., *Captain Poison*, Luis Marquina, Spain, 1949.

Montiel, S., *The Man of Tangier*, Robert Elwyn, Spain 1950.

Montiel, S., *Red Fury*, Steve Sekely, Mexico, 1951.

Montiel, S., *Need Money*, Miguel Zacarias, Mexico, 1951.

Montiel, S., *Women's Jail*, Miguel M. Delgado, Mexico, 1951

Montiel, S., *Martin Corona is Coming*, Miguel Zacarias, Mexico, 1951.

Montiel, S., *The Lover, Miguel Zacarias*, Mexico, 1951.

Montiel, S., *She, Lucifer and I*, Miguel Morayta, Mexico, 1952.

Montiel, S., *I Am Rooster Anywhere*, Roberto Rodriguez, Mexico, 1952.

Montiel, S., *Cinnamon Skin*, Juan J. Ortega, Mexico, 1953.

Montiel, S., *Why Don't You Love Me?*, Chano Ureta, Mexico, 1951.

Montiel, S., *Need Models*, Chano Ureta, Mexico, 1954.

Montiel, S., *Facing Yesterday's Sin*, Mexico, 1954.

Montiel, S., *I Don't Believe in Men*, Juan J. Ortega, Mexico, 1954.

Montiel, S., *Veracruz*, Robert Aldrich, Hollywood, 1954.

Montiel, S., *Where the Circle Ends*, Alfredo B. Crevenna, Mexico 1954.

Montiel, S., *Serenade*, Anthony Man, Hollywood, 1955.

Montiel., S., *The Run of the Arrow*, Samuel Fuller, Hollywood, 1956.

Montiel., S., *The Last Couplet*, Juan de Crudina, Spain, 1957.

Montiel., S., *The Violet Seller*, Luis Cesar Amadori, Spain, 1958.

Montiel., S., *Carmen of Ronda*, Tulio Demicheli, Spain, 1959.

Montiel., S., *The Last Tango*, Luis Cesar Amadori, Spain, 1960.

Montiel, S., *Sin of Love*, Luis Cesar Amadori, Spain, 1961.

Montiel, S., *The Beautiful Lola*, Alfonso Balcazar, Spain, 1962.

Montiel, S., *Queen of the Chantecler*, Rafael Gil, Spain, 1962.

Montiel, S., *Nights of Casablanca*, Henri Decoin, Spain, 1963.

Montiel, S., *Samba, Rafael Gil*, Spain 1964.

Montiel, S., *The Lady of Beirut*, Ladislao Vajda, Spain, 1965.

Montiel, S., *The Lost Woman*, Tulio Demicheli, Spain, 1966.

Montiel, S., *Tuset Street*, Luis Marquina and Jorge Grau, Spain 1968.

Montiel, S., *That Woman*, Mario Camus, Spain, 1969.

Montiel, S., *Varietes*, Juan Andoino Barden, Spain, 1971.

Montiel, S., *Five Pillows for One Night*, Pedro Lazaga, Spain, 1974

Sevilla, N., *Cry of the Bewitched/Yambao*, Mexico, 1957.

Young, D. And the Culinary Arts Institute Staff, *Montgomery Ward– Adventures in Microwave Cooking*, Culinarts Institute, U.S., 1976.

ADDITIONAL READING

Funk, W, Dr. and Lewis, N., *30 Days to a More Powerful Vocabulary*, Pocket Books, 1971